Dear R...

I'm del... ...Bestselling Author Collection for 2024! In celebration of Harlequin's 75 years in publishing, this collection features fan-favorite stories from some of our readers' most cherished authors. Each book also includes a free full-length story by an exciting writer from one of our current programs.

Our company has grown and changed since its inception 75 years ago. Today, Harlequin publishes more than 100 titles a month in 30 countries and 15 languages, with stories for a diverse readership across a range of genres and formats, including hardcover, trade paperback, mass-market paperback, ebook and audiobook.

But our commitment to you, our romance reader, remains the same: in every Harlequin romance, a guaranteed happily-ever-after!

Thank you for coming on this journey with us. And happy reading as we embark on the next 75 years of bringing joy to readers around the world!

Dianne Moggy

Vice-President, Editorial

Harlequin

Robyn Carr is an award-winning, #1 *New York Times* bestselling author of more than sixty novels, including highly praised women's fiction such as *Four Friends*, *The View from Alameda Island* and *A Family Affair*, as well as the critically acclaimed Virgin River, Thunder Point and Sullivan's Crossing series. *Virgin River* is now a Netflix original series. Robyn lives in Las Vegas, Nevada.

Nina Crespo lives in Florida, where she indulges in her favorite passions—the beach, a good glass of wine, date night with her own real-life hero and dancing. Her lifelong addiction to romance began in her teens while on a "borrowing spree" in her older sister's bedroom, where she discovered her first romance novel. Let Nina's sensual contemporary stories feed your own addiction to love, romance and happily-ever-after. Visit her at ninacrespo.com.

DREAMING OF A BRIGHT CHRISTMAS

#1 *NEW YORK TIMES* BESTSELLING AUTHOR
ROBYN CARR

Previously published as *Informed Risk*

BESTSELLING AUTHOR COLLECTION

Harlequin®
BESTSELLING
AUTHOR
COLLECTION

Recycling programs
for this product may
not exist in your area.

ISBN-13: 978-1-335-01244-9

Dreaming of a Bright Christmas
First published as Informed Risk in 1989.
This edition published in 2024.
Copyright © 1989 by Robyn Carr

A Chef's Kiss
First published in 2021. This edition published in 2024.
Copyright © 2021 by Nina Crespo

Harlequin Enterprises ULC
22 Adelaide St. West, 41st Floor
Toronto, Ontario M5H 4E3, Canada
www.Harlequin.com

Printed in U.S.A.

CONTENTS

Also by Robyn Carr

Sullivan's Crossing

Virgin River

Visit her Author Profile page at Harlequin.com
for more titles!

DREAMING OF A BRIGHT CHRISTMAS

Robyn Carr

For Beth Gibson, with affection.

Chapter 1

Chris heard a loud thump. The furnace had turned on; soon warmth would begin to flow through the rickety little house. She wrinkled her nose, then remembered that heaters always smelled of burning dust and soot the first day they operated. She returned her fingers to the laptop keys, and her concentration to the last chapter of her story about a twelve-year-old boy named Jake. After seven rewrites, Jake was finally about to enjoy some resolution to the previous 122 pages of pubescent tribulation he'd suffered in his first year of junior high school.

This was her fourth attempt at a young adult novel, and Chris knew she was getting closer. Of earlier attempts editors had used such words as *brisk, lively, smooth*. Also words such as *awkward, unresolved, clumsy in places*.

She stopped typing and wrinkled her nose again.

Should it smell *that* bad? She had asked the landlord if the furnace should be serviced or cleaned before she set the thermostat, but he'd assured her it was fine. Of course, he said everything was fine, and this old rattrap was anything but. To be fair, she had never actually seen a rat, but she *had* swept up plenty of suspicious little pebbles, which she assumed were mouse turds. The traps she set, however, remained—thank you, God—abandoned.

She and the children had made do with oven heat until now, waiting as long as possible before turning on central heat. Utility bills were hard on a Christmas budget, and, when you got right down to it, hers was hardly a budget. But the temperature might drop to freezing tonight, and sleeping bags alone wouldn't keep the kids warm.

She looked at the kitchen clock. Nearly midnight. Her eyes were scratchy, but tonight she was determined to finish the last chapter. To be published...finally? Much of this great push, she had to admit, was for Jake himself, a great kid who deserved a resolution that was not awkward or clumsy in places. As did she.

As for publishing, the responses she collected had been consistently more encouraging, asking her to send future work. "Write what you know," a writing instructor had advised. Chris certainly knew what it was like to be twelve, to be struggling for self-reliance while simultaneously fighting feelings of incompetence. She knew this dilemma even better at twenty-seven.

The shrill siren of the smoke detector interrupted her musings. The sound wrapped strangling fingers around her heart and squeezed. Stunned, she looked up from the gridlock of library books, photocopied magazine articles and laptop on the kitchen table. Through the kitchen door, her wide eyes quickly scanned the little living room with its two beanbag chairs, old television, clutter of secondhand toys and card table littered with the remnants of the macaroni-and-cheese dinner she had given the kids hours earlier.

And there, from the floor vents in the living room, poured smoke.

She bolted from the chair, fairly leapt to turn off the thermostat and raced into her kids' room. She grabbed one in each arm—five-year-old Carrie and three-year-old Kyle.

"There's a fire in the house," she said, hustling them through the thick smoke and toward the door. "We have to get outside, quick." As she rushed past the smoking vents, she prayed the situation wasn't as grim as it looked. Maybe it was only dirt? Soot? Dead bugs? But she didn't pause in her flight out the front door.

Only when they were safely outside did she stop to take stock of her predicament. The neighborhood was dark. Even in broad daylight it left something to be desired; at night it seemed almost threatening. There was not so much as a yard light shining. Her seven-year-old Honda sat on the street, and she opened the car door, nearly threw the kids inside and reached into the back seat for a blanket. "Wrap up in this, Carrie. Wrap Kyle up, too. Come on, that's a girl. I have to get someone to call the fire department. Don't get out of the car. Don't. Do you hear?"

Kyle started to whimper, rubbing his eyes. Carrie pulled the blanket around her little brother and nodded to her mother. Then she began to comfort Kyle with little crooning, motherly sounds of "'s'okay…'s'okay…"

Chris slammed the car door shut and ran to the house next door. Like her own house, it was small, ramshackle and in need of a paint job. She rang the bell and pounded on the front door. After a minute or two she gave up, ran to the house across the street and began ringing and pounding and yelling. She was panicked. How long do you wait for someone to get up? She jumped from one foot to the other. No light came on there, either. "Come on, c'mon! Anybody home?" The porch light across the street went on, where she had begun. "Damn," she muttered, turning away from the door to run. The porch light behind her came on. "Jeez," she hissed, doubling back.

A sleepy, unshaven and angry-looking man opened the door. He was holding his robe closed over boxer shorts. That was when Chris remembered she was wearing only an extralarge T-shirt, moccasins and her undies. Purple silk undies, to be precise. That was it.

"Call the fire department," she begged her unsavory-looking neighbor. "The furnace is on fire. My kids are in my car. Hurry. Hurry!"

She turned and ran back to her car. She opened the door. "Are you okay?" They looked like two little birds peeking out from under the blanket.

"Mommy, what about Cheeks?" Carrie asked.

"Cheeks is in the backyard, sweetie. He's okay." She lifted her head to listen. "He's barking. Hear him?"

Carrie nodded, and her yellow curls bounced. "Can Cheeks come in the car with us?"

"I'll get him in a minute. You stay right here. Promise?" Again Carrie nodded. "I'll be right back. The fire truck is on its way. Pretty soon you'll hear the siren."

"Will our house burn down?"

"Burn down?" Kyle echoed.

"It'll be okay. Stay here now. I'll be right back."

Chris knew it was stupid to go back into a burning building; people died that way. But under these circumstances, she rationalized, it wasn't entirely stupid. First of all, she had seen only smoke, no other evidence of a bona fide fire. Second, the house was so tiny that the kitchen table, where her laptop and all her research lay, couldn't be more than ten steps inside the front door, which she intended to leave open in the event she had to make a fast getaway. Third, she wasn't going inside unless it looked relatively safe.

She heard the distant trill of the siren. The station was only about a mile away. She would be quick. And the smoke was not terrible, not blinding or choking. She had a plan.

She filled her lungs with clean air and bolted toward the kitchen. Even if the whole house burned to a cinder, the refrigerator would remain intact, like the bathtub in a tornado, right? Since she couldn't possibly gather up all her materials and her laptop and get them out of the house in one trip, she opened the refrigerator door and started heaving papers into it. It wasn't even supposed to be a long book. How had she ended up with so much stuff? And the books—the sourcebooks and expensive reference volumes—went in next. One marked *Sacramento Public Library* landed in the butter dish, but she didn't have time for neatness. She yanked out a half gallon of two-percent milk to make room for a pile of photocopied pages—the sirens were getting closer— and replaced a jug of apple juice with the large, old dictionary she had gotten at a garage sale. The sirens seemed to be winding down.

Suddenly Chris started feeling woozy. The laptop,

she thought dimly. Could she carry it out? But things started to blur. She looked toward the vents. That sucker, she thought remotely, was really smokin'…

The first fire engine stopped behind an old green Honda, and the men sprang off. The truck with ladders and hydraulics was right behind. As his men pulled a hose to a hydrant, Captain Mike Cavanaugh glanced at the burning house and approached the man in boxer shorts and a ratty bathrobe who stood on the curb. The furnace, he'd been told. He saw heat waves come off the roof. A furnace fire could have started in the basement, but in these old houses without fire-stops there could be an attic fire already. The ladder company would go up. Over his shoulder he called, "Take the peanut line in to fog it, and we'll open up the top." Then he turned to the bathrobed man. "Anyone in the house?"

"It ain't my house. Some woman's house. She's only lived there a couple of months. Them's her kids, there."

"Did you call it in?"

"Yeah, she was pounding on my door, said her furnace was on fire and her kids was in the car."

Mike felt someone tugging on his coat, and looked down. The face that stared up at him jarred him, almost cut through him. A little blond girl with the face of an angel, a face something inside him seemed to remember. She wore pajamas with feet, and beside her was a similarly attired little boy, one hand dragging a blanket and one hand holding on to his sister's pajamas. "Our mother's in the house," she said. "She told us to stay in the car."

"Then you'd better get back in the car," he said. "I'll get your mother." He spoke gently, but he broke into a run, pulling at the mouthpiece of his air pack so he could cover his face. "There's a woman in there," he informed a firefighter nearby. "Number 56 will initiate rescue. Take over incident command." The man, Jim Eble, turned to pass the word.

"Women," Mike muttered. Women invariably thought there was something worth saving in a fire. Usually a purse or some jewelry, but sometimes they were goofy enough to go back after a pair of shoes, or a robe.

Even these thoughts left him totally unprepared for what he found just steps inside the front door: a small woman, her thick, wavy hair in a fat ponytail, wearing only slippers, an oversize T-shirt and purple—yes, purple—silk underwear. He knew about the underwear because she was actually bending over, digging in the refrigerator, in a house cloudy with smoke.

He tapped her on the shoulder. "What are you, hungry?" Through his mask it came out something like "Bflust uurrr doooo, flungee?"

When she turned toward him he instantly recognized the ashen pallor and the glassy eyes. She coughed, her knees buckled, and he put his hands on her waist. She folded over his shoulder like a duffel bag. He supposed she might toss her cookies down his back; it wouldn't be the first time.

He pointed that purple silk rump toward the front door. It was right beside his ear, creating an indelible impression even in the midst of chaos.

Once he got her outside, he put her down by the rear of the engine and pulled down his mask. "Anyone else in the house?" he barked.

"Cheeks…is in…" she wheezed and choked "…the backyard."

"Cheeks?" he asked.

"Dog...wirehaired terrier," she managed. She gagged and fell against Jim, who held her shoulders and backed her up to the tailboard of the engine so she could sit down.

"I'll get the dog," Mike said to his friend. "Furnace is in the basement. We'll have to go down. Right smack in the middle of the house. That's not a new roof." He headed toward the backyard.

"Here," said Jim, pushing a mask toward Chris. "You'll feel a little better after some oxygen."

Chris decided this fireman was much gentler than the one who'd deposited her on the sidewalk. But his voice seemed to become smaller and more distant as her head whirled and her stomach flipped. She abruptly leaned away from him and lost dinner and several cups of coffee in the street. Bracing a hand on the tailboard, she heaved and shuddered. The man handed her a bunch of gauze four-by-fours to wipe her mouth. "Sometimes you feel a lot better after that." He touched her back. "It'll be okay now. Take it easy."

Chris, mortified, accepted the wipes and mopped her nose and mouth, meanwhile dying of all kinds of embarrassment. A large green trash bag miraculously appeared and covered the mess. All of this, she assumed, must be standard business at a fire.

"Is our mother sick?" Carrie asked in a small voice.

"Mama?" came Kyle's echo.

The fireman hunkered down and smiled into their little faces. "Naw, not really. She smelled too much smoke, and it made her sick to her stomach. She feels better now. Dontcha, Mom?"

She straightened up, eyes closed, and nodded. She

couldn't speak yet, but she felt her pea-green face turning red. The irony was not lost on her that her house was burning down, and all she felt was shame because she was wearing practically nothing and had thrown up in the street.

"Our mother is going to be upset if her book burns up," Carrie told the fireman.

"Well, now, we can always get another book, can't we? But it sure would be hard to find another mommy as special as this one. That's why we *never* go back into a house where there's a fire."

"Our mother is *typing* her book, and it takes a very long time and is very hard to do," Carrie informed him rather indignantly.

As the fireman glanced at Chris, she stretched her T-shirt down over her thighs. She was recovering now. "Never mind that, Carrie. The fireman is right—I should not have gone back into the house. It was very dangerous and very stupid." She looked up at the fireman. "I don't suppose you have a drink of water?"

"Well," he said, standing and looking around, "water is pretty hard to come by."

She noticed three different hoses reaching across the lawn toward her smoking house and shook her head.

"I'll ask a neighbor," he said, moving away.

A minute or two later he returned with a paper cup. After she had taken a few swallows she noticed that he was holding a blanket toward her. "Thanks," she said, trading the water for the cover. "If I'd known you were coming, I would have dressed."

"No problem," he said. "Besides, you don't have to be embarrassed by those legs," he added as he turned away. The blanket, thankfully, reached her ankles.

"Whoa!" came a baritone shout, followed by a crashing sound.

Part of the roof where men had been poking opened up, and flames leapt out. Two firefighters came shooting out the front door of the house, then two others dragged a larger hose in. They were everywhere—inside, outside, on the roof.

It was amazing, Chris thought. Just a few minutes ago she'd only seen a little smoke. Now there was a great deal more than smoke; red-orange flames were eating up the little house.

Out of the darkness the tall fireman who had saved her life approached them with a silver ball of fur that went *grrrr* in his arms. He handed Cheeks to Chris. Cheeks, very particular about who carried him around, snarled and yapped in transit. He was cranky.

Carrie and Kyle pressed closer to Chris, and her arms wrapped around them reassuringly, enfolding them in a circle of safety she herself didn't quite feel. As she drew Kyle up onto the tailboard and hugged Carrie closer with her other arm, she saw that all the neighbors she had never met were up, watching her house burn down.

"Maybe we should have a block party," she muttered, kissing one child's head, then the other, then getting a dog's tongue right across her lips and nose. *"Phlettt."* She grimaced.

"Do we have a second alarm?" one fireman asked another.

"Yep." Just that fast another huge rig rounded the corner, bringing the total to four. They had not heard the sirens, Chris assumed, because of the general pandemonium immediately around them: shouting, engines, radios, gushing water and the hissing, creaking, crackling sound of everything she owned in the world turning to ash.

This new fire truck blinked its headlights like a great behemoth, and soon its ladder and basket rose like a stiff arm over the tops of the eucalyptus trees. A hose that was threaded upward began to pour water down on the little house.

Fire fighting had turned to demolition, from Chris's point of view. She flinched at the sound of crashing glass and splintering wood as windows and doors were smashed in. She looked back to the mounting traffic. Police cars blocked the street, and an ambulance had arrived. Chris and her kids and dog sat quietly on the bumper of engine 56.

Tears ran down her cheeks. There it all went. And there hadn't been very much. Five weeks until Christmas. She was twenty-seven years old, and this was the third time in seven years that she stood by, helpless, hopeless, while everything she had, everything she thought she *was*, disappeared—this time, before her very eyes. First, when her parents both died in a small plane crash. She had been twenty, and an only child. Then, when Steve walked out on her without so much as a goodbye after having used up her every emotion and every penny of what her parents had left her. Now this.

"Mommy, where are we going to sleep?"

"I…uh…we'll work that out, baby. Don't worry."

"Mommy? Did our sleeping bags burn up? How can we sleep without our sleeping bags?"

"Now, Carrie," Chris said, her voice breaking despite her effort to fake strength, "don't we always m-manage?"

The house was fifty-six years old and, because of

the landlord's minimal maintenance, badly run-down. It didn't take much time for it to look like one big black clump. Chris sat watching, stunned, for less than two hours. She wasn't even aware of being cold.

The last fire truck to arrive left first. The neighbors went to bed without asking if there was anything she needed. Hell, they went back into their houses without *introducing* themselves. A policeman took a brief statement from her: the furnace came on after she set the thermostat, then it made smoke. Not much to tell. He gave her a card that had phone numbers for Victims Aid and the Red Cross and headed back toward his car. The disappointed ambulance was long gone. Kyle snored softly, his blond head against her chest, the fireman's blanket that she wore wrapped around him and Cheeks. Carrie leaned against her, wrapped in her own blanket, watching in fascination and fear. She was silent but wide-eyed. It was after 2:00 a.m., Chris estimated, when she found herself sitting on the bumper of engine 56 with no earthly idea of what she was going to do next.

The fireman who had saved her life stood in front of her. He seemed even taller now that her house was a mere cinder. His hair, thick and brown and curly, was now sweaty and matted to his scalp. Dirt and perspiration streaked his face. His eyes were deeply set and brooding under thick brows, but there was a sympathetic turn to his mouth.

"If you take this fire engine out from under me, I have absolutely no idea where I'll sit."

"You don't know any of the neighbors?"

She shook her head. If she attempted to say a word about how all the neighbors had just gone off, she might cry.

"Is there someone you can call?"

She shrugged. Was there? She wasn't sure about that.

"You can go to the police station and make some calls. Or we can wake up a neighbor so you can use their phone. Or you could come to the firehouse and—"

"The firehouse," she requested abruptly. "Please." She couldn't face a police station tonight. Or her ex-neighbors. At that moment, looking up at the man who had carried her out of a burning house and even managed to rescue Cheeks, she had the uncanny feeling that he was all she could depend on.

"Got any family around here? A husband? Ex-husband?"

"Oh, there's an ex-husband…somewhere," she said.

"Don't I know you?" he asked.

She frowned.

"Iverson's," he said. "The grocery store."

Of course, she thought. Before tonight, that was the only thing she had known about the local firemen. They shopped for their groceries together, finicky and cohesive, in much the way women went to restaurant rest rooms together. Chris was a checkout clerk at Iverson's grocery store, and it had always amused her to see the truck pull into the parking lot and five or six big, strapping men wander in to do their shopping for dinner. "Yes. Sure."

"Well, you must have some friends around here, then."

How that followed, she was unsure. Did being a clerk in a grocery store ensure friendship? She had only moved to Sacramento from Los Angeles in late August, just in time for Carrie to start school. She had a few friends at work, but their phone numbers, which she'd rarely had time to use anyway, were in that big ash heap. And she couldn't call anyone in L.A. She'd live in a tent in the park before she'd go back there.

"I'll think of someone on the way to the firehouse," she emphasized. "There are probably fewer criminals there than at the police station." She looked down at her slippered feet. "I'm not dressed to fend off criminals tonight. How long can I use the blanket?"

For the first time Mike remembered the purple panties and was glad it was dark. His cheeks felt warm. *He* felt warm. It was a vaguely familiar feeling, and he liked it. "Until you're done with it, I guess. You can get some things from the Red Cross. I'll get the officer to drive you to the firehouse. We can't take you on the engine."

"What about my house?" she asked.

"Well," he said, looking over his shoulder, "what house?"

"Won't it be looted or something?"

"Lady, there isn't a whole lot left to loot. You have any valuables that might have survived the fire?"

"Yeah," she said, squeezing her kids. "Right here."

He grinned at her approvingly; it was a great, spontaneous smile of crowded, ever-so-slightly protruding, superwhite teeth. A smile that did not hold pity but humanity. And one deep dimple—left side. "You got the best of it, then." He started to turn away.

"The refrigerator," she said, making him turn back. "Did the refrigerator go?"

"Well, it'll never run again."

"I don't care about the refrigerator itself," she said, her voice gaining strength. "I put my laptop in there. And research papers. There's a book on the computer. It's the very last thing of any value I—" She stopped before her voice broke and she began to blubber. She hugged her children tighter. Inside she felt like a little girl herself, a defenseless, abandoned, pitiful orphan. *Won't someone do something, please. Why, oh, God, why does my luck get worse and worse, and just when I think I might make it, it goes wrong and I don't even know what I did to deserve this and, oh, my God, my kids, my poor kids.*

"Is that what you were doing?" he asked her.

She looked up at him. Brown eyes? No, green. And crinkled at the corners.

"What…what did you think I was doing?" she asked.

He reached into the engine cab for an industrial-sized flashlight. "I had absolutely no idea. I'll go see if the fridge made it."

She stood suddenly, struggling to hold on to Kyle and Cheeks. "Well, be careful."

The hoses were being put away, and the shortwave radios were having distant and eerie conversations with one another.

He came back. He had it. A laptop she'd salvaged from her former life. He showed it to her, smiling. It wasn't even singed. "It's got butter on it. And something red. Ketchup, I think."

"I don't believe it," she breathed.

"Well, I hope it's good. It almost cost you way more than it could possibly be worth. Don't you know better than to go into a burning—"

"The sleeping bags? Toys? Clothes?"

He shook his head, exasperated. "Really, there wasn't time to save anything in there. We tried, but… Come on, let's get you into the squad car. These old houses, jeez."

Chris walked ahead of him in the direction of the police car. She carried Kyle and Cheeks while Carrie held on to Chris's blanket, trailing behind. The fireman followed with the laptop. "I've known women to go back for their purses, but I couldn't imagine what you were doing in the refrigerator! They'll never believe this one. You're lucky, all right."

"I'm not feeling all *that* lucky."

"Well, you ought to. That old house went up like kindling."

Taking her precious laptop, Chris managed to get into the police car without saying anything more, and they followed the fire engine to the station. The policeman carried Kyle inside, but Chris was stuck with Cheeks because of his obnoxious attitude. She struggled to hold the terrier and her laptop.

Inside the station she was taken into a little living room that boasted two couches, several chairs, a desk, a telephone and television and even a Ping-Pong table. This must be where they lounged between fires.

The big fireman, out of his coat now, suspenders holding up his huge canvas pants, a tight T-shirt stretched over his enormous chest and shoulders, was standing in the living room as if he were the welcoming committee.

Carrie tugged on his pants. "Our mother types on her book every night because she is trying to be a book writer and not work at the grocery store anymore."

"Oh?" the fireman said.

"And it's worth a very lot," Carrie informed him proudly.

Chapter 2

After the other firemen were finished, Mike Cavanaugh took his turn in the upstairs shower to wash away
the acrid odor of smoke that clung to his hair and skin.
While he lathered his hair he thought of his mother,
who lived nearby. She would have heard the sirens and
might be lying awake, wondering if her firstborn was
all right. Mike knew this because his father had told
him; his mother had never admitted it. He could give
her a call, his father had suggested, making Mike suspect it wasn't only his mother who worried. But, hell,
he was thirty-six years old. He was not going to call
his mother after every middle-of-the-night alarm so she
could fall back to sleep without worrying. Besides, it
would start a bad pattern. If he obliged, sometimes his
phone call would come fifteen minutes after the sirens,
occasionally it would be hours. Calling would become

worse than never calling. Sooner or later she would have
to get used to this. He had been a firefighter for more
than twelve years.

He did, however, check in with his parents during
the daytime. And he had bought them a multiband radio
scanner so they could listen to the radio calls. He wasn't
as stubborn as he pretended.

It had been 3:00 a.m. when he left the woman—
Christine Palmer, he'd learned when they finally had
a moment to exchange names—and her kids in the rec
room. He'd given her a couple of pillows and blankets
to tuck her little ones in on the couches, and some extra
clothing for herself—the smallest sweatpants and sweatshirt that could be found. He'd told her which line to use
to make her calls. He'd told her to go ahead and close
her eyes for a while if she could; the men would be
getting up for breakfast and a shift change in a couple
of hours—around 6:00 a.m. She could have someone
pick her up in the morning so as not to upset the kids'
sleep any further.

Upstairs in the sleeping quarters there had been some
grumbling. It was not customary to bring homeless fire
victims to the firehouse. It was very rare, in fact. Jim
had said it might set a bad precedent. Hal had said the
kids might be noisy and rob them of what little sleep
they had left. Stu had said he suspected it was that little purple tushie Mike had carried out of the house that
had prompted this innovative move. Mike had said, "Go
to sleep, girls, and try not to get on my nerves." Mike
was in charge tonight.

He couldn't stop thinking about her, however. It
wasn't the purple silk butt, even though that did cross
his mind from time to time. It was the way she seemed

unusually alone with those two little kids. He thought he'd picked up a defiant loneliness in her eyes. Blue eyes, he remembered. When she thrust out her chin it gave her otherwise soft face a sort of challenge. It was peculiar, especially during a catastrophe as exciting to the average man or woman as a house fire, not to have people rally around the victims. Even in neighborhoods where folks were not well acquainted or friendly, it was odd not to have someone break out of the crowd and ask all the right questions, take the family in, call a church or a victims' aid organization. The Salvation Army. But Christine Palmer seemed to hold them all at bay with her look of utter isolation.

Mike could have called the Salvation Army himself. Or the Red Cross. He'd taken a shower instead. His first reaction had been to distance himself from this little family; their aloneness made *him* feel vulnerable. But he felt them pulling him like a magnet. Now he decided to go downstairs and see if she was awake. He wouldn't bother her if the lights were out. Or if her eyes were closed. He was just too curious to go to sleep.

Christine Palmer was a curiosity—an attractive enough one, to be sure—but it was that precocious little blond bombshell who'd gotten right under his skin. He had had a daughter once. And a wife. They had been dead for ten years. Joanie had been only twenty-three and Shelly three when a car accident stole them away and left holes in Mike's soul. He had felt a charge, like a shot of electricity, when that Shirley Temple reincarnate tugged on his coat. What a kid. He felt a giddy lightness; then a familiar, unwelcome ache.

When his foot touched the bottom step he heard a predictable *grrrr*. Then he heard "Shut up, Cheeks." So he knew she was awake. Mike stood in the doorway of the rec room and saw that Cheeks was sleeping on the end of the little boy's couch, right on the kid's feet. He liked that, that the dog guarded the kids. He felt as though these kids needed that. They slept soundly; the boy snored softly. Christine Palmer sat at the desk nearby, her feet drawn up and her arms wrapped around her knees. The phone book was open in front of her, and her back was to him.

The terrier stiffened his front legs, showed his teeth and growled seriously. She turned to see Mike standing there, surprise briefly widening her red-rimmed eyes. Then she turned away quickly and blew her nose as though it was humiliating to be caught crying after your whole world had burned up. "Shut up, Cheeks," she commanded sternly. "Down." The terrier obliged, but he watched.

"Has he ever actually bitten anyone?" Mike asked, working hard at sounding friendly and nonthreatening.

"No," she said, wiping her eyes before swiveling the chair around to face him.

She had pulled sweat socks up to her knees over the sweatpants, probably to take up some slack; she was drowning in the smallest sweats they could find. Small boned, but with a wiry toughness that showed. She was a very pretty woman. Her blue eyes were fierce, her thick, light brown hair willfully wavy, springing loose around her face. If they hadn't just been through a fire and if he hadn't caught her crying he would wonder if contacts gave her eyes that intense, penetrating color.

"Cheeks is only crabby," she said. "He's not dangerous. But I don't mind if strangers are wary around my kids."

"Why'd you name him Cheeks?"

"His mustache. When we first got him, Carrie grabbed him by that hair around his mouth and said, 'Mommy, look at his cheeks,' and it stuck." She shrugged and tried to smile. The rims of her lips were pink, and her nose was watery. "This is very embarrassing," she said, becoming still more fluid.

"Look, it was a bad fire. Of course you're upset."

"No…no, not that. I… I have no one to call. See, I'm new in Sacramento. I only moved here the end of August, just before Carrie started school. I got a job at Iverson's about a month, no, six weeks ago. I only know a few people. I don't know anyone's phone number except Mr. Iverson's at the store. I have a baby-sitter for Kyle and for Carrie after school, but she doesn't have—" She stopped. *Anything* was the next word. The baby-sitter, Juanita Jimeniz, was the mother of another grocery-store clerk; the Jimenizes were practically destitute themselves. There were more family members living under one roof than there appeared to be beds. No help there.

"I could give you a lift to the bank after my shift change if you—"

"My checking account has $12.92 in it."

"Where'd you come from, then?" he asked, moving to sit on one of the chairs near the desk. Cheeks growled, watching. Mike wasn't convinced he wouldn't bite.

"Los Angeles."

"Well, that's not so far away. Maybe someone there could send you a few bucks? Or invite you back down till you get, you know, reestablished?" He felt his heavy brows draw together, and he tried unsuccessfully to smooth out the frown. His mother had warned him that he looked mean, threatening, whenever he got that brooding look, his heavy brows nearly connecting over the bridge of his nose. But his forehead took on contemplative lines now because he was confused.

Something about Christine Palmer did not sit well. She appeared indigent, yet he'd shuffled a goodly number of indigent families off to Victims Aid, and she didn't fit. People totally without resources, without family, friends, money, without memberships in churches, clubs or unions, did not usually rush into burning buildings to save the books they were writing. Strange. What's missing from this picture? he asked himself.

"L.A. was also…pretty temporary," she said.

Her hesitation and her downcast eyes made Mike think she was lying.

"Mrs. Palmer, are you in some kind of trouble?"

Her head snapped back. "Yeah. My house just burned down, my car keys are in there somewhere, I have no money—oh, I *had* forty-two dollars and some cents in my purse for groceries for the rest of the week till payday, but I imagine that's gone, too. And I lied about L.A. I was there for more than three years. I had already borrowed as much as my former friends were willing to—" She stopped abruptly, took a deep breath and quieted herself. "There was no farewell party, all right? I didn't actually do anything wrong, I just…had a run of bad luck. An unpleasant divorce. My ex is a… scoundrel. It gets rough sometimes."

"Oh," Mike said, pretending to understand. "Make any calls to the Red Cross? Victims Aid?"

She nodded. "And two crisis counseling centers, four shelters and a church group that's helping illegal aliens. Do you know what? My house burned down on the first freezing night in Sacramento. Everyone, it seems, has come in off the streets."

"No luck?"

She shrugged. "I have two more numbers here. The Opportunity Hotel and a place called Totem Park. Do you suppose you have to sleep outside in Totem Park?"

"I know so," he said, frowning. "Here, let me try the hotel," he offered, pulling the phone across the desk. She turned the pad on which she had written the number toward him. He glanced at the sleeping kids as he waited for an answer on the line. Their shiny yellow heads were clean, their pajamas the warm and tidy kind. They were obviously well cared for, with healthy skin and teeth. Bright, alert eyes, when they were awake.

This particular shelter, called a hotel because they took a few dollars from people who either overstayed or could afford it, was possibly the sleaziest place in the city, Mike knew. Some people actually preferred the street to places like this; protection from the other homeless was difficult to provide. Even though she didn't have anything to steal, Christine Palmer didn't look tough enough to fend off an assault. He glanced at the kids again; the ringing continued on the line. The shelter was filthy, nasty. He wondered if there were rats.

Finally there was an answer. "Hi, this is Captain Mike Cavanaugh, Sacramento Fire Department. We're trying to place a homeless family—woman and two small kids. Any room down there?"

The man on the line said yes.

"Oh, too bad. Thanks anyway," Mike said, making his decision and hanging up quickly.

"I'll call Mr. Iverson in the morning, when the store

opens. He's a pretty decent guy. Maybe he'll advance me some pay or something."

"Are you *completely* orphaned?" He didn't mean to sound incredulous, but he came from a large family himself and had trouble picturing a life without relatives. Cavanaugh. Irish Catholic. Six kids.

"My parents are dead; I'm an only child. There's this unmarried aunt back in Chicago, where I grew up, but she probably hates my guts. We parted on very unfriendly terms a long while back." She gave a short, bitter laugh. "Actually, it was all my fault. But I'm sure if I grovel and beg and apologize enough, Aunt Florence will invite me and the kids back home. Chicago. Ugh. I hate the idea of crawling back to Chicago, all ashamed and sorry." She slapped the laptop on the desk. "I was going to go back, you know. Patch things up with Aunt Flo, who is the only family I have in the world besides the kids. But later, hopefully with my tail straight up and not tucked between my legs." Her voice quieted. "I'm not a bad writer. Some people have liked my work."

"'It's worth a very lot,'" he said, quoting the little girl.

"Oh, to her," Chris said, her voice becoming sentimental, almost sweet. "Carrie's my biggest fan. Also the greatest kid in the whole world. Never lost faith in me—not once." A large tear spilled over.

"No one, huh?" he asked her.

"I'm sure I'll think of something in the morning. I've been called resourceful. Gutsy, even. Probably nice ways of saying I'm contrary and not easy to get along with."

He laughed. She wasn't nearly as hysterical as she could be, under the circumstances. Nor as scared. And he could relate; he wasn't always easy to get along with, either. "Just so you get along," he said.

"One way or the other."

"Well, this doesn't look good," he supplied.

"No, but them's the breaks, huh? I'll think of something. I hope."

According to six o'clock news stories, Mike considered, this was how it happened: some perfectly nice, smart, clean, decent individual hit a cultural snag— illness, divorce, unemployment. Fire. Then, with no money for rent deposits, utilities turn-on, child care or retraining, he or she was suddenly living out of a car. After about three weeks of living out of a car, no one would hire them. Then, if they did land a job by some miracle, they couldn't work it because there was nowhere to shower, leave the kids or do the laundry. A mean social cycle. No money, no job. No job, no money. The forgotten people who were once accountants or engineers.

The press indicated the homeless situation was getting worse every year. The reported living conditions were terrifying. Hopeless and vile. The one common link among these people seemed to be aloneness, lack of family. Mike had family. Boy, did he.

"You know what?" he began. "Maybe we could help you get a news spot. A little—"

"What?"

"You know, get channel five to do a spot on the fire and your circumstances."

"What? What are you talking about?"

"Donations to a post-office box or bank or—"

"*Be* on the news?"

"Yeah, because your house—"

"Oh, *please*. Please don't do that. I'd die!"

"Well, it's nothing to be ashamed of. It's not like it was your fault, you know."

"No. No. That would be awful!"

Okay, he thought, she's hiding. From the ex? She didn't look like a bank robber or kid— Kidnapper? He wondered if the ex had gotten custody. Yeah, he decided. That was probably it. Well, maybe. Whatever, she was hiding something. He wondered how much.

"Tell you what. I live alone. You could use my place for a couple of days. It's a roof."

"What?" she said, almost laughing. "Come on, that's not your usual policy. In fact, judging from some of the looks we've gotten, I'd say you don't have a whole lot of fire victims in your rec room, either."

"It's not usual," he admitted. He shook his head. He had surprised himself as much as her with the offer. But Christmas was coming, and the kids were clean, cute, precocious. She had some secrets, but he was sure they weren't the dangerous kind. Bad luck, she had said. Most of all, they had no one. No one. Well, what the heck, he was someone.

"Fact is, none of this has been policy. The only other time we brought a fire victim here in the middle of the night, it was a relative of a firefighter. Upstairs they think I've gone soft in the head."

"We'd better get out of here."

"Naw, no problem. Here's the deal, Christine. Can I call you Christine? Chrissie?"

"How about Chris."

He nodded. "Well, here it is, Chris. I'm a little soft in the head. You seem to be having some rotten luck, and I don't have to know what happened to you, but that little girl of yours reminds me of my little girl. She was a lot like that one," he said, jerking his head toward the sofa. "Blond, opinionated, had an IQ of about four thousand. She died in a car accident with her mother about ten years ago. She was only three. And hell, it's almost Christmas."

Chris stared at him. She had only lost a house and everything she owned. Suddenly it didn't seem like much.

"So," he said, watching her watch him. "I don't spend all that much time at my house. I sleep here when I'm on duty, I have a cabin I like to use when I have a few days off in a row, and I have family all over Sacramento. It's a pretty good-sized place, I guess. Three bedrooms. You could make a few calls, get some things like insurance paperwork started. You might say a few things to that landlord about the furnace, and he might settle with you real quick, but there could be a lawsuit in it. You didn't hear that from me, okay? And then, before you grovel to your old-maid aunt, you'd have a little edge. There don't seem to be many alternatives." He shrugged. "It would be too bad to have to take those kids to one of those crappy shelters. Most of them are pretty awful."

"Your house," she said, her voice barely a whisper. She looked at him a little differently. She judged his size and musculature.

"My parents live just around the corner, and I could stay with them when I'm not here. I might be soft in the head, but I'm pretty safe. Anyway—" he smiled "—you have *him*," he said, glancing at Cheeks.

"Gee, that's…really generous of you," she said, but she said it cautiously, suspiciously. Mike wondered if she had been abused by the ex. He wondered *how* abused.

"It's a pretty well-known fact that firefighters have a weakness for little kids. It's up to you. I live alone, but I have this house. I didn't even want it, to tell you the truth, but my family started hounding me about doing something with my money—real estate, you know. Sometimes you have to do something just so that everyone in your very nosy family will get off your back. So they talk you into buying something, investing. Then they stop worrying and start calling you moneybags." He chuckled to himself. "In my family, everyone minds everyone's business but their own. It's an Irish tradition."

"What will your very nosy family say if you take in this completely unknown, whacked-out, poverty-stricken divorcée with two kids and a dog?"

"Oh, I don't know. They'll probably shake their heads and say, 'It figures.' They gave up on me a long time ago; I'm the one they always shake their heads over. They call me ornery. Probably just a nice way of saying I'm not easy to get along with," he said, and grinned that big grin again.

"You?"

"Yeah. Don't I seem ornery?"

She tilted her head and looked at him. He smiled confidently through her appraisal. "No," she said after a moment. Gentle. Generous. Never ornery. "But they know you better than I do."

"They have their reasons, I suppose." Reason number one, they couldn't get him remarried after Joanie and Shelly were gone. Not a one of them—not three brothers and their wives, not two sisters and all the friends they had in Sacramento. Tough, he told them. He had never liked dating, and he kept his few liaisons to himself; they had never come to much, anyway. Though he missed Joanie and Shelly, he no longer minded being alone. He had gone through school with Joanie, married her when he was twenty and she was eighteen. And he had known he was going to do that the first time he kissed her.

He had liked being a husband and father. And he wasn't anymore.

What he also liked was to hunt, a reclusive sport. He liked the department's baseball team, the gym, the little one-room house in the mountains, and sitting in front of a television set with his dad and brothers when they couldn't get tickets to a game. He liked to read, and he liked to putter under his car. He was solitary but not antisocial. Sometimes he needed sex, someone to make love with, but he didn't like doing it with strangers and there hadn't been very many women over the years who'd become friends. It had been quite a while, in fact. He was a little disappointed in himself for that, but he had become a man who put his energy into a lot of physical things and thereby coped with a primary physical need left unmet. The longer he waited, the less urgent he felt.

He was a quiet, private, sometimes lonely man who had no one to spend his money on except his mom and dad, his brothers and sisters and their spouses and kids. Uncle Mike. He knew what he was becoming—the odd uncle, gentle with some, crotchety with others. Difficult and sometimes short-tempered. Like Cheeks.

"What do you think? Got any better ideas?"

"I…uh…it's hard for me to take…you know, charity. I don't know if…"

He tilted his head toward the sleeping kids. "They

won't know the difference. You oughta see some of those shelters. You've got a job, so pay me a little rent if you want, later, when you get it together. Or maybe you could do a few things around the house? Like cleaning or laundry?" He tried not to draw his eyebrows meanly over his nose, which happened whenever he lied. His house was immaculate, and his mother did his laundry. She insisted.

"What if I'm a crook or something? What if I hotwire my old Honda, clean out your house and haul your TV and stereo off to Mexico?" She was weakening.

Mike laughed. "They'd never let you across the border with that dog." Cheeks growled on cue. "God, he's a piece of work. If he bites me, he's out. Does he, um, make any mistakes?"

"No," she said, smiling. "He's really a very good dog, just crabby. And the kids are pretty good, too." And there it was. Without her saying anything more, he knew it was decided. She and the kids would move in tomorrow.

In the morning, while Jim scrambled eggs for the whole crew, Carrie tugged on Mike's sweatpants. He looked down into her pretty blue eyes. "Our mother says we're going to stay at your house for a little while, because our house is burned."

"Do you think you'll mind?" he asked her.

"No," she said. She smiled at him. "Do you want us to?"

"I invited you, didn't I?"

"We always pick up our toys and our dirty clothes," she informed him. "Kyle is just learning, but he's learning very good."

"I'm sure you're very neat," Mike said. "But I'm a little bit sloppy."

Carrie's expression changed suddenly. She looked over her shoulder toward her little brother, who was sitting on the couch with his thumb in his mouth. Then she looked back up at Mike's face. "Our toys burned up," she said, her expression stoic.

"Oh, didn't I tell you? I must've forgotten. I have toys. They're at my mother's house, but she'll let you borrow them. If you promise to pick them up, of course."

She smiled suddenly, and her eyes became very like her mother's. "We'll pick them up. We're learning very good."

Cheeks growled.

"Can you make him stop doing that?" Mike asked her.

"If he gets used to you, he stops it. You must not hit him. It will make him mean."

"He already sounds mean."

"Yes," she said, smiling a wild young smile that was tangy with innocence and made Mike feel warm all over. "But he only *sounds* it," she added with a giggle.

He wanted to crush her in his big arms. He became afraid of himself, his hard and trembling shell, his gushy innards. He was an uncle who had cuddled many nieces and nephews since he'd lost his own child, but he suddenly, desperately, wished to hold a child who *needed* to be held.

He picked her up, gently. His loneliness, his aching desire for a family of his own, pressed against the backs of his eyes. What was he doing with this child in his arms? A long time ago he'd stopped trying to replace what he'd lost. After ten years, he'd built a strong enough wall that he didn't have to face what he had lost. But holding this little girl shook loose the bricks he had used to build his wall.

Everything they had was gone, and it hadn't been much to start with. Yet these people were not the destitute ones.

Chapter 3

Mike opened the front door for them but did not go in to show them around. He and Chris had talked on the way over. He said he had a lot to get done on his days off, and she had important decisions to make, phone calls to place. Calls that Mike suggested might be easier if he wasn't there to listen.

"You go ahead and look around," he told her. "You won't have any trouble recognizing the two extra bedrooms. The one with the desk and the couch, well, the couch folds out into a bed. And keep the kids out of the garage, okay? There are power tools out there. I'll be back around lunchtime."

"Look, I feel kind of funny, going in alone and everything. There's no reason you should trust me, you know. I mean, it's not too late to—"

"Is there anything you're looking for besides a way to take care of your kids?" he countered.

"No," she answered.

"That's what I figured. Just make your calls. I'm going to stop by the house you rented. If I found an ash that might have been a purse, would your car keys be in it? Maybe a crispy cell phone?"

"Yes, keys. No phone—too expensive." She smiled. "Hey, that would be great. Really, I don't know how to thank you for all this."

"Don't worry about that. I don't usually do things I don't want to do. It just isn't that big a deal."

"It is," she said, peeking into the house. "It's a very, very big deal."

"Naw." He shrugged. "The place just about stands vacant. I'll see you in a few hours, then. And listen, I'm going to be pretty tied up for a couple of days, so I hope you can handle all your reorganizing without my help." As if it had just occurred to him, he added, "Since I'm going to stay with my folks, take…uh…the master bedroom, if you want."

Then he vanished. Chris cautiously placed Cheeks on the floor inside the front door. As she and the children stood watching, he ran down the stairs from the foyer into the carpeted living room. "Please, God," she said, "don't let him pee." He scooted around the floor like a windup toy, his whiskers flush against the rug, zooming a pattern of certainty that no other dog had marked the place. He paused for a long while at the coffee table leg. "I'll kill you," Chris warned. The terrier looked over his shoulder at her, then zoomed on.

As Cheeks sniffed and scooted around downstairs, Chris and the kids peeked up the short flight of steps leading to the bedrooms. The three of them were all a little frightened of the fireman's house. It was quiet, new, immaculate, not theirs. Chris finally stepped across the parquet entry onto the thick gray carpet that flowed down the steps.

The living room was decorated in masculine colors of blue, gray, dark purple and dark rose, mostly velour. Walnut accent tables held a few decorator items—an unused ashtray, a scented candle, coffee-table books. A fireplace with a great granite hearth took up most of one wall. Even the logs in the tray beside it looked impossibly clean.

The kids stared at the entertainment center as if it were a rocket ship. Stereo, DVD player, large HD television, DVDs, CDs, speakers, knobs by the dozen, dials, all enclosed in smoky glass. Spotless, smearless, dark glass. And paintings—prints, actually. Could he have chosen the prints? Also behind glass. Two McKnights. McKnight was known for his happy, homey, bright settings of rooms devoid of people. No hazy pastels, but sharp-featured living-room scenes crowded with things, not people, paintings of rooms that seemed to celebrate themselves with vibrant aloneness. Like Mike?

"My God," she muttered, "I might have to feed you kids in the bathtub."

"He said he was a little sloppy," Carrie told her, "but I think he's learning very good."

"Yeah," Chris replied absently. "Don't touch anything. See that coaster there, on the coffee table?" She pointed. "That brown thing that you put your glass on so you don't leave a mark on the table?" They nodded. "That's the only thing in this room that I can afford to replace."

"Are we going to put our glass on it to not leave a spot?" Carrie asked.

"No," she said. "You're not going to eat or drink anything in the living room." She looked around fretfully.
"I'm going to keep a bottle of Windex strapped to my
belt."

"I never eated in the bathtub," Carrie said.

"Ate. And I'm kidding. Maybe."

She felt a lump in her throat and turned them around
before they could look with envy at the living room any
longer. "Come on, let's see if we can find where we're
going to sleep."

Upstairs was not the showplace the downstairs was,
but it, too, was immaculate. The bedrooms were large
and airy and practically unfurnished. The only furniture in one was a set of twin beds, with not so much as
a lamp or cardboard box in addition. The other room
had a love seat, which, upon inspection, Chris found
was the hide-a-bed. And there was a desk where Mike
paid his bills. The desk had a glass top. Underneath
the glass were a few pictures. One was a picture of a
woman and child, and by the woman's hairstyle, Chris
guessed it was them. She stared at it a long time, the
ones he had lost. Her heart began to split into a bleeding wound. Poor guy. How could you lose that much?
It was incomprehensible. She had buried her parents
before becoming a mother. She had since decided that
the overwhelming pain of that still could not approach
what a parent must feel when burying a child. Her throat
began to close.

"Is that me with the lady?" Carrie asked.

"No," she said, her voice soft and reverent. "No, honey.
That's Mr. Cavanaugh's little girl and his wife. They died
a long, long time ago. Way before you were even born."

"Does he miss them, then?"

"Yes, of course. This is his private stuff, all right?" Private feelings. "I don't think we should ask him questions about it. Okay?" Chris crouched so she could look into Carrie's eyes. Her own wanted to water, but she tried not to cry over borrowed heartache. "In fact, I don't think we should even mention we saw the picture, okay? Please?"

"Okay. Can we watch TV?"

"Sure," she said, straightening. "If I can figure it out. Come on. Back downstairs, where you may sit on the floor and touch nothing."

"I thought you said we could touch that brown thing?"

Chris was not in awe of Mike's moderate, tasteful wealth, even if her children might be. She was in awe of *him*. There was stuff to steal here. How was he so sure she wouldn't? How did he know she'd be careful? How could he do this, trust her like this? He knew nothing about her, nothing at all. Except that she was alone and had nothing. She felt a trifle insecure about using his discriminately chosen, carefully placed things, but her chief insecurity was that she didn't deserve this charitable act.

Chris had grown up in a house that would make Mike's place look like the maid's quarters. The fireman's house, in fact, was much like the place she and Steve shared the first year they were married. The kids wouldn't remember anything so comfortable, however. The comparison to what they *did* know made her shudder, and the tightness in her throat grew into a lump of self-pity as she took the children downstairs to deposit them in front of the television while she made some calls.

Mr. Iverson excused her from her job for a few days and agreed to give her a hundred-dollar advance on her salary, which he would deduct from her pay over an extended period of time. She gave him the phone number where she could be reached and called the babysitter. Juanita asked her if there was anything she needed. In spite of the fact that they needed everything, she said nothing. Juanita, good-hearted and hardworking, had too little to share. At Carrie's school, the secretary offered the names of places that might offer help. Chris didn't mention she had already tried most of them, but simply informed her that Carrie would not be back for a while. Actually, she didn't know where Carrie would go to school next, and she was grateful it was only kindergarten.

The call to the landlord was another story. Not a story of compassion, either.

"Well, Mrs. Blakely, when do you think Mr. Blakely will be able to return my call?"

"I'm sure I don't know, Mrs. Palmer. He's a little upset about the house, you know. We don't know how that happened."

Chris laughed hollowly. "It happened because the furnace was old, in poor repair and hadn't been serviced in a good many years."

"Ah, I see. You, of course, have the arson report?"

"Arson report?"

"Could you possibly have been…smoking?"

"I don't smoke! Hey, listen, I've got two little kids, and we could've all been killed! We didn't even get the car keys out of that old house, it went up so fast! Would you like to take down this number, please?"

"I'm sure we don't need your number, dear, as long as the police know where you can be found."

"What?"

"Well, we don't want to make any accusations, naturally, before the investigation is complete, but I'll take your word that you won't leave the area."

Chris was stunned for a moment. Then, thanks to the finesse she had learned too late from her missing ex-husband—who she hoped was at that very moment being subjected to some incredible Chinese torture that would leave vicious scars—she let out a knowing sigh.

"Mrs. Blakely," she said smoothly, "my lawyer suggested that I find out when your husband will be available for a settlement meeting. We should probably talk before any further medical tests are run on my children so that you'll be fully and fairly apprised of all possible expenses and punitive suits that could be forthcoming."

"Tests? What kind of tests?"

"Smoke inhalation. Possible internal injuries. Possible brain damage. And, of course, stress, trauma, emotional—"

"What is that number?"

She recited Mike's phone number.

Click.

Chris's husband had been a con man. A wheeler-dealer. A schemer. A crook, a louse, a liar. But she couldn't prove it. The sad truth was that she knew where every freckle on his body was located, she would be able to pinpoint his very individual male musk in a stadium holding twenty thousand people, but she had not known what he did for a living. Or what he did with her money. The word *incomprehensible* popped into her mind again, associated with catastrophic loss and the fact that she knew nothing at all about a man she had been married to for four years. Because she had been inside-out-in-love and feeble with idealism and ignorance.

While her children watched a nature program on a cable network, Chris brooded about her past. It was checkered indeed. Poor Aunt Florence.

Chris's grandfather had started a furniture business as a young man; he had started his family as a much older man. By the time Chris's father was twenty-two and married, Grandfather was nearly ready to retire. His company, Palmer House, was respected and very successful. Chris was born into a family that included her young parents, her elderly grandparents, her father's younger sister and piles of money.

When Chris was small, her aunt, Florence, spoiled her, played with her, babysat her and bought her lacy undergarments and expensive pop-it beads to match every dress. When Chris was older they went on trips together—to Hong Kong, London, Tibet. They bought everything of leather, gold, silver and jade that they could carry or ship home. When Chris was eighteen Flo made a down payment on a car for her. A Jaguar.

What she remembered most vividly, however, and missed most painfully, were the letters and phone calls. While Chris was at Princeton, she e-mailed and called Flo daily. And Aunt Florence replied—consistently. Chris, studying literature, couldn't believe that her job for four whole years would be reading all the greatest books ever written. She was a straight-A student. She loved books, always had, especially Regency and Victorian romances, from Austen to Brontë. And she loved the inexpensive love stories you could buy at the A&P

for $5.95. So did Aunt Florence; they agreed that everyone deserved a five-ninety-five happy ending. They often discussed the books the way other women discussed their favorite soaps.

They had been so close, the best of friends, confidantes.

Florence had never married—the "old-maid" aunt. Except that Aunt Florence was only fourteen years older than Chris. More like an older sister than an aunt, actually. Five-year-old Chris had sobbed for hours the day Flo left for college; she sat by the front bay window all afternoon awaiting Flo's first weekend home. Flo was brilliant, sophisticated, fashionable and rich. She was also bossy, fiercely independent, ambitious and stubborn as a mule. Devoted, sometimes controlling. Loads of fun or a pain in the butt, depending. Such was the deal for an aunt and niece who were more like siblings. Flo couldn't help it that she was the elder.

Chris, her parents and Aunt Florence had always lived on the same street. Flo had kept the old Palmer family home on the upper river drive after her parents—first her father, at the age of seventy-two, then her mother, at sixty-four—died. Flo was only twenty-one then, and Chris vaguely remembered an argument over Flo's living alone in the big house when she could just as easily move in with Randolph's family. Flo, predictably, won.

Chris's mom, Arlene, whom Chris still ached for, was the nurturer of them all. Chris longed to revisit the smells from her early childhood: her father's cologne, her mother's cooking and baking, Flo's furs. Arlene had married Randolph and, she joked, Florence. And indeed, Arlene was like a wife to both of them, representing both Randolph and Flo at charity functions. A

society wife—philanthropic, on a number of boards—
and caretaker in one. Randolph and Florence had inher-
ited the family business and worked at it. Arlene hadn't
"worked" technically, except that no one ever worked
harder at taking care of a family. And that was all the
family there was. The Palmers of Chicago. Randolph,
Arlene, Florence…and Christine.

Then it happened. Arlene and Randolph. Dead. They
were in their forties—too *soon*. Chris came home from
Princeton to help Aunt Flo bury them, to pack up what
they wore and wiped their noses with. It had been black
and horrid. She didn't go back to school. What for? For
literature?

She met Steve at a nightclub. Steve Zanuck—they
called him Stever. Hotshot, arrogant, sexy Stever. He
was a few years older than she, and Aunt Florence became instantly bitchy, as if she were jealous of him. As
if she didn't want Chris to be in love. Flo believed he
might be no damn good, as she so tactfully put it. Chris,
who needed love, assumed that her grieving aunt had
turned mean and selfish. Steve had said that Florence
was clinging and manipulative. The pot was definitely
speaking of the kettle. So Chris slept with him, married
him and sued her Aunt Florence, the executor of her
parents' estate, for control of her trust. What had happened? Had she been having an out-of-body experience?
Had he drugged her? With sex and flattery. She was so
vulnerable and alone she was just a big dope. She had
somehow managed to stay asleep for four whole years.
Dear God, what an imbecile she'd been.

Trying to emerge from that nightmare had produced
some growth and even a little dream or two, like writing,
but also immeasurable loneliness. At one time she had

had more friends than there seemed time for. The past few years, though, had been largely solitary. Trying to make it on her own, to develop independence and self-reliance, had led to a fundamental absence of people in her life.

She looked at the back of her children's blond heads; they stared up at the television, transfixed by luxury. Kyle's toe stuck out of a hole in the foot of his pajamas. And that was all he had now. So, to prevent their being hurt or further deprived, she might have to call Aunt Flo. For them.

She had hoped, somehow, that she could reverse her circumstances. She could never recover her entire lost legacy, but she could be at least a self-supporting single mother, couldn't she? And so here she was, lying in this bed she had made, because she had to take responsibility for her own mistakes. And because, when Flo was proved right about Stever, her sensitive remark had been, "Well, you just couldn't listen to me, could you? You had to let that slimeball run through everything Randy left for you before you could even figure it out! Will you *ever* learn?"

Probably I will learn, Chris thought. Probably I have.

That was why calling Flo was on the very dead-last bottom of her list of possibilities. She loved Flo, she missed her desperately, but she didn't expect her aunt to be very nice about this.

Of course, she deserved Flo's anger, her scorn, but...

Perhaps Flo would forgive her? Be somewhat kind?

Perhaps she would hang up, like the landlord's wife. Or say, "Chris who?"

"Hi, Ma," Mike yelled as he walked through the living room toward the kitchen. "Ma?"

"Yes, yes, yes," she called back from the kitchen. "I'm up to my elbows in dough. Come in. Come in." She pulled her hands out and turned to look up at him. She frowned. "You look hungry. But good."

He laughed and kissed her forehead. "I weigh one-ninety-five, and I'm not hungry." He took a cookie from the cookie jar. "Not real hungry, anyway."

"You must have had a quiet night," she said softly, quickly looking away from him and back to her kneading. "No bags under the eyes."

"Not so much as a peep," he replied, leaning against the cabinet, watching her back. She glanced over her shoulder, and he smiled. Then his shoulders shook. They both knew she had been awake, stayed awake, and they both liked that to some degree. "Where's Dad?" he asked. But she didn't have to answer. The toilet flushed, the bathroom door opened, and Mike's father, a short, muscular and thick, bald-headed Irishman carrying a newspaper, wearing his eyeglasses on his nose and his leather slippers on his feet, came down the hall into the kitchen. His name was also Michael.

"I thought I heard lies being told," he said. "Mikie, my boy, 'not a peep' went by the house at about the witchin' hour, round ninety-five miles an hour, followed by the second bell."

"Oh?" Mike's mother said without turning around. "I didn't hear it. I sleep like the beloved dead."

"We went down Forty-second Street, as a matter of fact, four blocks east," Mike said. "House burned down—one of those little ones over on Belvedere."

"Everyone okay?" his mother asked, turning around. "And the firemen?"

"Everyone is fine, but as a matter of fact, that's the

reason I stopped by. Last night's fire. Ma, I've gone and done the craziest damn thing; they just might lock me up for a lunatic. The woman who was burned out is a young divorcée with two cute little kids, just three and five years old. They had nowhere to go, and I loaned them my place. Can I sleep over here tonight? Maybe a couple of nights? Until they get settled?"

"Your house?" she asked. She decided to take her hands out of the dough altogether and wash them. "You gave this family your house?"

"No, Ma, no, I didn't give it to them. I offered them a place to stay until they can make some plans. See, she's pretty young, I'd say about Margie's age, under thirty. And she has no family except the kids. It's so close to Christmas, and the shelters are—" He stopped. His parents were looking at him as though he'd slipped a gear. At any moment he expected his mother to feel his brow.

He didn't know how to explain how it made him feel to think of those kids in one of those crappy shelters. *Or* how it made him feel to think of them in *his* house. Something peculiar and personal had already attached him to them. Maybe he wouldn't have done it if the woman, Chris, had been totally unappealing. He briefly considered her appeal; not a bad-looking woman, and feisty. He had gotten snagged on their helplessness, on them, all three of them, even that stupid dog. No way would they get that dog into one of the shelters, and the kids needed the dog. He had no idea what was happening to him.

"Crammed," he finally said. "The shelters are crammed full."

"They could stay here," his mother said.

"No, Ma, no. My place is fine."

"This divorcée? She's pretty?"

"Ma, she's a little short on houses right now, and I'm hardly ever there. Anyway, I'm sure it'll only be for a few days. Oh," he said, looking at his dad, "do you have an hour or so you can spare? I need a hand; her car is still over at her house. There's been an inspection and cleanup crew going through the mess, and they found her purse and keys. Maybe you could drive my car so I can ferry hers back to my place?"

"Sure," he said slowly, looking over his glasses at his son, maybe considering putting him in a rest home until he became stable again.

"Okay, then."

"Okay, then," his parents replied in unison.

"Anything we can do to help?" his mother asked. "How are they for clothes? Do they need clothes?"

"Well, since you asked, you know that box of toys and coloring books and things you keep here for when the kids come over? I think her kids would love to borrow it. What do you say?"

"And some bread, maybe? Rolls?"

"No, Ma." He laughed. "There's plenty of food. Just some toys for the kids."

"Clothes, then?"

"No, really…"

"So what do they have for clothes, then?" she asked.

"Mattie, never mind," said Big Mike, who was far smaller than his son, whom they called Little Mike. Big Mike stopped his wife as though she was getting personal. Mattie—short for Mathilda—and Michael Cavanaugh looked with deep concern at their eldest son, who stood nearly six foot two and was about as wide as a refrigerator.

"Don't worry, Ma," he said, touching the end of her nose with a finger. "They aren't naked. There are no naked women and children running around my house. I can stay the night here? No problem?"

"Sure, Mike, sure. Let me give you some rolls to take to her. I'll roll a few, and you tell her to let them rise and have them for her dinner. Do you take dinner here, or there, with her?"

Mike thought his mother stressed *her*. After all, his sisters, Margie and Maureen, had brought home plenty of good Catholic women who were not divorced with kids. "She'd love some rolls, Ma. That's nice. I'll bring Big Mike back in about an hour, okay? Then I'm going to go back to my place to make sure that anything kids can get hurt on is locked up—the tools and all that. I'll have dinner here. I'll be back around five. I won't put you out, huh?"

"You never put us out," she said, patting his cheek. Actually, she slapped his cheek, but she did so affectionately.

An hour later, when the car exchange had been accomplished, Big Mike walked into his house. Mattie came out of the kitchen, wiping her hands on a dish towel. "So?" she asked her husband.

"There is a dog, too," Big Mike said. "A woman, pretty, two kids, both, like he said, cute, and a little dog with no manners."

He walked past his wife to his favorite chair and picked up the newspaper, which he had already read twice. Big Mike had been retired for a year and still had not done any of the projects he had been saving for retirement. "Do you think the dog will hurt his carpet?" Mattie asked.

Big Mike sank into his chair. He shook the paper. It always read better after a good shake. He looked at his wife of almost forty years over his glasses.

"Mattie, four times you saw your boys fall in love and get married. Two times you took our little girls to the bridal shop and took me to the cleaners before you let me take them down the aisle. Why do you act like you don't know nothing about your own kids? That dog could make Tootsie Rolls on Little Mike's head and he don't care. You pay attention then, Mattie," he said, shaking his paper again. "Little Mike's gonna keep even the dog. And it's a terrible dog. His name is Creeps."

"Rolls?" Chris asked.

"Listen, just count your blessings that she didn't come over here to dust you, dress you and feed you with her own hands. All I had to say was you've been burned out, and my mother almost adopted you all, sight unseen."

"That would be nice," she said. "Your dad looked, well, I don't know…reticent. Hesitant." Suspicious.

"Suspicious." At least he said it. "I've never done anything like this before. At least he didn't frisk you." He went back into the garage, brought in two more bags of groceries and put them down.

"Why would he want to frisk me?"

"Well, my mom and sisters have been parading nice Catholic old maids past me for ten years without any luck at all. And then I go and invite you and your kids to move into my house," he said with a laugh. "When I told them what I'd done, the first thing my mother said was, 'So, is she pretty, this woman?'" Mike decided Chris could find out how his mother felt about divorcées later, or maybe never. "I told you, they shake their heads over me. I'm sort of a special project. Since Joanie died, anyway."

He left again, brought in two more bags. "You want me to put this stuff away?" she asked.

"Please," he said, getting still more.

"Gee," she said, "this is because we're here. You shouldn't have done that. I feel—"

"Hungry, probably. The rolls have to rise. Put them in the sunlight—there, on the windowsill."

He brought in more bags. Eight. He felt very big across the chest, bringing so much food into his house. Taking care of people, really. It was not like giving things to his siblings or folks, who all tolerated it very patiently, even gratefully, but, no kidding around, they didn't *need* his giving. They could get by fine without his gifts, his interference. What he gave his family was extra, not essential, like this. Today was the first time since he'd lost his family that he'd stocked so much; it filled him right up.

Next he brought in different kinds of bags. Then the box of toys, which he took into the living room for the kids. In the kitchen Chris was trying to figure out the cupboards. "I can't really tell where things go, Mike. You don't have a lot of food here."

"I almost never eat here. My mom would die of grief if she couldn't feed people all the time. I go over there almost every night. Here, I keep chips, beer, coffee, pop, cereal and eggs. And toilet paper. I don't even get a newspaper." He took out his wallet, unfolded some bills. "I ran into your landlord, and he told me to give you this to tide you over. I bought a couple of things for the kids, so you don't have to take them shopping in their pajamas. I would have picked up something for you, but I didn't know…you know…"

She looked at him in disappointment. "Mr. Blakely?"

"That his name?"

"That's not true, Mike. You didn't run into him."

He didn't seem to mind being caught in a lie. "You sure?"

"I talked to his wife. They're thinking of suing me. They aren't going to be generous about this."

"Suing *you?*"

"It would seem. I'm going to have to fight them."

"The son of a bitch. Here," he said, holding out the money. "You can pay me back out of your settlement. You ought to fry the bastard."

She smiled but hesitated to take the money. "Thanks. Why didn't you just say it was yours straight out?"

"I was afraid you wouldn't take it. You suffer too much, Chrissie. It's almost like you want to."

"No," she said, feeling a slight shiver at the sound of the nickname. Her dad had always called her Chrissie. "No, it's just that I have an extraordinary amount of bad luck for someone who doesn't take drugs or pick up hitchhikers. And I don't want to take so much from you that I feel guilty."

His face lit up. "I didn't know you were Catholic."

"I'm not," she said, confused.

"Oh. You mean other religions borrow guilt when they don't have enough, too?"

"Come on," she said, taking the money.

"I think these will fit the kids," he said, picking up the department-store bags. "I didn't even want to take a chance guessing your size… You'll be okay in that sweat suit, huh? It isn't high fashion, but it isn't pajamas."

"People shop at Iverson's in worse than this. Why are you doing all this?" she asked him, a gentle inquiry.

"I don't really know," he said, the enormous honesty of it causing his dimple to flatten. He didn't break eye contact with her, even though he knew the heavy brows were probably making him look dangerous. "But I am. I want to. Just let it go. Okay? Please."

"Mike, I appreciate this. It's very generous and kind of you, but—"

"In the closet in the room with the desk, there's a printer. You can connect your laptop. You'll have to buy paper. And there's a wireless connection—just jump on. And here's a house key, since you'll be coming and going."

"Mike," she said slowly, "do you have some crazy fantasy about all of this? About these poor, destitute little kids and you're the big strong fireman who—"

"Don't," he said, holding up his hands and looking as though something had just poked him. "Don't, okay? Don't start all that. My family has been dead a long, long time—I don't have a lot of fantasies anymore. It's almost Christmas, for Pete's sake. I'm not trying to make you feel too grateful or too guilty. I don't have any big plan here. It's just sort of happening. They're good kids—they're too young for bad luck. Just get things back together. I don't expect anything. Let it be."

"Well," she said, "it's a lot to do…for a complete stranger."

"Did you find everything? Bedrooms? Bathrooms? Towels? Need to know where anything is?"

"No. You have a wonderful house."

"Well, you have your keys and some clothes for the kids. Go get something for yourself, have a good supper, take a bubble bath or something. Relax. There's some liquor in the dining-room cabinet, if you drink. So the heat's off for a while, okay? Your run of bad luck has been replaced by a little good luck, huh? And, Chris? I wouldn't hurt your feelings for the world, but you smell sort of like a ruined brisket."

Chapter 4

In one bag from the department store were three pairs of corduroy trousers, three shirts, pajamas, underwear and socks and a pair of tennis shoes, close enough to the right size, for Kyle. Pants, shirts, undies and tennies for Carrie were in a second bag, these in pink, lavender and white. All the price tags were removed, as was done with presents. "How did you feel, Mike, buying these things for the children?" she had wanted to ask him. But even had he stayed while she went through the bags, she would have lacked the nerve.

She suspected, or imagined maybe, that he would say it felt like something he had needed to do for a long, long time. She remembered how he had looked after the fire, his features rigid from hard work, wet with sweat and smeared with dirt. He had seemed so physical, rugged, dominant, yet there had been this tenderness all along. His kindness and humanity had glowed like a light in his soft green eyes. It was as though he did things from the heart, not necessarily prudent or logical things. What was prudent about running into burning buildings to save lives?

She had been pulled out of a fire; there was hardly any position more vulnerable than that. He had pulled her out, taken her in. There was hardly anything more masterful.

He had so quickly, so bravely told her about his missing family—not flippantly, not melodramatically—openly. Raw with honesty but no longer stinging with pain. An uncomplicated man who could speak in simple terms; he gave shelter, just like that. Because he was hardly there anyway, because the kids were too young for bad luck and because the shelters were awful…and because he'd had a daughter once. This gave her comfort and hope; her own pain was still fresh, and she looked forward to a time when she could calmly discuss all that had happened as the distant past rather than a current event.

"Here's the deal, Chris, your daughter reminds me of my daughter...."

He had locked up his tools in the garage with new padlocks before leaving again. To keep the children safe. He asked if she would mind leaving him notes on the refrigerator, taping up her schedule so he would know if she was out for errands, working, whatever. He didn't mean to pry, but he would have to stop by for his things now and then, and he didn't want them to be tripping over each other or getting in each other's way, surprising or embarrassing each other. And he gave her his mother's phone number, plus his cell number, which he wouldn't be able to answer when out on a call. It seemed to Chris as though she was being given everything, including space and privacy, when he should probably be asking her for references.

She had told him as little as possible about herself, secretive because her life story was so complex and astonishing. Mysterious Chris, so alone with her kids and their mean little dog. Him she had sized up within a day.

His eyes were a little sad, which was easily accounted for. He didn't have a mustache now, but in a photo she had found while looking for a TV schedule he had a thick brown mustache. He had been photographed in a T-shirt that read SACTO #54; he'd been younger, his cheeks shallower, his eyes wider, not yet experienced and crinkled. He'd been prettier, not more handsome. That was the man, she imagined, that Joanie had fallen in love with. A strong, lean, hopeful youth.

She liked his older looks. He had cozied; his manliness, the strength of maturity, even his sadness, gave him a depth a woman would be tempted to sink into for comfort, for pleasure. Every plane on his face reflected seasoning, seasoning by pain and sorrow but also by compassion and abundant love. When Mike Cavanaugh had offered to provide for her and her kids, and then did so, the gesture had settled over her like a warm blanket. He seemed sure, capable, sturdy. Here was a man, she thought, who wouldn't collapse when leaned on. He was a complete stranger to her, but she felt perfectly safe. She hoped she would not become drugged by the feeling.

She had felt safe at other times in her life. She had felt the security of an only child; then suddenly she was an orphan. She had depended on her aunt's unconditional love, then felt betrayed by Flo's rage. And then—three strikes and you're out—she had felt safe because she'd had a bunch of money and a husband she loved and a baby and what could go wrong?

She had obliquely asked Mike if he were trying to compensate for his losses. And he had said, "Don't, okay? Just don't. Just let it be, okay?" And then that little breathy way he had of saying, "Please?"

There was more, Chris knew. She felt a familiar pull. She was attracted to his power, his arms, his tanned face and curly hair, his bright, imperfect smile. The dimple. It had been such a long time since her body spoke to her of needs that she was shaken by this sudden, spontaneous awareness. And she sensed his feelings were not very different. Oh, this was supposed to be for the kids, but he looked at her in a way that made her think he was trying not to look at her in *that* way. She couldn't help but wonder what his motives were. Maybe he wanted a woman. Or a family. He couldn't replace what he'd lost, but he could try to recapture some of those emotions he had experienced when they were alive. The feelings of usefulness, companionship. This he could do by providing shelter. The thing he didn't know was that he was exercising a need to provide on a woman who had a terror of dependency.

"It's a roof," he had said. She would try to remember what it was. And she would remind him, if necessary.

Chris scribbled a note. "Gone to shop, post office, Iverson's, babysitter's and burned-down house. Be home all evening. Thanx. Chris."

She hiked up the sweatpants, pulled down the sweatshirt and was grateful her moccasin slippers had rubber soles. On her modest shopping spree she bought two pairs of blue jeans, blouses, some underwear and tennis shoes. She had purchased the barest minimum, and all on sale, but still the money Mike had given her was nearly depleted.

She stopped to pick up a new smock from Iverson's Grocery so she could get back to work. Her boss and co-workers offered sympathy and help, which touched her deeply but did that other thing, too: made her feel even worse. What right had she, after all, to such concern, such sympathy? She had been an heiress, for God's sake, and she had bungled it. She felt like an impostor. She longed for her mother, as she often did. Her mother would understand.

She dropped by Juanita Jimeniz's house to explain her time off and to plan a new babysitting schedule for when she could get back to work. Then she went to the old house, which was roped off to keep the neighborhood children out. Her own children stayed in the car. The house was hopelessly destroyed, but some of the books that had been shoved in the refrigerator had survived. She took them back to Mike's house but left them in the garage to air out.

She fixed herself and the kids a simple, cheap dinner; she didn't want to use up too much of the food Mike had bought. She would repay him, in any case. Then she soaked off the burned-brisket smell and washed her hair with Ivory Liquid—she had been too cheap to buy shampoo. She borrowed very little of what belonged to Mike and was not fooled by the appearance of new, unsqueezed toothpaste in the bathroom he probably never used. In fact, there were many new, unopened items in that bathroom, while he had a bathroom off the master bedroom full of half-used things. She didn't think he had much call for Jergen's Lotion or baby powder, yet it was available for her.

She scrubbed the kids, gave them ice cream, snuggled them for a while. She tucked them in early. Then she lounged, indulging in a weak bourbon and water. She wore her jeans because she wouldn't spend her limited funds on sleepwear. The soft, deep velour sofa was decadent; the movie channel was as entertaining as a producer's screening room. And she waited.

For Mike. Because she had left the note, she wondered if he would stop by. To see how she was holding up? To see if she needed anything? To see if she had ripped off the TV? To see if the kids were okay?

But he didn't come by. He might not even have been there to read the note.

Her next day's note said: "Out for errands, home by six. Will be here all evening. Thanks for everything. Best, C."

But again there was no evidence that he had come home. And the phone didn't ring while she was there. It felt very odd. Being in his house was somehow intimate, as if he surrounded her and was everywhere she looked but still was far away and hard to reach. Like Santa Claus. Or God.

She looked for something to read and found a small library in the master bedroom, which she entered guiltily. She was afraid to intrude, to invade. His books, in a bookcase by the bed, were almost all men's adventure and spy novels. Cussler, le Carré, Ludlum, Follett, Shaw. Some horror by Stephen King. The book that was open on the bedside table was Dan Brown's latest bestseller. The books gave her a good feeling about him; he read by choice and for fun, entertainment, to imagine, to widen his vision. She wrote for similar reasons. Then she went to the study, where she made her bed from the couch. She opened the closet there. "Well, what do you know," she said out loud.

The printer sat on top of a small bookcase that held some very different titles. Collections of Dickens, London, Melville, Tolstoy, even Austen. There was an old copy of *The Jungle Book*, a children's edition of *Tom Sawyer*, and other classics. There were hardcovers and paperbacks. *The Little Prince*, and *Illusions*, by Richard Bach. Did he read them, or were they here for another reason? Had they been his wife's? She finally picked up a copy of *Moby Dick* and, caressing it, went downstairs to luxuriate in the living room again. And to wait.

For him. What kind of guy can do this? she asked herself again. Give a complete stranger, who's obviously in a mess, a key to his house? And be so unworried? It was pretty hard not to like this guy. She liked his house, his generosity, his soft spot for a couple of unlucky kids. The thing that bothered her the most was that she couldn't quite tell if she liked him as a friend... or a man.

Then it was Friday, her third day in Mike's house. She knew she shouldn't complicate things. But she wanted to know about the man who owned interesting books and clothed and fed them because it was "just happening." Her note said: "Will be at the library today until 2:00 p.m. Appointment downtown with landlord at 2:30. Do you like tacos? We'll eat at 5:30–6:00 or so. Join us if you can. C."

She was back at the house by four. On the bottom of her note were some pencil scratchings. "I'll bring beer. M."

She showered and washed her hair. She was eager for his presence, for his approval and his concern. She would promise not to take up his space for long, and maybe she would learn a little more about the man who locked the tool cupboards to keep the children safe, the man who kept classics in one room and new fiction in another. The man who would bring beer, even though there was already beer in the refrigerator. He had been here, but his presence had flowed through without leaving a mark. Had he been here every day? Waiting for just such an invitation?

No way could he flow through her life without leaving a mark; already, she would never be able to forget him. He had touched them all in a permanent way. The way life can be forever changed by the smallest act. A man gives a quarter for a cup of coffee, but instead of coffee the recipient makes a phone call for a job and ends up being president of the company, makes millions, tells the story in the *New York Times*.

When he arrived he rang the bell. Carrie let him in, and Cheeks growled.

"Hello, Mr. Cabinaugh," Carrie said. "Mommy, Mr. Cabinaugh is here for tacos. Our mother is being very careful with your house, Mr. Cabinaugh."

"Carrie, you can call me Mike," he said, picking her up. She was light as a feather. A six-pack in a brown paper bag was under his other arm. "Are you feeling better?"

"Was I sick?" she asked him.

"No, but your house burned down."

"Oh, that wasn't our house, we were *renting* it. We had a 'partment before. Are you feeling better?"

He smiled broadly. "Was I sick?" He liked the games precocious children played.

"No, but our mother says we've taken your house."

He laughed, delighted. His laugh rumbled through the house, and Cheeks nearly lost his composure, seriously growling. "I loaned it to you because I wanted to. Have you told *him* yet that this is *my* house?"

"Maybe if you give him part of your taco, he'll start to like you."

"No way. He can like me or not, I don't care."

"Maybe he'll bite you if you don't share," she said.

He looked at her in such shock that her giggle exploded. Both her hands came together in a clap; she'd teased him good.

"He won't bite you really," she said.

Mike wished that adults could look at one another the way children looked at people. A child's look was so unashamed, so blatantly invasive. They wanted to *see* you. They looked hard. Without flinching or feeling self-conscious, looking you square in the face to see what you were made of, what you were about. And they didn't care a bit that you saw them looking. If adults could do that, friendship wouldn't take so long.

"Maybe we should have a fire tonight," he said. "It's cold and rainy outside."

"Our mother says the fireplace is brand-new."

"It's been used. Come on," he said, even though he carried her into the kitchen where the sound of meat sizzling indicated Chris was working.

Tacos were not fancy by anyone's standards, but Mike thought the kitchen smelled wonderfully homey; she might as well have been baking bread. And she might as well have been wearing an evening gown; she cleaned up real good. But it was only a pair of jeans. His eyes went right to her small, shapely rear, although when she turned around to greet him he shifted his gaze guiltily to her face. She smiled and said hello, and he began to color because he had sex on his mind and was afraid she would know. It had been a while since he'd had that reaction. He hardly knew this woman, but he couldn't wait. He was somewhat ashamed, somewhat relieved. He had hoped that part of him wasn't all used up. He also hoped he wasn't going to be terribly disappointed when he didn't get things his way, which he suspected he wouldn't. He handed her the bag. "Smells good. Can we have a fire? The screen is safe, and I'll watch the kids."

"That would be good. I don't want them to be afraid of safe fires."

He cocked his head to look at her, impressed. "I thought you might be more nervous about it...after losing everything."

"I have them," she said, smiling. "The other stuff wasn't that valuable."

Kyle was sitting on the counter by the sink, and Mike grabbed him with his free hand. Holding a kid on each hip, he hauled them off to the living room to get the fire started while Chris fixed tacos.

She heard him talking to her children, and she peeked around the corner to see what was going on.

"We're going to stack the logs very carefully, like this, so they won't fall. What would happen if a log fell off the grate while it was on fire? That's right, it might fall right out of the fireplace and onto the rug. Uh-huh, we have to put some paper underneath, here, like this, to start the fire easier. Yep, the wood would burn without the paper, but the paper makes it hotter quicker. Paper burns very easily. Now, Kyle, is that very hot?

Yes, you must not go closer than this. The screen will be very hot, too, while the fire is burning. There, isn't that warm and pretty?"

Chris handed him a cold beer. "Thanks," he said.

"About ten minutes for tacos."

"The kids want a drink, too, don't you?" Both kids stared at him hopefully. "Chocolate milk?" Their eyes became wider, more hopeful.

"Uh, Mike, they should come into the kitchen..."

"They can't see the fire in the kitchen." He saw Carrie and Kyle holding back gurgles of desire.

"What if someone spills?" Chris persisted.

"So? We want chocolate milk by the fire. Don't we?" He looked at one, then the other, and they nodded very carefully. Carrie's tongue was poking out of her mouth, and her eyes beseeched her mother's sense of adventure.

"All right," she said. She heard them laugh, all three of them. When she was safely in the kitchen stirring chocolate into glasses of milk, a smile ran through her body. He was spoiling them, giving in. Thank you, God. He was gentle and giving and fun, and they would remember him forever. Chris had been worried about the total absence of male role models for them, but she had lacked the time, energy or courage for even the most innocent of relationships with men. Also, she had thought it necessary to keep them safe from her poor judgment. She had really messed up when she picked Steve. This was good; they needed a decent man to think about, to remember. As did she.

She brought them their drinks, a beer for herself. "I turned the meat off for now. It looks like we're going to have a cocktail hour here," she said.

"Good," he said, passing the milks. "Relax. Enjoy yourself."

She sucked in her breath and flinched as her younger child sloshed his drink to his mouth. Before long Kyle's indelible mark would be on the fireman's rug.

"I said, relax. I could throw a cup of chocolate on the carpet right now just to get it over with if it'll help you calm down. Don't be so nervous."

"It's just that everything is so nice. Practically new."

Mike knew, as he had known the very night her house burned down, that although she seemed to own almost nothing of any value, she was not a person who had done without all her life. She didn't come from poor people. He didn't know how he knew, but he did. *He* had come from poor, blue-collar Irish Catholics transplanted from the East Coast. His mother had fried round steak on special occasions; his father had said, "Chewy? Good for your teeth." The way Chris talked, or walked, or held her head, or something, he knew she had grown up differently. "It's new because it's hardly been used, Chrissie. That isn't necessarily good." That won him a grateful smile. "What did the landlord say?"

"He said he'd get back to me."

"What?" That made Mike a little angry.

"Actually, he offered me a few hundred dollars— my original deposit. But he wanted me to sign a paper that promised we were uninjured and wouldn't seek a larger settlement. I wouldn't sign it. I told him that I lost several thousand dollars' worth of stuff—none of it new, but none of it stuff that we could spare. It's not as though it was my fault, really, although I should have had some insurance. I would have expected him to be a bit more compassionate."

"Son of a bitch. Sorry," he said, glancing at the kids. "Now it'll only go harder on him. Sue him."

"I'm not really the suing kind," she said, and thought about adding, *anymore*. "But I will try to get a little more money out of him."

"A bunch of money. The fact is, you could've all been killed."

"I know," she said, shuddering. "I've given a lot of thought to that."

She had condemned herself for the risk she had exposed Carrie and Kyle to, living on pride as she was, struggling to be independent. Renting a cheap, crummy house in a questionable neighborhood when Aunt Flo would have taken them in—probably after a mere tongue-lashing and Chris's promise never to disobey again. Her kids could have more, be safer. It only meant admitting that she had been a fool, a senseless fool, and she had already been punished plenty for that.

But having more had never been the issue. Even though she had grown up rich, she didn't miss luxury all that much. She wanted to recover, not beg forgiveness. She wanted to make herself safe, not sink into someone else's provisions. She wanted to call Flo and ask if they could make up, *not* call Flo and ask for plane fare. She didn't want to be completely beaten, a total victim. She had been teetering on the edge before, ready to pick up the phone and call Chicago collect, but she always managed to steal one more day of independence. Pride. Her father's gift to her. Fierce and unyielding. And sometimes quite tiring.

"I haven't called my aunt yet," she said apologetically.

"No hurry on that," he said. "Did you find the printer?"

"Yes. And books—wonderful books."

"My brother," Mike said. "I'm the oldest one in the family and wasn't interested in college. I just wanted money and a man's work—my father's son, all right. The other kids are all hotshot brainy types. Tommy—he's about twenty-nine, I guess—is a professor. Big-shot professor. And a coach. Every time he was working on a book with his class, he wouldn't shut up about it. You'd think he was gossiping about the neighbors, he was so wound up and chatty. He'd always give me a copy." He laughed at himself. "I never let on that I read them, but I read them. Hell, with Tommy carrying on for weeks, it's like taking the class."

"I had a little college myself," she said. "Two years. I studied literature."

"Then you know," he said, as if there were a club for the few people who cared enough to discuss the little-known secrets about things that happened inside books, a small group who entered these classic stories, lived in them briefly but were forever changed, deeply touched.

During tacos they talked about Chris's writing, even though she usually tended to be secretive about that, too. She was slightly embarrassed about her novice status and the enormity of her ambitions. She wanted to be the next Judy Blume. Her love of books had begun these dreams, but it was the way creating a story of her own could take over her life, consume her thoughts, charge her with energy, that kept her enthusiasm so high. It took her away from her petty, surface concerns, while at the same time making her probe more deeply into her inner self than was possible to imagine.

She especially liked stories for kids; there was something magical about them, and she identified so closely with the emotional impact of their experiences.

"I don't think everyone remembers details from their childhood the way I do," she offered in partial explanation. "I remember what I was *wearing* the day Barbara Ann Cruise pushed me out of the lunch line; I remember the exact feeling of being third-to-the-last picked for the soccer team. It might as well have been last to be that unpopular. And the first boy-girl party, sixth grade. I *know* I was the only one not invited, and I was so miserable and hurt that my mother let me sleep with her. I remember those feelings so exactly that it's almost scary."

And, she explained, she loved kids in general. Loved what they had to build on, endure, traverse, overcome, become. Had she finished her degree, likely she would have chosen a field in which she would be working with children—probably teaching at the elementary level.

She was amazed at how she went on and on, how natural it felt, and how nice it was to have someone encourage her to continue.

"Do you want more children?" he asked her.

"I'd like to concentrate on doing all right with these two. I've got no real job skills, but I'm a good writer. Eventually I want to stay home with the kids and write for a living. Writing for kids is the only thing I've ever done that feels right."

Carrie and Kyle asked to be excused and ran off to play quietly.

"How about if you remarry?" he prodded.

"No chance of that," she said emphatically. "My ex went on a business trip and never came back. Before Kyle was even born. Now my future is in these two hands," she said, holding up her palms.

"Never say never; gets you into trouble."

"I'll be fine. I land on my feet. When times get real tough, I work overtime, or I clean houses. If I clean for people who are away working, I bring the kids along. And with that schedule, I can write. As long as I take care of the kids and do enough writing so that I feel I haven't given up every little dream I ever had, then I'm as happy as I expect to be." She watched his face. "Maybe I won't write great books," she said. "I'll write a few good books if I work very, very hard—books like the kind you have in your bedroom, books that entertain, that help people imagine, get away and expand a little. The kind you have in your study, people are born to write."

He smiled a small smile.

"I didn't sleep in your bed," she said.

"I know," he replied quietly.

They shifted their eyes away. She wondered how he knew, wanted to ask, but had too much fun with the fantasy. Had he rigged something? Left a pencil on the bed? Positioned the bedspread just so?

He had glanced away because he was embarrassed by how he knew. When she was gone, doing errands, he had lifted the pillows from his bed, hoping to smell her on one of them, disappointed when he had not. He had thought about the pillow on the hide-a-bed but had restrained himself.

He was relieved when the children chose that moment to interrupt. They all played a game of Candyland in front of the fire and watched a thirty-minute Muppets special on TV. Mike scratched Cheeks behind the ears, inadvertently creating a slapstick routine with the terrier. Every time he reached toward the dog, Cheeks snarled blackly, then allowed the scratch anyway. The game made the children laugh with uncontrolled passion.

At eight o'clock Mike turned off the television. The fire was dying down. He turned on the light behind his recliner, pulled the kids onto his lap, and opened a big Richard Scarry picture book. He began to read.

At eight-thirty Kyle was asleep on Mike's chest with his thumb in his mouth. But Mike was still reading. His shoes were off; his voice was growing slower and scratchier. Chris stood and hovered over them. "Come on, Carrie. Bedtime. I'll help you."

"Not yet, Mommy. I want to fall asleep here, like Kyle did."

"It would be better if you brushed your teeth and fell asleep in your bed," Mike said gently, kissing her forehead.

"Okay," she said, "but first finish the story."

"I'll read to you again next time. Let Mommy put you to bed."

Chris lifted Carrie out of the recliner. "Let me get Carrie settled, then I'll come back for Kyle."

"Okay," he said. He didn't offer to carry Kyle. He wanted to be left alone with him for a few minutes, alone in the dim evening with a child in his arms. Mike embraced the little boy tightly. He inhaled the smell of his hair, the redolence of child. Tangy. Sharp. Kyle snored when his thumb came out of his mouth. Mike put it back in. Childhood was so short.

Too soon, Chris took him away. Mike felt a choking sensation in his throat and something binding his chest. He reached behind him to turn off the lamp. The living room was bathed in firelight, glowing but dark. When Chris returned to the living room she said "There," in that way a mother does when her duties are done, even though she's still on call. Joanie had said it that way when she finally tucked rambunctious Shelly into bed; that kid wanted to go all night.

Then Chris sat on the sofa and looked at him. He knew he was caught in the shadows and that she might see the tear that had slipped down his cheek. He decided he wouldn't wipe it away because then she would know for sure. He wasn't ashamed of emotions like these, but crying was so intimate, and he didn't want to invite her in any further yet. He wasn't all that sure this was something she could share. She must have known, however, because she gave him a few moments of respectful silence while he suppressed his emotions. She did, after all, know of his losses.

"Did you read *Out of Africa*?" he finally asked her.

"Years ago. Way before anyone considered a movie."

"Me, too. It was Holden Caulfield's favorite book, remember? I read *The Catcher in the Rye* with my little brother Tommy's class. Then I read *Out of Africa*. This part wasn't in the movie, anyway. There's a place in the book where she tells about the veldt-sores you can get in Africa. If you're not careful, the sores will heal on the outside, but inside they get worse; they get infected and runny and full of poison. The only way you can get rid of them is to open them up, dig them out at the roots, leave them open on top until they get the proper scabs and scars."

He brushed off his cheek.

"You don't just get them in Africa," Chris said.

"Don't call your aunt yet," he said. "Please."

"It might be better if I called her right away."

"Please," he said again.

"Look—"

"There's plenty of room here. There's no hurry."

"But—"

"You need a place for them. For you. For now."

"It's not mine, though. It's hard to—"

"You wouldn't exactly be taking charity, Chrissie. This works as well for me as for you."

"Mike, what's happening here?"

"Stay awhile. Just awhile. I gotta get a scab on this, so I can scar. I'm way behind. I didn't do it on purpose, but I waited too long."

"Oh, jeez," she said through a sigh.

"Maybe I can grout the veldt-sores. If I can't, it's not your fault."

"What if staying here only makes new ones?" she asked him.

"No. I don't see that happening."

"Just what the heck *is* happening?"

"Nothing bad, I don't think. Big Mike calls things like this 'unconscious plans'—when you do something that looks to the whole world like it's crazy as hell and totally coincidental and you don't think it ran through your brain for one second first, but unconsciously you knew all along you were going to do it. Like I wasn't looking to help out anyone, for a family to move in here—there have been lots of burned-out families over the years—and I didn't know I was going to offer you a place to stay even when the shelters were full, and I sure as hell didn't know I'd ask you to hang around longer than you have to, but—" He stopped and shrugged. "But Ma says Big Mike is full of it."

A huff of air escaped Chris—it was almost laughter.

"I don't talk about my feelings very well," he apologized.

"You're doing fine."

"If things had been different, if I'd met you at the zoo, I'd just do something normal, like ask you out to dinner or offer to take you and the kids to a movie."

"You would?"

"But it isn't that way. You got burned out. You need a place to stay. Feels like it oughta be this way, like this is the natural order. That's all. I haven't brought a lot of food into this house before. I don't have to be quiet when I get up early. No one messes anything up; it's pretty quiet all the time. And it has one or two advantages for you and the kids, too."

"But—"

"Not just the kids," he added in such a way that she thought he felt he should be completely honest.

"Oh."

"I'm not making a pass," he said.

"This is crazy," she said, leaning an elbow on her knee and cupping her chin in her hand.

"Yeah, the whole world is crazy. Your ex left you when you were pregnant. Your only family hates you. Your house burned down. And some lunatic wants you to hang around awhile because…"

She waited for him to finish. When he didn't, she prompted, "Because why?"

"Because, why not?"

"Look," she said, taken aback a bit. What kind of reason was "why not?" "You've been very generous, you seem like a nice guy, but really, Mike, I don't know you, and you don't know me, and—"

"This is crazy, Chrissie, but I'm not. I'm pretty safe.

I mean, I pulled you out of a burning house, for Pete's sake. You want some references? Want to meet my mother?"

"I just want to know what you're after."

"An extension. Of tonight. It was a fun night, huh?" He grinned, proud of himself.

He had a contagious smile that made you smile back even when you didn't have a smile ready. It *had* been a nice evening. She had even had the fleeting thought that she liked him, desired him, felt comfortable and secure for the first time in a very long time. What she had *not* had was the slightest notion of this kind of invitation.

"And that's all?"

"That's all I have the guts to ask for."

"You're making me nervous," she said.

"Don't overthink it. Men say more daring things than that in singles' bars, right?" Again he grinned. He knew. She knew. He knew she knew he knew. "Won't hurt anything if we're friends."

"How long?" she asked him.

"How about Christmas? It isn't very far away. It could be fun, huh? For the kids, anyway. Maybe for me and you, too."

"Christmas?" she asked doubtfully.

"Shelters and places like that, well, they're sometimes... pretty dangerous. Dirty, a lot of unsavory types hanging around...people get hurt. It wouldn't be a good idea. Really. If you don't like the idea of staying here, you should call your old-maid aunt who hates your guts. I think it would be lousy for you to go to Chicago because then we wouldn't find out if we like each other—all of us, I mean—but all things considered, it would be no fun at all to visit you at one of those awful shelters."

"Christmas?"

"It might be nice for the kids to know where they're going to be for a while. To have something to look forward to."

"I find this a little scary," she admitted.

"No scarier than sleeping in your car."

"True. But—" She couldn't think of any buts. Even though she hadn't expected him to ask her to stay, she had known almost instantly why he had done so. Because he missed his family, because he wanted his home to be less lonely, because Carrie reminded him of his daughter…because he was attracted to Chris.

"But you understand." He looked at her with easy, unbrooding eyes, relaxed, trusting eyes. She'd have to be nuts herself not to understand that they'd started something. "Don't you?"

"Are you going back to your mom and dad's?" she asked.

"Yeah," he said, sitting forward and reaching for his shoes.

"You don't have to." He stopped. "If you'd prefer, I understand, but it's your house." She curled her feet under herself. "If what you're looking for is some noise, it'll break loose at about seven."

He leaned back, leaving his shoes where they were. "Thanks. Sure you don't mind?"

She shook her head. "I'd just like you to remember that this is temporary."

"I know."

"Don't get yourself all caught up in it."

Too late. "I won't."

"I appreciate the generosity."

"I appreciate it, too. Your part, I mean. I understand

why this would make you a little nervous. You probably don't trust men."

"Not a lot, no."

"Well, that's understandable. It'll be all right."

"Roommates. This is really astonishing."

"Probably nothing like this ever happened before," he said.

"Never."

"That hide-a-bed is okay? Comfortable?" He lifted one eyebrow.

"Perfectly," she said.

"I could take it. Or—"

"Don't even think it," she said.

This time his eyes sparkled with the grin. He was feeling a lot better. "Come on, Chrissie. You can't make me not *think* it."

She threw a couch pillow at him. And, in spite of herself, she laughed at him. Or at herself—it was hard to tell which. After all, she'd been thinking the same thing almost since she met him. It just scared her, that was all. But not enough to run for her life.

It was the middle of the night, and Mattie Cavanaugh was sitting up on the edge of her bed. She reached toward the bedside table.

"If you touch that phone," Big Mike said, "I will break your arm."

"Shouldn't we know he wasn't in a bad accident?" she asked.

"No, and I don't care if you don't sleep for a month. You leave the boy alone. He had a hard time of it. Some things his mama can't take care of."

"But we don't know this woman, this *divorcée*."

"Both arms," Big Mike said. "I'll break both arms."

"I hope he's all right, is all. I hope he's all right."

"He ain't been all right for ten years now. Lay down. Come on, here," he said, pulling her back into his arms. "If we're going to be awake thinking about what Little Mike's doing, maybe we should fool around, eh?"

"Fool around? How can I fool around with some old man when all I can think about is my son, maybe lying in a ditch somewhere?"

Big Mike laughed and kissed Mattie's cheek. "That isn't what you're thinking about, Mattie Cavanaugh. The priest is gonna get an earful at confession, eh? Nosy old woman. Come here. Closer." He was quiet for a long time. "It ain't the woman worries me so much as that dog, Creeps. That dog's gonna maybe take Little Mike's toe off."

Chapter 5

Chris had pulled out the sofa bed at 10:00 p.m. She left her door ajar to listen for the kids, although they always slept soundly. She had left the desk lamp on, propped *Moby Dick* on her knees and trained her eyes on the page. But not a word of it soaked into her brain.

She could hear the sound of the television downstairs. Also she heard him make two trips into the kitchen and slam the refrigerator door once. She heard water in the sink, lights clicking on and off and, finally, at eleven, the squeaking of the stairs. What in the world have I gotten myself into? she asked herself.

She heard his shower running. She had never heard of a man showering before bed. Unless... Just what was he cleaning up for? She heard a blow dryer. So his wet hair wouldn't soak the pillow? His mattress creaked softly, his light clicked off, and before very long she heard the purr of a soft snore that hit an occasional snag and tripped into a brief snort. Her shoulders began to ache from the tension of listening.

Chris's imagination always worked best late at night. For someone who was struggling to make it alone, she was the last person who *should* be alone. Night noises always grew into monsters; melodramas unfolded in her mind at the slightest provocation. Once the sun came up she was remarkably sane. It was, however, nearly midnight before she began to realize that as long as she could hear him snoring, he wasn't tiptoeing down the hall toward her sofa bed. What kind of guy wanted to have kids—someone else's kids—in his house? No, no, surely not *that* kind of guy! He seemed like a nice, normal fella—pretty good-looking, too. Just what un-usual habits had prevented his remarriage?

At one she put down the book, of which she had read four paragraphs, and turned off the light. She got out of bed and peeked down the hall. He had pulled his door to, but it was ajar a few inches, which was why she could hear him snoring. She got back into bed, but her neck was stiff and her nerves were taut. What if he *was* crazy? If she and the children suddenly disappeared, would Mr. Iverson, or Mike Cavanaugh's Irish mother, demand an investigation?

At about two, rather bored with the rapist, pedophile, murderer fantasies, she began to indulge another kind. He was a nice guy, a decent and friendly man who'd had his share of troubles but had not been destroyed by them. Only wounded. Chris had not had to listen to him long before she could actually feel his desire to heal himself. He had accomplished a feat that Chris still felt was slightly out of her reach—he was managing on his own—but it hadn't made him whole. He hadn't asked that much of her, she reflected, and a small part of her was even relieved to not be the only needy one.

She wanted to drift off to sleep, but his presence down the hall overwhelmed her. It was so long since she had shared her space with anyone but the kids. All she could think about was him—what he wanted from her and what he'd done with the past ten years. Why hadn't he found a fire victim with two little kids five years ago? Would his "unconscious plan" have fallen into place with someone else in similar circumstances?

At three Chris tried putting her pillow at the foot of the bed. Steve had never read to Carrie. He'd rarely held her. He wasn't at the hospital when she was born, and he only visited twice; he said he was in the middle of a deal. He didn't care what they named their daughter; Carrie was fine, he said. A person's name for a whole life…fine. After he had been missing for quite some time her lawyer finally found him in Dallas, living, she was told, very modestly. Struggling. Staying with acquaintances, friends. Driving a borrowed car. Wearing last year's clothes.

"What about my money?" she had asked the lawyer.

"He doesn't seem to have it anymore."

"But it was *mine!*" she had exclaimed.

"Did you have a prenuptial agreement, Chris? An account number somewhere? Anything? We could sue him, but you should be aware of the cost, and the consequences of losing…or of finding out there's nothing left anyway. So, Chris, did you do *anything* to protect yourself?" the lawyer had asked her.

The lawyer had then asked Steve if he would contest the divorce.

"Absolutely not," had been his answer. "Chris deserves better than me," the lawyer reported Steve as saying.

What a generous bastard he was.

"And the custody of the two children?"

"Two?" he had countered.

"Since you don't want to sue him for support," the lawyer had said to Chris, "I imagine it doesn't matter that he questions the paternity of the second child."

Oh, hell no, why would a little thing like that matter?

She turned her head. Her pillow had become somewhat damp from remembering. If she hadn't been used the first time around—lulled away from her home, tricked into betraying her own family, abandoned and humiliated— then maybe she would walk down that hall and curl up against that strength and power and comfort, just as her kids had. Because they weren't the only ones who needed to feel some of that. And they weren't the only ones who missed having a man around. Life was very big. Everyone needed a top and a bottom, a right and a left, a masculine and a feminine, a full circle that connects. Wouldn't it be nice, she thought, if she hadn't been so thoroughly educated in the perils of trust?

At three-thirty she noticed that Mike wasn't snoring, but she had decided he wasn't dangerous a couple of hours earlier, so she wasn't worried that he was sneaking down the hall. She hadn't stayed only because it was safe and comfortable for the kids, and she hadn't been afraid of him for one minute, not really. After those few hours of wild sleeplessness she had finally remembered that the only person she was frightened of was herself.

She fell into a jerking sleep, every muscle taut from insomnia, her brain throbbing from vacillating between the idea of reintroducing sex into her barren life and running away with her kids before she became tempted.

Morning had been around awhile when Chris awoke. She heard her kids talking quietly, and she sat up with a start. Her back was sore, and her head ached. An insomnia hangover. By the time she had fallen asleep she must have been in a double pretzel position. She rubbed her eyes; they were swollen from crying. She tried to smooth her wavy hair and reached for her jeans to pull them on. Then she heard *his* voice. He was up taking care of her kids. This was going too far.

Distracted, she failed to glance into the bathroom mirror to see how the night had worn on her. She immediately began looking for the kids. She could hear their voices coming from his bedroom. She stood at the door, listening.

"Do you shave your legs, too?" she heard Carrie ask him.

"Women shave their legs. Not men."

"Why?"

"No telling. Want shaving cream on your legs?"

"Yes. Then you'll shave them?"

"Nope, we're just practicing today. You have to be older."

"Kyle? Carrie?" Chris called, not entering his bedroom. "What are you doing in there?"

"Mommy, come and see us shaving."

"Shabing. Vrooom," Kyle added.

She thought about it for a second. "Mike? Can I come in?"

"Well," he said, dragging the word out, "I don't know if you should, but—"

She shot into the room. What had she expected? That he would be naked? She shook her head at them. Carrie sat on the closed toilet seat with shaving cream on her legs; Kyle sat on the sink beside where Mike stood shaving. They had their own bladeless razors to scrape shaving cream off themselves, and slop it into the sink. They smiled at her, all three of them. Mike met her eyes in the mirror.

"What are you kids doing?" she asked, looking at the biggest kid of all.

"Got anything you want shaved?" he asked. He turned around to face her, and his brows drew together a little. "Didn't you sleep well?"

She peeked around his shoulder to look in the mirror. Ugh. It must have been a worse night than she remembered. How did you apologize for waking up ugly?

"I've never slept on that bed," he remarked, turning back to the sink. "Is it terrible? Maybe I should take it. Or try the couch downstairs. Or maybe one of the kids, being pretty light, would be able to—"

"It wasn't the bed," she said, feeling stupid. "It was one of those nights, you know, when you're being chased all night long and wake up exhausted." And then she made a decision that the next time she heard rapists and murderers in the night, they were just going to have to get her in her sleep; she wasn't waiting for them anymore. It wasn't the first time she had resolved this, but maybe from now on she could make it stick.

"Chased? As in nightmares?"

Kyle had scraped off all his shaving cream and was ready for more. He grabbed the can and gave it a squirt. Bad aim. It snaked toward Mike's ear. Chris grimaced. Then she laughed.

"Not exactly nightmares," she said, reaching for a towel and wiping Kyle's face. "No more," she told her son. "You're done." She wiped Carrie's legs. "More like a vivid imagination."

"You overthink everything," he told her, starting to shave the other side of his face.

"Want some breakfast, Carrie?" she asked.

"We had pancakes already. Clown pancakes."

"Oh. Okay. Go watch TV."

He wiped his face clean. He turned around. "So, what chased you all night?"

"Just your basic neurotic fantasies."

"You want a lock for your door? Think you'd sleep better?"

"How'd you know?" she asked, amazed that he had seen through her that quickly, that easily.

"Well, to worry about things that *have* happened is one thing, but to worry about things that *might* happen... well, you seem to specialize in that. But you have a long way to go to catch up with Mattie."

"Mattie?"

"My mom. Guilt and worry. She's got a Ph.D. Dr. Ma."

"Well, gee, we're strangers, you know. All you have to do is read the newspapers to—"

"Chrissie," he said solemnly, touching her nose and leaving a little spot of shaving cream. "We're not strangers anymore. And we almost never were." She looked into his green eyes. "Chrissie, Chrissie, maybe you have good reason to be careful. Me, too. But honest, there isn't any reason not to get a good night's sleep. Take it easy. I like you guys. I'll take good care of you."

"I don't want to be taken care of," she said, though

not very vehemently. It was, in fact, something she still wanted very badly sometimes, something she hadn't grown out of naturally before her parents were suddenly killed. But she'd spent four years remembering that such wants were immature, grounded in ignorance, *and* double-edged. Let someone take care of you, and they might just take care of you.

"Fine," he said, smiling. "So, wanna chat awhile? Or can I take a shower?"

"But you took a shower last—" He smiled more deeply. "I think I'll go eat something," she said, turning away.

"I have the day off," he called after her. "Wanna rent a movie for the kids or something? I left two clown pancakes for you in the kitchen. There's coffee, too. Chrissie? Chrissie?"

She leaned against the wall outside his bedroom door, arms crossed over her chest. She didn't answer him. She wanted to eat the clown pancakes. Rent a movie. She wanted all of it. Oh, please, God, don't let me wake up for a while. Please.

There were a lot of things besides men and sex that Chris had given up. She had simply been too busy to notice. Leisure time had been the first thing out the door behind Steve. Things like walking around the mall, or sitting at a picnic table tossing popcorn to ducks. Things like sitting down to a meal *with* her kids rather than cooking something for them while she ate out of a pan over the sink. And friendship—having someone reach for your hand or give you a hug at precisely the right moment. These were the kinds of simple things that made life satisfying.

"I didn't think I was smart enough for college," Mike told her when they were walking around the mall. "I missed that gene the other kids got, the one that made them ambitious and convinced they were smart enough. I worked construction for a couple of years out of high school. Then I drove a truck until I got hired at the department. Like I said, I always just wanted physical work and a solid paycheck. That's all."

"But what kind of gene does it take to never doubt, not for one second, that you're going to get out of that burning building?" she asked him.

"I doubted it once or twice," he said.

"Too scary."

"Wanna know what's scary? Fear itself. I've seen two guys, in my twelve years, get scared. Too scared of the fire to do it anymore. They all of a sudden couldn't go in. Whew."

I can relate, she thought.

"That's why I try not to think too much."

"If you don't think about it, it won't happen?"

"Sort of. Ever read any of those books, you know, the how-to-get-through-anything, or how-to-love-someone-who-loves-someone-else, or—"

"Pop psychology?" she supplied.

"Yeah. Well, I went through about fifteen of them in the two years after Joanie and Shelly. *Love Yourself First. Grief Management. Living Alone Happily.* Think, think, think."

"Didn't they help?"

"Yeah. They gave me something to do while I was letting time tick away. I'd be right here, right now, doing exactly what I'm doing if I hadn't read a word. In fact, most of the ones I read about grief said you just have to admit your feelings and feel them. Hell, I couldn't *help* that."

She laughed sympathetically.

"How many of those books have you been through?" he asked her.

"Oh, twenty or a hundred."

"And did it ever turn out that your husband hadn't walked out after all? Did you ever slam the cover shut after the last page and find your life any different?"

"You're an analyst's nightmare," she suggested.

In the park, tossing popcorn to the ducks, she told him a little about herself and her divorce, though she remained cautious of the exact circumstances.

"He said he was going to a business meeting in San Diego," she explained. "Then the phone started ringing— people were looking for him. He didn't call. I was afraid he was dead. I called his office. They hadn't heard from him, his secretary said. I called the police; he wasn't missing long enough. I started dialing every hotel in San Diego. It was horrible. It was two weeks, then four. I started to find out how little I knew about him and his life away from me. I realized I was pregnant, and even though I had a little money and could pay some of the bills, I didn't know how to go about finding this joker.

"When I started calling some business acquaintances I'd heard him mention, I found out he'd done a lot of lying. The big wheeler-dealer was a con artist, and he'd skipped town. Literally." She decided not to mention that she herself had been conned.

"What did he do for a living?"

"He said he was a lawyer. I'm even starting to doubt that."

"And you never found him?"

"Once I had myself convinced I wasn't a widow but an abandoned wife, I hired a lawyer. The lawyer found him in another state. Do you know what I asked the lawyer to do for me? I asked him to ask Steve if he would please come home, for the children." She turned her head and looked at him. Tears filled her eyes. "He said, 'Children?' He didn't even know about Kyle."

That was when he reached for her hand. He gave it a squeeze and did her the courtesy of saying nothing.

"After he walked out on me when I had a one-year-old and was pregnant, I asked him to come home. Can you beat that?"

"Course you did, Chrissie. Whenever something bad happens, the very first thing you want is for it not to have happened."

"The kids don't even know him."

"Kids. They're always the lucky ones, huh?"

He put his arm around her shoulder. Carrie and Kyle hopped around while ducks chased them for popcorn.

"What I've been trying to figure out for the past four years is how I could have been that stupid. I believed everything he told me. I trusted him completely, even though he did all these things that should have signaled me he was a liar. Not being where he was supposed to be, not getting home when he was expected, not following through on any of his promises, not showing any real affection. He was so good-looking and entertaining and funny that I, big dope that I was, went right into a coma and didn't wake up until he left me."

Mike squeezed her shoulders. "I don't mean to butt in, Chrissie, but aren't you blaming the wrong person?"

"I don't ever want to be that stupid again, know what

I mean? Hey!" she said when he pinched her upper arm. "What was that for?"

"Just making sure you're wide-awake," he said, grinning.

Later that evening, after the kids had gone to bed, they stayed in the living room, Mike in his recliner and Chrissie curled up on the couch. He had made them each an Irish coffee. And they talked. About what he'd done with the past ten years. About his women.

"My mom thinks I've been celibate for ten years. That's fair, since I think she has. She's always worried I'm alone too much, but she has to know where I am every second, so I can't really be alone *with* someone, right?"

There had been only a few women in his life over the years. Sometimes he knew right away it wasn't going anywhere, and he'd end it after a couple of dates. No one-night stands; he'd never understood how people could do that. Men did it all the time, he knew, but it didn't appeal to him. There was a guy, Stu, he worked with, for example, who seemed to be hot to trot every minute. A married guy, no less.

Then a few years back there had been two women at once; he dated them both on and off for a whole year. One was a flight attendant who was out of town a lot, and with his twenty-four-hour shifts at the department, it was hard for them to connect. They seemed to get bored with trying. The other one he liked pretty well, but he knew she was on the rebound. She'd broken up with a guy she had really been in love with, then ended her affair with Mike when the guy came back. "My sister Maureen found out about me seeing two women at once and gave me a book about fear of intimacy. She's the family counselor. I told her to shove it."

"Well, that was a nice thing to tell her."

Then there had been the woman in Tahoe. An artist. She threw pots, painted, sculpted, did incredible and beautiful things, things no one would ever think of doing, and lived in a small adobe house furnished by her own hands. She had made the rugs, furniture, wall hangings…everything but the toilet.

"When I first met her I thought I'd died and gone to heaven. She's a little older than me—she's over forty. After a year of driving to Tahoe every time I got a few days free, if she had a few days free, too—she traveled and taught, gave workshops and all that—I started to figure out there was something missing. I *admired* her. *Envied* her. That talent, skill. Those ideas. Like a pioneer. I couldn't wait to get to her place and see what she'd done. I was actually surprised to realize I didn't love her. I *liked* her a lot—still do.

"She's one of the neatest people in the world. But you know what was missing? She needed absolutely nothing from me. There were things I could give her, like friendship, or like, you know, the physical stuff. But she never suffered without it, either. The last time I was in Tahoe and gave her a call for the first time in almost a year, she said, 'Mike!' real excited-like. 'You're back! Come on over!' Then I realized she had never once, in over two years, called me in Sacramento. A real free spirit. She needed herself, period. Amazing."

"I think that's where I want to be," Chris said.

"Would that be good? I don't know. What if everyone was like that, really? Totally without needing other people?"

"There might be a lot of people who were in places they *wanted* to be, not trapped in places because of need," she suggested. "Need weakens you."

"Lip service," he scoffed. "You say that because you had a bad experience needing somebody you shouldn't have trusted. But you were pretty young."

"Well, yeah, but—"

"I'm not talking about that trapped kind of needing; that's no good. I've never been trapped by anything, but I know it would be no good. I'm talking about give-and-take. Like, I could get by just fine without my family butting into my business every single minute, but there's not a one of them I could give up. Plus, I complain, but if they didn't butt in, I'd probably feel ignored. Do you know what I'm talking about?" he asked seriously, his brow furrowing. "If nobody needs you, then when you're gone, you just slip through the cracks and disappear, and everything stays the same. You've had a whole life, and you've made no impact."

"But your Tahoe friend has," Chris argued. "Her art!"

He drained his Irish coffee. "*I* don't have any art."

"You've saved lives in fires! That's impact!"

He got out of his recliner. "People I've rescued don't call me Sundays and say 'Come and watch the game.' They won't know I've gone when I go. I'm just doing my job, and that's not the same thing, is it? I sort of felt as if I was just doing my job with the artist—that she didn't need me for anything and wouldn't know I was gone if I was." He flipped on the TV. "Wanna see who's on Letterman?"

"Sure," she said, after a moment. "But did you need her, the artist?" she couldn't help asking.

"Yeah. I guess. I think that's why it ended as undramatically as it did; she didn't need me back. No connection."

No wonder he'd told his sister to shove it when she gave him the book. He wasn't as afraid of intimacy as he was of never having it again. That real, vulnerable intimacy of needing another person. And having that person need you back.

Chris couldn't dispute its worth. She had two little people depending on her, really needing her, and often that was what kept her going, kept her from self-pity. But, she wanted balance—to be able to lean on someone who wouldn't betray her or control her or collapse under the weight of her need. She knew, unfortunately, how unlikely it was she would find such a person. Thus, she was on her own.

Maybe Mike wasn't afraid of needing because he hadn't been let down. He'd been tricked by fate. There was a difference.

Many times she had asked herself, if Steve had been honest, loving, devoted and dependable but had died, would her loss and pain have been terrifically different? She never answered herself, because the answer seemed almost as shameful as what had happened to her.

"More Irish?" he asked.

"Yes, please." *Maybe it should be a double*, she thought.

Chris worked three six-hour shifts at the grocery store during the week before Thanksgiving. Mike worked two twenty-four-hour shifts. That left a lot of time to be filled with chores, cooking and watching movies or television. They shared the cooking, but Mike had her beat by miles; firefighters were great cooks, she had learned. There was time to talk—not only the kind of talking that's done when all is quiet and dim, but also the kind of casual talking you do while one of you is sweeping the kitchen floor and one is loading the dishwasher.

"What about that book of yours?" he asked her while she was folding some clothes. "Shouldn't you be working on that book?"

"I have sort of missed Jake—he's the twelve-year-old I've been writing about. He's had a rough year—seventh grade."

"Well, why don't you work on Jake while I make dinner. It's my turn, right?"

They had done it, as he'd said. They'd stopped the clock. She hadn't worried about the burned-down house or the kids or anything. She slept well; the sound of his snoring had become as comforting as the purr of a well-tuned engine. She threw his shorts in with her dirty clothes. He washed her old Honda when he washed his Suburban. He brought doughnuts home with him in the morning when his shift was relieved. She brought ice cream after work.

Chris turned off her brain. She refused to analyze. She scorned common sense. She was briefly, blissfully content. The dog ate Mike's socks, the kids spilled on the floor, there was warmth and an extra hand to wipe off a chocolaty mouth, to hold a tissue and say, "Blow." And in the eyes, the smile, the occasional touch of a hand, there was a pleasant tug-of-war of sexual possibility.

Chris knew that the past seven years of her life constituted a trash heap of problems that should be sorted out, organized, settled and resolved. No way she could make that mess go away. She should contact her estranged Aunt Flo; she should reaffirm her goals and sense of direction.

But she waited. She couldn't bear to upset the applecart, couldn't bring herself to spit in the eye of good luck. In fact, if real life would be so kind as to not intrude for a few short weeks, she had the potential to be disgustingly happy.

Chapter 6

There was nothing to prepare Chris for the Cavanaugh family. After having met Mike's father, she had been afraid to meet his mother. The prospect of meeting them *all* simply terrified her. But she couldn't think of how to refuse. She was scheduled to work until two o'clock on Thanksgiving day, and Mike suggested that, since he was not working, he would babysit until she was finished, and then they would have turkey dinner with the Cavanaugh clan.

Clan, indeed. What would they ask her? she wondered. Would they ask if she slept with him? Should she say no politely? Or indignantly? Or disappointedly. Would they ask her how long, precisely, she would be staying with him? Should she say: "Look, Mike is a good and generous man, and he needs my little family for a while, to complete his grief, as I need his strength and friendship, and you must not interfere"? Or should she say, "Until December 26"?

"So this is Chrissie," said Christopher Cavanaugh, the brother closest in age to Mike. "Glad you could come over. Well, you don't look too badly singed. Everything going okay since the big burnout?"

"We're getting it together, I guess," she said, weak-kneed and shaking inside.

"My wife, Stacy. Stacy, here's Chrissie. Palmer, isn't it? My partner's name is Palmer. Rusty Palmer. You know any other Palmers in Sacramento?"

She didn't.

Christopher Cavanaugh was an orthodontist. His wife, Stacy, managed his office. They had three children, the oldest in braces. Next came Matthew, about thirty-two. Wife, Maxine. Three kids, aged four, six and eight. And then Maureen, whom they sometimes called Mo, and her non-Irish, non-Catholic husband, Clyde. Maureen, a nurse, was in uniform because hospitals, like grocery stores and fire departments, did not close for holidays. She was a petite, feminine version of Mike: curly brown hair, bright green eyes, that notable, crooked Cavanaugh smile that seemed so perpetually full of fun. Then came Tommy, the professor-coach, his wife, Sue, and their two little kids. And finally Margaret, the twenty-six-year-old baby of the family, who was a graphic artist, and her husband, Rick, and her huge stomach, which would soon provide Cavanaugh grandchild number eleven.

Ten children. Fourteen adults. Mattie, on her feet the whole time, getting some trouble from the daughters-in-law about how hard she worked. They called her Mother, but her own children, to the last, called her Ma. It was an experience in itself, hearing an orthodontist say, "Ma, hey, Ma—we have any beer to go with this ball game?" And the kids called her Gram, like a metric measurement, nothing so precious or pretentious as Mimi or Grandmother. Everyone called their dad and grandfather Big Mike, and of course they called the bigger Mike, Little Mike.

Chris should not have bothered to worry about what they would ask her. They talked so much, all of them, that they could easily have ignored her presence, except that they included her quite naturally.

"The *prints?*" Margie howled. "Did Little Mike pretend he had something to do with the McKnights? What a hoot! He didn't even buy the ashtrays! I did the house. He wouldn't let me upstairs, though. I bet he doesn't even have a shower curtain."

"I have a shower curtain, brat."

"Oh, yeah? What color?"

"Never mind the color. You don't need to know the color. I'm not helpless."

"I bet it's brown. Or green. Come on, is it green?"

"It's red," he supplied.

Margie laughed and held her big belly. "Red? In a blue bathroom?"

"It looks good. It looks fine. Tell her, Chris. Doesn't it look fine?"

Chris had a vision of them—six of them born within ten years—growing up here, in this four-bedroom, one-bathroom house, fighting or laughing, yelling all the time, the way their kids were doing.

Mattie managed them all. She placed them where she thought they would be most comfortable. She set up a card table and put children with coloring books

there, at the end of the living room where her boys—
her men—watched the game, so that arguments over
crayons could blend with shouts over a touchdown. The
women stayed around the dining room and kitchen, talking about their houses, their kids, their work. That was
where Chris felt she belonged, yet didn't belong. The
bigger kids were in the garage-converted-to-a-family-
room with games. The family room had been added,
Chris learned, after the first three of Mattie and Big
Mike's kids had left home.

Carrie had been intimidated at first. She held back,
but Maureen swept her in with her five and three-year-
old. Soon Carrie was playing hard, behaving like a
normal child rather than a whiz kid. And Kyle talked.
Carrie was too busy to speak to him, so he spoke to
the others, snatched toys away and alternately offered
them, negotiating his terms. Here, among so many Cavanaughs, no one looked askance at the things children
did, whether sweet or mean.

The small house became hot, close, with so many
bodies that Chris felt at once trapped yet never more
alive. They touched, this family, hardly ever speaking
without hands on one another. Even the men. Except,
perhaps, Big Mike, who sank into the role of patriarch,
letting them come to him. The children came readily
and often. "Big Mike, will you get this apart?" "Big
Mike, what color is this color? Is this color red or *rose?*"
They climbed on him, asked of him, sought comfort
from him. He attempted to look a little aloof, a little
bored, but he wiped four noses with his own old hankie.

Chris, who had been afraid they would be suspicious
of her, saw Big Mike draw Carrie in, and she had to
look away before she wept with longing. Carrie, who

had watched all the other children take their minor accomplishments and miseries to their Big Mike, had approached him holding a picture torn from a coloring book. She stared at him; he had a newspaper in his lap, which seemed natural for him, even with his entire, huge family around him. As if he might read it, hide behind it, while they carried on their intimate family relations.

"Does Big Mike mean Grandpa?" Carrie asked him.

"Around here," he said, looking at her over his glasses.

"I don't have any Grandpa. Or any Big Mike."

He stared at her for a long, gloomy second. Then he said, "You'd better come up on my lap, then."

She went very easily, as if she had climbed onto that lap many times before. Together they looked at the picture she had colored. As if she was one of them. With so many, there were no favorites. Or they were all favorites.

It took three tables for the Thanksgiving meal: the dining-room table, fully extended, pockmarked and burned from many such dinners; the kitchen table for the smallest children, where their spills would create fewer problems; and two card tables in the family room for the not-so-small children. Christopher and Little Mike took sides against Tommy and Clyde in an argument over unions that went as far back as the air traffic controllers' strike. Rick and Margie tried to convince Big Mike about some investments that would yield him more from his retirement, even if there was a risk. It was perfectly clear that Big Mike had no concept of what they were suggesting, would not change anything about his retirement but loved their frustrated interference.

Watching them, Chris ached. She wanted to share with them the way they shared with one another—advice, arguments, concern, love. It was a family so tight, so enmeshed, so interdependent—original Cavanaughs and in-laws alike—that there was barely enough autonomy here to fit a gasp of surprise into. But no one seemed to mind. Not at all.

She wondered how they had done it, how so many people could achieve this kind of intimacy. But their closeness, so involved and intense, seemed to be a thing they simply had, not a thing they strived for. It was too effortless to be contrived.

Through snatches of conversation and questions freely answered she had figured out who was responsible for whom. Christopher had gone to college on a football scholarship. Dental school had been made possible through loans Little Mike, probably a young widower by then, had cosigned. Matt had borrowed for college with brothers cosigning, then Christopher had paid for nursing school for Maureen. Tommy had gone to school on Little Mike's and Christopher's money, and Big Mike and Mattie were able to manage for Margie. They had all done it together. Whoever had, gave. Whoever needed, took.

On the buffet were the pictures. A few studio portraits, six wedding couples in tuxedos and lace—yes, Joanie and Mike, too—but mostly school photos in their traditional tacky cardboard frames. And there was Joanie and Shelly, the same picture Mike had on his desktop, only larger. The young mother, the little blond angel.

All things considered, she thought, the Cavanaugh family had held together pretty well, lost little compared to what they had. The Palmers had been a family of four, after all, and had lost two, leaving the two survivors estranged. Half gone, half broken. Still, Chris felt a twinge of despair over Mike's losses.

Mike. He seemed to need little. Chris had been surrounded by ambitious people: her father, her scheming husband, her aunt Flo. Her mother alone had loved her gently. For a man to be content with simple things—some work, some play, some family, some privacy and some companionship—seemed to Chris to be of the highest virtue. He did not seem to long for easy money so much as comfort he had earned. Nothing too fancy, nothing too complex, nothing too frivolous.

The Cavanaughs had no idea how different she was, had no idea of her secluded, privileged childhood. She had gone to Tibet when she was fourteen, for heaven's sake. She had had none of what they had and probably much of what they longed for. Despite the differences, though, they did not allow her to remain an outsider. They drew her in, delighted to have an audience.

"So, the big shot, Chris, says to me, 'If you go down the clothes chute, I'll go, too. I've already done it three times,' he says. And he says, 'Come on, Tommy, you're skinny, you won't get stuck. Chicken?' And of course I didn't get stuck, but the big shot, who had never—I mean *never* done it himself, got stuck. And I had to go to the church, where Ma was doing volunteer work with the League women, and get her and bring her home to try and unstick him from the clothes chute."

"Yeah, sure. As I remember, *you* called *me* the chicken and said you'd tell about the names I'd carved in the dresser top, under the doily…"

"And how do you s'pose he got out? You think Ma got him out, Chrissie?" Tommy went on. "Oh, no, nothing so nice and neat as that. Ma had a fit, and I thought she was going to die of a heart attack, because the big shot had turned his head inside the clothes chute and couldn't turn it back."

"I called the police," Mattie said. "What could I do but call the police?"

"You shoulda called the undertaker," Big Mike said.

"Almost had to after you got home," Little Mike said.

They had to tear out the wall to get Chris out of the clothes chute. When Big Mike got home and the wall had been torn out, it was almost murder. But that was nothing compared to the time Little Mike was kissing his girl—Joanie, probably—in the front seat of his car in her driveway, thought he had his foot on the brake when it was on the gas and plowed through her dad's garage door and into his car.

The banter continued throughout the meal, through cakes and pies and ice cream and coffee, engulfing Chris, making her laugh, making her forget herself.

Preparing to leave the Cavanaugh house, however, stirred up her original anxieties. In this intimate, nosy family where everyone minded everyone's business but their own, wouldn't someone mention the new house-keeping arrangement Little Mike had introduced into his life? She fairly shivered with nerves as she cloaked her children for the trip back to Mike's house.

"Goodbye, God bless you, go to Mass. Are you going to Mass?" Mattie quizzed her brood as they departed from the Thanksgiving gathering.

"Yes, Ma," each of them said. Even Mike.

Chris wondered what Mattie was going to say to her. Go to Mass, perhaps? Are you Catholic? Where, ex-actly, do you sleep?

"You come again sometime, Chrissie," Mattie said.

"And the kids. Don't make them be too good, now. They're good enough, those kids."

"I won't. I mean, yes, they are. Thank you. Very much. It was lots of fun."

Big Mike said to Carrie, "Take care of that dog, now. You make Creeps behave himself."

"Cheeks." She giggled. "I keep telling you his name is Cheeks."

"I know, I know. Creeps. Good name for that dog."

During the quiet drive back to Mike's house, with the kids nodding off in the backseat, Chris knew what was going to happen later. She wanted him. She wanted to be part of something again.

She put her good-enough, happy, exhausted children into the twin beds in the fireman's house. They went to sleep instantly, but she waited a moment to be certain. She tried to warn herself about the danger of getting more deeply involved with this man, but she was drunk on family, on hope and life and pleasure. Lonely, weary, needy. A little afraid, but not afraid enough. All her alarms were malfunctioning; she could not summon the least ping of warning. She couldn't remember a time in her life, even way back when she had had a family of her own, that she had felt this secure. Mike's embrace was so wide. Had he known, she wondered, that by taking her to where he had come from, she would find the surety and peace of mind she needed to touch him, hold him, invite him in?

Downstairs, the house was quiet. A light was still on in the kitchen, but Mike was sitting in the living room, on the couch, in the dark. Waiting. He had known. Or hoped.

It would be a holiday from real life for them both, Chris decided. For just a little while there would be no tangled, complicated pasts for either of them. Nor need they consider their uncertain futures.

She went to the couch, knelt beside him, put her arms around his neck, kissed his lips. She meant for it to be light, preliminary, but he had little patience. He was a man, as he had said, who didn't think for a long time about things but simply did them when they were right.

"Oh, God, oh, Chrissie."

The arms that pulled her close were so caring. Powerful, caring, needing arms; this was the embrace she had wanted to fall into, to disappear within, where she would feel forever loved. His mouth, hard in wanting, covered hers with such heat that she felt wild inside.

"Mike," she whispered against his open mouth. "Mike."

They couldn't simply kiss for a while first, Chris realized, as if on a date. She lived in his house; she had come to him and put her arms around his neck. It was not a seduction and could not be misconstrued as one. It was surrender. Until now they had both reined in their desires, knowing it without speaking of it, until they were ready for all of each other. She would not have played with his delicate restraint; she wouldn't lean toward him, inviting, until she was prepared to take him into her body, and this unspoken fact was understood by them both. That was why his hands were fast and greedy under her blouse, her bra.

"I want to touch you," he said. "Every part of you. Every part."

His hands on her were desperate yet considerate as he squeezed her small breasts. He held her waist, his thumbs and fingers almost meeting. He pulled her onto his lap, across him, and her hands worked on his shirt, tugging open buttons, as frantic as his hands but less careful.

One of his big hands went under her, between her legs, his palm flush against her, pushing, rubbing. She wished she had come to him naked, saving time. Beneath her thighs and buttocks she felt him grow; she ached so deeply, wanted so much to be full of him, full of passion and love.

He lifted her. He carried her. She had never before been carried to bed. With her arms around him she kissed his neck, licking in the taste of him, floating in his arms up the stairs. As they approached his bedroom she lifted her head, glancing anxiously toward the bedroom where the children slept.

"Mike?" she whispered.

"We'll close the door," he said, entering and doing so.

They tumbled onto the bed together, their hands moving wildly over each other, struggling with clothing, desperate to get it out of the way.

"Do you want me to use something?" he asked her.

"Can you?"

"Yes," he said. "Sure." But he didn't stop kissing her or pulling at her clothing. He tugged at her jeans, her underwear, burying his head in her breasts, her belly, kissing, licking. She found the hard knot of his erection and unfolded him, rubbing him through his underwear, then beneath. He moaned. Then her jeans were gone, her legs kicking them away. Her panties flew off in pursuit. She tugged down his shorts, and he sprang out into her hand, large and hot and impatient. She folded her hands around him. She opened herself.

Mike rolled away a little, jerking open the drawer by the bed, retrieving a hard-to-open cellophane packet. "I can't wait. I can't wait, Chris."

"Me, either," she admitted, taking it from him and using her teeth to open it. "Is this ten years old?"

"Four days. Ahhh."

"You knew?"

"I don't think about things too much," he said, rising above her, sheathed, waiting.

"Don't think now," she whispered.

He pressed himself in, slowly, very slowly. Then, lowering his head slightly, he tongued her nipple. She locked her fingers together behind his head, holding him to her, and it happened. That fast. That wildly fast. Almost without motion, almost without any movement at all. She felt a pulsing heat and could not tell his from hers. Five minutes, maybe less. The moment they came together, tightly fitted to each other, wham. Incredible.

"That," she said when she caught her breath, "is almost embarrassing."

"Yeah? Well, what did you expect? A warm-up game?"

"Warm-up game?" She laughed.

"To tell the truth, I'm lucky I got up the stairs."

"You bought rubbers," she said, her tone accusing when it should have been grateful.

"Yeah," he said. "The eternal optimist."

"All along, you knew we would? You wanted to on that first night you invited me to your house?"

"Nope. Oh, wanted to, yeah, just about right away, but I didn't offer you the house because of that. And I didn't buy the condoms because I wanted to or because I knew we would. I bought them because things are complicated enough. And because if we got it into our heads we were going to, I didn't want you to say no at the last minute because there wasn't anything. So, what a Boy Scout, huh?"

"Yeah," she said, snuggling into the crook of his arm, not really wanting to discuss complications and what-ifs tonight. She had started to think responsible behavior was a thing of the past. Then Mike. "Thanks. I don't need any more problems."

"Who does? So, what do you need, Chrissie? Tell Little Mike."

"Ohhhh," she moaned, a laugh trailing on the end. "Little Mike...now maybe."

That was the sex and the brief conversation afterward. Then came the lovemaking, which was, like Mike, generous and serious and very physical. As with all things he did, he used earnestness and strength. He had power and control but was so soft and loving that Chris couldn't tell whether she was giving or taking.

She hadn't ever thought of herself as a little woman before this night. His hands turned her so deftly, so artistically, that she felt small, lightweight, almost fluid. And cared for, always cared for, as this man she had come to think of as quiet, a man of few words, spoke to her, comfortable with words that usually embarrassed people. "Like that?" he whispered to her. "Here?" "Now?" Or in giving her instructions. "Yes, here. Like this. Please, here."

He took his time. She, to her surprise, did not have nearly the stamina or patience he had. When she frantically begged, desperately squirmed, tried to stop his playing around and pull him into her, she could feel the smile on his lips against hers, and he said, "Okay, baby, okay. This is for you, and you owe me one."

His manner and tone were as sincere and good-natured in bed as at any other time in his day-to-day living. He seemed not to notice how skilled he was. She was astounded by his talent; she had not guessed at his abandon, the shameless fun he had making love. It intrigued her, for she had little experience and had never considered that men had such a good time with sex. It had seemed to her that men were driven by some need that, once fulfilled, was forgotten. She had not thought of men as giving of their bodies, until Mike. Mike was the only man she had ever known who was so completely sure of his feelings that, as a lover, he trusted himself and her completely.

Chris had thought of lovemaking as give-and-take; one gave, one took, alternating perhaps. With this man she was a participant. He pushed her up, up, up, ruthless in his determination to push her over the edge, relentless in his stubborn wish to blind her with pleasure, and then he held her tenderly in her shuddering release. And again. Sometimes there was a little request for himself. He had, after all, earned that much. "Come up, here, like this. Yes, just like this. For me, my way. *Oh, God.*"

Deep in the night, while she lay on her back beside him, he on his side with one large hand spread flat against her stomach, he whispered, "I love you, Chris."

She was silent. She bit her lip in the blackness but turned her face toward him. She had never felt so much love in her life as she had today, yet the words wouldn't come. Not even now.

He turned, fell onto his back, removed his hand. In the silent darkness, still humid with the past hours, he sighed deeply, with hurt.

"Mike..."

"Never mind. No big deal."

"I'm afraid to say—"

"What you feel? Come on. I didn't *ask* you for anything!"

"Didn't you?"

"No! Saying what you feel doesn't mean you're promising anything."

"I love you, too," she said, her voice small and terrified. "It's just that—"

"Shh," he said, calmer now. "It wouldn't be a good time to talk. Anyway, I already know what it 'just is.'"

She was awakened in the morning by the sound of Mike's moving around in the bedroom. She opened her eyes, and, as if he felt her awareness, he turned toward her. He had showered and shaved, and he was putting on his pants and fireman's T-shirt. He smiled at her, and she saw that his joy had survived the hurt of her reluctant words.

He came to sit on the edge of the bed. "I have to go to work," he said.

"I know."

"Stay here and sleep. The kids are okay—I checked them. Want a T-shirt?"

"Yes, please."

He fished one from a dresser drawer, held it for her when she sat up to put it on. He playfully pulled her hair, wild and woolly, through the neck, then kissed her lightly on the lips. "You taste like a good night of it."

"I feel like I fell down the stairs."

He laughed, proud of himself.

"Mike, yesterday was wonderful. The whole day. And night. Your family is…well, they're just plain incredible."

"My *family?*"

"And you." She smiled.

"Thanks. Any time."

"I think I should call my Aunt Florence. Let her know I'm all right. That the kids are all right. I haven't even contacted her in years. You understand."

"Family is family." He shrugged. "You gotta be good to 'em. You can't let family slip away. She deserves to know you're okay."

"Yeah, she does. Don't worry."

"One thing? Don't surprise me. Please."

His eyes were begging her, his brows furrowed over his nose. She thought about the long-ago phone call telling her that her parents were dead. She thought about the call Mike might have gotten. She remembered her shock and dismay when Steve had not come home. For the past several years she had put so much energy into deciding whether or not this person or that could be trusted, she seldom wondered whether she, herself, was trustworthy.

She summoned courage. She bravely faced the fact that she had crossed a certain line with him. Not ignorantly, perhaps foolishly—time would tell—but not unknowingly. Even if she remained afraid to trust, she must prove trustworthy. Must. If she wanted to be able to live with herself.

She touched his eyebrows with her fingertips, trying to smooth them out. "I won't do that to you. I'll make plans and talk to you. You won't come home and find me gone. I promise."

"That's all I ask."

Chapter 7

She could not help making the comparison. If Mike knew her thoughts, he would say she was overthinking it. But the last time Chris had made love, Kyle had been conceived. Sexy old Stever, the last of the red-hot lovers, devil-take-the-hindmost man of the world…had not really liked sex all that much. They had not made love often; he was busy and preoccupied. He had been talented, not sensitive. Expressive and creative, not tender. Chris had been drugged by his sexual skill, for he could satisfy her quickly and efficiently, but the satisfaction was fleeting; she always felt unfinished. There was a lot left undone. Orgasm and fulfillment, she now realized, were not the same thing. Maybe that was why she hadn't really missed that part of her life. Maybe it simply hadn't been that great. Perhaps her body had felt Steve had not really loved her long before her mind knew it.

She got out of Mike's bed before her children awakened. She went down to the kitchen, poured herself a cup of the coffee he had made and stepped out onto the patio in T-shirt and bare feet. And breathed. Down to her toes. Feeling wild with life, positively smug with gratification. She thought about the differences between then and now, the differences between Chicago and Los Angeles and Sacramento. The sun was brighter here, the air crackling clean, cool, clear. If she looked over the fence she would see the mountains. Los Angeles, on the other hand, would be balmy and thick with humidity and smog, sort of like a dirty piece of crystal. She would be happy never to see Los Angeles again. Chicago would be dank, dirty, old. Like a woman planning to start her diet on Monday, Chris decided she couldn't face Chicago before spring. Today—and maybe for one day only, but maybe for a week, or a month, or many months, who knew?—she felt she was where she ought to be. That was almost a first, at least since she had buried her parents.

Feeling she belonged prompted other comparisons, as well. Though she suspected she was not extremely clear-headed—she was, after all, nearly limping with pleasure—she remembered how wrong she had felt during the years of grappling with Steve and Aunt Flo. Clearly she hadn't felt right about what Steve talked her into doing; not only had she cried a lot, but she had frantically sought alternatives to suing her aunt, options other than completely estranging herself from Flo. Nor had Flo's suggestions given her a feeling of warmth and safety; she had ached at the thought of giving up Steve, only to be managed by Flo.

She had had to choose. Between her only family and

the only man she had ever loved. And the move to L.A. had been so painful and scary that she cleaved tighter to her man, her husband, in loneliness and fear. It had felt so wrong that she had struggled even harder to make it feel right. She had had to slam the door on her own feelings, her instincts. Now, barefoot on the fireman's patio after a wonderful night, she realized that when something was right, it just was. You couldn't make it so.

Then she heard the sirens. All her life she had ignored sirens, unless they made her pull off to the side of the road. Now, because Mike rode the engine, she took sirens far more personally. She had never realized there were so many emergencies in a quiet, residential part of town. Four times she heard that trill, that scream. Because the big firefighter had crept into her body and heart, she sucked in her breath in fear when she heard the sirens.

The nurturer in her wanted to keep Mike out of harm's way. In that and other ways she was like her mother. She had been certain nothing could satisfy her as much as to live the kind of life Arlene Palmer had lived. That was what had prompted her to fall in love with Steve; she had wanted someone to whom she was so intimately connected that his life became her life, and together they would create more life. That tendency helped make her a good mother; it also made her miss the aunt who was now her only family, even though Flo could be an ordeal in herself.

And then, of course, there was what she had done last night with Mike, which made her shiver in aftershocks this morning… She nested well.

And all of this made her hate the sirens. Mike went into burning buildings. Still, he was experienced, right?

He'd been a firefighter for more than a decade. A fire-man had not been killed in a fire in Sacramento in years. Years?

She went back into the house and turned on the TV to check the local news. There wasn't any—at least none pertaining to fires. Not satisfied that there wouldn't be, however, she played the local radio station while she got ready for work.

She had only been at her cash register for thirty minutes when it happened. The event that overturned all the safe, peaceful, nesting feelings she had decided to indulge for the past week, especially the past twenty-four hours. Chris had been in a better mood than usual, joking with the customers, bagging groceries quickly, clicking those old buttons like a demon. Then she pulled one of those gossipy rags past the cash register between a box of Tampax and a pound of hamburger, rang up the price and saw the tabloid cover. Her face stared back at her.

Missing Heiress Speaks from the Grave.

No! She picked it up, stricken. The customer held a pen poised above a check. Chris threw the tabloid after the other groceries. Please, God, no. She rang up the total, and the customer, unaware that Chris's life had just flashed before her eyes, wrote out the amount. Chris stood frozen, panicked, paralyzed. Just when she started to think things were going to be okay, she tripped over some major event. Like smoke pouring out of the vents. Like this.

On automatic pilot she bagged the groceries, then checked two more shoppers through her aisle. At the first lull, she spoke across the partition to Candy, a college student who worked weekends and holidays. "I have to take a quick break. I'm closing for a minute, but I'll be right back."

She locked her register and grabbed a copy of the scandal sheet. Her face stared out between equally poor pictures of Robert Goulet and Dolly Parton. Good Lord. In the worst of times life had not seemed as grotesque as this. She raced to the bathroom, closed the door and read.

"You should never be surprised," Aunt Florence had once said, "at what you read about yourself in the newspaper if you have a lot of money. Or fame. Or whatever." Chris wanted no part of money or fame; she had simply wished to disappear and re-create herself. But it looked as if she were stuck with her past.

In Chicago, where the Palmer family had been considered among the upper crust of local society, their names had occasionally appeared in the society column. They had had a minor scandal once, too—a manager of one of their stores sued Randolph for wrongful firing—but it hadn't come to much. And of course Chris had had a debutante's ball, there had been the death of her parents, and then her horrid suit against her aunt and the estate. But that had been the extent of press coverage on the Palmers.

Now, however, someone had written a book about her and Steve Zanuck. Steve, her ex-husband, was apparently dead. As was his wife, Mrs. Zanuck. Months ago a luxury yacht headed for some Caribbean island had left Miami and never been seen again. Recently a piece of the vessel with the name of the boat on it had been found. The authorities suspected an onboard explosion.

Chris was not that Mrs. Zanuck; yet, she realized, not everyone knew that.

According to the article, Aunt Florence was not certain whether or not it was her who perished. *"The last time Florence Palmer talked to her niece was in 2006, when Christine Palmer Zanuck, then a Los Angeles resident, was discussing divorcing Zanuck."*

In 2002 Chris had married Steve in Chicago. A small ceremony with only a few friends. Florence had grudgingly gone along with this; she was even a little relieved that they didn't want a big wedding, since she didn't expect this "fling" to last. Chris had been twenty. And absolutely dumb with passion.

She had gotten pregnant instantly. Was pregnant, in fact, when she turned twenty-one and Steve insisted that the hundred grand per year she received from her trust fund would simply not do. Not when there were millions, at least, to be had, and he was an attorney, for goodness' sake! They had very politely asked Aunt Florence to fork it over, please, so that they could get on with their lives. She had said no.

It had taken a while for Chris to be completely convinced by her charismatic, con-artist husband that it would be logical to sue the executor of the estate, the trustee, for that money. And it had taken two years for them to win the lawsuit. Chris had already had precious little Carrie when she was given 3.75 million. And they moved to Los Angeles, where Steve was going into business.

The high life, then. What had she been high on? She lived in a palatial house on the side of a hill and went to many parties and opening nights. They went on cruises—Steve more often than she because she wanted to make a home with her child. Steve invested in films and other things and, according to his secretary, had a legal practice. Oh, Chris had seen the office and staff on occasion, but Steve didn't like to discuss business with her. And she, big dummy that she was, had plopped her entire fortune into a joint account. She trusted him. Why wouldn't she? In her grief and loneliness, he was all she had.

She began to suspect him of having an affair that year, for his attention toward her, his desire to keep her perpetually happy, had started to flag. Affair? That would have been easy by comparison. So she asked him to set up a trust for Carrie, and he said, "Sure, babe, we'll get that taken care of pretty soon." He was very busy with clients; he had a lot of socializing to do. She became pregnant with Kyle. Steve had to leave town on business. The phone calls began to pour in. Where was Mr. Zanuck? Bills had to be paid. The mortgage was due. The office had been closed. The secretary had vanished. The film company he claimed to be investing in had never heard of him.

Too ashamed to ask Flo for help, Chris had not known what to do besides call a lawyer. The long and short of it turned out to be that, during the first three years of marriage, the degenerate monster had lived on the hundred grand a year from her trust, and during the last year he had been busy either losing, spending or stealing her money. She had never been entirely sure whether he had converted it, moving it out of her name and into his, or whether he had actually *lost* it. But it was gone. Out of all that money she could only lay her hands on one account of around thirty thousand dollars. Was this an oversight? Or had he left her a few bucks purposely so she could take care of herself while getting a divorce? The rest was really and truly gone.

Kyle was born, and when she came home from the hospital, her house was locked against her. For the next two years she rented one tiny apartment or another, working as a receptionist, housekeeper or waitress, living mostly on the goodwill and generosity of friends she had made since moving to L.A. But those friends had been lied to, if not swindled by, Steve Zanuck, too, and, burned, they drifted away from her. The attorney stuck by her for a while, believing he was eventually going to get a big hunk of dough out of either Steve or Aunt Florence. Instead, he got most of the thirty thousand.

Steve Zanuck never reappeared in Chris's life. Though he was found, the money wasn't. Chris was left exhausted, afraid, weak. Once she understood what had been done to her, she committed the unpardonable sin in her lawyer's eyes. She wanted the divorce, period. The jerk she had married didn't even know or care that he had a son. She wanted to be Chris Palmer again. She refused to ask Flo to bail her out, refused to have Steve Zanuck prosecuted, refused to hire detectives to track down the money. "Let me out," she had said.

Though she couldn't ask Aunt Flo for help—not after what she had done to her—she did call her right after Kyle was born. "Yes, Flo, I'm all right, I guess," she had said. "And you were right. I married a real scumbag."

"Are you coming home?" her aunt had asked, her voice tight.

"Maybe when I can get myself together a little bit. I just had another baby."

"When are you coming?"

"I don't know. As soon as I can."

"Are you going to divorce that bastard?"

"Yes," she had said, and cried. Cried her heart out. And for what? For grief; he was gone, and she wanted him back. For fear; she was alone, all alone, unless you counted Flo, who was very angry. For shame; this was her fault, really. And maybe for love; though he made a mockery of that, she *had* loved him. "I am. I will. And… I'm sorry."

"I should think so."

She had hung up on Flo then, not answering the phone when her aunt rang back.

She should have gone home right then. She should have taken the little money that was left, gotten on a plane and told Flo to do whatever she wanted to do. Hire the lawyers, lock Steve up, have him knocked off, anything. The broken bird should have flown back under Flo's wing. Her aunt might have been angry, bossy, outraged, but she loved Chris. It wasn't Flo's fault that she didn't know how to give the unconditional, selfless kind of love and caring that Arlene had found so natural; that didn't mean it wasn't real love. And Flo would have forgiven her, eventually. But Chris had screwed up so badly and wanted so desperately to salvage something, she had only made it worse.

Every day since Kyle was born, for three long years, she had lived day to day, barely able to afford anything, but had not called on Flo for help. She had tried to find a way to rectify her mistake, to pull herself out of it. She wasn't sure she even knew why. Pride, maybe. Guilt and humiliation, probably. Also, a deep wish not to have Flo take care of her, which meant Flo would run her life.

Now this article. Someone had written a book about her, and within the book were dozens of little-known facts about her husband. It said that Christine Palmer was one of possibly four women he'd married. Wives with money. Wives who had disappeared. They didn't disappear, Chris wanted to say, they only ran out of money and became clerks and housekeepers. She ought to buy a copy of the book, find out what that weasel had done with her money.

But first she had to talk to Mr. Iverson. And Florence.

"You mean I gave you a hundred bucks and you're worth millions?" Mr. Iverson said. He held the paper in his hand. She sat across from him. He had an office, sort of. Two walls in the shipping area in the back of the store. A cluttered desk. A computer.

"Read a little farther," she said. "I was ripped off. I married this jerk who took me for my inheritance, and I am now a destitute grocery clerk with two fatherless children. That's who you gave the hundred bucks to."

He read farther. "Says here you're probably dead."

"Well, I suppose that's the *current* Mrs. Zanuck."

"Jeez. Who wrote this book?"

"I haven't a clue."

"Maybe you ought to read it."

"I was thinking that myself." She watched while his eyes roamed the page. "Look, I'm really sorry about this, Mr. Iverson, but I didn't exactly do it on purpose, you know? I'm going to have to get in touch with my aunt—I can't have her thinking I'm dead. I'm probably going to have to go home. Chicago." She swallowed hard.

"You want some time off? Jeez, you don't want to work here. You're an heiress, for crying out loud. What are you going to do? What about my hundred bucks?"

"Oh. That. Look, don't worry about that, okay? Here," she said, digging into her purse frantically, trying to pay her debts and retain her dignity. She stopped suddenly. This was what she'd been doing for more than three years. Trying to assure people that she wasn't a no-good, taking-you-for-a-ride con artist. She slowed down. People had helped her, had always said don't worry about it, but in the end they worried they might not get their loans back. They were, in fact, more suspicious of her when they found out she'd come from money than when they believed her to be poor, pitiful and down on her luck. It was as though she had no business being so stupid if she was so rich.

Well, they were probably right about that.

She pulled sixty-three dollars out of her purse. "Okay, here's sixty. And I worked the other day—six hours. That's forty-two. And I'll ask Aunt Florence to send me something. But that's one-oh-two, right?"

"There's taxes."

She sighed and gave him the three she had left. "Let me know if I owe you," she said quietly.

"How do I reach you?"

He instantly thought she'd run out. Would Mike see the paper? Would *he* think she'd run out? Would he *want* her to run out, now that she was someone else? People got crazy when they found out there was more to you than what was on the surface. And here was this terrifically nasty article, plus a book. Mr. Iverson was looking at her as if she were Patty Hearst.

"You can reach me at the same number," she said even more quietly. "I'll let you know if it changes."

She picked up the kids at the babysitter's and went back to Mike's. She told Juanita not to expect them unless she called but didn't quite say goodbye. She never had, she realized. To anyone. Anywhere. She always acted as though she was just going down the block to buy a candy bar and would be right back. And if she didn't do that to people, they did it to her. She was going to have to stop that. At once. Stop running, stop pretending that she would have this fixed in a minute. It was now officially bigger than she was. She would have to either fold her hand or learn to blame the right person. She didn't *do* this. It was done to her. Help.

That was her thought as she placed the call. She was thinking hard about it, about her promise to Mike, when she dialed direct rather than collect. She wanted to negotiate with Aunt Flo, if possible.

But when she heard Flo's voice, when she felt the tie that bound them tighten around her heart, she forgot negotiations. What she said, through her suddenly rasping tears, was "Oh, God, Flo, I'm sorry. I'm so sorry! I never meant to hurt you like I have. Never!"

"Chris! Chris, where *are* you? Are you all right?"

"I'm all right. I'm in shock. I just read about myself in the paper, and I'm in total shock. I didn't know I was missing, didn't know I was the subject of a book, didn't know that Steve— I'm in California," she said, not mentioning Sacramento.

"California? We tracked him as far as Texas."

"Oh, I've been alone for years, Flo. Years."

"Where in California? I have been looking for you *forever!*"

"Flo, I didn't know that…honest. I thought you were still mad, which you have every right to be. I wasn't hiding, I was trying— Listen, listen, one thing at a time.

I'm not going to hang up in the middle, I promise. But first, is he dead? Is he really dead?"

"Oh, who knows? Who cares? Three years, Chris! Good God, how could you? Even after all we'd been through, you had to have known that I..." Flo's voice caught and drifted away. Chris couldn't quite imagine her aunt crying. Flo could be angry, wildly happy, or her usual—completely composed. But cry? Make her pillow wet and wake up ugly, like Chris did? Was she in pain?

Chris, the nurturer, tried to comfort. "Oh, Flo, I kept trying to get it together, to salvage something. He wiped me out, naturally. And I have two little kids. Carrie is five now, and Kyle is three. I've been working, trying to get on my feet so when I did go home I wouldn't feel like such slime. I was wrong. I should have called you. But I...just couldn't get up the nerve."

"What about Steve? When was the last time you saw him? Did he leave you anything? Anything at all?"

"I haven't seen him since before Kyle was born. He ran out on me, left me holding the bag. I don't know what he did next. I hired a lawyer who tracked him down, finally, in Dallas. I got the divorce. I never got anything back. Except my name. I got my name back."

"Your name? Palmer?"

"Yes," she said through her tears.

"I guess that explains why I couldn't find Christine Zanuck."

I screwed that up, too, she thought. *Figures.*

"Come home," Flo said. "I'll send the money. I'll wire it. I'll come and get you. We can deal with this. We can—"

"Wait. Hold it a second, Flo. I'm coming. I'm coming home, I promise, but—"

"But? You said that before. You said 'as soon as I can,' and weeks went by. Then I couldn't find you. Then—"

"No, no. No, I won't do that to you again. No, Flo, but listen. It's a little complicated."

There was silence, then a short laugh. "How is it that doesn't surprise me?"

Chris started to cry again. "I'm like a bad penny. Why do I do this to people? I never meant to hurt anyone. Never."

"All right, all right, calm down, Chris. Try not to be childish. This isn't the worst thing, God knows. At least you're all right. First, give me the number where you are—the real number. Please don't lie to me."

Chris grabbed for a tissue to blow her nose. "No, I won't lie to you." She sniffed again and recited the numbers. "Now look, Flo, listen, I want to come home, I mean it, but I'm not ready yet. I can't just pick up and run. I won't. For the moment, the kids are more comfortable than they've ever been. I don't want to jerk them out of here. They're—"

"Out of where?" Flo interrupted.

"I'm living with a man. He's been very good to us. I can't run out on him."

"Who is this man, for goodness' sake?"

"His name is Mike. Mike Cavanaugh. It's real complicated."

"I bet. So bring him, too. Who cares? Or I'll come there. Chris, after all this—"

"Let me try to explain." She took a deep breath. "I moved from Los Angeles to Sacramento in August. I rented a house and got a job. The house caught fire and burned to the ground. Mike Cavanaugh was the fireman who carried me out of the house, and he let the kids and me move in here with him until we could get resettled. Since then it's gotten kind of, well, kind of—"

"Oh, God."

"He's a wonderful, generous man. He's calm. Sensible. He's good to the kids, and they adore him. It's the very first time a man has— He's been very good to me, too. I'm not going to stay here forever, but I promised him that I'd stay for a little while. See, he lost his wife and daughter in a car accident about ten years ago, and he's been all alone since then. And here I was, all alone with my kids, and we—"

"God Almighty."

"This is important, Flo. For both of us. It's as if we're both in some kind of recovery. This is the most comfort and safety I've felt since before Mom and Daddy were killed. It's not necessarily permanent—we don't have any long-term commitment, but—"

"Chris, listen to me. Here's what you do. Tell this nice man you appreciate everything he's done and you'll stay in touch with him when you get to Chicago. Tell him—"

It was all coming back to her. *Chris, here's what you do.... Chris, you wear the beads on the outside of your blouse, but on the inside of your sweater. Chris, you don't study only literature, you have to have a few business courses. Chris, you don't just marry the first man you*—"Are you listening to me? Tell him you'll call him every night, all right? Visit him. Let him visit you! You've been *missing* for three years, and I am your only family! He'll understand. Do you hear me?"

Chris started crying again. "I'm not telling him that," she said. "I don't want to."

"Chris, now listen to me…"

"Flo, please, don't. Stop making my decisions for

me!" She blew her nose again. Carrie found her, in the kitchen, pacing with the phone in her hand, crying her eyes out. Carrie tugged on her jeans. "Flo, listen, I haven't made this mess on purpose, but ever since Mom and Daddy died I've been bouncing between people who want me to do things *their* way, to take sides, to choose. Like now."

"Chris, you're getting—"

"Just this morning I told Mike I was going to call you so you'd know where I was and that we're all right. He thought that was good, but he asked me not to surprise him, you know, like run out on him without any warning. Don't you understand, Flo? His wife and baby— they were *gone*, without warning! And I know how that feels because Steve… Oh, please, try to understand. He saved my life. And I… I told him I was going to stay a while. Just a while. I can't keep doing this, Flo. I love you. I want to see you desperately. I want to make up for hurting you so much. I just don't want to hurt him, too. I'm sorry."

And she hung up. She blew her nose. "Mommy?" Carrie asked, her little chin wrinkling. Carrie would cry if Chris was crying; children didn't need to know the reasons.

Damn. She had hoped to find Flo tractable, reasonable. She had wanted Flo to be glad to hear from her, relieved to know she was safe and happy, period. She had wanted Flo's humor, generosity and spirit, not her commands. She *needed* Flo; Flo was her only link to her roots. She even liked Flo's take-charge manner on occasion; it sure came in handy in foreign airports. But that was where she wanted Flo to stop. She didn't want Flo to keep taking charge of *her*.

The phone rang. Chris laughed through her tears. "Hello."

"Dear God. You really are there. I don't know why I try. You are the worst brat."

"I really wanted to talk to you, you know. But I want to talk when you start listening and stop ordering that *I* listen to *you*." She was amazed at the strength in her voice. Yes, this was why she hadn't called before. Yes, she was sorry she'd hurt her aunt so deeply, frightened her so much. And she did love her, but she wasn't going to be pushed around anymore. By anyone. "I shouldn't have hung up, but I was upset. I would have called back. Do you want to talk a while now? If you can listen and I can keep calm?"

"Please tell me exactly where you are. Tell me I can fly out there and see that you're all right, that you're alive and well, not living with some lunatic. Or some jerk like that Zanuck masterpiece. Please. I deserve some peace of mind, after all."

"Sure. But, Flo, you're going to have to hold back a little. I want to see you very much, but you're not going to keep telling me what to do. I'm going to make my own mistakes and pay for them myself."

"That," said Flo, "is the understatement of the year."

"Will you give me a couple of days, please?" Chris asked patiently. "Before you come? So I can get Mike ready for this? So I can explain what kind of mess I've made?"

"Two days?"

"Yes. And, Flo, you're going to have to understand that I have business to finish here. I might be ready in a day or in a couple of—"

Flo sighed heavily. "You want my promise that I'm

going to leave you and the children with this—this fireman?"

"Flo, do you know anything about that book? *The
Missing Heiress?*"

"I just read it."

"Is any of it true?"

There was a moment of silence. "Only the really bad
parts."

Mike was hoping to run into Chris at the grocery
store when he and the guys went shopping for dinner,
and he couldn't hide his astonishment when he inquired
about Chris's whereabouts and the clerk said she was
gone. Quit. Poof.

Well, he thought, maybe Aunt Flo had come through,
wired money. Then, back in the rig, Jim handed him
the newspaper. "Isn't that your Christine Palmer?" he
asked gently.

My Christine Palmer? So I had thought, briefly.

Back at the station Mike took the paper into the bathroom with him. He read it. Christine Palmer Zanuck,
heiress to a multimillion-dollar furniture empire, possibly dead—one of four women Steve Zanuck had married
and swindled. The Palmer fortune, excepting Chris's inheritance, was still sound and in the possession of Florence Palmer, who did not know where her niece was but
had been actively hunting for her for three years. Even
after the horrible ordeal of their lawsuit, Aunt Florence
longed only to know that her niece was alive and well.

He left the bathroom.

They had two alarms in a row. One turned out to be
nothing—a smoking stove. The other was a burning

car, no injuries. He kept quiet, doing his job, straining his muscles, his mind elsewhere.

"Well," Jim said. "That her?"

"I guess so. Yeah, must be."

"She still at your place?"

"She didn't say she was leaving."

"You seen her lately?"

"Yeah, I saw her. Before I came to work." Jim probably knew, Mike figured, that he'd left her in his bed. The other firefighter knew how early they reported for their shift. It was pretty unlikely that Mike had gone from his parents' house to his house for coffee at 6:00 a.m.

"Think she's still there?"

"Well, I suppose so. I'm not afraid she's going to rip off the television, if that's what you mean. Especially now."

"Want to call? Take a couple of hours of personal time to run home?"

Want to? Oh, did he want to. So bad he could hardly stand it. But if he rushed home to check on her, what did that say about *him?* That he had not known what he was doing when he asked her to stay with no strings. That he could talk about love and trust but couldn't act on it. "Nope," he said. "She's a big girl." It was her life.

He lifted weights that afternoon. He thought it through. Long and slow.

He believed in people. He believed in love—in saying it, showing it, trusting people. And when he loved, he loved hard, totally and with faith.

He had known right off that Joanie was the one for him. The second time he'd felt that way was with Chris. With Chris he hadn't felt giddy the way he had with the flight attendant, desperate the way he had with the woman on the rebound, or entrenched the way he had with the artist. He had felt secure and strong and exact. So he had done what he had done—given everything he had. He didn't hold back a little, save a little, like for a rainy day, in case he had been mistaken. Nope. He'd plunged in with everything he had—every tear, every passion, every possession, every hope.

Kind of stupid to think you'd be more relieved to find out she'd kidnapped her own kids than to find out she was rich. *Stinking* rich.

He didn't want to push his own needs onto anyone. He didn't want Chris to save him, exactly. He just wanted her to tell him the truth or refuse to answer. That simple, two choices. Don't say it if you don't feel it. When he had asked her to stay a while and she had said okay, even though she'd been afraid of what it would mean, what it would become, it had meant she'd stayed because she wanted to. And when she said, "I love you," it meant she did. Oh, he knew she was reluctant to say that, and he knew why. Maybe he shouldn't have pushed her, but he had, and she'd said it. Simple. She didn't say she would stay forever, he didn't ask her to, and unless something happened to change her mind, she would probably go. But not without saying goodbye.

No alarms through the night, but he didn't sleep. He almost picked up the phone to call her about fifty times. But she had the number. He'd *told* her to call if she needed him. You can't be any plainer than that.

Long and slow, he thought about it. By morning he thought he knew what he felt. He wanted to take care of her, protect her and love her because it felt good. He wanted to have some time with her and those two little kids because if he could remember what it felt like to be loved and depended on as a man, a provider, a lover, maybe he could get on with his life. Finally. He wanted to hold her without holding her down.

He didn't hang around the station for breakfast. He drank a quick cup of coffee and went home. The old Honda was in the driveway, but he didn't breathe a sigh of relief—not yet. If Aunt Flo had recited the numbers on her American Express card, there might be a note on the refrigerator telling him to sell the car for his trouble. *Please, God, no. Please, God, all I ever wanted was the straight line.*

He unlocked the door. They might still be asleep; it wasn't even seven.

But Chris unfolded herself from the couch, already dressed. Her eyes didn't look a whole lot better than his. She picked up the tabloid that lay on the coffee table and carried it toward him, her lips parted as she was about to speak. She was going to tell him the whole thing. But he didn't want to hear it right now. He didn't care about anything now. She was there.

"Come here," he said, opening his arms, so relieved he was afraid he was going to shout. "Come here and fall on me. I didn't sleep all night."

"Me either," she said, and a sniffle came. "There's so much to tell you."

"You're here. Tell me later. There's lots of time."

"You saw this, then?"

"Oh, yeah. Kind of hard to miss. And they told me you quit Iverson's."

"But you didn't call here?"

"You said you wouldn't surprise me. I had to believe you."

"How could you believe me? Especially after all this?"

"You maybe left a few things out, but you haven't lied to me. I would know."

"Oh, Mike. Oh, hold me. Please."

Which he was glad to do. Ah, that was relief. To believe and find that you were right. "Any of it true?" he asked.

"Some of it," she said. "Like the part about me being dead. That part's probably true. I'm probably just watching this film in purgatory."

He laughed at her. He squeezed her tighter. "Naw. If purgatory felt this good, there wouldn't be any Catholics."

Chapter 8

Firefighters do not think in rainbow shades of many possibilities but in simple light and dark. Hot and cold. Perhaps good and evil. Chris began to understand that Mike Cavanaugh lived in a yes-or-no world that he laboriously kept neat and uncomplicated. It began to make perfect sense to her, the way he thought, even if she didn't think that way herself.

Firefighters don't stand around the outside of a burning building and draw straws to see who goes in, who climbs up on the roof, or who drives the rig. Everyone has a job; he does it. They are decisive, with practiced instincts about safety and danger. They do dangerous things that no one else would dare, but they know it and they know how. They are men and women of skill and strength. They *never* overthink things.

On the Saturday morning after the tabloid story

broke, they curled up on the sofa with cups of hot coffee, talking until the kids woke up. He heard the whole long story about Chris's marriage, lawsuit, divorce and Aunt Flo's desire to come to Sacramento if Chris would not go immediately to Chicago.

"I told her I was staying here for a while, that the children are safe and comfortable here. She doesn't understand, of course, because the kids would be safe and comfortable in her house, but—"

"Did you tell her why you were staying?" he asked.

"Because the kids—"

"Did you tell her you love me?"

She looked at him for a long time. "In the past," she explained, "I haven't used the best judgment based on that emotion. My instincts, which I'm only just beginning to trust, say we're safe here. It isn't very logical, and it probably isn't fair to you, but if you still want us to stay a little while—"

He was either acting on instincts that told him he was safe, or he was using his skill and expertise to enter a danger zone. "I want you to stay."

"Aunt Flo wants to fly out, see me, make sure I'm all right. She's a pretty forceful person, Aunt Flo and—"

"Chris, if you want to be here and I want you here, old Aunt Flo will just have to live with it. All that other stuff, about your instincts and your judgment, well, I think you ought to take your time with that."

"Well, she'll come here, then. Monday."

He shrugged. "I can't blame her. She's family. She's worried about you. We'll manage."

"My family, Mike, is nothing like your family."

"That's a relief," he said with a laugh. "I have the weekend off," he said. "Why don't we take the kids to

the cabin? It's nice and cold in the mountains. It's snow-
ing. It's quiet. Monday, huh?"

But no more running away or disappearing. That
was another thing about firemen. Maybe they didn't
borrow trouble, but they liked to face the fire, not have
it hiding in a basement or behind a closed door. Sometimes it came at them from above or behind or beneath.
When they walked or crawled into a smoky, stinging,
blinding problem, they liked to know where it was. So
he suggested to Chris that she call Aunt Flo and tell
her that she was going to the cabin, that she would be
away from the phone, and give Mrs. Cavanaugh's phone
number in case there was any emergency. And find out
when, on Monday, Aunt Florence should be picked up
at the airport.

Then they drove for two and a half hours to the
mountains, to a place called Pembroke Pines, just north
of Lake Tahoe. At Mike's cabin in the woods they could
talk and play and worry in peace.

Mike swung Kyle up onto the back of the mare.
"Hold on here," he told him, placing the boy's hands
on the saddle horn. "Hold on, now."

Chris held the reins of Carrie's horse. Mike's nearest
neighbors, the Christiansons, had loaned him the horses.
Mike and Chris walked together, leading the small, gentle mares on which the children were perched. Cheeks
trailed along, barking and snarling. They trudged down
a sloppy dirt road in the Saturday afternoon sunshine,
talking more like old friends than new lovers.

"Big Mike once saw that movie, *It's a Wonderful
Life*. My dad gets an idea about something and makes it
into a whole philosophy. Hurray for Hollywood, huh?"

"I liked the movie, too," Chris said.

"So that was how he handled us. Every single problem, from the fumbled pass during high-school football to death and despair. 'So Little Mike, what one thing would you go back and change, huh? What one thing that *you* could do would make it all turn out different?' And I would say, 'Well, I woulda studied for the test, that's what.' 'There you go,' he'd say."

"I should have paid more attention to the movie," Chris said.

"So, Chrissie, what one thing would you go back and change?"

"Ah! What wouldn't I change!"

"Your lousy ex? Wouldn't have married him, huh?"

"Starting there..."

"No Carrie and no Kyle. See, that's how this little game works. You go ahead and change something in your past, and you remove a big hunk of your future. That's the trick. You have to be real careful what pains you're going to trade for what pleasures. This is not as simple as it sounds."

"So what about you? What did Big Mike tell you?"

Mike laughed. "Oh, he had me so mad I thought I might deck him. Big Mike hasn't always been a little old man, you know. Even ten years ago I couldn't beat him arm wrestling. Yeah, he put me on the spot with Joanie's death. 'So what would you change? Never having met her? Never having married her? Never having Shelly...for even a little while?' For a long time I believed that would have been easier, better. Then I decided that if I could change anything, maybe I would have gotten up at night and changed the baby's diapers more. Or maybe I would have fought with Joanie about

money just a little bit less. Maybe I wouldn't have asked
her to join the Catholic church just so Ma would relax
about the whole thing. But I don't know. I try to think,
would that have made losing them feel any different?
Easier? Harder?"

"And what about this?" she asked, taking his hand.
"Starting to wish you hadn't been on duty that night
my house burned down?"

"Oh, heck no. No, I really needed this. It shook things
into place. I'm thirty-six. I had a bad deal, and I gotta
get past that. I hadn't been with a woman in a long time.
And before that I'd been with some without really being
with them, you know?"

"Terrible waste," she said.

"In case you're interested, I feel like a big dope about
it now. I was afraid of what I wanted from life. I want
a lot, Chrissie. I want a family again."

"Whoa, boy," she said, shivering.

"You get worried when people tell you what they
want, don't you?"

"If I think they want it from me, I do."

"No, that isn't it, I bet. You want it, too, and it scares
you half to death. That's just what was happening to
me. For ten years. I wanted a family again, but what if
I tried to get one, got it and lost it again? After about
ten years you decide to either play the hand you're dealt
or stay out of the game."

"So," she said, "you're getting back in the game?"

"Me? I shouldn't have tried so hard to be alone. So,
now that I remember, I'm not giving up on it again."

"I don't think you should."

"You're my first choice," he said, grinning at her.
But he did not ask her to make him any promises. "Just

having you around has been real good for me. It's like waking up."

"But will it always be good?"

"Chrissie, you'd make a great Catholic, no kidding. You borrow more trouble than Ma does. Never thought I'd meet a woman who could compete with Ma for worry and guilt."

The cabin, one open room with a large hearth and shallow loft, was equipped only with the necessities. But while the wind blew outside, the fire was hot. All four of them had to use sleeping bags in the central room. The loft wasn't a good place for the kids to be alone, in case they woke up in the night and began to wander. And downstairs alone, with a fire that had to burn all night, was an even worse idea.

"Why didn't you tell me the whole thing right off?" he asked her late in the night while the kids slept nearby.

"Because it's so shocking," she said. "People find the whole thing just plain incomprehensible. I told a couple of friends I met after Steve was gone, trying it out. The first thing they can't understand is why I didn't go after Steve, have him at least put in jail. People think you can do that, no sweat. You can't. He'd lost community property—proving he did it on purpose or stole it might have been impossible. Next, they wondered, if I had this rich aunt, why I didn't just call her right away. Say, 'Send a few bucks, you can afford it.' But a few bucks wasn't the thing I needed most. Pretty soon people look at you strangely, like you've made it all up. I began to feel weird, like a fraud or something, so I stopped telling anyone, which made me a real impostor. I might have had acquaintances but fewer and fewer real friends. With real friends you share personal things about your life. And my life was becoming more and more impossible to believe."

"But you decided to call Aunt Flo. Before the newspaper story," he pointed out.

"I wanted to call her because of the Cavanaughs. I had family once—very different from yours in a lot of ways, but tight, close, intimate family. Once Flo and I were very, very dear to each other—we were like best friends, in a way. There had been lots of other friends in my life, too—friends from high school and college—but I lost touch with some once I married Steve and moved, and the rest after the divorce because I was so embarrassed about how stupid I had been. When things settle down, I should probably try to get in touch with some of them.

"But first I have to deal with Flo. We didn't start to butt heads until my parents died and she took over as my parent. She began telling me what to do, what to feel, I guess because she felt responsible for me. Probably half the reason I married Steve in the first place was because Flo told me I couldn't.

"But I'm not really like you were. I'm not afraid of what I want. I'm more afraid I want all the wrong things. I'm afraid that I really and truly lack judgment. That I am really and truly incompetent."

"All you lack is confidence. It'll come back. Give it time."

"We're not talking about climbing back on a horse here, Mike. We're talking about lives and futures. Mine. Theirs."

"Ours."

"Don't," she said.

"You can hurt yourself more than one way, Chrissie. You can hurt yourself by making a wrong choice and loving some creep who just wants to use you, or you can hurt yourself by not loving someone who would be good for you."

Loving or not loving, she thought, was something she seemed to have no control over. But she had to try to have control over her *life*. "I'm not too worried about what's going to happen to me," she told him, "because I'm going to take my time and not rush into anything. But I would hate myself forever if I somehow hurt you... or them." She glanced at her children.

"One of the first things I noticed, Chrissie, is that you take good care of them. You're a good mother. That doesn't sound incompetent to me. I think," he said, pausing to kiss her nose, "you can be trusted with human life. I'm not worried about what you'll do to me."

"When Aunt Florence comes, Mike, would you like me to go stay with her at the hotel, or stay with you?"

"I would like you to stay where you want to be. But remember that your aunt has been through a lot, Chrissie, and you have to be careful with her. She's your family, and you gotta be careful with your family. You be nice to her, be gentle. But you can also tell her that you're a grown-up woman, a mother yourself, and you have to be where you have to be."

"She said almost the same thing about you."

"Oh?"

"She said, 'Oh, Chris, you just tell that nice man that you're very grateful for everything and that you'll call him, even visit.'"

Mike frowned his dangerous frown. "Well," he said

with a shrug, "even if Aunt Florence turns out to be a real bitch, we can handle it."

Yeah, Mike could probably handle just about anything, she decided as she tried to fall asleep.

She had always been attracted to independence and mastery. Her father, her lousy ex-husband, even Aunt Flo. Mike was like them all in many ways.

The next morning Mike wandered off, returning with firewood. Later, Chris heard a noise behind the cabin and found him repairing the pump. He puttered quietly, but when there was something to talk about, he opened up. It was all right when they didn't talk, too. One of the things that Chris learned was the kind of quiet she could have with intimacy. She had never had that in her marriage.

Mike took the kids for a nice long walk after breakfast while Chris cleaned up the dishes and rolled sleeping bags. They held on to his hands and toddled off, asking a million questions as they went out the door.

This was why she didn't leave. Not because she had any illusions about happily ever after, but because she was briefly visiting with her desires, the ones she was afraid were stupid and impossible.

For a short time she could indulge the fantasy of having a man for herself and for her kids. A man with enough love and caring to embrace a family. That was what she had thought she saw in Steve, but what she had seen was a lot of energy, not a lot of love. She had been too young and filled with grief to know it.

She had given her kids plenty of love and nurturing, even though she had been bereft herself, but they had lacked some vital things. A happy mother, for starters.

She worried about that a lot; what had they learned from her loneliness? Were there hidden emotional scars that would hinder them later, making it tough for them to form critical relationships? Would they not know how to make a family of their own because in their formative years all they had seen was their mother's tired, frustrated struggle? The absence of a father figure? Deprived of the sight of adults touching each other, showing easy and natural affection that came of love? What about a smile on their mother's face because a good man had made love to her?

There was no kidding herself, after making love with Mike she had felt different—relieved, soothed, fulfilled. And when a woman felt good, she mothered better. Did they pick up on these things?

And Mike provided. It wasn't just the things he provided, like cable TV or the new jackets, boots and mittens they had needed to go to the mountains. It was also the zone of calmness, sanity. His trust and confidence. She could see that they sat differently on his big lap, more secure because of his size and self-possession. They had hungered for a father, and for now they had a big fireman to show them what it might be like.

She wanted a life like the one they were pretending. To cook while he worked and to surprise him with something special. Or to not cook and have him complain. She wanted to be there to talk about the fires with him and take a casserole to Mattie and Big Mike's. She wanted to take her kids to the park, be a room mother, buy a chair she didn't need and argue over the expense, complain about the way he never wiped out the sink, and make love regularly. Then she wanted to work on her books and maybe have another baby. And be up through the night and nag that he took her for granted and have him say he was sorry and never would again.

She wanted a stupid, happy 1950s marriage that was fraught with give-and-take and pleasure and trouble, and sensible women did not want that anymore! Especially women who had jumped into that bonfire and been badly burned. She did not make any sense to herself.

He hadn't asked her to stay forever. She hoped he wouldn't too soon, but she knew he was sneaking up on that. She felt it. The fact that she would be tempted only made it worse. But she couldn't stand to think about leaving him, either. She was in love with him. And she knew it. If only she could have a little time to think.

But Flo was coming. Better think fast, Chris.

Late on Sunday night, when they were back in Sacramento and getting into bed, he asked her, "What time are you picking her up?"

"Noon."

"Bringing her here?"

"No, I made a reservation at the Red Lion."

"I'll be at work. Till Tuesday morning."

"The kids and I will spend the afternoon and evening with her, but we're coming back here, if that's all right."

"Stop acting like I'm going to change my mind. Old Aunt Flo doesn't worry me nearly as much as she worries you."

"That's because you don't know her."

"What's she going to do? Punch me out? Come on, relax. You call me if you need me. If she tries to kidnap you or something, we'll take care of Aunt Flo."

"Make love to me," she said. "Please. And don't make love to me like it's the last time."

"Is it? Is there any chance it's the last time? If it is, don't lie to me, that's all I ask. Just tell me the truth."

"I don't want it to be," she said, but tears came to her eyes. "I swear, I don't want it to be."

"That's good enough for me."

The Sacramento airport was small, tight and busy. Chris parked her car as close to the terminal as she could, but it was still quite a walk. She held hands with Carrie and Kyle. They were solemn, though they didn't exactly know why. They had been told about Aunt Flo, Mama's aunt from Chicago whom they had never seen before, whom Mommy hadn't seen in five years...since court. She didn't tell them that part.

Chris was so nervous about the reunion that she didn't even indulge in people-watching. She simply found them seats right outside security and waited. And waited.

The plane was late, but Flo got off quickly. She would have flown first-class. Naturally.

And there she was, more stunning and powerful than Chris remembered. She was five foot eight and still wore heels. She was dressed in a mauve suede suit and a low-cut lacy blouse. She wore boots—probably eel-skin. Her coat, slung over her arm, had a white mink collar. Flo wore as many dead animals as she pleased. Her diamond stud earrings glittered behind her short auburn hair. She was gorgeous, aristocratic. Forty-one years old. Good old Aunt Flo. Be nice to her now.

Chris saw her aunt spot them: she in her blue jeans, T-shirt, ski jacket and tennis shoes, no makeup, her hair pulled back into an unsophisticated ponytail; and two little kids who wore practically new but nonetheless rumpled clothes. Not a designer label among them.

The two women rushed toward each other and embraced. Chris was reduced instantly to tears. It was like meeting her past, her longed-for, frightening, grievous, essential past.

"Chris!"

"Flo! Oh, Flo!"

A camera bulb flashed.

"Oh, hell!" Chris gasped.

"Ms. Palmer, how long have you waited for this reunion?" "When did you first discover the whereabouts of your niece?" "Who died on that yacht, Ms. Palmer?" "Where will you be staying?" "Was any of the fortune recovered, Mrs. Zanuck?"

Chris grabbed her kids, one with each hand. She took only two steps before she looped an arm around Kyle's waist, lifted him onto her hip and headed down the concourse. Flo trotted after them.

"My God, Flo!"

"You think I invited them?"

"How did they know you were coming?"

"How the hell should I know? They know everything. Ever since that damn book came out!"

"Can't you get rid of them?"

"How, exactly? Let's just get out of here. Where's the car?"

"It's in the parking lot! Did you think I pulled the limo up to the curb?"

"You had to wear jeans? And those...shoes?"

"What do you think? That my designer is all tied up? Jeez, my house burned down! Anyway, who cares what I'm wearing? I didn't know it was going to be a damn press conference."

"Stop swearing. They'll hear you swearing."

"*You're* swearing."

"My luggage. Oh, forget the luggage. I'll send someone for it later."

"What if *they* get it?"

"Oh, they can't get my luggage. Later," she said to a reporter. There were only about six, but it seemed like six hundred. "I just want to spend some time with my niece. I'll give you a statement later."

"You will not!" Chris said.

"Just come on, all right?"

They were followed to the parking lot. They were half running, dragging Carrie along.

"Get a shot of the car! Get a shot of them getting into the car. Man, will you look at that car!"

They were not followed from the airport, but by the time they had Flo settled in her suite—after warning the manager about reporters, having someone sent to the airport for the luggage, and making various other arrangements for Flo's comfort—Chris was exhausted. And disgusted. She began to remember the photographers at the courthouse. When she won, she had had tears in her eyes, sensing if not admitting her betrayal. But Steve had been whispering in her ear, "Don't cry, for God's sake. Smile. Tell them you have no hard feelings, that you love your aunt, you know. Come on, we won."

We. There had never been any *we*.

Flo hadn't cried. "There should be no question of my motives or my relationship with my niece. I only attempted to protect her future as was spelled out in my brother's will. She didn't sue *me*, after all. I happen to think that it's a mistake for her to contest her father's wishes, but the court has made its decision, and we'll certainly abide by it." To Chris, later, Flo had said, "I am too angry to even talk to you. You just don't know how foolish you are."

In Flo's suite, Kyle bounced on the big round bed and Carrie carefully manipulated the buttons on the television. Flo spoke on the phone, ordering room service. Chris slouched in the chair.

"Well, they're sending up some sandwiches and sodas for the kids, salads for us, and I ordered a bottle of wine. We should toast this occasion, hmm? Then I think we should go shopping. I'm renting a car, and—"

"Tell me about the stupid book."

"Well," Flo said, sitting down gracefully, sliding into the chair and crossing her long, beautiful legs, "the 'stupid' book is exactly that. It is contrived almost solely from old newspaper articles and gossip and isn't nearly as revealing as it claims to be. I'm sure a great deal of it is made up. And I think it's been thrown together and rushed to print in the few months since that yacht has been missing. All of the pictures are previously published photos, and—"

"Pictures?"

"Oh, yes. How they got a baby picture of you is beyond me. Stole it, probably."

"Who did this? And why?"

"The author's name, Stephanie Carlisle, is a pseudonym. This is her third such exposé. She writes a decorator column for a Miami newspaper. The Miami paper ran a small piece about a missing yacht, a missing woman and an investigation of a man by the name of Steven Zanuck, the name under which the missing yacht was chartered. And I think I can tell you how this all started. That weasel's third wife, not his fourth, was the daughter of a Texas millionaire. Naturally. Her father began investigating him, not liking in the least who his daughter had fallen for. I think it's pretty certain that Steve took her off to Miami when things were getting a little hot in Dallas. We think, for example, that he might have married her before he was divorced from you. And we also suspect that he didn't divorce his first wife at all—a woman he married when he was only twenty-one and living in San Francisco. Precocious little devil."

"What? Who was that?"

"Sondra Pederson, daughter of a rich Swedish shipper. But that one wasn't as messy as the other ones. He managed to get a bunch of money before Daddy flew from Sweden to San Francisco and simply collected his brokenhearted daughter. She's alive and well and living with her family in Stockholm. That hasn't been mentioned, however. It would probably hurt book sales."

"Jeez. It figures."

"He wasn't a lawyer. No record of his ever having attending law school or taking the bar exam."

"Why didn't we know any of this sooner? When I was stupidly trying to win my fortune?"

"Believe me, if I had been able to find one thing on him, I would have used it. He checked out. There was a Steven Zanuck who passed the bar after graduating from law school in New York. There was even a yearbook picture that resembled your husband. He was pretty good at this little scam. And, although I thought he was a weasel and a creep, I didn't know the worst of it. It was that Texan, Charles Beck, who dug up the real dirt. And I think it's possible his family paid the biggest price."

"You think they're really dead, then? Steve and his—"

"Fred."

"Fred?"

"His name wasn't really Steve Zanuck. In San Francisco his name was William Wandell, and in Texas he was Steven Wright. He kept a place and a small business under the name Zanuck for a while, kind of living a dual identity. It probably had something to do with monies he had received as Zanuck. His real name is Fred Johnson. And the real Steve Zanuck, a nice young tax attorney with a practice in Missouri, isn't real happy about all this, either."

"Fred?"

"Terrific, huh? Well, I always knew he was no damn good. Just couldn't prove it. I hired detectives and lawyers, and they didn't figure him out, either. Real slick, this lizard. I ought to sue them. Incompetents."

"Is all this in the book?"

"This business about his aliases is our little secret so far. We're going to have to do something about that hair." Flo reached across the small table and plucked at Chris's hair. Chris withdrew. "You know you shouldn't wear your hair all the same length."

Chris put her forehead in her hand, leaning her elbow on the small round table. "Fred," she moaned. "This is simply impossible."

"It'll blow over. There's a little money, I think. The Texan found some money, but maybe it's not in this country. I wonder what the scum was saving up for?"

"Does he have a lot of children, too?"

Flo glanced at Kyle, bouncing, and Carrie, sitting entranced in front of the big TV. Her features softened.

She looked back at Chris. "Not that I know of," she said gently. "You should have called me so much sooner."

"I know. I know." But then I wouldn't have been pulled out of that fire, she thought. She almost told Flo about the philosophy behind *It's a Wonderful Life*, but she held her tongue. Sophisticated Flo, who'd climbed to a mountaintop in Tibet to learn about meditation from the masters, would have a tough time swallowing something as effective as playing the hand you're dealt. "Well, I figured you were pretty mad, Flo. I was trying to make it on my own, I guess. I've been working, taking care of the kids and writing."

"Writing? What?"

"Never mind that. Not my life story, I promise. I was trying to take care of myself, trying to figure out what I really wanted to do. I'm getting a little tired of feeling stupid. I just wanted to make it on my own for a while. I thought I'd done enough damage. I wasn't planning to *never* call you."

"Well, you should have called me. I was worried sick. Now, when are you coming back home?"

Chris began telling her story. She tried to explain how for the first time in so long she felt free but coddled at the same time. This wonderful man and his lovely family had embraced her, and though they didn't have many luxuries, within their tender assembly there was such a rich intimacy, such love.

Room service arrived. They set up the kids at the table, and Flo brought the wine to the sitting room where Chris was telling her tale, knowing she sounded like a romantic fool. Yet another chapter in Chris's novel of misguided fortunes, fantasies and foibles. Flo poured wine and sat listening, pulling a long, slender cigarette from her snakeskin case, inhaling, the smoke curling up past her perfectly enameled nails, past her rose-colored lips, over her artistically fashioned copper hair. Listening to this story of love and woe.

"I always wanted to have a family," Chris said. "A family like my family was. Even before Mom and Daddy died, I always figured that whatever I ended up doing, I'd be doing it in a home with a husband and children."

"Well, you have children," Flo said.

"I should have listened to you. I shouldn't have married Steve—I know that. But I did, I have them, and in Mike's home and in his family the kids have a sense of belonging. For the first time. I can see a change in them already—they feel more loved, more secure, at ease."

Flo did not comment.

Chris told of parks, ducks, movies, stories read. "Imagine Carrie not knowing that men don't shave their legs! And they love his cabin, the horses they rode. The cousins at Mattie and Big Mike's."

"I can't come up with cousins," Flo said, "but the horses shouldn't be a big problem."

"It's more than horses and cabins and movies. As for me," Chris said, "I had been lonelier than I realized. I had let myself become friendless. I hardly even noticed that I had lost touch with old friends who probably would have stood by me. Then, meeting the Cavanaughs, I saw the potential to have family and friends again." She smiled almost sheepishly. "They liked me. Right off. Without knowing a thing about me.

"And Mike," she went on. "Logically I knew that all men aren't men like Steve… Fred. But I had stopped believing it was possible for someone to care for me, no matter whether I was rich, poor, smart or dumb. This guy just opened up his heart and his home, no questions asked. It had nothing whatever to do with my bloodline or checkbook balance. I can't tell you how it feels to have this man not give a damn about all that."

Flo stamped out the cigarette. She sipped the wine.

Then, Chris tried to explain, he had needs, too. He wasn't asking her for anything, really, but because his life had not been a picnic, this unit they had formed, the four of them, was helping him, too. He was finally getting in touch with what he had lost, what he could have, and was thinking in terms of having a real life again— one filled with love, people, give-and-take. Before Chris and her kids, Mike had cut himself off, afraid to feel, afraid to be involved.

"The long and short of it is, I'm simply not ready to leave him. That doesn't mean I'm planning to stay forever—I haven't made commitments—but the four of us, well, we're comfortable with one another when none of us has been completely comfortable for years. We're recuperating from past hurts. It might not sound very practical, but it's a good feeling to be needed."

"I love you, Flo. I know I haven't been very good family, the way things have gone. First the lawsuit, then disappearing like that. I'm sure you've been at the end of your rope with me, and I want to patch things up. I want to have our old relationship back. I want to be friends again. You're the most important person in my life, my only family. But I'm not going to do everything you tell me, and I'm not going to leave Mike's house until I'm ready. Until we're healthier. All four of us."

Her eyes were locked tightly on Chris's. Chris realized Flo probably thought her niece still had a screw loose, as though she had moved from one absurd situation to the next. But for the first time in seven years Chris felt sane. And—another first—she felt tough enough to deal with Flo. She lifted her chin, waiting.

"Well," Flo said, as composed as ever, lifting the wineglass, "how long do you think this is going to take?"

Mike had finally talked about it. He had told Jim some of this incredible tale. He had come right out and said it, that though he probably sounded like a lunatic, he had fallen for this goofy woman and her kids. And it was true, like the story in the paper said, she had been pretty well kicked around by that jerk she had married, but she hadn't known it was all a scam from the start. Young, you know, grieving over her dead parents, no one but her old-maid Aunt Flo, and then along comes this good-looking, fast-talking lawyer, and bam! Before you know it the whole family falls apart over money. Figures, huh? Money and sex, the biggest problems in America.

And yes, he had said, he'd told her to stay for as long as she wanted. He hoped it would be for a long time because he liked it; it was good to take someone to his mom and dad's, not go alone. They loved the cabin, all of them. Especially the kids. For a few years now he'd been thinking of building a room on. Maybe this spring he'd get started.

These complications from her past? Well, he had said, who didn't have a past, huh? His past, for example, wasn't very tidy, all things considered. She had to try to reconcile with her aunt, keep her family together somehow. She hadn't taken any of her aunt's money, of course, only her own. She didn't need money right now, but everyone needs family. So he had encouraged her to be as patient and kind with old Aunt Flo as she possibly could. This would all work itself out.

The afternoon paper arrived. Mike had been playing Ping-Pong with a couple of the guys. Jim walked in and stopped the game, spreading the paper on the game table. At least it wasn't the front page. The headline said *REUNION*. The airport scene. Blue-jeaned Chris was being embraced by a tall, fashionable woman who looked to be about Mike's age. She wore jewelry everywhere, *big* jewelry. She carried a fur coat and a briefcase.

"Old Aunt Flo," Jim supplied.

"Holy shit," Mike said. Then he picked up the paper and took it into the bathroom.

Chapter 9

Mike entered his house quietly. He peeked in at the sleeping kids. Cheeks, the great watchdog, asleep on the end of Kyle's bed, didn't even greet him. Cheeks was exhausted from spending the entire night eating a pair of Mike's socks. He was sleeping with the remnants still under his chin.

When Mike found Chris in his bed, still asleep, he felt his chest swell with pride. He felt as though he were in possession, as if he had won. He didn't mean to feel that way, but he did. He wondered how many more mornings he'd leave his shift wondering what he'd find at home. He sat down on the edge of the bed, gently, and kissed her. "Hey, sleepyhead," he whispered.

She moved a little, moaning. "You had fires," she sleepily informed him. "I can't sleep through those sirens."

"I can't sleep through them, either." He laughed. "I'm

going to have to sleep today though—I'm bushed. I saw Aunt Flo."

"You saw her?" Chris asked, coming awake, sitting up. "Where?"

"In the paper. Your picture was in the paper."

"Oh, yeah, I should have thought of that. There were reporters at the airport, but we ditched them. Was the story awful?"

"There wasn't much of a story, no quotes or anything."

"That's a relief. They didn't make anything up."

"Any particular reason you didn't tell me that Flo wasn't some crotchety old bat?"

"Is *that* what you thought?" she asked with a laugh. "Well, don't worry, I won't tell her. No, Flo is everything every woman dreams of being. Intelligent. Sophisticated. Independent. Beautiful. Rich. Successful." And a few other things, she thought, like belligerent, possessive, domineering.

"How old is she?"

"Oh, about forty. Maybe forty-one."

"Jeez. I had no idea. I was expecting this little old lady, like from *Arsenic and Old Lace*, just a rich old biddy who couldn't understand true love because her libido had dried up."

Chris laughed again.

"How was it? The reunion?"

"There were three things we had to get out of the way—first, how ashamed and sorry I am for having sued her, abandoned her and worried her half to death. Second, this business about my ex-husband and that stupid book. And finally, how I'm not getting on a plane with her this afternoon. Then we had a lot of fun reminiscing. I've missed her so much. We had such fun together when I was growing up. My mom would say that she had married Randolph and Flo. We were a famous foursome. And Flo was always there, spoiling me, pumping me up, taking my side. Auntie Flo," she said sentimentally, shaking her head. There had been affection, such hilarity, such joy in their relationship— so much lost since the death of her parents and the lawsuit. Chris longed to have it back. "My best friend while I was growing up. She's more like an older sister than an aunt."

"So. Not this afternoon, huh?"

She kissed him, quick and cute, on the lips. She wrinkled her nose. "You stink. Awful. Smoke?"

"And a bunch of other things. I would have showered at the station, but we had a shift relief in the middle of a fire."

"What other things?"

"God knows. Sweat. Mud. Good old Jim ought to take an emesis basin into a fire with him, for starters."

"A what?"

"You know, that curved little pan they give you in the hospital when you have to throw up. It's amazing— everything hits your turnouts, but you still come away smelling like all of it. Jim shot me with the hose to clean me off, but I still need a scrub, huh?"

"Oooo. I guess I thought only the victims threw up."

"Bet you also thought only the victims swallowed a lot of smoke, huh? I'll take a quick shower."

"Were they bad fires?"

"One was at a paint store. Those are almost the worst—chemicals and all. That one will be on the news—horrible mess. It took hours in the middle of the night, but it was just about over by the time I left. The other two were pretty good fires."

"Good fires?"

"Manageable fires, no injuries, easily contained."

"Do you like fires?"

"I like to put water on fires."

She watched while he stripped off his shirt and pants, heading for the shower in only his briefs. She remembered the young fireman in the photo she had found, the leaner, trimmer man. But though he was thicker now, he was firm and graceful. He walked with such purpose, even without clothes on.

"Mike, have you ever gotten hurt in a fire?"

He shrugged. "Not bad."

"This is really dangerous, what you do. You could be killed."

"Don't overthink it. I know what I'm doing or I wouldn't do it." He yanked down the briefs.

"*Overthink* it? What about firefighters' families? What must they go through every time they hear the siren? What if you—"

He stood in the bathroom doorway, hands on his hips, not in the least distracted by his nudity. "Chrissie, being born is dangerous. Joanie and Shelly were driving to the grocery store. If you're going to worry for a living, worry about something you can control, for Pete's sake. I'm going to shower. *I* can't even stand the way I smell."

While the shower ran, she thought about those two things. One, he could get killed in a fire. Two, if she were paid for worrying, she'd be a millionaire.

"Tell me about Aunt Flo," he said, standing in the

bathroom doorway with a towel wrapped around his lower body, using another to dry his hair.

"I invited her to dinner. Is that okay?"

"Here?"

"Would you rather not?"

"No, it's okay. But—"

"She is not going to relax until she looks you over, Mike. She simply can't believe I'm planning to stay here for a while. And I thought we'd all be a lot more comfortable here than in a restaurant or something. I'm cooking."

"I'm getting into bed," he said, moving to close the bedroom door and then tossing the towel to the floor. "When did you tell her you'd go back to Chicago?"

"I didn't say when."

"What did you say?"

"Want to know how I sold you, huh? Well, I told her you were this big, handsome brute who—"

"Actually," he said, pulling back the covers to climb in beside her, "I want to know how you sold her on not dragging you off to Chicago."

"I said we were getting healthy here," she replied, her voice soft, her words serious. "All four of us. Is that true?"

He thought about it for a minute. "Yeah, I think that's true. Yeah, that's okay." He pulled up the covers. His eyes looked bright, but dark circles hung under them. Fires. His eyes, scorched but excited, tired but revved up. She wondered how long a man could do this work before it took its toll. "But you never told her that you love me."

"She thinks I'm crazy as it is."

"Well, in that case, I hope this is a long illness," he said.

"How long do you think you'd like it to be, Mike?"

"Oh, thirty, forty years. I want to keep you."

"Forever?"

"If I can."

"I can't make that kind of commitment. You know that. It's way too soon."

"Well, it's an open invitation."

"How can *you* do that—ask us to stay here permanently? You mean, you want to marry us after knowing us such a short time?"

"Are you going to hold that against me?"

"No. But I'm not rushing into anything."

"Just so you're not rushing *out* of anything."

"You haven't even met my family. My 'family' will blow in here at about six-thirty tonight with twenty-two midgets carrying her train and polishing her crown. I think the term *formidable woman* was invented to describe Flo. Then you might add some conditions to this not-very-romantic proposal."

His hands went under her T-shirt, which was his T-shirt, and he squirmed closer. "You want romance, Chrissie? I'll give you romance."

"Mike, why would you bring up marriage so soon? Really, why?"

"It's what I want. I think it's what you want. I think you want to be a real family. I want to take care of you."

"If I wanted taking care of, I could call the Red Lion. Flo would be thrilled."

He squeezed her breasts and moved against her thigh. "Oh?"

"That's not enough, wanting to take care of someone."

He shrugged. "We can think about it for a long time, or a short time. But, Chrissie, life is short. You just never know how short. And I love you. I haven't loved anyone like this in a long, long time."

"What if you don't feel that way in another month?"

"Look, if you're not sure how *you* feel, that's one thing. You had a hard time of it, I know, so take your time and decide how you feel, okay? But I know how *I* feel, and I know that this kind of feeling doesn't come and go that fast. They trip around a little from time to time—every marriage on record has ups and downs. But love is love, and I'd rather live it than give it lip service."

"And you didn't feel this way about the other women you've been with?"

"Nope. I wanted to, but I didn't. Boy, when it hits you, it about knocks you over." He smiled. It was a feeling he liked.

"I'm afraid of being in love," she whispered.

"Really? Afraid of being in love? Or afraid of loving someone who's going to hurt you?"

"Isn't that the same thing?"

"Depends," he said, shrugging, his eyes getting that tired, drained look. He was going to nod off. "Are you afraid of me?"

"You know I'm not."

"Then it's not the same thing." He put his head on her shoulder, holding her close, snuggling up tight.

"Actually," she said almost to herself, "what I'm really afraid of is depending on someone too much. Really needing, *counting* on, someone. Giving in so totally. Because the next stage seems to be taking it all for granted, expecting it will stay safe and satisfying forever until the only thing about yourself you're sure of is who you are in relation to the person you feel you belong to.

Whether he's a great guy or a jerk, it could—whoosh—disappear, leaving you suddenly on your own. Do you know what I'm talking about, Mike? Mike?"

He had fallen asleep.

"Marriage!" Flo said, in a combination of shock and distrust. Chris sat in the beautician's chair, Florence stood behind. The kids were with a sitter, a *bonded* sitter at the hotel. "Are you even close to seeing how ridiculous this is becoming? Marriage! Layer it," she instructed, pointing a long, polished fingernail at the back of Chris's head. "But leave some of the length. No bangs. Brush it *back*, so."

"I can tell her how to cut my hair, Florence."

"Tell her then," Flo said, hands on hips.

"Well, I'd like you to cut it shorter around the top and take only about an inch off the length so that it still touches my shoulders, and—"

Flo smiled. "That's what I thought."

"I wish you wouldn't tell me what I want to do all the time." Especially when you're right, she almost added.

"Marriage, huh? He suggested marriage this soon? You certainly didn't accept?"

"Not because I wasn't tempted."

"Chris, you're going to have to be sensible at some point in your life, and now would be a good time. A little shorter on top, here," she instructed the stylist. "You're on the rebound, you can't enter into another marriage."

"Rebound? I've been alone for nearly four years!"

"Yes, but you haven't really recovered from that yet. In fact, you don't know for sure if you're divorced, widowed or still married." The stylist stopped, eyes widening. Flo dismissed her curiosity with a hard stare. The comb moved again. "There," Flo told the technician, "that looks good. Real good."

They shopped for clothes and accessories. Makeup, nail polish, files, perfume, bath oils, shampoos and rinses. Chris turned before a full-length mirror in the department store. She looked very different in tailored dress slacks, a loose angora sweater, heels and hose, makeup, a sculptured hairstyle and even a necklace. A thick, curving gold collar. Very chic.

"I'm not on the rebound. I've been on my own for four years. I haven't had any kind of serious relationship, but that doesn't mean that I didn't meet and know men. I've worked several different jobs in the past few years. I even had a couple of dates. And Mike hasn't met anyone he wanted to marry, but that doesn't mean he doesn't know women. You've got this all wrong."

"What kind of a guy offers his house for the night because a woman is burned out, and then, lickety-split, asks her to marry him?"

"Oh, you're right, only a real pervert would do a thing like that!"

"What if this has something to do with your money?"

"I don't have any money, Flo."

"*I* have money. And what's mine is yours."

"No, it's not, Flo. We aren't the same person, remember? All my money, which was Daddy's money, hit the trail."

They walked between the shops in the downtown Sacramento open mall. As they were passing a window, arms laden with shopping bags, Flo drew Chris up short. "Look," she said, standing behind Chris and taking her parcels, giving her a full view of herself. "Do you feel any different? You look great."

Chris looked at herself in the shop window. She fingered the necklace that cuffed her neck——not solid gold, but a very nice piece of jewelry nonetheless. Classy, like Flo. "Yes, Flo," she said, meeting her aunt's eyes in the glass. "I feel different. I look more like your version of me than mine. And your version looks better." She turned around, staring into her aunt's eyes. "I don't quite know what to make of that."

"Why don't you simply enjoy it?"

But Chris had had plenty of time to think about what she needed to be happy, and it wasn't fancy clothes. She needed family. She needed to be connected to people she loved, people who cared for her and counted on her. She also liked to sit behind a typewriter and imagine. She imagined best in a sweat suit or jeans or a man's T-shirt. Grubbies. It might be nice, she thought, to dress up after a grueling day at the keys, but it wasn't necessary in order to become whom she was becoming. What she needed a lot more than a nice pair of slacks and a necklace was someone to talk to about the book she was working on—and for that it didn't matter what she was wearing.

Who wouldn't enjoy nice things? Oh, boy, there it was again. It was difficult to maintain an idea of what you could do on your own when you were being taken care of. That she would enjoy nice things so much more if she could get them for herself and also give them was difficult for people like Flo to understand. And there was no way to refuse Flo's generosity, for Flo spending on Chris was part of their history. But it was already starting to feel loaded. She kept waiting to hear the bait line: "After all I've done..."

You suffer too much, Chrissie, he had said. *It's almost*

like you want to. No, that wasn't it. Chris hated to suffer. She wanted balance. Give-and-take. Take *and* give.

"Why haven't you ever married, Flo?" she asked.

"I never saw the need."

"Need? Is that what marriage is? Something you need?"

"You tell me. You're obviously thinking about doing it for the second time."

"I'm not really ready to make any long-term commitments; I only said I was tempted. And Steve… I mean. Fred, doesn't count. I was a victim of temporary insanity."

"Nothing counts *more* than Steve, or Fred, or whoever the heck he was, because you should have learned something from that—something about how impetuous you are when it comes to this kind of emotion. Lord, running back into a thunderstorm again before you're even dried off."

"I think you mean jumping from the frying pan into the fire," Chris supplied, laughing. "Almost literally. Don't worry, Florence. I learned far more than I bargained for." What she did not add was that she was finally *un*learning some of the suspicion, distrust and paranoia Steve had left her with.

"In fact, I know a lot of women who marry regularly. And dreadfully. Like a bad habit. I don't know what moved you to marry the first one any more than this second one, whom you've known for less than—"

"Don't change the subject, Flo. We both know you have a low opinion of my choices. I want to know about *you*. Do you have any kind of personal life these days? You look like success personified—wealth, beauty, intelligence, et cetera. I met some of the men you dated, or rather 'attended functions with,' but that was years ago. What's the deal, Flo? Are you a lesbian?"

Flo gasped and stopped walking. "Christine!"

It made Chris laugh to have shocked her aunt, but this was more of their history. Chris would be daring and in need of discipline, and Flo would be sensible and ready to give it. Big and little girl. Teacher and student. Yet as much as Chris admired Flo's composure, her command, her savoir faire, Chris neither envied nor wished to become Flo.

"Are you lonely?" she asked her aunt.

"No," she said. "Certainly not. I've missed *you*."

"But when you're not either fighting me in court or hunting for me, what is your life like?"

"You may wish to remember, dear, that my older brother died and left me a horrendous business when I was only thirty-four. The next several years were a tad busy with very demanding work and trying to figure out what to do about you."

"It might have been better for you if you'd written me off as a loss."

"Ha! The only family I have—a young woman who is in perpetual trouble, my brother's child, once my dearest friend. Why would I write you off? I knew we'd be together again someday."

"But who do you spend Christmas with?"

"Usually with friends."

"Ah. Do you have a lover?"

"Chris, believe me, if I thought it were any of your business, I would—"

"Come on, Flo, you know all *my* dirt. Come on, what do you do when you snake out of all that eelskin? Do you have anyone special and dear? Has your whole personal life been on hold so you could manage Palmercraft and Palmer House and the Perils of Pauline?"

Flo sighed. "I have the same friends I've always had. I've been seeing the same man for years. Literally years. We're both very busy, but we do quite a lot together. We're very good friends. We travel together sometimes."

"Who?" Kate said.

"Kenneth Waite."

"Kenneth Waite? Isn't he the president of some big advertising agency? What is it? Multimega—"

"He's the owner now. Waite Commercial Resources, Inc."

"How long?"

"Oh, I think he's been the owner for—"

"No." She laughed. "How long have you been seeing him?"

"Forever. I don't know. Fifteen years."

"But isn't he married? Wasn't his wife a friend of Mother's? Wait a minute…"

"As I said," Flo went on, "we are two busy people with a great many commitments. There's not a lot of room in either of our lives for romance. There never has been, although Ken has been divorced for years— seven or eight, I think. We're simply very good friends."

"You were having an affair with a married man!"

"His marriage left a good deal of room for that. And my responsibilities have never left room for much more."

"How well organized, Florence," Chris said, shaking her head. "Are you going to get married? Ever?"

"It doesn't seem necessary, even since Ken has been divorced. We're pretty independent people."

"It sounds so distant. So…uninvolved."

"Not everyone has an overactive libido."

"Come on, don't make any cracks about my poor old neglected sex drive. Stever might have awakened it, but he certainly left it in a coma. I couldn't even fathom an interest in sex for years. Have you any idea what it's like to be absolutely insane with passion and then find out the lousy creep probably didn't even *like* you? Talk about impotence! Or frigidity, or whatever. It comes as a real blow. Here you are, willing to do anything short of crawling through cut glass for one more kiss, only to learn he was just using you. Honestly, I bet Steve, or whoever, didn't even *like* me. Whew."

"Well, I tried to tell you, but you—"

"But what about you?" she asked as they reached Flo's rented Cadillac. Chris leaned on the roof, looking across at Flo. "What's your excuse? How come you never fell in love? Dumb, embarrassing love?"

Flo tossed her bags into the backseat and put her elbows on top of the car. She rested her chin on her forearms and looked at Chris. "What is it, huh? What do they offer you that I don't understand? No kidding, what does this big, dumb fireman have that has made you gunky with devotion? A schwanz as long as a fire hose?"

Chris erupted with laughter, covering her mouth.

"This big?" Flo asked, putting up her hands, indicating something of inhuman proportions. "Or is it their vulnerability, the things they need from you? Old Stever needed a few bucks, and this guy needs to play house for a while. Or is it really just some primitive man-woman thing, some bonding that I didn't get the gene for? Come on, tell old Aunt Flo, you little slut."

How she loved her! There weren't many people who

knew this Flo. The people who read the society pages expected a Princess Diana sort. But Flo operated a huge furniture business. That meant she could speak many languages; she could communicate as well with the governor's wife as with an upholsterer with an eighth-grade education. She was tough, slick, sassy. No way Mike was ready for this dame.

"Regardless of how utterly stupid I was to have married Steve," Chris said, "it's important to remember that it was a simple mistake. It's important to remember that I was young, vulnerable, and he wasn't just a bad choice—he was a criminal. Mike is a decent man.

"It's risk," Chris said. "Not the kind of risk you take to sneak to a hotel behind your husband's back, or the kind of risk required to put your money in his account, for that matter. It's the risk of your emotional self. It's exposing yourself to a person who will accept you as you are, embrace you as you are. It is the risk, Flo, of being naked in an emotional way, and betting that you won't get cold." She was quiet for a second. "I feel nice and warm," she said softly, "all the time now."

After meeting her aunt's eyes over the roof of the car, Chris opened the door and slid into the passenger side. Flo stayed above for a few moments before getting into the driver's seat.

"Christine," Flo began seriously, "would it not be just as good to buy a nice, thick parka? Mink, perhaps?"

Mike had napped and then gone to his folks' house. When he walked into the kitchen through the garage door, Chris was stirring something at the stove. He looked her over and smiled. "Wow. You look different. Gorgeous."

She turned her lips toward him for a kiss. "I let Florence have me 'done.'"

"She didn't change anything on the inside, did she? When's she coming?"

"Anytime now. And, Mike, listen... Oh, forget it, there's no point in trying to prepare you. Just try to roll with it, okay?"

He took a beer from the refrigerator and walked into the dining room. He looked at the table. "What's this?"

She followed him. "I hope you don't mind," she said. He lifted a new plate. "Flo gave me a bunch of money after she shopped me to death and told me to get something I wanted, something frivolous. It's no big deal for Flo, and it made her feel good to give me the money. And this was how I wanted to spend it. On you, sort of."

His table wore a new linen tablecloth. New ceramic plates in lavender, royal blue and beige sat between new flatware and linen napkins in china rings. There was a new lavender vase filled with fresh flowers. Wineglasses. Mike felt funny inside, a little dizzy maybe. New dishes—because she was staying and wanted a nicer set? Or was his slightly imperfect, chipped set of ironstone too flawed for this event? But he said, "Looks nice."

The kids called his name and ran to him, and his dizziness went away. He picked them up, both of them, and went into the living room where they had things to show him—toys, books and gadgets. He was relieved to see that they wore the clothes *he* had bought them. Cheeks wandered over, tail wagging, and nudged him for a scratch. I got to *him*, Mike thought. If I can impress this mutt, I can handle Flo. Can't I?

And the doorbell rang. He remembered something.

He remembered Joanie's dad saying hello but looking at him with that if-you-touch-my-daughter-I'll-kill-you look. Mike had been a mere boy. He had gulped down his nerves. He wanted to kick Cheeks in the ribs for not growling at Florence.

"So, this is the fireman," Flo said, smiling very beautifully. "Well, there's hardly anything I can do to repay you for saving my family."

Yes, you can. Leave. Go away and turn into a surly old woman. I'm good with cranky old ladies. They love me. "Just doing my job," he said, taking the proffered hand.

"And thank God you were," she added, gliding past him into the living room. She had packages. She probably didn't go anywhere without presents. She was dressed casually—gray wool fitted slacks, a fuzzy red sweater, gray pumps out of some kind of skin and a rich leather blazer. Rings and things. She smelled heavenly, expensive. But she did crouch to receive the children. "There are my angels. I have presents. It must be your birthdays."

"It isn't our birthdays." Carrie giggled, reaching for a bag. "And you know it isn't our birthdays."

"Is it Christmas?" Flo asked.

"No." They laughed.

"Then somebody must love you. No, no, you have to give a kiss and hug first."

Mike ached. He wanted to be happy for them, for them all. What was wrong with him? Where were his heart, his convictions about family? Where, for gosh sakes, was his courage?

"Here you are," Chris said, coming from the kitchen. "And you've met Mike?"

Chris kissed the cheek Flo turned toward her. They looked alike, suddenly. None of their features, for Chris was small and fair, while Flo was big and bronze. It was their style. Chris, in expensive clothes and pumps, was very different than she had been in a T-shirt and jeans, hair pulled back, no makeup. She was now more like her rich aunt.

The kids were being fed something simple in the kitchen, after which they would be excused to play or watch television, while the adults sat at the newly appointed dining-room table. Mike sat with the kids while they ate, playing with them, talking to them, watching Flo and Chris in the kitchen together. They were like his sisters and sisters-in-law when they got together around the pots. They lifted lids, gossiped, laughed, helped each other—like good friends, like family. Flo and Chris recited a litany of names he had never heard before—old family acquaintances, friends from high school and college. They were still catching up. But he felt like an outsider, something he had never felt when the women in his family played this companionable game around the food.

For the first time he wondered if he should have gotten himself into this. He was scared of this woman. He was afraid he was going to lose Chris and Carrie and Kyle...

"Wine?" Chris asked him when they were all seated.

"Sure. Thanks."

"Well, Mike, Chris tells me you had a dangerous fire last night. No one was hurt, I hope."

"No, no injuries."

"But it must be very dangerous, this work."

"We're trained for it," he said. He saw that he wasn't helping. Here she was, trying, and he was so suspicious, he was going to hurt his own case. You couldn't come between family. Chris had tried to blend into his; until now he hadn't known how hard she might have had to try.

He had to concentrate not to shovel food into his mouth too fast. Firefighters know the minute they sit down to a meal, the alarm will sound. He was going to try to be more refined. He would eat like an accountant. "Fire is dangerous and unpredictable, but our training, which is ongoing, prepares us to make intelligent decisions. We don't take risks foolishly is what I'm saying. But still, there are times…"

"Like in saving people, I suppose. Rushing into a burning building to rescue someone. Don't you ever stand there, looking at the fire, and think 'Wait a minute, here'?"

"That's the thing we don't do, as a matter of fact. Number-one priority is protecting life. Number-two is saving the structure. But we don't go in looking for people unless there's a reason to believe someone needs to be pulled out. Usually the person who calls in the alarm informs us on the scene."

"And you wear gear? Like oxygen masks?"

"Air packs," he said, "if there's time."

"And if there isn't time?"

"Look, that's the job." He shrugged. "Time is the only advantage there is, and we don't waste it thinking things over a lot. Firefighters don't rush into a wall of flame because it's fun. We all have our jobs at the fire, we take informed risks. We've been trained to recognize possible and impossible situations. We only get into trouble when something unforeseen happens—part of the structure collapses, or an on-site explosion occurs. That's the danger."

"So," Flo said, lifting her fork, "you pretty much rush into things, huh?"

Chris gulped. "Mike's been a firefighter for twelve years," she said. "He's very experienced." She took another sip of wine. "More wine?" she asked. They shook their heads.

"It's always an informed decision. Rapid but experienced."

"Have you ever been wrong?"

Mike stared at Flo for a long moment, using his heavy, brooding brows in that frightening look of his. But Flo met his eyes as if to say she was every bit as tough as he was. Tougher. This lady had played ball in the major leagues.

Chris drained her glass and refilled it.

"Everyone has been wrong, made mistakes. But if you fold your hand after your first mistake, you fail to learn anything, how to do it right the next time."

"You should meet Mike's family, his brothers and sisters," Chris attempted. "They—"

"So," Flo continued, ignoring Chris, "tell me, Mike, does this job require…um…a college education?"

Mike's cheeks took on a stain. "No," he said. "At least half of the firefighters in our company have degrees, but I don't."

"And if you had some disability? If you couldn't fight fires anymore?"

His mouth became grim. "I'm sure I'd manage."

"Really, Flo…" Chris said.

"Hmm," hummed Flo. "I suppose it must be the big-city firefighters who have the most precarious careers. Out here in the suburbs, it can't be as bad."

"Not as many bells as in, say, Chicago. But—"

"But this matter of doing dangerous work and the disability situation must be a major factor when you consider, for example, taking on a family."

"That would certainly be a consideration, Flo," he said evenly. "But usually not the first one."

Flo leaned an elbow on the table. "And what would the first consideration be?"

"Whether or not I could stand to be under the same roof with the other person, I guess."

Chris could tell he was trying, answering Flo's most prying, unreasonable questions with patience and honesty as if this were his steady girl's father. She wanted to tell Mike that he didn't have to prove anything to Flo. She wanted Flo to shut up, to let Mike off the hook. But it was bedtime for Carrie and Kyle, so she excused herself to take them upstairs and tuck them in, reluctantly leaving Mike and Flo at the dining-room table.

She heard snatches of their conversation: intelligent decisions...danger is danger... There are challenges that won't get you killed...

She returned to the table to find it was Mike's turn. He had been trying, but now he was getting mad. He asked about furniture.

"The Palmers began selling furniture more than forty years ago. We started manufacturing a specialized line of indoor/outdoor furniture only twenty years ago—Palmercraft. It's been very successful."

"That's what I hear. Lots of money. That must make life pretty easy."

Chris grimaced. "My grandfather didn't have much

when he started. He built the business from his garage
and—"

"I don't dislike success, if that's what you mean.
But it is hard work. Chris herself has a vested interest
in the business."

"Oh? She never mentioned that."

"Because I don't!" Chris said, but she might as well
have told Cheeks. These two were not listening to her.

"Well, you already know that business about the will,
but there's more to it than that. The will was written before Chris was of age, and it provided for her. The family
business was given to me because it was understood that I
would always take care of Chris's needs should anything
happen to her parents."

"Take care of her needs," he repeated. "Her needs
before she became an adult, I trust."

"My thinking is that the furniture company is half
hers."

"Really? I suppose she'd have to go to Chicago for
that."

"Chicago is her home, of course."

"Oh. I thought her home burned down."

"More wine?" Chris asked in frustration. They ignored her. She filled her own glass and stared into it.

She wanted to stop them. Flo knew Chris was not
interested in the furniture business. Flo would happily
take care of Chris forever; in fact, if Chris showed up
at the factory one morning to take an executive position, her aunt would probably give her a title, plenty of
money, and have her emptying wastebaskets to keep
her out of trouble. Flo controlled everything. But it was
moot; Chris would never even consider it. After all, she
had run through almost four million dollars indulging a

naive passion for a thief. She didn't want to be responsible for any more family money. The only money she
wanted was money that belonged to her.

If these two stubborn people would stop sparring
over her for a few minutes, she could probably explain
her position better than either of them could. She would
return to Chicago at some point soon—maybe not permanently; time would tell—but she did want the kids
to see where she had grown up, and she wanted to re-
acquaint herself with some of her past. But she didn't
want to move in with Aunt Flo and have her life managed. She also didn't want to live with Mike if he was
going to insist on telling her what her priorities should
be. What she wanted was simply their love, as they
had hers, while she reconstructed a life that belonged
to her. You couldn't share your life with anyone unless
you had one of your own.

"There is a lot of unfinished business in Chicago
that—"

"—could probably be handled by a good accountant," Mike interrupted.

"There's nothing wrong with a lucrative business,
but I was talking about home, family—"

"Home is where the heart is."

Chris refilled her glass as their conversation grew
more competitive. Thank God for the wine.

"I think you're suggesting, Mike, that Chris ignore
who she is and where she came from to stay here with
you, when you hardly know her and can hardly provide
for her in the manner she is accustomed to."

"Oh, *that* manner—a crummy little firetrap in a rotten
neighborhood, struggling to make ends meet because she's

too proud or too scared to call her rich aunt? I can probably compete with that life-style. Yeah, I'm suggesting—"

"Stop it," Chris said, but she slurred it. They looked at her as if she had just arrived on the scene. Their images swirled before her eyes, but she got up from her chair with as much dignity as was possible, given the fact that she was completely sloshed. "When I make up my mind what I want, I'm sure the two of you will let me know."

She walked a crooked line from the dining room. "I'm going to bed. I accidentally got drunk trying to ignore the two of you. G'night."

Chapter 10

When Chris awoke she had the headache she deserved. On the bedside table was a note under a bottle of aspirin. The fireman had gone off to fight fires. The note said, "I'm sorry. I had no right. Love, M."

After two aspirin and two cups of coffee she called Flo. "Shame on you," she said to her aunt.

"Chris, I'm sorry. I didn't realize we were talking about you as if you weren't even there."

"Yes, and it was awfully familiar. I felt like I was in the middle of a custody battle. I'm not going to do this with the two of you. I'm furious."

"Come and have breakfast with me. I want to work this out."

"Well, as long as you're ashamed and sorry, let me dress the kids. Give me an hour."

"An hour?"

"I have a headache."

"I can imagine."

No, you can't, she wanted to say. She didn't know how she had managed to delude herself that there was any possible way Mike and Flo would hit it off. It wasn't that they were so terribly different—in fact, they had much in common. But in their strength, possessiveness and competitiveness, each seemed to have what the other wanted. Her.

And what did she want? The thought of giving up either Mike or Flo was excruciating, but...

Chris drew herself a bath, the water as hot as she could stand it. She hadn't been in the tub long before Carrie woke up and wandered in. "Morning, sweetie. Want to have breakfast with Auntie Flo?" Carrie nodded, rubbing her eyes, and positioned herself on the closed toilet seat to take waking up slowly. Chris leaned back in the hot water and closed her eyes.

When Chris was six years old she had wanted to be a singing ballerina. A star. She'd had wonderful fantasies about wowing her friends with performances—Shirley Temple fantasies with full production sets.

At twelve she had wanted to be a chemist. She saw herself in a lab coat and glasses—and when she took the glasses off she was beautiful, a gorgeous intellectual smarter than all the handsome young scientists around her. Soon she discovered that chemistry involved math. *C'est la vie.*

At sixteen she hungered for travel and decided to be a flight attendant. Flo took whole summers off two years in a row to accompany her around the world, to help her fill that need for expansion, appalled by the prospect of Chris's serving drinks on an air carrier.

At eighteen she was in college, reading her heart out.

Flo bought every book that Chris wanted to discuss. They talked on the phone for hours each week. Flo traveled to New York often to take Chris and her friends to plays, museums, art galleries and on plentiful shopping trips. All Chris's friends idolized Flo. Chris was not interested in business, but she wanted desperately to be like her Aunt Flo.

Carrie wandered over to the tub and started playing with her bath toys. "Carrie, I'm taking a bath."

Carrie was now pushing an empty shampoo container under the water, filling it and pouring it out. "I won't get you wet, Mommy."

Chris laughed. "Move down by my feet then," she said, wondering how she'd come to have such a headache over the people she loved.

At twenty Chris wanted to be the woman behind the man, as her mother had been. She would raise a beautiful family for this sharp young lawyer who had not even given his real name. But all she wanted was to be *his*.

She touched Carrie's curls.

"Mommy, you'll get me wet." Carrie looked up and smiled. "Should I get in?"

"You can have your own bath in a few minutes."

At twenty-five she had to start thinking differently. A divorced mother, short of cash and deep in debt, she couldn't remember who she was or what she wanted. More than to simply survive, though. She began writing, not masterpieces but simple stories for young adults. She wanted to give back some of the fantasies she had used through the years to sustain her impossible, illusive fancies. She knew she was fanciful. Hopeful and idealistic. She had almost lost that because of Steve, and it was what she liked best about herself. Hopeful idealists changed the world. They could also be perfect victims.

Chris was unlike Flo, who had been born to control, and unlike Mike, who addressed life expediently as a series of "informed risks." Chris made up stories for kids who, like her at six and twelve and sixteen, were dreamy, desirous and always wondering the same two things she wondered. One, what was going to happen next? And two, would it all work out?

It didn't take long for her to realize that she loved the way she felt when she was writing, and soon she knew she was fulfilling some kind of inner need and being alone was so much less lonely. Suddenly she found herself working harder than ever to learn how to do it, to make it right, to make it more than right. She took night classes whenever possible, she read how-to-write-and-market-your-book books and articles every Sunday in the library while the kids paged through picture books beside her. She read, studied, typed, tore her work apart, typed some more, scrapped it again. She *had* to get it right, because if she succeeded, she could be happy, she could make money to support her little family, and she could do it in a way important to *her* and the woman she was becoming.

Carrie scampered out of the bathroom, dripping water from her wet sleeves, and scooted back in with more bathtub toys. Chris watched and smiled as Carrie splashed and sang off-key. She decided then and there, looking at her older child, that she would never again call her marriage a mistake. Carrie and Kyle were healthy, smart and her greatest accomplishments. If she had to do it all over again, would she pay almost four million dollars for them? In a heartbeat.

"Mommy?"

"Hmm?"

"Mommy, where is my daddy?"

Chris felt her cheeks grow hot. "Well, Carrie, remember I told you that he went away when you were a baby? I don't know where he is. I haven't seen him or talked to him since he went away."

"Does he miss us, then?"

"I… I don't know, honey. But he should miss you, because you're wonderful."

"Mommy? Where is Mike?"

"He's working. We won't see him until tomorrow morning."

"Do I remember my daddy?"

"Well, I don't think so. Do you think you do?"

She shook her head. "Is my daddy the same as Kyle's daddy?"

"Yes," Chris said, appalled. "Of course."

"Is Mike supposed to be our daddy now?"

"Mike… Mike is our very special friend, Carrie, but I'm not married to him."

"He likes us to use his house," she said, smiling at her mother.

"Yes. He does."

"Will he go away from us, then?"

"No, Carrie. No, we will always know where Mike is, and he will always know where we are. Always. Even if we don't use his house forever. Even if we get a house of our own. Do you understand?"

"No."

"Well…" She'd better get used to answering difficult questions, because the older the kids became, the more serious the questions would be. "Well, even if we get our

own house again, we will be good friends with Mike.
We'll visit him, talk to him on the phone, see him sometimes. I'm sure of that. Do you understand?"

"No. I like Mike's house, and he likes us to use his
house."

"Yes, but—"

"Can I watch cartoons until I have my own bath?"

"Yes. If you want to."

Of course she doesn't understand, Chris thought.
Neither do I. She worked the drain release with her toe.
So, twenty-seven years old, soaking out a headache,
what did Chris want? Not a lot, actually. She wanted
to keep the rain off her kids' heads, first. She wanted
to reconcile with Flo so she could be rooted once more
with the people, events and emotions that had shaped
her. She wanted a man like Mike—the Mike who loved
so deeply and with such involvement that loss made
veldt-sores in him—to love *her*. To love them all. And
she wanted a few hours a day to become the person she
was destined to be—a creative, caring, independent
woman. There should be room for all of that without
any crowding. It wasn't much to ask. It was not a tiny
bit more than those people she loved could afford.

Flo, though sometimes brassy, flashy and bossy, was
not really a snob. Chris had been surprised at Flo's treatment of Mike, intimidating him, making it appear that
he wasn't good enough. None of the Palmers, though
well-to-do, had ever behaved uncharitably toward another human being; they had never taken their privilege
for granted or placed themselves above others. Mike, too,
had surprised her with his reverse snobbery—jabbing at
Flo for having so much, insinuating that bounty made
life too easy, accomplishments too effortless.

Grabbing at her was what they'd both done, and it made her very nervous, claustrophobic. Well, in another half hour she'd have it out with Flo.

"I don't know what to say," Flo said at breakfast. "I regret making you unhappy by pressuring Mike that way, but I honestly don't think I'm wrong. He doesn't have much to offer you, and I think you should be more practical."

Chris swallowed coffee as if swallowing fury. "Because he doesn't have a college education? You ought to be ashamed of doing that to him."

"I wasn't doing anything to him. Good Lord, Chris, if anything should happen to him…"

"No, that isn't it. If anything should happen to Mike, I'd have *you*. You're more afraid nothing will happen to him, that I'll stay with him forever. Just as he was afraid you were going to win and take me away. Well, I've got news for the two of you. This is a no-win situation."

"Chris, I'm not in a contest with this man. I feel responsible for you—I simply want you to reappraise the situation."

"Responsible? I'm not twelve, though you treat me as though I am. You keep forgetting that I've managed to keep my children and myself without state aid and without calling you. I did it myself. I didn't do it in designer labels, but I did do it. And reappraise what?"

"Your future plans. There are a lot of things I'd like you to consider. Your education, for instance. If you want to complete college, I think you should. Or if you'd like to consider business, I would be delighted. Whatever."

"Whatever? Or one of those two things?" she responded drily. Chris reached for Kyle's plate, automatically cutting his room-service pancakes for him. "Flo, I have future plans of my own that don't include either of those two things. Besides, I don't want to decide my whole future in the next week, so I wish you'd stop listing my options for me."

Carrie tipped her milk and it sloshed onto the table, flowing toward Flo. Flo jerked into action, mopping, her movements almost as natural as Chris's. Flo didn't seem to worry about her expensive slacks; she merely acted, as if she had been mopping up Carrie's spills since birth. Flo had only known her children for three days, Chris reflected, yet they seemed bonded. Connected by blood. Chris shook her head absently. Flo didn't scold Carrie; she simply took care of her. The way she wanted to take care of Chris. The scolding hadn't started until Chris began trying to take care of herself.

"I'm only trying to help," Flo said. "I have no ulterior motives."

"Not consciously. You just want to do for me, show me your generosity and love. So does Mike. He wants to give and have me receive. Here I am being offered so much, from two people I care deeply about, and last night was a nightmare. When I saw the two of you together, I felt as though I didn't know either one of you."

"Well. Are we *both* sorry?"

"Yes," she said, swiveling in her chair to begin cutting Carrie's pancakes. "I haven't spoken to Mike yet, but he wrote an apologetic note before he left for work. I won't see him till tomorrow morning."

"Do you have any idea what you want, Chris?"

"Oh, yes," she said, laughing humorlessly. "I want to see if I can recapture the little bit of sanity I felt between the fire and the *Missing Heiress*. I felt… I felt alive, full of feelings that for once didn't conflict or frighten me. I had a sense of family—there was Mike and his people drawing me in. And even though I was too proud or stubborn to call you yet, I was getting closer. I had safety, pleasure, hope and desire. I felt protected but independent. And then it all changed."

"Come now, let's not get melodramatic, Chris. Did I make our reconciliation difficult? I may not have cozied up to the fireman too well, but—"

"Difficult? Heavens, no, it was just the opposite. Our reunion was so ideal I was spinning from it. You forgave me for all the trouble I've caused you when I'd half expected you to refuse to speak to me. I felt like a baby you'd waited seven years to give birth to."

Flo sighed. "I suppose I've failed again somehow," she said.

"When have you ever failed at anything? The fact is, you offer me so much that it's impossible for me to live up to it."

"Christine, let's not—"

"But it's true! You want so much for me that I find it hard to want anything for myself! You can dress me, style my hair, discuss my future, spoil my kids. We've barely talked in seven years. Do you even know me, Flo? Or are you trying to create me?" She felt her eyes well with tears. "I'm sorry. I didn't mean to cry about it."

"You're overwrought. You need—" She stopped herself.

Chris wiped her eyes. "You see? If you keep doing that, I'll have to keep fighting you. I want to have our friendship back, Flo, but with give *and* take. As it stands, the only thing I can give you is obedience, and I'm too old to be happy with that."

Flo pursed her lips, and when she spoke, her voice was scratchy. It was the closest Chris had ever seen her come to crying. "I just don't want you to be hurt. I don't want to lose you. Again."

"I'm going to carve a little niche out of this world that's all mine. Not a big chunk—just a little niche. I don't want to buy the world a Coke or conquer outer space, I just want to take care of my kids and work on becoming the best of who I really am. There's more to me than being your child, Stever's latest con or Mike's charity case. That's what I was working on, Flo, when the house burned down."

"This has something to do with this idea of writing?" she asked. "Because if all you want is to be independent, to be able to write—"

"No. Yes. I mean, I was writing, and I plan to keep writing—I'm even crazy enough to think I'm going to succeed at it. What I have to do is make sure the decisions I make belong to me. I want to pay for my own mistakes. I want to take credit for my accomplishments. I don't want to be taken care of anymore."

"What I'd like to know," Flo said slowly, "is why it is reasonable for you to live in the fireman's house and eat his food and take his presents, but it's wrong for you to—"

Chris shook her head. "You don't get it, do you? I'm not going to give my life to him the way I did with Steve, and I'm not going to keep taking from him, either. I'm willing to share my life, my space, all that I am, but *share*, Flo. With you, with him and, hopefully, with others, because I've been alone way too long."

"And you can't come with me and share your life with him, only the other way around, is that it? He sounded as determined about what you need as I did, you know."

"If that turns out to be true, then it won't work."

"Why would you take that chance? Why not—"

"Because I love him." There. She'd said it. Shouldn't lightning strike or fireworks go off?

"That's ridiculous," said Flo.

"But it's true, just the same," she replied, exasperated.

"You're setting yourself up for some real trouble, Chris," Flo solemnly predicted. "You're going to get yourself hurt all over again. You hardly know this—"

"No, I'm not. I'm not setting myself up for anything at all. When I give up and let other people take over, then I'm in for it. I may be a lot of things—impetuous, idealistic, maybe even foolish, but dammit, I'm going to see if this is what I think it is. And if it isn't, I'll cry and be done with it. I won't lose four million dollars, I won't get pregnant, and I won't forget what I want from life. I'll cry. There are worse things."

"What about the kids? What about what they'll—"

"The kids," she said, "already love both of you." Carrie looked up. Her eyes were round and large; she knew there was something serious going on, but she didn't know what. "They shouldn't have to give up Mike to have you, or vice versa."

"He's awfully possessive."

"Said the pot," Chris quipped.

"We've never had any kind of family life together, Chris. Within a year of Randy's and Arlene's death you were gone. With that—"

"I got married. Maybe you didn't approve, but the reality is that I grew up and got married. And get this—

I'm *glad* I did, because I have Carrie and Kyle. I'm a grown-up now, Flo. I can't go back to being the child you can spoil and discipline. We have to get together a new set of rules for our family life. I don't want to be all you have. I don't want you to be all I have. Go home, Flo," she softly advised. "It's the only way I can come home to you, which is all you really want, anyway."

"When is that going to happen, Chris? I don't want us to be estranged forever."

"It's never going to happen the way you think it should. When I go back to Chicago, I'll be a visitor or finding my own place. Flo, let go of me. Love me for myself, not for what you can do for me. Please."

They reached a tense compromise. Flo set up a checking account for Chris with a tidy sum deposited; she simply couldn't leave any other way. Flo took Chris's word that if the worst happened and the fireman turned out to be a big lout, Chris and the kids would rent something *decent*—with smoke alarms and everything. And they decided that if Chris remained in California through Christmas, Flo would have her tongue removed or her lips sutured shut and would return in time to celebrate with them all. She would be nice to Mike or else. Chris promised to call Flo frequently to reassure her they really were reunited.

And she still cried at the airport.

Mr. Blakely's address was in the phone book. Chris took the kids out for a hamburger and then pulled up to the landlord's house at just about the dinner hour. She was not in the least surprised to find he and his family occupied a substantial piece of real estate while they rented out hovels in poor repair. Still, she felt tension grating like sandpaper against her backbone—the backbone she was only just remembering she had. She wanted to do this exactly once.

"Hello, Mrs. Blakely. I'm Christine Palmer. Is your husband at home, please?"

"I don't believe we have any business with you. You can have your lawyer—"

Chris unfolded the tabloid so that her picture flashed in the woman's chubby, ruddy face. Mrs. Blakely looked like a mean, unhappy person; she had frown lines and downcast eyes that could flare wide in surprise, like now. She was about four weeks behind on her strawberry-blond dye job; her gray roots moored her frazzled mop. The house they lived in had been custom-built and appeared both well cared for and expensive. Mrs. Blakely, a fiftyish woman, looked out of place in the doorway. She was heavy, sloppily attired in a floral cotton house-dress, and held a smoldering cigarette between her yellowed fingers.

"I'm the 'missing heiress,' Mrs. Blakely, and if you let me see your husband, we can complete this transaction in a few minutes. Then I will leave you alone. If you force me to call my attorney about this, it will cost you, because I am angry."

The woman stood still for a second, stunned. Then she slowly turned like a rotating statue. "Henry," she called.

He, too, looked out of place in such a decorous environment. He wore a white undershirt, slippers, baggy pants with his belly hanging obtrusively over his belt, and he had a nasty cigar in his mouth. The slumlord.

Mrs. Blakely passed the tabloid to her husband, who looked at the picture and then Chris, taking the cigar from his mouth. She gave him a minute to get the headline, but no more. "We can settle this in five minutes, Mr. Blakely. Your faulty furnace not only destroyed my every worldly possession, it nearly killed us all. In fact, I was rescued from the burning house. Now, I am not a difficult person, only fair. I would like some refunds and some restitution. There is the matter of the deposit—the first and last months' rent—the rent I paid for the month of November, and lost valuables." She reached into her purse. She unfolded an itemized list and held it out to him. Her children stood stoically on each side of her. "I take responsibility for fifty percent of the possessions lost in the fire because I did not have renter's insurance, which I should have had. I will take five thousand dollars now, or I will take you to court and sue for pain and suffering, as well. And I can get the best lawyer in the country."

"Um…maybe you'd better come in."

"No, that won't be necessary. I'll wait right here. It won't take you that long to write a check."

A teenager shrieked from inside the big house. "Mother! Where is my—"

"Shut up, Ellen! Just a minute!" Mrs. Blakely barked.

"I oughta check with my lawyer before I—" the landlord began.

"That won't take long, either. Here's what he'll tell you—if you have been approached with an itemized list of damages and you have made restitution in that exact amount, she really won't have a leg to stand on in court if she comes after you for more. Unless, of course, there are injuries, which there were not. Now, let's get this over with, shall we?"

Mrs. Blakely glared at Chris from behind her husband. She crossed her arms over her ample chest while Henry Blakely shuffled away with the list in his hand. The worst of it, Chris believed, was the fact that they had no remorse for the danger they had allowed in renting poorly maintained property. That the rent had been low did not absolve them. The malfunctioning furnace was Henry Blakely's fault, and he had never even called to see if Chris and her children were all right. Mrs. Blakely, who should be flushing in shame at her husband's callous evasion of responsibility, stood like a sentry in the doorway while the unrepentant man went in pursuit of a phone call or a check or a better idea.

These people were poor and didn't know it, Chris decided.

"Here," he said, handing her a check in less than ten minutes. "I don't want to hear from you again."

"Oh, you won't, believe me." And she walked away from them, pity for their selfishness leaving a sour taste in her mouth.

She was up, dressed and had the coffee brewed when Mike came home from the station early in the morning, beginning his four days off.

"We're on our own for a while?" Mike asked when Chris told him Flo had gone. "What does that mean?"

"I've convinced Flo to back off and give me some room. She acted like an ass. I'm really sorry."

"Not that I was any Prince Charming. I don't usually act that way around anyone."

"Neither does she."

"She, uh, spoke with some experience," he said.

"Oh, she's a born fighter, don't get me wrong. But she's

not the snob she appeared to be. She wants me back, wants me home. It's been a long separation."

"But you didn't go."

Chris sighed. "Not because I don't love her. I need Flo in my life. She can be a real pain, but we have a lot of good history, too. The Flo you met was not my generous and strong friend, but a terrified mother lion afraid of losing her cub. I apologize for her."

Mike nodded, then changed the subject. "I had this idea about Christmas," he said. "The kids like the cabin so much, I thought we might go there, have a real Christmas, chop our own tree—"

"What about your family?" she asked.

"They could spare my presence for one year. What about yours?"

"She'll come back, Mike, if this is where I am through the holidays. You don't have to accept Flo, but I can't reject my family any more than you can reject yours. Flo has never been with the kids for the holidays."

"Maybe I should call up to Pembroke Pines and see if the caterer is busy. Or will she bring her own staff?"

She flinched.

"Sorry. It's just that she made me feel so damned inadequate. Middle-class. I've never felt that way before. I guess I wanted to be the one to give you a chance to rebuild your life."

Chris bit her lip. "Maybe we should talk about this. Maybe you found me easy to care about when you thought I was helpless, destitute. Is it harder for you because I'm not? Just how far do you want to go to see if this crazy thing is real?"

He didn't hesitate to think it over. "I want to go all the way to the end. Wherever that is."

Chapter 11

"Mrs. Cavanaugh is cooking an Irish stew," Hal said, placing the plates around the table.

Mike turned from the pot he was stirring and grinned at Hal. "It's spaghetti," he said.

"Everything you cook tastes like Irish stew."

"Hey, lay off," Stu said. "I love Mrs. Cavanaugh's Irish spaghetti."

"I'd put my cooking against yours any day of the week," Mike challenged Hal. "My red beans and rice against your chili."

"Against my potato soup, and you have a deal."

"Name the day and put some green on it."

"Hey, how are things with the heiress?"

Mike stirred the pot again. "Don't call her that, okay?"

"Uh-oh. What's the matter, Little Mike? Chris go home to Auntie Flo?"

"I'd go for the aunt," Stu said. "In a minute, I'd go for the aunt. My wife would write me a note."

"My wife asked me to make a play for the aunt, and then send money."

"The auntie has gone away, for now, while Little Mike thinks about the furniture business."

Mike dumped the spaghetti into a colander. "You wanna eat, dog-breath?"

"No kidding, what's going on? You getting married?"

"Married?" he asked, as though amazed. Was he that transparent? "I've only known her a few weeks."

"What's taking you so long?" Hal asked.

"I'd have her in front of the priest," Stu said. "She's loaded, right? She's cute, too—I saw that much. Stupid me, I shoulda gotten into that house ahead of him."

"You're married already, Stuart. Although I know you tend to forget that from time to time."

"I have these blackouts. Spells."

"Yeah. You keep getting engaged."

"Naw. I go steady sometimes. A little."

There was laughter. Mike rinsed the spaghetti. He had a hard time with Stu sometimes—didn't like the way he handled personal business. Otherwise he liked him. Good firefighter. A little green about life, but good in a fire. If Stu knew what it was like to lose a family, he wouldn't waste precious time away from his; he wouldn't fool around on his wife. Hal, young like Stu, still less than thirty, got a big kick out of Stu's antics, but Hal didn't fool around. He was serious about his young family. Mike liked that. Hal was a good cook, too. He had a little business on the side when he wasn't fighting fires, which was typical of firemen.

Jim Eble was Mike's closest friend besides family.

They were nearly the same age and had worked the same rig for five years. They were alike in personal values as well as sharing many favorite pastimes. But Jim couldn't go fishing with Mike too often because he drove an ambulance part-time when he wasn't on duty; he'd be paying for college educations before long.

Mike was the only one, in fact, who didn't work at something else when he wasn't here. His income was plentiful for a single man, and with all the other kids in the family married and off doing their family things, he used his days off to make sure his mom and dad had everything they needed. And he liked to go to the cabin. Maybe he didn't have another business, but things like hunting, fishing, camping and riding took time. There was no work he liked more than this work. The furniture business? In a pig's eye.

"Don't let 'em get to you, Little Mike," Jim said while they did the dishes.

"They don't get to me. They're having fun. That's okay."

"Things are okay with Chris, then?"

"Yeah, I guess. I mean, she's the same person I pulled out of the house, right?"

"Well, is she?"

"Yeah, sure."

"Hey, Little Mike, don't let the bull from these guys get in your way, huh? You know what you want, right?"

No, he didn't know what he wanted. He thought he knew, but now he wasn't sure. Sure that he loved her a lot, yes. But all that other stuff, money, was getting to him. Getting him down.

How good he had felt when he carried bags and bags of groceries into the house to fill them up—to fill them up because they were empty. He had felt like a man, a dad, a provider. Maybe it wasn't his right, but he had. He liked to put himself to use that way.

That was what firefighters did; they helped people who needed help. It didn't stop after the fire was out or the victim saved. They had their charities, individually and as a group. They were called upon to teach kids, help little old ladies, organize benefits. Brave men and women. Firefighters helped people much more gracefully than they accepted help.

Then Chris didn't need so much anymore, and things changed. It wasn't his feelings for Chris and the kids and that stupid dog that had changed; it was this terrible discomfort he felt in his gut because he wasn't in charge anymore. Because without him they could survive just fine. He wanted to be the one they needed the most. He wouldn't have thought this would be so hard. This was a side of himself he didn't like.

Packages in Christmas wrap had arrived from Aunt Flo, in case Chris and the kids were still with him by then. Without opening them, he knew they were expensive presents. When he took his jacket out of the hall closet to go to work this morning, he had looked at Chris's jackets. More than one now. He had spent a lot on the jackets he bought for Chris and Carrie and Kyle so they could go up to the snowy hills. Now, in the front closet, was a new suede coat. Auntie Flo had probably paid ten times as much. He felt reduced.

Chris looked different now. Even though she looked better than ever, he wanted it all to have come from him. It was unfair, and he knew it, but it was still fighting inside him. He thought about his family and knew money shouldn't bother him so much. His brother Chris had a lot of money. Orthodontics was a good-paying profession, and Chris was a clever investor. Money could be loads of fun. He thought about his sister Mo who made way more money than her husband, and how stupid he thought it was that they should ever argue about it. What was the difference how much or whose or where it came from if it put food on the table and provided for the future? So why, he asked himself, was he feeling the opposite of his own beliefs?

On the first night he stayed with her in his own house he had opened up a secret part of himself and told her about his deepest pain. The shamelessness of it didn't humiliate him; he was ready to be as frank about his weakness as he had been obvious in his strength. But now, when he had this little injury inside over her money and her aunt, he didn't talk to her about it. He didn't say, "I'm in pain because you're buying new sheets when I want to buy them for you. I hurt because I feel not good enough. I'm afraid I can't give you anything." He said, "Looks nice." Then he sulked. And his pain popped out somewhere else. He yelled at the dog for chewing his socks, when he would have gladly fed Cheeks a thousand pairs for a feeling of security.

Jealous and stupid, he chided himself silently. He hoped he would get over it, because he was afraid to expose himself to Chris as the selfish jerk he really was. If she found out how tough this was for him, how much he hated that witch, Florence, how much he prayed Florence would somehow hit rock bottom, leaving Chris poor and needy again, she would leave him. She would have to. How could she stay with a man like that?

He tried to think of what he had instead of what he wanted, because he still had Chris in his bed at night, and through their intimacy an important part of his identity had returned to him. Sex with her was better than any sex he'd ever had because he loved her so deeply and wanted her so completely. Sometimes he felt surly and unaroused because of self-pity, but once it got rolling, it was fabulous. He tried not to imagine how good it would be if they had years to perfect it. They had already developed fun, lush games...

"Come on, smoky, put out this fire."
"In a minute, in a minute."
"Why do you wait so long?"
"I thought I was making *you* wait."
"I already didn't wait—twice."

And...
"Hug me for a while. Just hug me like you're not interested in sex."
"Hug you until you beg me to move, huh?"

And...
"I'm not even going to take off my shirt until you tell me what you want. No, until you *show* me..."

Well, actually, those things had happened before Flo and the money. Since then he had felt inadequate, insecure. But if Flo and the money disappeared, he would be all right again. Virile. Even with his troubles, bed was still one of their best places these days. Because of the way their bodies worked together like an efficient factory that ran on its own energy. Once it got going and he forgot his anger, she didn't ask him what was wrong and he didn't sulk or worry. He wanted it to go on forever.

He was terrified. He thought he caught a glimpse of the end.

"Flo is coming in on the twenty-third, Mike. She promises to be good. Shall we do Christmas here? Should we take her to your mom and dad's?" Chris had asked.

You can't turn family away at Christmas. You can't. Even if they're awful family. But Flo at his mom and dad's? "Let's do it here. My folks can spare me one year."

He didn't ask her if she was going away after the holiday. He didn't ask her if she was staying. She didn't mention her plans. She didn't ask him if his invitation remained open. Everything seemed to be moving out of reach. Except the money.

Chris had decided she had better not let her ex-husband get away with anything, for Carrie and Kyle's sake. It had been their grandfather's money. Flo could handle it. Chris didn't need it, didn't want it, but it could be put in trust for the kids, and some kind of dividend could be paid while they were growing up to help provide for them. They would never be poor again.

Mike had actually hoped he would be forced to take a second job to finance their college education. Like he had done for Tommy. Stupid thing to wish for, huh?

Chris didn't need that money because she was going to sell books. She loved writing, she was going to start selling, and she had big plans. A career. A good, satisfying one.

One way or the other, Chris was going to be well off. With or without him.

"Why don't you and Chris and the kids come over

for dinner?" Jim asked as they washed and dried the last pot.

"Yeah, maybe. There's a lot to do with Christmas, though."

"Yeah, I suppose. Is her aunt coming out here?"

He was slow to answer. "Yeah. Not till the twenty-third, though."

"Little Mike, take it easy. You're not going to marry the aunt, you know."

"Who said I was going to marry anyone?"

"Uh, Mike? Joanie wasn't Catholic when you asked her to marry you, was she?"

"No. Why?"

"Did you tell her that was part of the deal, if you got married?"

"No. I wouldn't do that. I just told her it would make things a lot easier if she would think about it."

"Was it hard to ask her?"

He chuckled. "Yeah. Until I did. I guess I thought she'd get mad."

"What'd she say?"

"You know what she said. She did it, right? She said that wasn't too much to ask."

"Try and remember that, huh?"

Remember what? To ask for what I need? If Chris finds out how much I need, it'll scare her to death. Hell, it scares me to death. I cover up all my needs by filling the needs of others. I give a lot better than I receive.

Remember what? That people make changes in themselves in order to make a couple? I'm trying. I'm trying to change what I feel, but it hammers away inside me that I can't give her as much as Aunt Flo can—as much as she already has, for that matter.

Remember what? That when you lose the one you love, the one you counted on, you lose a part of yourself? Believe me, I remember. That was why I stayed alone.

I remember.

The bell came in. Truck and engine and chief. Mike's heart got a shot of adrenaline. He would only think about fire for a while now. Thank goodness.

Chris was scared to death of Christmas. Tomorrow Mike started his four days off over the holidays—quite a coup for a firefighter, to have so much time. In a couple of days Flo would return. If they could get through this, amicably, maybe they could get through the rest. She hoped. But Mike was so distant and quiet that she feared Flo's presence combined with Mike's cautiously suppressed anger was going to drive the last nail into the coffin.

The tree was up in the living room. It was bulging with presents, more presents than she had ever seen in her life. Every time the UPS truck pulled up with another load from Aunt Flo, Mike went out and bought more. There was no telling who would win this contest. Meanwhile the kids were having a time like they had never had. Mike, fortunately, did not seem to discriminate against them because they had wealth and Aunt Flo. His lap received them as dearly as ever.

She had asked Mattie if she could drop by their house. She wasn't sure what she was looking for exactly, but maybe some Cavanaugh wisdom would teach her something about Mike that would make things work. She was willing to do anything—short of changing who she was. Since she felt she had only just discovered the real Chris Palmer, and since she had only just discovered she liked her, she would not abandon herself again. It wouldn't be worth it. Becoming who you thought people wanted you to be made a mockery of real love. Henceforth she would only settle for the real thing.

"Chrissie, you look so different. You're doing your hair different now, huh?" Mattie asked, after she greeted Chris and the children that evening.

"I just got it cut."

"You brought us presents. Oh, Chrissie, you shouldn't have done that. Really. We have so much. Bring everyone in. Come in, come in. I have a bundt cake."

"We brought the dog—I hope you don't mind. Carrie wanted Big Mike to see the dog."

"You brought that dog?" Big Mike asked, walking toward the front door with his newspaper in his hand, hiking up his low-riding pants. "You brought that Creeps to my house?"

Carrie and Kyle giggled happily, looking up at him. How did the children know he was funny, when he never smiled? How did they know he was making jokes? Cheeks stood just behind them, right inside the door, his tail wagging while he growled.

"I don't know why you bring him here. He hates me."

"He doesn't really hate anybody, but he's very crabby."

Big Mike hunched down and reached between the children to scratch under Cheeks's chin. Cheeks growled louder; his tail wagged. "This dog is a mess," Big Mike said. "Look at him. He wants to be petted, but he makes all this noise. What a terrible dog he is. I think somebody hit this dog in the head, huh?"

"We think somebody was mean to him when he was

a puppy," Carrie said. "We think it was a *man*. He's always crabby to men, but not to girls."

"You're so tough, aren't you, Creeps. Come on then. Come on, Creeps," Big Mike said, straightening and walking into the living room, the wagging, growling dog following, the children giggling.

"Come in and have coffee, Chrissie. It's so cold. We might even get a little snow."

Chris took off her coat and tossed it over a chair. The kids were already sitting at Big Mike's feet, laughing as he said the dog's name wrong and made him look stupid, growling while he was being stroked.

Chrissie carried the presents into the kitchen. Mattie, who had waddled ahead of her, already had a coffee cup filled. "These are for the whole family, Mattie, but they're mostly for you. We picked them out together, and I want you to open them early."

"You shouldn't have, really. We have so much already."

"Go ahead. It isn't much."

It only took Mattie a minute to get inside the first box. Chris had tried to get exactly the right thing. A Christmas platter, a decorated lazy Susan, red napkins in green holly rings—enough for the whole clan, plus extras.

"I thought maybe you would like something like this. You have everyone here at Christmas, right?"

"Perfect, perfect. How nice you are to do this, Chrissie. How nice. Everyone will love it. Yes, they all come here, though I don't know why. Chris and Stacy have a big place with lots more room. They could have Christmas there, but they don't." Mattie lowered her voice to a whisper. "I think they don't like Big Mike to drive so much. At night, and all." She resumed in her normal voice. "Everyone comes here to this tiny house where we can't even move, but they come. I don't know why."

How they care for one another, Chris thought. As if they had secrets from one another, which they didn't. "I know why," she said, smiling. "This is where they belong. I love watching your family together. You're right, Mattie. You have so much."

"We've been blessed, me and Big Mike. Oh, we had our troubles like everyone else. Broken bones, for instance." She laughed. "You don't have four boys without broken bones. And the like. But we do okay, I think. Kids. They put you through it, huh?"

"You know, you've probably seen all that stuff in the paper about me, and Mike might have mentioned—"

"He told us a little bit about your aunt coming, but we don't ask him, Chrissie. It isn't our business, this with your aunt and all."

"Well, still, I'd like to explain some of that." Big Mike came into the kitchen to fill his coffee mug. "I want to tell you both," she amended, "that I haven't been taking advantage or—"

"You never mind about that, Chrissie," Big Mike said. "You don't need to tell us anything."

"It must seem so bizarre, all this 'missing heiress' nonsense. That's not really what I am at all. I was out of touch with my aunt because I was sure she would be too angry to even speak to me. I didn't know I was 'missing.' And I'm not an heiress. My aunt still runs the family business, which was half my dad's, but, well, it's not Exxon or anything. It's worth a lot, I guess, but that doesn't mean I'm really rich."

They looked at her, Big Mike by the coffeepot with his mug in his hand, Mattie at the kitchen table with her.

"I'm really not as different as I must seem."

"You don't seem different to us, Chrissie. We don't care about that story."

"But Mike..." Her voice drifted off for a moment. "I think Mike might have some trouble with it. I'm looking for a way to make him believe that I'm the same person who checked groceries at Iverson's. It's too bad it all came out so fast, and in such a bizarre way."

"Little Mike is a pretty smart boy," Mike said. "He doesn't do things he doesn't want to do. And he doesn't believe a lot of stories."

"Well, the stories are pretty much true," she said. "It just seems that Mike liked having us with him a lot more before he found out where I came from."

"You don't have to tell us about this," Mattie said, almost entreating Chris to shut up.

Chris was afraid she might cry. I love him, she wanted to say. I love him and I want him to love me the way I am, whether dead broke or monied.

"The boy likes to take care of everyone," Big Mike grumbled. "He does that with us, too. He's always taking care of us. He built that storage shed out back. He comes over, says he bought this storage shed. I say I don't need a storage shed, but he wants me to have it. So fine, I tell him. I have it. Thank you very much. But he can't let it go at that. He has to build it, too. Then he can go home, right? No. Then he has to put my lawn mower and things in it. Now he can be done with it, huh? No. He comes over to use the things he put in it. Sometimes he has to clean it out. And fix the roof. And trim the trees around the house. And paint this and that. Whew," he said, waving a hand. "He just likes to be useful."

Chris smiled in spite of herself. "How do you handle him when he gets like that. How do you act?"

"I act like I always act. 'What do I need some damned storage shed for?' I say. He builds it anyway."

"That's Little Mike," Mattie said, laughing. "We should slice up this cake."

"You just tell Little Mike you don't need it—he'll force it on you anyway."

"But," Chris said, "I can't do that."

"No, I guess not. Then you tell him to stick it in his ear if he doesn't like it."

"Don't tell her what to say, Mike," Mattie said. "Never mind him, Chrissie. He doesn't know what he's talking about. He's an old man who gets himself into all the kids' business. He gives them marriage counseling. If they listened to him, they'd all be getting divorces. Never mind him. We just want Little Mike to be happy, is all."

"Me, too," she said.

"Then everything works itself out, huh?"

"You want to make him happy, huh?" Big Mike scoffed. "Tell him, 'Stick it in your ear, I don't want a damned storage shed,' or whatever. He'll be happy." Big Mike went out of the kitchen.

Mattie got out plates and started slicing pieces of cake. You couldn't come to this house and not eat, Chris decided. They fill you up in any way they can.

"What's hard for Mike," she told Mattie, "is that he wants very much to do for us, give to us. It makes him feel good."

"Yes, he's that way. He does for everyone."

"I think he's afraid there isn't anything I need anymore. With this business about my aunt, about money."

"Well, I didn't raise the boy that way, Chrissie. Little Mike knows the important things money can't buy. I made sure my kids knew that, growing up. We didn't have too much then, when they were little, but I was real careful that they knew what's important. And I was real careful they knew people learned that two ways. One way was if they didn't have a lot of money but they had a good life. The other way was if they had a lot of money and that wasn't all they needed."

Mattie put a plate and fork in front of Chris. "He's a bullheaded boy, Little Mike, but he's pretty sharp. Don't listen to the old man, just give Little Mike some time to remember about that. A little time. He had some trouble in the third grade. In the seventh grade, too, if I remember. Maybe remembering things takes him a little time."

It might serve just as well, Chris thought, to tell him to stick it in his ear. "A little time," she repeated.

"He'll catch on eventually." Mattie laughed. "Will the kids eat the cake?"

"They'd love it," she said. And then the sirens came. Time stood still. The shrill noise mounted. They lived near the firehouse. Mattie continued slicing cake and an odd staticlike sound came from the living room.

"What's that?" Chris asked.

"We turn on the scanner sometimes when we hear the sirens. We worry a little bit, but we don't tell him. He knows it, but we don't tell him. He likes to think he's on his own."

Mattie's hand went into her apron pocket, and something in there rattled softly. Chris knew without asking that they were rosary beads. "Bring your cake," Mattie said. "We'll listen."

Big Mike said it was a house fire. At first it didn't sound too serious. She heard Mike's voice on the radio. The engine, Big Mike explained. Then the truck with the hydraulics. Another engine—maybe it was getting a little hot. Then another alarm. Police and ambulances. Chris started getting nervous following the fire by radio calls like this. She would never have one of those things, never! Then she wondered if she could get to Radio Shack before they closed to get her own.

Next the hazardous materials squad was called in. There had been an explosion. Mike's company was initiating rescue, though it was not Mike's voice they heard. And then, with eerie screeching through the little living room, came the news that there were firefighters down.

"God!" Chris said, straightening. "What do we do now?"

"Shh. We listen, that's all."

"Will they say the names?"

"No, they don't."

"Oh, God, why can't he be a house painter? This is horrible. Horrible!"

"No, they know what they're doing. They know."

"I don't know if I can take this."

"What would you change?" Big Mike asked. "What one thing would you change?"

"I would have sent him to law school," Chris said.

"Oh? He's been a firefighter twelve years now," Big Mike said. "If I had had the money to send him to law school, maybe about twenty-seven people would be dead. He takes chances, yes. About twenty-seven people, alive right now because he didn't go to law school, should thank me because I didn't have the money."

Because, Chris thought, he goes into fires to pull people out whenever he has to, no matter how scary and dangerous. And he can't think in terms of luck or miracles, because how often can you expect your luck to hold or a miracle to happen? He can't think about being heroic; he's just doing the job he was trained to do. An informed risk. Like love. Please, God.

Mattie rattled her beads.

Chapter 12

Engine 56 was the first on the scene, followed by the truck with hydraulics in close pursuit and another engine on its way. Two engines and a truck were standard equipment response for a house fire. There were no cops yet. The firefighters could count on an automatic response of two squad cars; they could also count on beating the cops to the fire. Mike's company's average response time was three minutes.

A civilian stood on the curb. He would have called in the alarm. The neighborhood was old but high-rent. The houses were all two-story, Victorian styles, around sixty to seventy years old but usually in excellent repair. The biggest problem with the houses here would be basement fires that could spread to the attic because of the absence of fire-stops. A maze of kindling.

This particular house had a nice big circular drive and an attached garage, from which smoke poured.

"I don't like 'em," Jim said, speaking of garage fires. Garages could be full of surprises; people stored paints, thinners, gas cans and such there. Not to mention cars.

As men sprang off the truck and engine, the neighbor jogged over. He was a little breathless, nervous. "There was a bunch of kids around here earlier—might've been a party. They have a lot of traffic around this place."

"Do you think there's anybody inside?" Mike asked the man.

He shrugged. "Could be. People coming and going all the time—parties and stuff. Could be a bunch of drunk teenagers in there."

Jim returned to the engine with a gas can in his gloved hand. He had gotten it from the driveway. He shook his head and set it down. This one might have been set; people didn't often leave empty gas cans in their driveways. Mike talked to the man briefly to determine when he had noticed the smoke, whether he'd seen anybody around—standard questions. He called for the peanut line to fog the site of the fire, while the ladder-company men approached the place with axes and pike poles. The truck men would cut the utilities and open it up; engine men would set up hoses and water. They pulled out tarps that would be used to protect the contents of the house from water, mud and other internal damage.

But the number-one priority was life. Structural consideration was always number-two. Jim was moving quickly, despite a hundred pounds of turnouts and equipment on his body, to the front door, next to the garage. He applied a firm shoulder to the door, pushed it open and went in.

Judging from a big bay window that faced the street

and smaller windows above, the house might have a living room or dining room on the ground-level front, kitchen in the back. The front door and garage were to the right, bedrooms upstairs. Maybe as much as three thousand square feet, and a basement and attic. And this one just might have been torched.

The chief's car pulled up, and he relieved Mike with the civilian. Mike was moving to join Jim in the house when it blew. The garage door cracked down the middle, and debris flew down the drive. Two firemen en route to the site fell like dominoes. There was a medley of curses around the truck and engine while two firefighters ran to the felled men to pull them away. But they were rolling over to stand up on their own steam.

Mike crouched away from the explosion for a second, but he couldn't take his eyes off the front door. It was no longer accessible, but blocked by debris and rolling gray smoke. Flames were licking out of the place where his best friend had gone in.

Then the chief was there beside him. "We have a man in the building," Mike told the chief. "Number 56 will initiate rescue; tell engine 60 to take over incident command. I'm going after Eble. Jim."

The chief called in a code 2 for the hazardous-materials squad. They didn't know yet what they had to deal with. They didn't know yet what had exploded or whether there was more. They'd use as little water on it as possible until they knew more about it.

Mike couldn't get in the front door, but the flames from the garage had not yet reached the living room window. A shovel lay in a flower bed at his feet, and he picked it up and smashed the big bay window. He hurriedly cleared the glass and climbed in, covering his mouth with the air pack mouthpiece. This meant, un-fortunately, that he couldn't call out to Jim.

These old Victorian monsters were built like mazes with lots of rooms clustered amid stairwells and hall-ways. Jim would probably have gone through the down-stairs quickly, looking for people, and then headed for the upstairs bedrooms.

The first thing that struck Mike as odd was the total absence of furniture. What kind of place was this? Peo-ple coming and going, but no furniture? To have a lot of company, you had to have a couch to sit on. He got a sick feeling in the pit of his stomach. He was guess-ing what was wrong.

Typical of these old houses, there was a front stair-case, now blocked by debris from the explosion and with flames climbing in through the damaged wall that separated house and garage. But there proved to be an-other set of stairs behind the kitchen. Mike took them quickly. At the top he looked down a hallway, with bedroom doors on each side, to the landing of the front stairwell. There he saw him, lying twisted, half on his side, half on his back, maybe dead, maybe unconscious.

Jim's blackened and bleeding forehead was either injured from flying debris or hurt by his fall but not burned. And he was alive, thank God. His red, water-ing eyes stared up into Mike's face. A wooden chest of some kind lay on top of his leg, a board across his ribs. His arm was stretched out toward his leg, as if he'd at-tempted to free himself. He was wearing his air pack, but his eyes were filled with agony.

Mike tossed off the trunk as though it weighed two pounds rather than fifty and threw off the board. He couldn't let Jim lie there or take the time to immobilize the leg. He grabbed Jim's collar and dragged him backward a little way before bending down to lift him. He heard the awful growl of his friend's pain. More than 260 pounds of Jim Eble in his arms made Mike's heart pound, his muscles strain and bulge, but this was his best friend. There was no lighter load.

He started back the way he had come, toward the rear stairwell, but upon passing a bedroom door that was ajar, he looked in. There he saw what it was about. The room was filled with tables, glassware, sacks, tanks, tubing. A drug lab.

He grabbed the doorknob with the hand under Jim's knees and pulled it closed. And then he got the hell out of there.

He exited the building from the back door and carried Jim around the house to the front, where the equipment was parked. The chief met them. Mike couldn't talk until he laid Jim gently on the ground and pulled away his mask.

"Got a drug lab on the second floor, front bedroom. Maybe propane gas tanks in there. Do we have a code 2? They on their way?"

"Yep. I'll tell 'em when they get here. And a second alarm. How's Eble?"

"Jim?" Mike said to his friend.

"Goddamn trunk," he groaned. "Came flying at me, hit me in the back of the knees." He coughed. "Crunch," he said, tears pouring down his cheeks.

Mike heard the chief telling the police to empty out the neighborhood for a half-mile circumference, and the ambulances started arriving. There were three firefighters down, but Jim had the worst injury. His leg was almost certainly broken, his head was cut and scraped and his jaw was already starting to swell. He had arm and shoulder pain as well, maybe a dislocation of the shoulder. The paramedics began cutting off his turn-outs, trying to start an IV, applying bandages to his face.

Mike stayed nearby for a few minutes, looking on. He thought briefly about what Mattie and Big Mike were hearing on the scanner. On-site explosion. Code 2. Firefighters down, ambulances dispatched. Injuries. Second alarm. Arson-investigation team called in. Additional police backup. Evacuation of neighborhood.

Mike guessed what had happened. A home drug lab, doing a big business in the area, especially for kids, and somebody got ticked off—maybe wanting a bigger piece of the action, or maybe unhappy they weren't being extended any credit. Someone had decided to set a little fire, burn them out. The do-it-yourself chemists were using propane gas and had extra tanks stored in the garage.

If the firefighters couldn't contain the blaze in the garage, keep it on the lower level, it might reach the lab. It could turn this area into a gas chamber. Hydrogen cyanide, probably.

The Firebird—hazardous-materials men—came around the drive.

When the paramedics moved away from Jim for a few moments, Mike crouched beside him and asked, "You okay?"

"Damn. No. Got an aspirin?"

Mike smiled in spite of himself. "I gotta get back into the fire."

"Yeah," Jim panted. "Get the SOB. Please."

"You bet, bud."

Not a good fire. Oh, it would have been okay if there

hadn't been chemicals that might blow, or injuries. Mike had tackled fires in old Victorians like this one, with hallways and rooms like mazes, twisting and turning and ending up blocked. Once inside you didn't know how you'd gotten in or where you might get out. It was a challenge. But this one was no good and it had to be stabilized before the heat got to the lab. Otherwise...

They managed to get the hose in the front door, over the debris, and hit the garage from all sides, while above, the men opened up the roof with pike poles to let the smoke and steam escape.

Mike fought it like fighting time. With vengeance and anger. The Hazmat squad in their rubber splash suits wandered through the upstairs, isolating the bad stuff, moving some of it out. Mike rallied to the race. It was a race to beat the fire before the fire beat them. And he wouldn't take a break, wouldn't call for relief.

He had not felt this good, or this bad, in a long time.

Dawn was dirty. The truck company would be left along with the Drug Enforcement Administration when engine 56 roared out. They smelled pretty bad. The structure was mostly intact; a lot of damage to the ground level, but the flames had never licked up against all those chemicals and gases. The DEA pulled orange tape across the site. A couple of lanky teenage boys were being cuffed and put in the back of a squad car. Arrests. For arson? Or for home chemistry? Mike hated to see anybody get away with either one. Especially since it had hurt a firefighter.

Different kinds of fires led to different kinds of feelings, especially about injuries. When you had a man injured saving a life in a legitimate, accidental fire, that was one thing. You felt proud, somehow, that one of you could be there, doing that. But when a good fire-fighter was downed in a torch job, or something like this, a vendetta among underworld slime that poisoned society with their drugs, it was like there was no justice. Putting out the fire just wasn't enough.

Mike noticed that Stu, dragging along in his filthy turnouts on his way to the engine, paused at the squad car. He took off his helmet and his gloves and stared into the backseat of the police car. He spit on the ground, then moved on.

It took a while for the talk to start after a bad fire. At first it seemed there was nothing to say. Then there was so much to say, you couldn't shut anybody up. But it was shift change. Not very many men would shower at the station; most of them wanted to get home, get out of there, before the next shift had time to think of a lot of questions.

There was one question, though, that no one would leave before having answered. And so Mike reported.

"Jim's got scrapes, a broken collarbone, broken femur," he said, tapping his thigh. "But he's all straightened out, no surgery, casted up, and higher than a kite on morphine. He'll be in a while, and it's too soon to know if there's any disability, but the doctor doesn't think so. Nice clean break."

Then he told everyone what a good job they had done. Then he thanked God for that little bit of luck that had Jim Eble all the way upstairs instead of on the steps when that propane blew. Five seconds, either way, would have cost them all dearly.

Chapter 13

Mike went to the hospital when his shift was relieved.
It could have been much worse than it was, but he was
not surprised that Jim's wife, Alice, fell against him,
releasing some of those pent-up tears. Hearing your husband was down in a fire was the dreaded news. Finding out he was alive was a huge relief, but temporary,
because next you had to know how alive he was.

"It's only a couple of broken bones," Mike said.
"How's he doing?"

"He's doing great," she said, sniffing, "but I thought
I would have a breakdown. Thank God he's all right."

The newspapers sometimes ran stories about downed
firefighters—basically they covered the fire, part of
which was a firefighter hurt and hospitalized—but they
didn't often follow up with stories about the ex–firefighter
locksmith or shoe salesman. The stuff they didn't print

was the terrifying stuff. Like the early-retirement injuries. Firefighters paralyzed by a fall. There were sprains, breaks and smoke inhalation—and then there were horrific injuries that made you wonder if life was the best deal for the poor guy. Like the firefighter, some years back, who had been rendered brain damaged by carbon monoxide gas from a leaking air pack. Freak things.

Then there were the heart attacks. It wasn't only from breathing smoke or straining the muscles; it was from the alarms. The stress, not from the fire—but from the constant shots of adrenaline that presented the flight-or-fight conflict to the body. Like getting an electric shock on a regular basis. Young men, sometimes, fell because of this.

"You doing okay?" Mike asked Jim.

"No, I'm not doing okay," he said, trying to smile but giving a lopsided grimace through bandages that covered his right eye and chin. His arm cast was elevated, his casted leg hefted off the bed by weights and pulleys. "This had to happen right before my time off. Some luck, huh?"

"You're not going to be in here over Christmas, are you?"

"Hell, no. I refuse to be. Everybody else okay?"

"Yeah. You left early, so you don't know. They're still out there, but it's down to cleanup now. You were the big injury of the night."

"What some people won't do for attention."

"For once you didn't puke."

"Didn't have time. Never saw it coming, in fact. Boy, that sucker blew, huh?"

"Not a good fire. There were arrests before the sun came up, though. Nobody's getting away with anything."

"Yeah. Sure."

The response was cynical. They both knew that the little guys with the lab might get arrested, but the big guys who financed or set up or sold the stuff would probably never be discovered. Street drugs. Chemicals. Ether. Et cetera. Who would have believed they'd come up with something more volatile, more unpredictable, than a paint-store fire? Home drug labs.

"I owe you, bud," Jim said.

"You owe me nothing."

"I owe you big-time. In fact, you oughta get a medal."

"Don't you dare. I hate those damn things. Medals are for cops. They eat that stuff up."

"Go on," Jim said. "Get out of here. I want the nurse."

"What for?"

"Do I need a reason? She's gorgeous, that's what for."

"I think he's going to be fine," Alice said with a sniff.

"Yeah, he'll be all right. A minute, huh, Alice?" She nodded and stepped outside the room. Mike paused. He thought.

"Don't," Jim said.

Mike looked down. They were good at living dangerously, living on the edge of life and laying it all on the line. They were bad at being vulnerable, because in this they were unpracticed. You couldn't admit vulnerability and act completely in control at the same time. Those gears did not mesh. This was why Mike was in trouble with Chris, and he suddenly knew it. He didn't know what to do about it or why it had to be that way, but he knew what it was. It was one thing to tell her about weakness and pain that was ten years old; it was quite another to look her right in the eye and admit the fear and shame of the moment.

He looked at his best friend who had suffered severe bodily harm. He was about to try out emotion on him. Scary thing. What if you admitted your fallibility when you were most apt to be fallible? Could you run into the burning building then? That's why they never talked about it. They were all afraid of the same thing—that if they thought about it too much, they'd come apart like a cheap watch.

"Don't start," Jim said.

"I have to. There are so many things I couldn't have faced without you. You know that."

"You face whatever you have to. You have before. You will again. Just don't start this."

"You're my best friend," he said, almost choking on the sentiment. He wanted to talk about the fear he had, a fear even worse than the fear that Jim had been killed. The fear of being all alone again. And the relief that he wasn't.

"You need more friends," Jim said.

"They can't take me. You can."

"Just take the thank-you and don't get sloppy. I'm in pain. I don't want to play with you now."

"Okay, then. But you're coming back."

"Sure. Of course. It's what I do. Anyway, lightning never strikes in the same place twice."

"Yeah." Mike laughed, remembering the old joke. "Because the place isn't there anymore after the first time."

"I'm here," Jim said, solemn.

Mike touched the fingers that stuck out of the cast. He wanted to do more, maybe hug him. But he had done all that he could reasonably do. *You're here, old buddy. Thank God.*

"See ya," he said.

"Don't bother me over Christmas. I'll be busy."

Mike knew what that meant. It meant that Jim didn't want him to feel obligated in any way; he should feel free to pursue his holiday plans without feeling obligated to visit the injured firefighter, his best friend.

He stopped for coffee with Big Mike before going home. He felt grubby even though he had cleaned up. And tired, but too wired to want to sleep. And angry—about the fire, about near calamity, about the difficulty of life sometimes. And about Aunt Flo coming tomorrow…two days before Christmas. It had been building in him. He even wondered if his worry had been distracting him when they got to the fire. Otherwise, he might have been in the house and Jim might have visited *him* in the hospital. He was usually the first one in when there were people inside.

By the time Mike got to his house, it was nearly 11:00 a.m. Chris was pacing. She gave a gasp and ran to him, putting her arms around his neck and hugging him.

"Hey," he said, laughing. "Hey."

When she released him, there was fury in her eyes. "Why the hell didn't you call me?"

"Call you? What for?"

"I was worried sick! I told you I can't sleep through the sirens! You know I can't."

"Well, gee whiz, I was busy."

"You weren't too busy to call Mattie!"

"So? Did Mattie call you, tell you everything was okay?"

"Yes, but you could have called. Where have you been?"

"Look, Chris, don't get like this on me, huh? I'm wiped out, I'm mad, and I don't need this."

She ran a hand down her neck. "Okay. Sorry. I was worried. I was scared."

"Well, who knew you'd be worried? I figured you'd be polishing the goddamn silver."

He stared at her for a minute, then he turned to go through the kitchen and to the stairs. He wasn't going to his room to sleep; he thought he'd better get out of sight. He was already sorry, but he wasn't sure he could stop it. He should have known it would start oozing out of him sooner or later.

He passed a pair of chewed-up socks on the stairs and picked them up with a curse. He slammed his bedroom door. *Oh, please,* he thought, *not now. Don't let me do this. Not like this.*

But there was a new comforter on his bed. He gritted his teeth. Pillow shams. He wanted to shoot the place up. He went to his closet to change his shoes. Hanging on a hanger was a new shirt with a sweater hanging over it. He touched it. There were new pants. A new set of clothes. To wear while they entertained the aunt over Christmas?

He opened the bedroom door and called her. Loud. Angry. *"Chris!"* Then he closed the door, waited and seethed.

Chris opened the bedroom door and stepped in. "What?"

"She didn't really leave, did she. She just stepped behind her big ugly checkbook for a while, that's all. She might have seemed to leave, but she really just left you a big pot of money as a reminder of where it's at, huh?"

"She left me some money, but—"

"So you could decorate the place and make it good enough for royalty, is that it? You know, Chris, it's getting on my nerves to come home and find new towels, new sheets, new dishes—like my stuff isn't good enough for you. It's starting to really burn me up! If you want to buy a few things for my place, why don't you try asking me if I want any of this crap? Huh?"

"Look, I wasn't trying to—"

"And don't buy me clothes!" He was shouting now. He took the two hangers out of the closet and threw the things on the floor. "I'll dress myself! I'm sure it won't meet the standards of Her Majesty, Florence, but it meets *my* standards. If you want to buy me clothes, buy me some damn socks. I think the damn dog has eaten the last pair."

"I didn't buy you that because of Flo!" she shouted back. "I bought it because of *me!* I liked it. I wanted to do something nice. I'll buy socks, okay? Two thousand pair!"

"Like I don't have anything nice?"

"You have wonderful things! I don't have any problem with your house, or the way you dress, or— Jeez, I just wanted to give you something!"

"Well, I don't want anything from you, because anything you give me is coming out of Flo's pocketbook. And I've had it up to here with her!"

"What has she done to you that you didn't do right back to her?"

"Besides rub my nose in my middle-class existence? Besides outfitting you and the kids for your next appearance at court? Besides laying all these little traps for you, like your lost money? Not a damn thing, really!"

"I'm not spending Flo's money, you big dope. I'm—"

"Don't you *ever* call me a dope! Don't ever, ever—" He stopped. He knew without looking in a mirror that his face was red, his fists clenched. He took a deep breath.

"I didn't mean you were a dope in general, you dope. I meant you're acting stupid over this situation, which could be a good situation if you'd let it, but you're too stubborn and bossy to bend a little."

"Oh, man," he said, letting a mean laugh erupt. "I was a dope to think you could ever fit into a regular kind of life."

"Just because I came from a wealthy family doesn't make me *ir*regular. You didn't even know my family; you only met Flo when she was feeling threatened. You don't back a Palmer into a—"

"I didn't back her into anything. I sat there and took her abuse. *You* sure didn't stand up for me. I guess I know where *you* stand!"

"You, apparently, don't know anything about me! Did you hear me standing up for Flo when you went after her? You two were the ones determined to do battle."

"I don't want to feel this way," he said, his teeth clenched. "I don't want to feel shoddy. I don't want to care, but I do care that I'm a firefighter and she has a damn empire waiting for you. I don't like the whole damn hoity-toity, highfalutin show we have to put on! Like I can't take her to Ma and Big Mike's because they're not good enough!"

"But they *are*. They're better than good enough!"

"I don't want you to be able to buy and sell me ten times over. Even if you wouldn't, I don't want you to be *able* to!"

"You're doing this to yourself! Nobody is doing this to you! You're being a snob. It's you. Not me. Not even Flo!"

"It was good before there were all these *things*. Before I came home every day and found new *things*."

"I can't do this. Stop it, Mike!"

"Is that how it would be?" he asked her. "There's something wrong and you can't deal with it? You can't fight it out? Chris, if there's a problem, *we* have a problem. What do you think? Think it'll go away? Huh?"

"You want to give it to me? Is that it? Yell at me for a while because you're mad? It was okay when I needed everything from you, huh? When I had nothing at all. Destitute, needy, sad little divorcée—you could tell me then, 'Go work on your book,' 'Be who you want to be,' 'Be where you want to be.' But you can't live with the real me, huh? Because my aunt's money makes you feel like less of a man? Maybe because you feel like a man only when someone's hanging on you, thinking of you as a hero, but you don't have any interest in someone who can stand on her own two feet."

The room was silent.

"Yeah," he said. "I don't want to feel that way, but I do."

"You feel different? Now?" she asked softly, tears coming to her eyes.

"I wanted—" He felt his throat closing up on him. "I wanted to hold on to a family that needed to be held. Not—" He stopped again to swallow before going on. "Not one that didn't need me."

"I don't have everything I need," she whispered.

"Then do something," he entreated. "Change it back."

"I can't. Don't you see? You loved the Chris who

didn't have anything. I don't want to be that Chris. If you don't love me as I am, you were loving a fantasy, a hard-luck story."

"I did *not* love a hard-luck story! It was this feisty little babe making it through tough stuff that a lot of stronger people couldn't. But it wasn't true. You weren't gutsy—you were *rich*. You always have been—you just didn't have it *on* you!"

"Oh, God," she said, shaking her head, "I should have known. I never should have stayed here. You think I've changed, but you're the one who's changed. I'm the same person, and you don't like me as much."

"No, you don't like it when it doesn't go your way. You gotta have it smooth as glass every second. That's it."

"Oh, yeah? I've been real spoiled, all right, the past few years of—"

"Oh, don't give me that bull! You never starved. You could always have called *her!*"

"Maybe I should call her now!"

"Well, maybe you should!"

They both looked stricken by what had been said. But it was too late to take it back.

Mike suddenly didn't know what to do. He yanked open the door. "I gotta have air. Gotta cool down." Reluctantly, helplessly, he left the bedroom and the house.

Mike drove around for a while but ended up at his mom and dad's. He'd pretty much known he would. It was years since he had sought his father's advice. Years since he had talked about his troubles. Years since he had admitted he had any.

"You oughta see what's under the Christmas tree,"

he told Big Mike. "I've never seen anything like it. And it's my fault as much as Aunt Flo's. But it'll never stop."

"It'll stop," Big Mike said. "You'll run out of money pretty quick."

"Do you know what she's got? I mean, like millions of dollars!"

"Did you stop playing the Lotto? I thought you went for an idea like millions of dollars."

"That's different. It would have been *mine*."

"'Mine,'" Mattie said quietly, half pretending not to get into this. "Kids say that when they're two. Usually they get over it."

"Ma, it isn't like you think. I thought a lot of money didn't mean that much to Chris, but she flaunts it now. I mean, she's buying things for my house all the time. Like when Flo was coming for dinner, she bought this whole new set of dishes, new tablecloth—the works. Flo can't sit down at a regular table? God forbid there should be a chipped dish. Can you imagine what it would be like if she came here? With the rest of us?"

Mattie shrugged. "She would sit down and eat or not. Makes no difference to me."

"Oh, you think that, but it isn't that way. It feels different to be surrounded by money. If I stay with Chrissie now, she'll build us a mansion."

"How terrible a thing, Mikie my boy. Just think of it—the pain of living with some money. Terrible break for you."

"Come on."

"So what would you change? What one thing?"

"The money. And the aunt."

"How would you do that?"

Okay, he thought. I can't make those changes. "Maybe I wouldn't have offered my house in the first place."

"Okay, if that makes it all better, okay. But for a minute there I thought you liked it. Maybe I was mistaken."

"I think you were." Big Mike *was* mistaken: it had been more than a minute, and he had more than liked it. He had felt restored, alive—before this whole issue of who had what and who was in charge got in his way. He'd already let it out, though, and if Chris couldn't face it any better than he could, then it couldn't be resolved. If you didn't know where the fire was, you couldn't put water on it.

He complained for a while longer, but he didn't tell them that the big problem was him. Probably they already knew. Stubborn and bossy. He liked to control things. On the other hand, *he* didn't want anything to do with a woman who would be controlled. The prospect for reconciliation didn't look good.

His parents said things like, "So what do you want? That she give the money away so you don't have to worry about it?"

"No, not that, but—"

"Maybe she should give it to you. Then it would be *yours*."

"No, but—"

I only want to feel good again, he thought. *In control. Useful. Helpful. Needed.*

At four o'clock he was ready, he thought, to go back to his house. His mother slapped his cheek affectionately. "Try not to be too stupid about this, Mikie."

"That will be hard for him, Mattie," Big Mike said.

"Don't do that. Don't say that. Chrissie called me a big dope."

Mattie kissed his cheek. "Did you see Jim? He's all right?"

"I saw him. He's doing fine, considering."

"Terrible thing," Mattie said. "Life is too short. Sometimes when you come that close to losing someone, sometimes it makes you want to shake everything up so you can fix it, huh?"

He thought for a minute. Was that why? He'd thought about losing Jim and then become afraid of losing Chris and the kids. Knowing that having them the way he did wasn't feeling too good, he'd wanted to shake it up. Maybe then they could put the pieces together right. But, no. He'd just made a big mess of things.

"Yeah, Ma," he said.

When he left the house Big Mike settled, shook the paper and hid behind it. "So?" Mattie asked her husband.

"That Chrissie. Good judge of character, that girl. He's a big dope, your son."

"He's always my son when he does something stupid."

"Was he the one who put Matthew in the clothes chute?"

"It was Chris in the clothes chute, and he put himself there after making Tommy go first."

"Was it? You're sure?"

"You think he's going to be all right?" she asked.

"I don't know. I'm betting on that terrible dog. I bet you anything that if she leaves, she doesn't take that terrible dog."

"I think you hope," she said.

The house was filled with the good smells of cooking. Chris was standing at the stove. This was not what he had expected. He had come in through the garage, and now he stood just inside the door and looked at her. "I don't know how to say I'm sorry about what I said."

"You said what you felt. You can't be sorry for that."

"I'm sorry I said anything. I don't want to feel that way. I wanted to work on feeling different before I said anything."

"But you were telling the truth?"

He nodded.

"Then I'm the one who's sorry," she said. "I cooked dinner, a special one. Do you think we can bury it for one night?"

"One night?"

"I think we should have an early Christmas. You, me, the kids. Flo is planning to get in at two tomorrow. If I can't reach her and get her to cancel—I've been trying—the three of us will meet her and go back with her. You two are incompatible. This isn't good for anybody anymore. I wanted it to work, Mike. And I'll never stop loving you."

"Is it because we're too different?"

"No. Because the differences are tearing us apart. And I don't think I can fix this."

"Try. Please. I'm willing to try."

"I don't think you can, Mike, and the past ten days— maybe the next ten years—you against Flo, against where I've come from, what I can provide..."

"But you don't have to provide. You—"

"I *do* have to. I have to give, too. And not just hot food and grateful sex. I have been working, working hard, so that I could make it on my own. That effort is as much a part of who I am as any other part of me. I don't have to live in a big fancy house or be like Flo or be able to afford the finest of everything, but I do have to be able to earn money, spend it, save it as I choose. I want this whole business about the amount to be irrelevant, like at Mattie and Big Mike's. Where whoever has gives, and whoever needs takes. Not just money, but all of it. I can't live with a man who will put restrictions on what I, too, could provide."

"You could give me a chance to try to—"

She shook her head, then walked toward him. Her arms went around his neck. "You mean struggle with this until it either works or crashes down around us? You wanted to be the one, you said, to give me what I need to build my life. Oh, Mike, you can't. Neither can Flo. I've got to do that for myself. Being loved because you're helpless is not very different from being loved because you're rich."

"You're comparing me to *him?* Chrissie, your husband didn't love you—he *used* you. He didn't say he'd try to change. You're just running away."

"Not exactly. I'm going to spend Christmas with Flo, but I'm not going to move in with her. I have some money from the landlord, and if I don't sell a book soon, I'll get a job. I've done it before. I want to do it on my own. I can share my life, Mike, but I don't want to be owned. I don't want to be kept down. This situation is hurting both of us too much."

"Chrissie, I have a bad temper. I'm bossy and stubborn, like you said. I got jealous. But maybe I can change some of that. Let's—"

"Look, I'm leaving, not dying. Maybe some of this can be worked out—a lot of it works already. But not while I'm in your house. I don't know which was harder, having you try so hard to be perfect and patient, or hav-

ing you blow up like you did. Let's let the dust settle.
We'll e-mail, talk on the phone. Maybe after a while…"

"Don't leave. Don't."

"I have to. I think the kids and I have been through
enough for now. For now, let's not put ourselves through
any more fighting. Maybe later, when things have
calmed down, when this business with the 'lost money'
is settled, when my book is published, you know…
maybe we can work it out. It's been wonderful, and I
love you. Let's try to part friends. I'm not going to disappear. If it's meant to last longer, it'll survive a separation while we both decide what we need. Let's not put
ourselves through a rough Christmas."

"Is it what you want?" he asked. "Would you love me
better if I had some house plans drawn up…if I wanted
to help you spend your money?"

"Mike, it isn't either love me for my money or love
me because I'm broke. It isn't either-or. This is who I
am. I am sometimes broke, and sometimes it looks like I
have a lot of money. I want to be okay either way. I think
it's the only way. We did what we set out to do, huh?"

"What if I beg?"

"Then that would mean you weren't telling the truth
when you asked me to stay just long enough so I could
get back on my feet and you could remember what you
wanted again."

He shrugged. "I never asked you to promise anything, it's true. I said open invitation."

"But you made that offer to someone else. I'm not who
you thought I was. That book. My stupid ex-husband.
Will you be all right?"

"In a while."

"No veldt-sores?"

Open, bleeding wound. But he was one tough guy. "Those are taken care of now. But I think I drove you away when all I wanted was for you to stay."

"Maybe you couldn't help it, what with wanting one thing but being stuck with another. It's my fault, too. I should have told you that first night you asked me to stay. At least I should have told you before we..." She held back tears, looking away briefly. "It's been pretty rugged around here since Flo came and my past became my present and we forgot we only had one small, simple goal: I needed a roof, and you needed to get in touch with what you really wanted. We got a little carried away. I don't want them to hear that kind of fight again," she said, her head nodding in the direction of the living room.

"I suppose."

"Kiss me, Mike. Kiss me so I'll never forget how wonderful it feels."

Carrie's chin quivered. "Mommy says that we're going to our Auntie Flo's for Christmas."

Mike picked her up. "Does that make you sad?"

"No. Cheeks makes me sad."

"Why?"

"He's going in a kennel for Christmas. Because he can't go on the airplane. He doesn't have a box."

"Oh, no, he's not. He'll stay with me. He can come to the cabin with me for Christmas. Okay?"

"You don't have to do that, Mike. Cheeks is pretty hard on your socks."

"I like him. I'll buy him a bunch of socks for Christmas. How's that, Carrie? Can I keep him for you while you're away?"

"Yes." She smiled. "And then you can bring him when you visit us. When are you going to visit us?"

"Oh, I don't know. Pretty soon, maybe. When are you going to visit me?"

"Pretty soon, too. Mommy says we will *always* know where you are. We bought you Christmas presents, and we're going to open them tonight. It is a 'practice Christmas.'"

Let it be, he thought. *Don't let me tempt fate by showing either too much joy in their presence or too much pain in their departure. Let them be happy, leave happy, as they were happy within my arms. All of them. And then, in my memories, I will be less lost.*

Dinner was ham and things. Christmas ham. And a fire in the fireplace. And eggnog, cookies and an Irish whiskey, neat, for the grown-ups, which would either untense some tight nerves or loosen their tongues or start the tears flowing.

They only opened presents from one another; Flo's were put back in the boxes they had been shipped in to be carried back to Chicago. Chris had already made plane reservations. It was a miracle she was able to book them this time of year, but she called a travel agent and paid top dollar for first-class. It was all set.

And the opened presents would also be packed and carried away because, as Mike knew, they wouldn't be back soon. The kids were thrilled with their bounty. And Mike was surprised to be given things he had not thought they knew how to buy. A gun-cleaning set. Riding chaps. A rod and reel. And a big packet of socks. "We'll go fishing when you visit, huh, Kyle?"

"Fishing!"

"Our mother doesn't like guns very much," Carrie said. "But she said you are very careful with them."

"I am. When you're very careful and you know what you're doing with guns, as with fires, they're not so scary." Why then, he wondered, had they been so reckless with what they so briefly, so blissfully had? Had they never considered love volatile?

"Will I ride the horses some more?"

"Yes. Yes, you will. And I'll take pictures for you and mail them to you. And pictures of all the Cavanaugh kids. And Big Mike and Gram. And I'll call you at your Auntie Flo's. Okay?"

"Okay!"

"Should we read a story? One of our favorites?"

"No, the new one. Read a new one."

"Okay, a new one, then." Which he did. A long, long one. But when they fell asleep, both of them, he did something he had never before done. He woke them. "Carrie. Kyle. Wake up a little bit. I'm going to take you to bed. It's my turn to tuck you in. There we go." And he hefted them up in his big arms and took them, together, to the beds upstairs.

There was an ache in his chest, but he would not give in. "I love you very much, Carrie," he told her. "And you can visit me whenever your mommy wants to." And then, "I love you very much, Kyle, and I promise to take you fishing if your mommy will let you go." And he held each one tight, kissed each one on forehead, cheeks, lips, chin. They were too tired to notice how desperately he behaved, and for this he was grateful.

He returned to Chris. She handed him another Irish. "I wish I had done better," he said. "Maybe you'll change your mind. Maybe when things are a little settled, you'll come back and work on this with me. I'm a big dope, but I'm not hopeless."

"Maybe. The timing has been all wrong. I'm not the coward I appear to be, Mike. And I'm not choosing between you and Flo—I'm only getting some distance from both of you while I think things through."

He lifted his glass to her. "That's probably good. Me and Flo, we've been lousy to you. You okay about the dog?"

"Carrie feels a lot better about it now. Do you think we'll have something to talk about on the phone? Do you think we'll keep whatever it was we had—"

"*Is*, Chris. Whatever it *is*. We haven't lost it. We just got sidetracked. Me. I got pigheaded. Our family's famous for it."

"But you're letting me go. Not arguing about it."

"I said I'd try. I don't know if I can change, I can only try. I became a different person when I started to compete with your big bucks. I didn't like the person I was becoming, but I couldn't get rid of the feelings. I want you to be where you ought to be. Here, there—it's all the same. I'll love you no matter what."

"I think if it's the real thing, we'll come back together."

"Yeah, well, you hit the nail on the head. I'm afraid if you go, you'll never be able to come back."

"Why?"

"I don't know. Because you'll find out what I've known all along: you're tougher than you think, and you have the moxie to make it on your own."

"You might find out something, too. You might find out you don't need all these complications."

"No, that's your line. I said I'll go all the way to the

end. I just didn't know it would be such a short trip."
He sighed deeply, fighting the feeling that the last shovelful of dirt was being tossed on the grave. "Like you said, we did what we set out to do. If you can stay, stay. If you can't...well, you're the one who thinks. I rush into things."

"Well, I could have gone earlier. I could have called Flo; then you wouldn't be feeling like you've lost something now."

"I feel fear, Chrissie, not loss. Afraid you'll decide leaving was the smartest thing you did. I want you to regret leaving, then decide it's worth it to come back. I just can't promise that I'll ever be easy to live with. And I might never like Flo. I can't make myself even *want* to like Flo. Just like Cheeks might never stop eating socks. Such is life. I'm sorry. My best isn't much sometimes."

"But I love you so," she whispered.

"Then show me. Here. In front of the fire. Show me where to touch you. Let me put out the fire one more time..."

Much later he whispered to her, "I can't say goodbye, Chrissie. Not to the kids. Don't make me do that."

"Okay. Whatever you want."

"Then I want you to sleep in my arms. And when you wake up, be smiling. It wasn't long enough, but it was good."

Chapter 14

When Chris awoke Mike and Cheeks were gone. She didn't have the time for the luxury of lying still and contemplating the past month and the decision she had made to end it; there was a great deal to be done before going to the airport. She hadn't made contact with Flo—where *was* her aunt these days?

As she hurried around the house gathering up their belongings, scraping their presence from his house, she could not still her mind. What was going to prove the most difficult to live without? The way he was with the kids? Like he should have a dozen. Natural and decisive, he never made hesitant or wrong choices for them. He spoke their language, found the right pastimes, the right jokes, and practiced affirmative discipline that showed them how good they were, how smart.

Or would it be even harder to live without the way he was with Chris's body? As though he had known it for twenty years and was, at the same time, just working up a sweat in the first round. How could you feel wild and nurtured at the same time? Frenzied yet companionable? Out of your mind with out-of-control passion but perfectly safe? You could feel this way with a man who trusted easily and gave everything he had.

Or would the hardest thing be giving up that fanciful, foolish, idealistic notion that one could have a unit of people bonded by love, fraught with ups and downs, fronts and backs, joy and pain, a circle that actually closed around them and was tied with the knot of trust? The belief that it could be settled, ironed out, renewed. Yes, that might be hardest. Had she really fantasized fighting and then making up? Sure. Before she had lived it. Before his temper had erupted and the first punch he threw hit her square in the only identity she had.

She had not, after all, asked him to become different from the man with whom she had fallen in love. Had she?

When she went into the kitchen she found his note. "I did all the things I have to say. Love, M."

That was Mike. Mike was better with actions than with words. When he was forced to confront his feelings, they were pretty hectic. What he wanted, she guessed, would be for them to forsake Aunt Flo, the money, the past. She almost wished she could.

There was quite a lot to pack, plus Christmas presents, opened and unopened. Then there was the car, which she took to a used-car lot. She did not strike a bargain, but she did get a ride to the airport with all their things.

"You're doing *what?*" Flo nearly shrieked. The airport was a mess. Hundreds of frustrated travelers fighting for space on overcrowded planes, airlines offering money for people who would give up their tickets. Chris held four first-class seats. Nonstop, Chicago.

"We're going back to Chicago. Today. It'll be a long wait—we don't leave until five-thirty, but—"

"Christine, what in the world are you talking about?"

"Don't start on me, Flo. It didn't work out. I made a last-minute decision. I tried calling you, but—"

"You were so damned hell-bent to stay with this big, dumb fireman."

"Don't call him dumb. He isn't dumb. He's the smartest man I've ever known in my life."

"Well, then, why in the world are you doing this? Did something terrible happen? Did he hurt you?"

"Of course not. Of course he wouldn't hurt me. He's the gentlest man I've ever known."

Flo rubbed her forehead with her fingers, exasperated. "I'm sure I'll understand all this eventually." Chris shook her head, struggling with tears she had been alternately fighting and giving in to all day long. "Me," Flo said. "It's me. He can't take me. What a wimp. I knew he was a wimp all along."

"No, no, it isn't that. I mean, he is intimidated by you and your money, but it isn't anything personal. Not really."

"Well, then, so what? I'm not crazy about him, either. So what else is new? That's the way it goes, right? You don't like your aunt-in-law. Big deal."

"And the money."

"What about the money? Does the money matter? What matters is how people feel about each other, not how much they can spend. What happened? *When* did this happen?"

"Florence, *please*. Don't interrogate me. Please."

"All right. All right. Let's get my bags and go get a drink. We're going to be here for hours. Chris, when you go off the deep end, do you absolutely have to take everyone with you? Where is that stupid dog?"

"He kept the dog," she said.

"He *what?* He kept the kids' dog?"

"No, no, nothing like that. The dog was going to have to go to a kennel, and Carrie was upset, so Mike said he'd take care of Cheeks. He can ship him later or something— I don't know."

"He kept the dog so Carrie wouldn't be upset?" Flo asked.

"Yes, something like that. And I think he secretly liked the dog."

It took an hour to collect Flo's baggage and recheck it on the next flight. Then they found a corner table in an airport bar. The kids sipped soda. Flo had a Bloody Mary, but Chris couldn't drink; her stomach was still jumping. The kids, fortunately, were very resilient. They were excited about the plane ride, about Aunt Flo's house, and they were sure they would see Mike again soon. Chris was less sure, but she didn't tell them that.

"Now," Flo said, "let me see if I have this right. You are leaving because now that you have money of your own, he is intimidated by your ability to be completely independent of him? Is that it?"

"Yes," she said, blowing her nose. "It's just like with Steve—I mean Fred. Oh, damn, I'll never be able to think of him as Fred. It's just another way of using a person. I met Mike's needs by being needy."

"And you felt used?"

"No. Yes. I mean, I didn't feel *used*, but he was angry

about the money. Angry—can you imagine? He came right out and said it, too. He resented my money. He didn't want me to buy things for him anymore. He said he'd like it better if I couldn't."

"I know men who like having fat wives. It's testosterone poisoning. They're all defective."

Chris blew her nose again. Now that she was with Flo, the tears kept coming. "Well, everything was fine until he thought about going through life competing with my big bucks. It hurt his pride, I guess. It made him feel middle-class, less of a man. I wasn't prepared for that. Here was a man, I believed, who understood for better, for worse. I certainly can't change who and what I am. I *want* to contribute. I've worked hard at being able to contribute. If he can't take my inheritance, would he be any better at coping with a successful writer? It's all the same thing."

"Too bad he wasn't willing to work on that. I don't happen to think having money is the worst crime a person can commit."

"Well, he wanted to try, but I could tell he wouldn't be able to do it."

Flo was fairly slow to respond. "There were undoubtedly many other things."

"No. Everything else was wonderful."

"There is, obviously, some reason you *knew* he wouldn't be able to change?"

"It's part of his nature to want to do for people. When he doesn't feel needed, he doesn't feel loved. There would be a lot of trouble. I don't have the stamina for it."

"I see." Flo leisurely sipped her drink. "Well, you did the right thing, Chris," she said coyly. "He wasn't good enough for you."

"Yes, he was! For a while he was the best thing that ever happened to me. You were right—I should have learned more from my mistake with my ex-husband."

"And I'm relieved you did. Just in time, too. You'll be much happier on your own. You don't need that crap."

Tears spilled over. "Oh, I don't know about that. I've been on my own for a long time. It's been pretty lonely. For a while, having you and Mike—my old family, my new love—it was so hopeful, so— Well, I just don't see that I have any choice. Regardless of what I think I want, I don't want to raise my children in a home where there's so much conflict, so much restriction on who can do what."

"Lord knows you don't need conflict and restriction after all you've been through. If anyone deserves a happily-ever-after life, it's you. You'll be much better off. Besides, I'm sure he wouldn't change."

"I won't know that, of course, because I— Well, I just couldn't risk it, Flo. I'm tired of fighting."

"He's probably relieved that you're gone. In fact, I wouldn't doubt that he's actually pleased. After all, his life was the way he liked it before you came along."

"He was lonely. I don't think he realized how lonely—"

"But these complications with money are too much for a man like Mike," Flo said. "He likes everything simple. He wants to be the big man, water down the big fire, bring home the bacon…"

"He doesn't like to think about things for too long," Chris said.

"No, and solving this problem would take a while. He wouldn't like that."

"He likes to face things straightforwardly—"

"Can't talk about his feelings," Flo said. "Come on,

let's go down to the gate. This place is a madhouse. I don't want us to get bumped because of overbooking."

They began to gather up their things. They walked, a row of four, holding hands with the kids. "But he does talk about his feelings," Chris said. "He doesn't think he's very good at it, but really he is. I honestly don't know what was worse, when he was trying so hard not to say how he felt, or when he came right out and—"

"Oh, well, water over the dam," Flo said. "I'm so glad you've finally come to your senses. You'll never regret coming home. Not for one tiny second."

"I'm not going to move in with you, Flo. I'll stay until I can get my own place, and then—"

"You can stay as long as you like, of course, but I think you ought to know, I've made a few changes myself. Remember your little philosophy about betting you won't get cold? Ken and I have decided to get married."

Chris stopped dead in her tracks. "Really?"

"Uh-huh. Ken has always wanted to get married. I was the one who was too busy or too independent or, really, too scared. It's a big step. That's where I've been the past couple of days—with Ken…working this out." Flo nearly blushed.

"I'm happy for you, Flo. If you don't know him after all these years, you never will."

"I will never be accused of being impetuous, that's for sure. You're the one with that trait. I may be slow at deciding what I want, but you, darling, leap before you look. You couldn't possibly have known Mike very well."

"Oh-ho." Chris laughed. "Within a week I knew almost everything about him."

"He was holding back some vital information, though.

Like not being able to accept you the way you are. It's a good thing you saw that in time."

"I had no idea he was holding back. In fact, he always seemed to give everything that was inside of him."

"You must have been pretty shocked, then, by the way he laid it on you about the money thing. After thinking he was so stable, so transparent, hiding that little tidbit…" Flo stopped at the gate. "Look at this place. An hour and a half until our flight, and it's mobbed."

"He didn't hold back for long. He put it on the line. He said what was the matter with him and wanted to fight it out."

"You don't need that, Chris. Life is tough enough."

"I wouldn't have lasted long. I hate to fight."

"No self-respecting Palmer wants to fight. Fighting lacks decorum."

"You're a born fighter," Chris disagreed.

"I'm a born *winner*. I don't like laying everything on the line. Never have. Probably why I never married. Look at that—they're *already* offering to buy back tickets. Good thing you booked us first-class. We are checked in, aren't we?"

"He wanted to face it. He wanted to try to work on it. He didn't want to feel the way he felt. What can I do about what he feels? I can't change his feelings. I can't—"

"I think maybe we'd better get our seat assignments," Flo said, "or we might have a problem. Oh, I'm so relieved, Chris. You would have been simply miserable through the holidays."

"I didn't want to argue through Christmas…"

"Last night must have been hell for you," Flo said. "The big jerk."

"Last night was..." Chris stopped. Tears spilled down her cheeks again.

"I could just kill him for hurting you this way. Here I thought he was a generous, strong man who wasn't afraid of anything, but when it came down to the wire, he just couldn't—"

"He *did* give me everything he had. Even the bad stuff."

"Well, honey, don't defend the big jerk. I think you got out just in time. And I'm certainly relieved that we don't have to deal with that dog."

"The kids are really going to miss the—"

"I wondered what I was going to do about that dog. That is not the most agreeable animal. Growly thing."

"Oh, he's noisy, but inside he's—"

"Where there's smoke there's fire. That dog had a hidden agenda, like the fireman. You *think* he's just growling, you *think* he's perfectly safe, then wham. He'll bite someone someday."

Chris's eyes widened, and she slowly turned toward Flo. She stared at her aunt's profile for a minute. Then Flo turned, and Chris met her eyes. "That dog will not bite if he's not abused."

"If you say so. But we're not going to find out at the expense of my carpet."

"I never had a fight with Steve," Chris said.

"Why would he risk fighting with you?" Flo asked. "If you didn't get along, you might have taken your money and gone home. I imagine he was very amiable. But don't think about that now, Chris. You're coming home. That's all that matters, right?"

Chris looked closely at Flo's eyes. "What are you doing to me?" she asked.

Flo put an arm around Chris's shoulders. "I'm agreeing with you, Christine. Don't you recognize it?"

"Flo…"

"If you're very careful, perhaps you can manage a life as tidy and enviable as mine. And maybe you'll be ready to take a few chances, again, when you're, say, about forty-one. What do you say, kiddo? Shall we get our seat assignments? Go home?"

It had been dawn when Mike arrived at his cabin with Cheeks. He had cried a little, then decided self-pity should be against the law. He wished he could have been stronger—strong enough to help them pack, take them to the airport, all of that. But he couldn't do it. His disappointment was overwhelming, and he would have broken down in front of them. There were certain things that children should be spared.

So he and Cheeks put on the coffee and built a fire to warm up the cabin. Later, they went for a hike. Then visited the horses. Cleaned up the cabin a little, shoveled some snow, cooked a steak on the grill, even though it was freezing out.

"Here," he said to the dog, giving him half the steak. "I'll give you a pair of socks later. For dessert."

What the hell, he thought. It had been a crazy, lunatic thing to do from the start—bringing her home like that, telling her to stay a while because it felt good. Who did stupid things like that?

Still, it might have worked. If she hadn't had money? No. It might have worked if he had not been bothered by her money. Or it might still have worked if she could stand that he was bothered. He might have gotten over that. If he had kept his mouth shut about it.

But he couldn't really live like that. It was about those changes, about that one thing that you would change to make things turn out differently. What if you got mad about the way someone squeezed the toothpaste but you could never say so? And if you said so, a whole major fight erupted and it tore you apart?

His whole family argued. At the Cavanaugh house you had better be able to hold your own during an argument, or keep your mouth shut. When something was wrong, you had better be able to either say what it was, fix it, or learn to live with it. You didn't grow up in a household crammed full of people and everyone politely tiptoed around saying, "Pardon me," "Oh, excuse me, did I do that?"

And in the firehouse, where the men were bonded by hard work, cooperation, danger, things were resolved quickly, too. You couldn't let bad feelings fester; it was critical to solve problems or learn to accept the fact that people had both virtues and flaws. Big ones and little annoying ones.

But Chris hadn't lived that way. Hadn't she told him that? There were only four of them—her parents and Flo. She was either struggling to be independent or giving in to let someone take care of her. Or she ran away. So it was just as well, then, that she left when she did. She would have gone eventually, at the first sign of trouble...

It wasn't just the money that made them different. It was the regard they had for risk. She could risk her life trying to save a dumb laptop, but she couldn't risk the discomfort of an argument, a fight. What did she think? That husbands and wives didn't fight? He had thought she *was* a fighter. Turned out it was only sometimes.

"So, what one thing would you change?" he asked the dog. "What one thing that *you* could do would make everything different?" He nudged the dog with his toe. Cheeks growled. "That's what I thought you said. Nothing. Not a damn thing. Because it wouldn't have been better if I hadn't carried her out of the fire. I would have missed out on a lot of good things if I hadn't fallen in love with her, and if I *had* kept my mouth shut, I would have opened it eventually anyway. It all would have turned out the same. Like she said, you have to be accepted just the way you are. And that's the way I am. And that's the way she is."

And I hurt, he thought, because I feel loss. But I am better for what I had. I had my arms full again; I had love that was deep and rich. And because of that, maybe it will come back to me. Maybe I can have it again someday. Just maybe. My amnesia is over. *We did what we set out to do, huh?* When I'm stronger I'll send her an e-mail and tell her...thank you. Despite the problems, because of you I am better than I was. I had been in hiding too long, and I needed to learn what a mistake that was.

He heard the sound of a four-wheel-drive vehicle coming up the road. He suspected it might be someone from the Christiansons' house. Probably they saw the light and pitied him, alone. Or maybe they thought he was with Chris and the kids and were stopping by for a friendly chat. He wished they wouldn't. He couldn't refuse to answer the door. You don't do that in the mountains. He opened the door and watched the car come up the road. It wasn't the Christiansons' car. It was a big new Suburban. Oh, hell, he thought, recognizing his brother Chris's car. Why'd they do that? He had said he wanted to be alone.

Cheeks growled and wagged his tail. The Suburban stopped, but the headlights stayed on. The door on the driver's side opened, and she got out. He could barely make her out with the headlights shining in his eyes. She walked toward him slowly, until she stood in front of him.

He tried to keep from feeling that he'd won the Lotto. "Have you come back?" he asked her.

"I was wrong. So were you. I think that means we're not finished yet."

"Is that Chris's car?"

"Well—" she shrugged "—no matter how hard I try to be independent, I just keep asking for help, don't I?" Her smile faded, and she looked up at him, tears in her eyes.

He opened his arms to her, and she filled his embrace. "I love you," he said. "I don't care how hard it is, I love you."

She cried and laughed but would not let him go. He lifted her clear off the ground. "I'm going to keep you happy for a long time," she said, her voice breaking, "because there is so much I need from you."

They stood in their rocking embrace for such a long time that soon the children were beside them, greeting the dog, plowing past them into the house, but they didn't let go of each other. Mike's face was buried in her jacket collar. Until the door to the Suburban slammed and someone said, "Ugh. Oh, *Gawd.*"

He looked over Chris's shoulder to see Aunt Flo ruining her fashionable pumps in snow up to her ankles. She couldn't move, of course, with her heels jammed into the packed snow. He laughed. It was tough for him to admit to himself, but he was even a little glad to see Flo. It meant they were going to face it, head-on, and work it all out together. That included family. And he felt strongly about family.

He let go of Chris—it figured that the first reason he would have for letting her go would be Flo. This time, though, he felt firm in his faith that he would hold her again and again, and he went to Flo. He looked her up and down with his hands on his hips. Then he scooped her up in his arms and carried her to the house. She complained the whole way, about her shoes, the snow, the cold, the long drive. He put her down inside. And once inside she looked around in silence, probably awed by the rustic sparseness of it.

Mike put his arm around Chris's shoulders. They watched the activity, the welcome fullness of it all. Cheeks was running in circles, barking. The kids were already looking in the cupboards for treats before even taking off their coats, and Flo was removing her wet shoes in front of the fire, grumbling.

"Did you bring the twenty-two midgets?" he asked Chris.

"Nope. She's going to do this without the caterer. Cold turkey."

"This ought to be good."

And it was.

* * * * *

Visit her Author Profile page at Harlequin.com
for more titles!

A CHEF'S KISS

Nina Crespo

Chapter 1

Six years ago...

Philippa Gayle buttoned her white kitchen jacket and brushed lint from her black pants. As she looked in the dresser mirror, she put on her chef's beret, tucking in her short dark hair, and adjusted the band until the monogrammed name of her hopefully would-be employer, Coral Cove Resort, showed clearly in front.

Last month in New York, she'd gone through two intense rounds of interviews for the position of sous chef at the exclusive property, beating out a dozen candidates to make it to the final stage—a month-long, paid interview audition.

Leaving her position as a cook at a hotel in Charlotte, North Carolina, and traveling to the private island just off the coast of Barbados was a huge gamble. But at age twenty-two, having a shot at her dream job made the sacrifice worth it.

Knocks echoed in the small bungalow.

Philippa walked from the bedroom into the adjoining living room.

The sun, just peeping over the ocean horizon and shining through the sliding glass door along the side wall, added a soft glow to the blue-and-cream decor.

Outside on the deck, Dominic Crawford leaned on the doorjamb. The breeze swaying the surrounding palms and yellow, flowering cassia trees plastered his blue button-down to his solid chest and ruffled the hem hanging over his tan shorts.

She opened the door, and the smile edging up his mouth and the intensity of his gaze stole words.

Madagascar cinnamon... His eyes were the same rich color of the spice known for its understated flavor, but there was nothing subtle about Dominic. He was six feet plus of dark-haired, naturally deep-tanned gorgeous.

Backing Philippa inside the bungalow, he shut the door behind him, grasped hold of her waist and kissed her. He faintly tasted of one of her favorite things—hazelnut-flavored coffee.

Sliding her hands up and around his neck, she fell into a kiss that sped up her heart rate.

If only she could forget about everything and just spend the day with him. But she was due in for the Friday breakfast and lunch shifts in the kitchen. And she couldn't be late.

Philippa eased out of the kiss. "Don't you have a boat to catch?"

"I do." Dominic briefly pressed his mouth back to

hers. "But I think I left a shirt here. A long-sleeved white one. Did you find it?"

Sinking her teeth into her lower lip, she attempted to hide a smile. "I did. But it's wrinkled. I slept in it last night."

"You did, huh?" His grin, along with his short, dark, tapered hair, brought even more attention to his eyes and the taut angles of his face. "If you would have let me sleep here last night, you could have had me instead of the shirt."

Laughing, she half-heartedly held him back as he nuzzled her neck. Heat and the inviting scent of citrus and amber emanating from Dominic made him even harder to resist. "Sleep was the last thing on your mind. And what about Bailey?"

His older sister, Bailey, had arrived on the island yesterday morning. Dominic and Bailey were taking a water taxi from Coral Cove to Bridgetown, Barbados, that morning to meet their parents who were flying in from New York.

He huffed a chuckle. "She wouldn't have missed me. She was snoring in bed by nine last night. But I'm missing you already. I wish you were coming with us."

"Even if I didn't have to work, it would have been wrong for me to intrude. It's your day off, and your family came to spend it with you."

"Intrude? Not even close. Once my parents get to the hotel suite, they'll spend the rest of the day working until it's time for dinner with one of their prospective clients."

His parents were financial advisors and ran their own firm. Twenty-seven-year-old Bailey, older than Dominic by two years, worked for them.

Dominic laid his forehead to Philippa's. "You could have sat by the pool with me and Bailey."

And that would have been as thrilling as being tossed into the deep end.

During dinner at Dominic's bungalow last night, a conversation she'd had with Bailey had felt more like a comparison analysis where, in Bailey's eyes, she'd come up short.

Bailey had pointed out that Dominic had graduated from Johnson & Wales University's culinary arts program with honors. Philippa had completed a culinary arts program at a junior college in Atlanta.

Bailey had bragged about Dominic interning in kitchens with award-winning chefs during semester breaks, while Philippa had confessed to working part-time gigs from food trucks to pop-up restaurants to catering companies to help pay her tuition.

Later on, Bailey had been sitting on the back deck talking on the phone. She'd been unaware of Philippa walking outside to bring her a piece of ice-cream-topped chocolate cake.

Dominic has been with her since he's been on the island. It's no big deal. She's second-rate compared to him...

The self-doubt and negativity Bailey's remembered comment had stirred up then came back to Philippa now. Pushing them aside, she smiled up at Dominic. "It's just one day. We'll be together tomorrow."

"I know." He released an extended breath. "But we really need to talk."

Just as Philippa was going to ask what about, the reminder she'd set for work beeped on her phone.

Slipping from his grasp, she took it from her pocket

and turned off the alert. "I better go. I want to get in early. You know how Chef LeBlanc is. I have to be ready for anything."

As she turned to retrieve his shirt from the bedroom, Dominic lightly grasped her wrist and tugged her back to him. "You *are* ready for anything. Remember that."

His sincerity made it easy to forget that they were rivals for the sous chef position.

From the moment they'd said hello to one another at the airport, waiting at the gate for the flight from Charlotte to Bridgetown, they'd been drawn to each other. In the days that followed, every glance, smile and conversation neither of them wanted to end had brought them closer.

Sleeping together had just naturally happened. But they were keeping things professional in public, always waiting until they were in their private bungalows to indulge their attraction.

She brought him his shirt, then nudged him out the sliding door. Before she shut it after him, he snuck in one last kiss. "I'll call you."

"You better." A short time later, smiling, she left by the front door and hurried down the palm-tree-lined path.

Ahead of her, employees who'd arrived by water taxi from Barbados walked into a three-story yellow building with white shutters known as the Hub.

Located near the center of the island, it housed support services, administrative offices, a suite of rooms for the general manager and a kitchen providing twenty-four-hour room service.

Philippa and Dominic had been placed in two of the resort's smaller bungalows so they could get a taste of guest life, but whoever got the job would have to live in Barbados.

In the Hub, Philippa found Executive Chef Liza Le-Blanc on the delivery dock, checking over crates of produce.

The brown-skinned woman with family roots in New Orleans and Hawaii shifted her attention from the delivery man opening a crate of mangos to Philippa.

Philippa suppressed the urge to glance down and check if her uniform was in order. The other day, she'd missed tucking a strand of hair under her hat, and Chef LeBlanc had brought it to her attention.

Chef LeBlanc nodded to the delivery man that she would accept the mangos, but she waved away the crate of carambola. "It's nearly a full house. I hope you're prepared for a busy day."

"Yes, Chef. I'm ready."

"Good. I have paperwork to finish, so you'll be in charge this morning."

Nerves knotted and pulled inside of Philippa. Supervisory experience was one of the weakest areas on her résumé. This could be one of her last chances to impress Chef LeBlanc and the higher-ups with her leadership skills before they made their selection next week.

Philippa joined the staff in the heart of the well-equipped commercial kitchen.

Cooks prepared an array of orders from scrambled-egg combos to Bajan salt bread filled with succulent ham to thick, rich smoothies made with fresh fruit and vegetables.

Off to the side, butlers in crisp aqua-colored shirts and black knee-length shorts waited for the orders they would promptly deliver to their assigned guests.

During a lull in the service, she reviewed lunch tickets stacked in an in-box near the butler's station, searching for special requests. Today, they fell into the "none of this, less of that" variety.

Last week, they were more unconventional. One of the guests had requested a tuna melt made with blue cheese, drowned in hot sauce and served on crustless, extra hard, cinnamon-raisin toast every single day of their stay.

The sandwich had resembled a crime scene on a plate, but she'd added a carrot-rose garnish and personally handed the meal to a butler with a smile. The guests came first, and Coral Cove aimed to please.

A chime dinged on her phone tucked in the front pocket of her jacket.

The dark-haired butler standing next to Philippa sent her a slightly startled glance. "No personal distractions during a shift" was one of Chef LeBlanc's main rules and she'd just broken it.

Crap! Philippa fished out her phone.

On the screen was a selfie text from Dominic, smiling in the hotel pool with a green dinosaur floaty wrapped around his waist.

Barely suppressing a laugh, Philippa turned her phone to silent and put it back in her pocket. She missed him already. Once the interview audition was over, how would she handle not living just a bungalow away from him?

They hadn't talked about what would happen when the interview process was over. They'd stay in touch, wouldn't they? Was that what Dominic wanted to talk about?

At the end of her ten-hour shift, she removed her apron, tired and ready for a walk on the beach. Maybe she could catch Dominic before he went to dinner with his parents and find out what was on his mind.

"Philippa." Chef LeBlanc beckoned her.

Weariness followed Philippa to the corner office. Hopefully, a double shift wasn't in her future.

Chef LeBlanc sat behind the desk, her expression more stern than usual. "Have a seat."

Anxiety rippled through Philippa as she sat in the chair in front of the desk. Breakfast and lunch had gone smoothly. Was she in trouble for not remembering to turn off her phone?

"We received a complaint from bungalow five about their breakfast."

Chef LeBlanc slid an order ticket across the desk, and Philippa picked it up. "A tomato-and-spinach omelet and a high-protein, berry-and-kale smoothie. No added salt or sugar. I remember this one. I saw the omelet being prepared to order, and I made the smoothie myself. Was something missed?"

"The smoothie was supposed to be made with rice milk, but it was blended with soy."

An image of the red-lettered, soy milk container in her hand as she made the smoothie flashed into Philippa's mind. Her mouth went dry. "I'm so sorry. I'll apologize to the guest right away."

"It's too late for that. The guest in bungalow five is the daughter of Coral Cove's newest investor. She complained to her father, and he called the general manager. I tried to convince them to give you another chance, but I was outvoted. I'm sorry, but this incident has taken you out of the running for the position."

Not sure she'd heard her right, Philippa sputtered, "So…my audition is over?"

Empathy came into the other woman's eyes. "Yes, I'm afraid it is."

Disbelief stunned Philippa into silence. She swallowed against the tightening in her throat. "Thank you for the opportunity. Working with you has been a great experience."

"You were impressive. Don't hesitate to include this interview audition on your résumé. I'm happy to give you a recommendation."

Chef LeBlanc taking an interest in her future displaced some of Philippa's sadness. "Thank you."

"I also have some advice, if you're willing to hear it."

"I appreciate any guidance you're willing to give me."

Chef LeBlanc sat back in the chair. "Managing a top-notch kitchen is a full-time commitment that comes with rewards and sacrifices. The reward is having your talent and creativity appreciated. The sacrifice is having to put most of your focus on the job. That doesn't leave room for much else…especially a personal life."

Was Chef LeBlanc just giving her general advice or did she know about her relationship with Dominic?

Philippa couldn't tell as she met Chef LeBlanc's steady gaze. "Thank you. I'll keep that in mind."

In her bungalow, fighting back tears, Philippa packed her bags on the bed. Messing up a simple ingredient change on an order. How had she made such a rookie mistake? But her relationship with Dominic had nothing to do with it. For the past three weeks, other than her hair being out of place and forgetting to turn off her phone, she hadn't made one major slipup until that morning.

Philippa's phone rang on the dresser, and she caught a glimpse of the caller ID on the screen. *Dominic.*

She wasn't ready to talk to him yet, not without getting all emotional. And now wasn't the time to break down and cry.

Per the agreements her and Dominic had signed at the start of the interview audition, as the unselected candidate, she had two hours to pack her things and leave. Human resources had already booked her a hotel room in Bridgetown near the airport. Her flight left in the morning.

Philippa let the call go to voice mail, but fifteen minutes later, Dominic phoned again.

She answered.

"Philippa…" Relief filled Dominic's tone. "Are you okay? I ran into one of the butlers in town. They told me what happened. I can't believe they're ending your interview audition over one mistake."

"But it was a big one. The guest was a VIP, related to an important investor. But I shouldn't have messed up in the first place." If only she'd reviewed the order one more time. Stuffing down sadness and disappointment, she shoved her work boots into a tight space in her carry-on. "I have to go. I need to finish packing. The next water taxi leaves in thirty minutes."

"I'll be waiting for you when it docks."

"Aren't you going to dinner with your parents?"

"You're more important. I'm staying with you tonight… and, hopefully, past the weekend. You could change your flight and we can hang out in Bridgetown or wherever you want."

"Don't you have to work?"

"I can't return to the kitchen until I officially accept

the offer. I told Chef LeBlanc I needed a few days to think about it."

"But you're going to accept it, right?"

"Yes, but my answer can wait. We need to talk about us."

Spending a few days with him figuring out their relationship status did sound nice. And she could drown her sorrows in rum punch over not getting the job while helping him celebrate the offer from Chef LeBlanc. He was going to make a great sous chef. And someday, an even better executive chef.

Managing a top-notch kitchen is a full-time commitment... The sacrifice is having to put most of your focus on the job. That doesn't leave room for much else... especially a personal life...

Chef LeBlanc's words came back to Philippa. She'd assumed that guidance referred to her time at Coral Cove, but did it concern Dominic? He was about to accept an important supervisory position. According to Chef LeBlanc's advice, if he wanted to be successful, he couldn't afford the distraction of a relationship, especially a long-distance one. And if she wanted to achieve her dreams of running a top-notch kitchen one day... neither could she.

The truth plummeted inside of Philippa, and she sank down on the bed. "I can't stay."

"If you're worried about the cost of changing the ticket, I'll pay. You can return the favor when I'm traveling to see you."

"The cost of the ticket isn't the problem." Forming the words made Philippa's heart so heavy, she forced herself to breathe. "We had fun these past weeks. Trying to make it into something more is too complicated."

"Are you saying you want to end it?"

The image of Dominic smiling down at her that morning flooded into Philippa's mind. Had she known that would be the last time he'd hold her, she wouldn't have rushed the moment.

Philippa squeezed her eyes shut and willed the image away. "Yes."

Chapter 2

The present

Philippa bumped her hand against the white mug on her desk and coffee sloshed over the side. As she dabbed the spill with a napkin, the scent of the hazelnut-flavored brew intertwined with the smell of charred bread wafting into her office.

Burnt toast and spilled coffee—trouble is on the way...

She'd read that line in a thriller novel once. But for a restaurant, those two things weren't the kiss of death. Bad reviews were.

Philippa closed the labor report on the desktop in front of her and tossed the soggy napkin in the trash. She had a meeting in ten minutes, but she'd check in on the breakfast service first.

After slipping on the lime-green Birkenstock clogs

just under her chair, she stood, put her phone into the side pocket of her black cargo pants and picked up her black leather padfolio.

A quick glance at her reflection in the tinted window overlooking the kitchen of Pasture Lane Restaurant, located at Tillbridge Horse Stable and Guesthouse, confirmed her green-and-black headband held her dark locs in place.

Beyond the glass, cooks in charcoal-gray uniforms and black ball caps prepared omelets and pancakes in the center cooking island. On the other side of the red-tiled space, more cooks chopped fruit in the corner prep area and took pans of baked muffins and croissants from the stainless steel, double ovens built into the wall.

A kitchen helper removed burnt bread from a conveyer toaster and quickly put fresh slices in the machine.

Philippa walked to the front of the kitchen to her sous chef at the expediter station, monitoring orders from the servers on a digital screen. "Everything okay, Jeremy?"

"Yes, Chef." The sandy-haired guy in his early twenties, who was just as passionate about weight training as he was cooking, took his attention from the screen. His usual confidence reflected in his blue eyes and his smile. "We're past the rush. Things are slowing down now."

"Good. I've got a meeting in the dining room. Find me if you need me."

"Will do." He went back to clicking through tabs on the screen.

Reassured Friday morning's breakfast service wasn't going up in flames, Philippa made the mental switch to her upcoming nine-thirty consult with the event organizer who had flown in from LA to Maryland last night.

They were working on the plans for a fifty-person, private, advance-screening party for the futuristic Western, *Shadow Valley*, the movie that had been filmed at Tillbridge last year.

The Tillbridge family, who owned and managed the horse stable and guesthouse, were looking forward to the event and the soon-to-be-released movie. The film was not only good for business, but Tristan Tillbridge, one of the owners of the property, was married to Chloe Daniels, a lead actor in the film. Her visit to the stable early last year to research the part had led to the unlikely pair falling for each other.

But Cupid's arrow hadn't stopped there. His cousin and Philippa's best friend, Rina Tillbridge, had literally run into her stuntman soulmate, Scott Halsey, on the set one afternoon.

A few months later, Rina's sister, Zurie Tillbridge and deputy sheriff Mace Calderone, a family friend, had faked being engaged to hide Tristan and Chloe's secret wedding plans from the media. In the end, the two had discovered they weren't just pretending but were in love.

Tristan, Rina and Zurie had endured so much in the past, they deserved to find love. As the next generation of owners overseeing Tillbridge, they were finally getting a chance to rebuild their family's legacy and their own futures.

Philippa walked into the front of the restaurant and gave the casually dressed patrons occupying the tables a cursory glance. One person stood out in the pale, wood-floored space.

The event organizer, Rachel Everett, sat in a less-crowded area near the wall of glass. But unlike the other guests captivated by the sunny, springtime view of lush grass and trees beyond the wood deck, the slim strawberry blonde in a fashionable teal pantsuit remained absorbed in her phone.

Rachel still hadn't decided on the menu. And she'd turned down the offer of a tasting as part of their meeting. With the event just a month and a half away, they should have made more progress. Hopefully, this meeting would clear things up.

"Good morning, Ms. Everett." Philippa gave the event organizer a friendly smile.

A pleasant expression came over the young woman's face. "Chef Gayle—good morning. Thanks for meeting with me today. Again, I apologize for the short notice about my visit."

"Not a problem. I'm glad we're meeting in person to nail down the details." As Philippa sat down, she glanced at the untouched basket of breakfast pastries on the table. "Would you like to order breakfast?"

Rachel held up a half-full white ceramic cup. "No, thank you. I'm fine with just coffee."

After waiting a beat or two for Rachel to kick off the meeting, Philippa opened her padfolio and woke up her computer tablet. "Did you get a chance to look over the menu suggestions I sent?"

"I did," Rachel nodded. "They were…decent."

Decent? The word jabbed Philippa like the tip of a sharp knife. That's how leftover takeout was described, not her well-thought-out catering menu that had received high praise from customers.

Philippa moved past the lukewarm assessment. "If you have something else in mind, I'm happy to consider it. Or maybe we should squeeze in time for a menu tasting to make it easier to decide?"

"A menu tasting isn't necessary." Rachel's pert nose twitched. "The party just needs items with more…" The organizer's expression morphed from finicky to thrilled. "You're here!" Jumping to her feet, she hurried to someone behind Philippa.

"Sorry I'm late," he replied.

The man's deep, smooth voice rumbled through Philippa along with disbelief. *It couldn't be…* She looked over her shoulder, catching a glimpse of Dominic hugging Rachel.

Air squeezed out of Philippa's chest and her heart sped up.

The embrace ended, and Rachel laid her hand briefly on Dominic's forearm, just underneath the pushed-up sleeve of his burgundy shirt. "I thought you were arriving yesterday. What happened?"

Smiling, he tucked car keys into the front pocket of his jeans. "I had to take care of a last-minute VIP booking at the restaurant."

"Ooh." Rachel leaned in. "Who was it?"

Dominic's low chuckle raised goose bumps, destroying Philippa's hopes that maybe he was a hallucination. "You know I can't tell you those details."

"Can't?" Rachel gave a subtle eye roll. "More like won't."

Philippa faced forward as Dominic and Rachel exchanged small talk about his flight.

Was he working in the area? From Rachel's reaction, she'd been expecting him. What if Rachel introduced them? How should she respond? How would *he* respond?

Rachel's breezy laugh reached Philippa seconds before the planner and Dominic got to the table. "Anyway, you're just in time," Rachel said to Dominic. "Chef Gayle and I were discussing the menu for the party. She'll be working under you. I can't wait to hear your fabulous ideas."

Working under him? Hear *his* fabulous ideas? As the reason why Dominic was there struck Philippa, shock gave way to irritation. She looked up. "I thought I was in charge of the party?"

"There's been a small change. You do know who he is?" Rachel pointed to Dominic, who had a slightly stunned look on his face.

Did she know him? Star of the cooking show *Dinner with Dominic*, owner of the celebrated LA restaurant Frost & Flame, the author of two bestselling cookbooks and runner-up on the cooking reality show, *Best Chef Wins Los Angeles*, five years ago.

Like every other culinary arts professional who paid attention to the industry, Philippa had heard of Dominic's exploits. But she'd avoided watching his show or reading about him as much as humanly possible. Being with him had turned her life upside down in ways she'd never anticipated.

As she met Dominic's gaze, an echo of the passion, regret and the heartache she'd experienced after she'd left Coral Cove, because they'd been together, reverberated in her chest.

But that was in the past. She'd earned her way to where she was—at the top of *her* game—and no one was taking that away from her.

Philippa stood. "I know exactly who he is, and I don't care. I'm the executive chef here. I don't work under anyone."

Chapter 3

Dominic, still reeling over seeing Philippa after so many years, didn't know what to say. "Philippa...hold up..."

Ignoring him, she strode toward the double doors with two small windows located at the back of the dining area.

Dominic looked from Philippa to Rachel. "You didn't tell her I was involved with the party?"

Rachel held up her hand, holding back the censure. "It wasn't intentional. You coming on board for this event was a last-minute change. Holland just requested you two days ago."

Holland Ainsley, the director of *Shadow Valley*, was a big fan of his restaurant and was good friends with Bailey, who was his business manager. One call from Holland to Bailey, and the movie screening event at Tillbridge had been added to his schedule.

The papers he'd signed had mentioned a restaurant on the property but not the name of the chef. He'd assumed whoever was in charge was okay with the plan of him being there.

Invading another colleague's space was the last thing he'd ever anticipated happening. No, seeing Philippa was.

Frustration, on his and Philippa's behalf, raised tingles along the back of Dominic's neck, and he rubbed over the spot. "I don't care if it just happened. Someone should have given her a heads-up about my involvement. Or I should have been informed you hadn't talked to her about it."

"I couldn't mention it to her before you signed the contract, and it was only finalized last night. But would it have mattered? I take it you two have a history?"

Catching on that his silence meant he wasn't going to comment, Rachel sighed. "Fine. I'll handle it. When I meet with Zurie Tillbridge tomorrow, I'll make sure she knows that Chef Gayle is being difficult, and that you would prefer not to work with her."

"Don't." The firmness in his tone earned him a brow raise from Rachel. "I owe Philippa the professional courtesy of an explanation and an apology. Hopefully, she'll be willing to talk to me so we can come up with a solution that suits us both."

"If that's what you want. You're in charge of the party." Rachel slipped her tote from the back of the chair. "I'm on my way to New York to see another client. I'll be back here tomorrow morning for a meeting with Zurie. I need to know Chef Gayle's answer before then."

Rachel left, and as Dominic wove through the tables, headed for the kitchen, he received more than a few double takes from patrons.

People staring at him. It had started during *Best Chef Wins Los Angeles* and had become a constant now that he had his own show. Bailey always reminded him that it was a small price to pay for his success. Small or not, it still made him uncomfortable.

At the back of the dining room, a dark-haired server wearing a T-shirt printed with MY THERAPIST EATS HAY glanced at him as she cleared dirty dishes from a table. Recognition dawned in her widening eyes. She froze.

Hoping to break through the awkwardness, he flashed a fan-friendly smile. "Hi. Chef Gayle—is she in the kitchen?"

"Uh, yes." The server pointed behind her. "She's in there."

"Thanks."

He walked through the double doors, and as the staff noticed him, the noise lessened and activity slowed.

Near the center of the kitchen, Philippa stood at a metal table, chopping a chicken into pieces with a cleaver. "This isn't break time, people. Customers are waiting."

The staff reanimated, but many of them shot curious glances his way.

As he walked to Philippa, a recollection flashed through his mind of the two of them in the kitchen at Coral Cove. When they'd been in proximity, it had been difficult not to stare at her. Whenever she'd caught him, she'd smiled.

In the present, Philippa barely spared him a glance.

"Guests aren't allowed in here. Let your server know what you need. They'll take care of it."

"I'd like to finish our meeting."

"Our meeting is over." She separated a leg and a thigh on a cutting board with one sharp stroke. "I'm no longer involved with the party." A slight southern lilt flowed through her words. That only showed up in her tone when she was stressed or irritated.

"I'd like to talk about the party. Privately. In your office."

He looked pointedly around the kitchen, and she followed his glance to her staff pretending they weren't listening to their conversation.

"Jeremy," she called out.

A muscular, sandy-haired guy came over to the table. "Yes, Chef?"

"Take over for me, please." After sharing instructions for what she wanted done with the chicken, she washed her hands at a small sink against the side wall.

At the entrance to Philippa's office, Dominic let her go in first. The faint alluring scent of sweet almond and shea butter trailed after her.

Emerging memories of smoothing sunscreen on her skin at the beach drew his gaze to her fitted chef's jacket, hugging her curves. Her favorite beachwear had been a burgundy bikini and a matching wrap she used to knot low on her hips.

A vision of her on the beach, laughing and untying the wrap, billowing and clinging to her sun-kissed toned legs, flashed in his mind.

He wiped the image from his thoughts seconds before she turned and faced him. "I'm listening."

"I'm sorry you weren't told that I was involved. That

never should have happened. The director of *Shadow Valley*, Holland Ainsley, is a fan of my restaurant. She requested me."

Philippa's expression remained neutral.

Determined to get through to her, he added, "If I would have known you were here, I would have called to discuss partnering on the event."

"I appreciate the apology, but my answer is still no. Two head chefs trying to manage an event never goes well. It only complicates things."

Too complicated was the reason Philippa had given for why they needed to break up six years ago. "We used to make a good team."

"Yes. We were a good team. But we're in different places now."

An insistent knock sounded at the door.

Frustrated over the interruption and Philippa's unwillingness to budge from her position, Dominic released a harsh exhale as he opened it.

In the doorway, Jeremy looked to Philippa. "Sorry for bothering you, but the dish-machine repair reps just walked in. You said you wanted to talk to them when they showed up."

"Thanks, Jeremy, I'm on my way."

As Jeremy returned to the kitchen, Philippa started to follow him.

As she passed by, Dominic gently caught her wrist, and a magnetic pull of awareness sucked a breath out of him.

From Philippa's wide-eyed look, he wasn't the only one who'd felt it.

He released her and let his hand fall to his side. "I'm

staying here at the guesthouse until Sunday morning. Meet with me so we can work this out. Please."

Softness mixed with a hint of sadness came and went from her eyes so fast he almost missed it.

A resolute expression came over her face. "I'm sorry, Dominic, but I've already made up my mind. Good luck with the party."

Later on, Dominic walked into the single room with a king size bed, his conversation with Philippa in her office still on his mind.

As he set his black overnighter on top of the navy comforter and tossed his key card on the dresser, more distant memories settled in.

She'd insisted they were too different to work together. Six years ago, their differences had connected them.

At Coral Cove, he'd been more experienced as a leader than Philippa, but the variety of places she'd honed her skills and her passion for food had made her a formidable opponent. They'd quickly realized they could learn from each other and that they had a lot in common, sharing similar visions from taste profiles to the presentation of food.

Neither of them had questioned what would happen when one of them got the job and the other one didn't. From his perspective, all that had mattered was figuring out a way for them to stay together once Coral Cove's management made their decision.

He'd assumed Philippa was on the same page. Finding out she wasn't had been a gut punch.

You're right. It was just a temporary thing...

That's what he'd told Philippa. But for weeks after she left, he'd struggled to forget her.

One night, during that time, he'd even called her, but she didn't pick up. That's when he'd accepted their relationship was truly over.

As Dominic's thoughts came fully back to the present, the distant view outside the window of two horses grazing in a green pasture came into focus.

With increasing responsibilities and the odd relationship in his life, he'd moved on. But seeing Philippa today...

The question he'd wrestled with, after their breakup, needled his thoughts.

Had he really been the only one who'd felt something special had existed between them at Coral Cove?

As much as he hated to admit it, he still wanted to know.

Chapter 4

Philippa scrolled through the time sheets on the computer screen.

A management restructuring had happened a few months ago, and she was no longer in charge of the guesthouse *and* running Pasture Lane Restaurant. But having fewer employees didn't mean she wasn't busy. Running Pasture Lane involved ordering, maintaining inventory, reviewing the financials, monitoring the staff, and above all, making sure the guests were satisfied. She really didn't have time to worry about anything else...like Dominic being somewhere in the building.

A whisper of tingles moved over the place where Dominic had touched her wrist, and Philippa rubbed the sensation away.

She'd thought about reaching out to Zurie to see if she knew about him taking over. But why interrupt Zurie's day off over this? The director of the film asked for Dominic, and as far as them collaborating, what she'd told him was true.

With the screening party for *Shadow Valley* just weeks away, they didn't have time to solve their idea-and-style differences. It made sense that she should step aside. That's what she'd explain to anyone who asked.

Not working with him had nothing to do with their past. She was over it. She never thought of him. Unless someone brought him up.

The first year after Coral Cove had been the hardest. For months, her mind had kept recycling thoughts of the two of them on the island, and just when she laid that all to rest, he'd been a contestant on *Best Chef Wins Los Angeles*.

At the restaurant in DC where she'd worked at the time as a lead cook, the staff wouldn't stop talking about the show or him. Apparently, he'd been a fan favorite, known for his confident-with-a-hint-of-cocky attitude and how good he looked in his chef's uniform. And her coworkers had also been caught up in his relationship with one of the show's contestants.

It had hurt to hear he was with someone, but putting Chef LeBlanc's advice in place, about remaining focused on her job, had tuned most of it out. And staying on task had helped advance her into a sous chef position at the restaurant.

The only other time Dominic had come up was a couple of years ago when Rina had purchased his first cookbook and kept raving to her about it. Telling Rina that she knew him and wasn't interested in his recipes had been the first time she'd acknowledged their acquaintance to anyone.

And then there was Chloe's bachelorette party last year. *Dinner with Dominic* had come up in the conversation, and everyone had raved about him...except her. Actually, Rina had been the one to bring him up then, too.

Philippa's phone chimed on her desk with a familiar ringtone. It was Rina. Why wasn't she surprised? "Hey, what's up?"

"Don't 'what's up' me. Why didn't you call and tell me Dominic Crawford was in the area? I had to hear it from one of my customers."

"It couldn't have been that important since you're just calling me now."

"I just got the chance. I've been running around so much I can barely keep up with myself." As a co-owner of Tillbridge and the owner of Brewed Haven Cafe in the nearby town of Bolan, Rina stayed busy.

"How's the new online ordering system working out? Things must be booming."

"The last few days have been a little hectic, but it's nothing we can't handle. Now, stop trying to change the subject and tell me about Dominic. Why was he at Pasture Lane?"

"You honestly don't know?"

"Why should I?"

"He's preparing the food for the screening party."

"Really? No one told me, but I missed Monday's meeting with Zurie and Tristan. Are you excited to work with him?"

"We're not working together. I've been replaced by him."

"Replaced? Since when? Did Zurie tell you this?"

"No. I found out from the event planner this morning, but I'm fine with not being involved. Two head chefs—"

"Hold on."

A muffled conversation between Rina and someone else came through the line.

Rina returned. "I have to go. They need me. Come by the house for dinner tonight. I want to hear the full story about this thing between you and Dominic."

"There is no thing between me and Dominic."

"Okay, then come over and tell me about the thing that's *not* happening between you and Dominic. I'm making spaghetti Bolognese."

"With fresh garlic bread?"

"Do you really have to ask? Seven thirty good?"

Philippa mentally ran through her schedule. She'd have to go there straight from Tillbridge. "That works."

"See you then." Rina ended the call.

Mumbling to herself, Philippa laid her phone on the desk. "I do not have a thing with Dominic."

Philippa shone a flashlight into the darkness illuminating the garden in Rina's backyard. "Have you found them yet?"

"No." As Rina walked farther down the row of plants, the yellow tie holding her braids and the matching Brewed Haven T-shirt she wore with a pair of jeans reflected in the light. "I know I spotted some red peppers out here this morning. Where are they?"

Relaxing on the couch with a glass of wine, wearing her T-shirt and a pair of borrowed sweatpants from Rina's closet—that's how Philippa had envisioned waiting for the delicious dinner Rina had promised. Not gardening in the dark.

Philippa swatted a bug flying near her face. "Do we really need red peppers?"

"Yes."

Leaves rustled on the bushes near the back fence.

Philippa swung the light that direction. "What was that?"

"Relax. It's probably just a couple of raccoons. I saw them out here this morning...when I noticed the peppers."

Knowing Rina, being happily distracted by wildlife in her backyard was the reason she hadn't picked the darn peppers in the first place. "Hurry up or I'm giving the harmless, rabid raccoons the flashlight, and they can help you."

"As long as they hold the light steady. I won't mind. Found them." Rina sang out as she held up her claim.

"Good. Let's go." Philippa hiked across the yard toward the welcoming light shining from the white, two-story clapboard house.

Rina caught up with her. Humor was in her sepia eyes, and a wide smile covered her pretty brown face. "Why are you in a hurry to leave the garden? You always say fresh is best."

"Fresh vegetables are best, but normal people pick theirs in the daylight. Dinner better be worth braving the wild animals hiding out in your backyard."

Rina playfully nudged her arm. "You know it will be."

They went through the side door of the house into a small, lighted entryway.

Rina set the peppers on an empty built-in shelf, then pulled off her yellow boots with goofy-looking chickens printed on them.

After slipping off the pink-and-white, polka-dot garden boots Rina had loaned her, Philippa followed her down the hall into the beige-and-white, country-chic kitchen.

The delicious smell of tomatoes, basil and garlic hung in the air.

After they'd washed their hands, Rina stirred the meat sauce simmering on the stove.

Philippa rinsed off the peppers in the sink. Surprisingly, Rina hadn't leaped on the topic of Dominic already. If Rina didn't mention it, she wouldn't. As far as she was concerned, the matter was closed. He was cooking for the party, and she was steering clear of him.

"How do you want these cut?" Philippa asked.

"Julienne strips. They're going into the salad that's in the refrigerator. The way the plants are growing, I'm going to have to give some of the tomatoes and peppers away. That plant-food recipe the gardener at Sommersby shared with me is amazing. You really should have gone with us the other weekend. It was so relaxing."

Sommersby Farm Vineyard and Winery was located a few hours away from Tillbridge. Not only did they grow grapes and produce wine, but they also maintained a small orchard and a modest crop of seasonal vegetables that they served in the restaurant on the premises.

Philippa put the peppers on the white marble cutting board on the counter. "It was a couples' weekend for you and Scott and Zurie and Mace. Being there alone would have been awkward."

"I'm pretty sure you wouldn't have been alone. The gardener asked about you." Rina spread garlic-seasoned butter on the inside of a sliced baguette.

Philippa tried to picture him in her mind. "Is he the one I met at Brewed Haven?"

"You didn't just meet him. He asked you out. Too bad you didn't take him up on it. It might have made today a little less uncomfortable."

Philippa pulled a cutting knife from the butcher block. "What does the gardener have to do with today?"

"I just meant that if you would have been seeing someone, maybe your confrontation with Dominic wouldn't have been so dramatic."

"Dramatic? What are you talking about?"

"Someone told one of my servers that you told Dominic you wouldn't work with him if he was the last chef on Earth."

"What?" Philippa glanced at Rina. "Which someone is spreading that around?"

"It's not one particular person."

"Of course not." Philippa cut open a pepper.

It never was with gossip, and that was a huge part of the problem. Like the telephone game, the rumor started with one person, but by the time the story made the rounds, it was an insanely twisted version of the truth.

Rina popped the bread in the oven. "So I guess the part about you holding hands with him in your office isn't true either?"

"No, we…" Philippa paused in slicing the pepper. She and Dominic hadn't been holding hands. He'd been holding hers, sort of. But it could have looked like they were holding hands from outside her office. Especially since she hadn't pulled away. "What people are saying, it wasn't that way at all."

"But what went on today, does it have something to do with you and Dominic being in a past relationship?"

Philippa went back to cutting the peppers. She'd admitted only to Rina that she knew Dominic. Not that they'd been together. And still Rina's spidey-sense had homed in on something. "How long have you known?"

"For a while. Honestly, I guessed. Hearing Dominic's name always made you irritated or sad." Rina stood beside Philippa. "Whatever happened between the two of you, I could tell it went deep."

Gratefulness for Rina choosing not to pry despite what she suspected mixed with the need to finally tell the truth. "Six years ago, he and I were the last two candidates for a sous chef position at a private island resort. The interview audition was a month long, and we got close. I know. Don't say it. Getting involved with him under those circumstances wasn't smart."

"No judgment here. I'm sure getting together with him felt right at the time."

"It did. But it wasn't. I made a mistake with one of the guest's orders and was sent home a week early because of it."

"And you think the relationship was the cause?"

Philippa took the salad from the refrigerator and brought it to the counter. She hadn't thought so at first, but weeks after leaving the resort, it was clear. "Being with him impacted my future. I should have thought it through before getting involved with him."

"And now the party at Tillbridge has brought him back into your life. No wonder you don't want to be involved."

"No. Dominic is *not* back in my life. And I'm fine with him handling the party. It's better this way. Two head chefs trying to run things can be a pain. And I'm sure everyone will be a lot more excited about the event now that a well-known chef is preparing the food."

"I'll accept any reason you give, and so will Tristan and Zurie, but as far as everyone else..." Rina offered up a shrug. "You not being involved with the party might feed the belief that you hate him."

"I don't hate him." Philippa dropped the pepper strips into the bowl. "I just don't want to be..." *around him.*

Finishing the sentence in her head red-flagged the truth. Dominic had been her greatest weakness to date, and she wondered if he still was. What if the spark of awareness she'd felt when he'd touched her that morning mushroomed into something she couldn't ignore? What if she started remembering all of the things she'd worked so hard to forget?

Rina nudged Philippa's shoulder with hers. "Not wanting to work with your ex because it's too awkward is valid."

"But you're right. If I don't, it could fuel this silly rumor about me hating him and create more gossip. You know how I hate being involved in rumors."

Whispered conversations behind her back. Knowing smiles and innuendos. Even more-distorted versions of the truth being talked about around town.

Helplessness settled over Philippa. "What am I supposed to do?"

"I don't know what the right answer is, but I get it." Empathy showed in Rina's eyes. "My parents used to say tough choices are like a rainstorm. You can't stop it from coming, but you can decide how you're going to get through it."

Chapter 5

As Dominic talked on his phone to Bailey in California, he glanced out the window of the guest room at Tillbridge. Heavy gray thunderclouds shadowed the early morning sky. "I'm not doing the party."

"What?" Bailey's tone rose an octave. "You can't back out. We've already signed the contract."

"And I'm sure it has an out clause, just like every other contract you've negotiated for me."

"Of course it does." Bailey gave a derisive snort. "Did you really wake me up for this?"

Dressed in jeans, Dominic snagged a gray pullover from his overnight bag sitting on the bed. "I waited three hours to call you. I've been awake since 4:00 a.m., my time. I couldn't hold off any longer. Rachel needs to know I'm out of the event before her meeting at Tillbridge early today."

"We're not telling Rachel anything. You can't make a decision like this on a whim."

"I don't do things on a whim, and you know it. If the situation had been handled properly with Philippa in the first place, there wouldn't be a problem."

"Ahh, the truth emerges. I'd wondered how long it would take before she became an issue."

Dominic paused before putting on his shirt. Bailey knew about Philippa being there? "The only truth that's emerged is that you held back information from me. Why didn't you mention Philippa was the chef here before I signed?"

"What happened between you two was in the past and it was personal. Signing this contract is about what's taking place now—a business opportunity—and how much money is on the table."

Money. Was that all Bailey thought about? Sometimes he wondered if giving a damn about anything other than a lucrative contract had been completely removed from her DNA. As financial advisors, not even their parents were that single-minded about money. Was Bailey adopted?

"I don't care about the money." He sat on the bed to pull on his black high-tops. "I care about me being used in a way that treats Philippa unfairly. It wasn't right."

"Right or not, this situation isn't just about you anymore. Once you agreed to become involved, Holland and her people upped the ante for the event. It's gone from fifty to a hundred and fifty guests donating a lot of money to see the film plus an exclusive, deleted scene, added back in, just for this audience. She's giving the proceeds from the event to her scholarship fund for women in film. And we've made a bigger commitment, too. The production and creative teams have already moved forward with the plan to film farm-to-fork episodes of *Dinner with Dominic* in Maryland."

One of the things that had excited him about the screening party was the access to local farms near Tillbridge. He'd envisioned developing a menu for the event featuring fresh food and preservative-free ingredients sourced from the area. Tying the menu to a few special episodes of his show had been a perfect fit. Or at least it had been until the situation with Philippa.

Last night, he'd thought about taking another shot at changing her mind, but he kept coming back to her two-head-chefs-managing-an-event excuse. It was flimsy, and it pointed to one explanation that went beyond contracts. Philippa didn't want to work with him. Period.

He'd encountered jealousy and animosity from rivals, and he hadn't cared, but Philippa's refusal to collaborate… That struck in a way he couldn't just shake off.

"Look." Hints of exasperation hung in Bailey's tone. "Could the way you were brought on as the chef for this party been handled differently? Absolutely. Can I get you out of this contract and smooth things over with Holland by making a huge donation to her scholarship? Probably. But there are influential people in her circle who won't be so forgiving. When you first started out in LA, Holland endorsed you. Not returning the favor by doing this event will come across as—"

"Ungrateful."

"Or selfish. You're the chef everyone wants to hang out with. No one wants to be around the chef who has his own hit show but won't help film students in need."

"I am willing to help but not by doing the party. I'm sure you and the new publicity firm you just hired can put another spin on it." Or at least they should, considering how much he was paying them.

"We could try to swing it around with a few rumors about Philippa being the difficult ex-girlfriend. You not wanting to bring that type of negativity to a positive event would definitely gain you sympathy points."

"Whoa, hold up. You will not spread rumors about Philippa. Put the blame on me."

"And tarnish your reputation right before we're about to enter into contract negotiations for the show *and* drop the announcement about you opening a restaurant in Atlanta? Don't think so. I know the whole running-into-your-ex was a curveball, but you have to set that aside and think about our investors, along with everyone who supports the show."

People depending on him seemed to be the reasoning for every decision he made. Dominic closed his eyes a moment, trying to envision a time when that wasn't the case. He'd been carrying the responsibility so long, he couldn't.

"Well, then." Bailey yawned and gave a relaxed sigh. "I'm going to get a couple more hours of sleep. Think about the angles. I'll hold off on calling Rachel. Bye."

Bailey ended the call. From the lightness in her tone, she assumed she'd won the argument. Maybe she had.

His brand. His reputation. And what was believed about him, true or not, impacted the people around him and not just the ones he employed. Now it had affected Philippa, too. She'd been moved aside by Rachel so he could take over the movie event.

Fighting a tiredness that tempted him to lie back on the mattress, Dominic rose from the bed and grabbed his phone and wallet from the nightstand. Making decisions half asleep and hungry always made him cranky. He needed food and coffee.

Dominic went to the door. As he walked out, he pulled up short to avoid running into someone.

Surprise flitted across Philippa's face as she remained poised to knock. She lowered her hand. "You're here. Good."

Dressed for work in her chef's uniform, Philippa blew past him, and her alluring scent trailed after her.

She crossed to the other side of the room near the window and faced him. "I want to talk about us working together on the *Shadow Valley* screening party."

Confusion over why she was there, along with jetlag, made him slow on the uptake. "You said you weren't interested."

"I know, but I might be with a few stipulations."

They were negotiating. That was an improvement.

He shut the door. "What did you have in mind?"

Philippa paced near the window. "First, we oversee the production of assigned items with separate teams."

"That's reasonable. Splitting up the menu is more efficient." And from a who's-in-charge perspective, it would eliminate the issue of her working under him.

"Second. My staff is excited about the possibility of meeting you and maybe working with you during the party. Their eagerness is understandable, but it's also a distraction."

A distraction for them or her? He set his things on the dresser, leaned back against it and crossed his arms over his chest. "What's your solution for that?"

"Well, of course, I don't have a problem with members of my staff working the party. That was part of my plan, along with bringing over workers from the Brewed

Haven Cafe. But I think the excitement of you being around would die down if you did something special for the staff, like a cooking demo. You could answer their questions, and sign autographs."

So she wanted him to play the part of celebrity chef. It was an expectation he'd come to accept. But from the tension emanating from Philippa, she was the one playing at something. Was she not at ease with her suggestions, or was she not at ease with him?

Philippa paused, awaiting his response.

He shrugged. "I don't have a problem with that either."

"I also think trading sous chefs and lead cooks during the planning of and during the event itself would be an advantage. Our people are familiar with how we work. They can meet on our behalf, if we're busy, and help keep us in sync during the event. And having the experience of working with you is something my staff will be able to add to their résumé."

"Trading staff sounds like a good idea, too." Dominic uncrossed his arms and pushed away from the dresser. He ambled over to Philippa. "And I'm sure my sous chefs will find it just as beneficial to learn from you. Maybe they could team up with your people in Pasture Lane's kitchen a few nights while they're here. Experiencing how another operation works is always valuable."

"I don't have an issue with that."

"Good. It sounds like we've made progress." Dominic took a step closer.

As she stared back at him, softness filled her eyes, and he glimpsed the Philippa he used to know. The woman who'd been passionate about food and her convictions about life. A passion he'd felt whenever he'd kissed her and held her in his arms.

Philippa's gaze dropped from his. She intertwined her fingers in front of her so tightly, her skin grew taut over her hands.

Was she concerned about her proposition? He was on board with all of it. As if reacting to muscle memory, his own fingers slightly twitched with the urge to cup her cheek and reassure her they were in a good place in their new working relationship.

Dominic tucked his hands in his front pockets. "I'll let Bailey know what we've discussed. She'll ask Rachel to draw up a new contract outlining the terms. Unless you'd prefer to initiate things?"

"No, that's fine. But I do have one more thing to ask."

"Name it."

Philippa lifted her head. Resoluteness filled her expression. "This alliance is strictly professional. Our past doesn't factor into it. There's no need to talk about Coral Cove."

"That's fine with me. As a rule, I don't talk about my private life with other people."

"I don't just mean we won't discuss Coral Cove with other people. We won't talk about it with each other. Ever."

What she'd just spelled out about them working together, along with not talking about Coral Cove lined up in his thoughts, revealing a pattern. The terms she'd set minimized their contact, limited their communication or kept them apart.

Take the win... Bailey's practicality laced through the voice in his mind.

He'd gotten what he'd wanted—a solution that kept

his image intact, took care of everyone who depended on him and was also fair to Philippa.

But it didn't feel like a win. Avoiding their past or pretending it never existed felt like a betrayal of what they'd meant to each other six years ago.

But it was only a betrayal to him, wasn't it? Philippa hadn't felt the same way about their relationship. And he needed to accept that.

Taking physical steps away from Philippa and mental ones from their past, Dominic walked to the dresser for his phone. "If that's what you want. That's fine with me. I'll text Bailey now. You'll have a new contract by tomorrow."

Chapter 6

A week later, animated conversation traveled over the hustle and bustle of the kitchen into Philippa's office. She paused in working at her desk and looked out the window.

Cleaning up after Saturday brunch, the staff was more jovial than usual, their excitement palpable over what was taking place in a little over an hour. Dominic's cooking demo.

Jeremy and the dark-haired, lead line cook, Quinn, laughed as they conferred with Teale and Eve, the culinary producer and production designer for *Dinner with Dominic*.

The two women on Dominic's staff were setting up the demo and helping with the development of the menu for the private screening party. They had arrived earlier that week with the advance team to scout out locations to film segments of the show.

Teale, an upbeat twentysomething with short brown hair and a generous smile, had been the one to tell her they were filming episodes of *Dinner with Dominic* in the area.

The last time Philippa had spoken to Dominic was that past Saturday in his guest room at Tillbridge, when she'd outlined her terms for them working together.

He'd left the next day without saying goodbye, but as promised, the new contract had arrived on her desk. Once she'd signed it, things moved at lightning speed.

That Monday, the sous chefs Dominic had assigned to work with her for the movie screening event had called to introduce themselves.

An assistant also emailed Dominic's notes for the party. His farm-to-fork theme had reminded her of the conversations they'd had at Coral Cove about their dream restaurants. They'd envisioned visiting farms and local producers to find what they needed to create dishes full of natural flavor. Did he remember that?

But she'd never know if he did recall those moments, since they weren't talking about the past. Or maybe they weren't interacting directly at all. So far, their meetings, including the one tomorrow morning, were group meetings with him and his team.

He was keeping things strictly professional…just like she'd asked.

A sudden restlessness came over Philippa. The laughter reverberating through her office added to her aggravation. She needed to clear her head and stretch her legs.

She left her office and veered left instead of right. Walking past the dish room, she went out the side door at the rear of the kitchen. In the light-tiled, white-walled hallway, staff in blue coveralls navigated cleaning carts onto the service elevator.

Farther down, she shared a brief smile with a red-haired groundskeeper on a ladder, swapping out a flickering florescent light bulb.

She exited the hallway, entering a wide corridor behind the lobby of the guesthouse.

A couple examined tourist brochures in a gold-tiered literature stand.

Philippa amped up her smile to customer friendly and exchanged hellos with them.

She passed a shorter adjoining hallway where the business center, a meeting space and the fitness room were located. Up ahead on the left corner was the closed, glass double-door entrance to Pasture Lane Restaurant.

A green paper, printed with the notice that the restaurant was closed for the rest of the afternoon and would reopen for dinner at five, hung on the inside of the door. She should look in on the setup before Dominic arrived. But honestly, she probably didn't have to check. Earlier that day, everything had been ahead of schedule.

Jeremy, Quinn and Teale, all in their early twenties, had hit it off as soon as they'd met, and Eve, a Black woman in her fifties who radiated health and self-confidence, fit right in with them. They clicked as a team.

Jeremy and Teale were at the point of finishing each other's sentences…just like her and Dominic had at Coral Cove.

Not ready to go into the restaurant yet, Philippa kept going and made an immediate right.

Tile transitioned to polished dark-wood flooring.

Gold-framed paintings of horses running and grazing in rolling fields and near mountains hung on white walls.

Up ahead, close to a small seating area off to the side, Dominic smiled as he took pictures with a group of people.

He's already here... Philippa's heart stuttered with a spark of happiness. She reversed her steps around the corner.

Curiosity made her peek back at Dominic and the crowd.

The charcoal chef's jacket and pants he wore looked tailor-made for him. Paired with his dark boots, he made a sexy fashion statement.

The warmth of excitement blossomed inside of her. It wasn't that she was glad to see him. She was just happy that he was able to make it.

Philippa glanced down at her own lime-green chef's jacket and black pants. They didn't look new like Dominic's clothing. And her pants had a dusting of flour on them. She'd jumped in to make more Belgian waffle batter during brunch. Doing so had freed up a kitchen worker to start cleaning a bit earlier so they could be ready to attend the demo.

"Boo!" The unexpected greeting came with a tap on her shoulder.

Philippa barely stifled a shriek. "Rina, what the...?"

Dressed in her Brewed Haven T-shirt and jeans, Rina had undoubtedly come directly from the cafe. She laughed. "Who are we peeping at?"

"I wasn't peeping at anyone."

Rina squeezed past her to check for herself. "Oh, I see. You weren't peeping. You were drooling."

"I was not." Heat fused into Philippa's cheeks. "I

was on my way to the front desk, and when I saw him with guests, I didn't want to interrupt."

"All of them aren't guests. The woman pushing ahead of everyone, she works as a groomer at the doggie day care spa in Bolan. Wait, all the groomers from the spa are here, and the owner is, too. And that guy works at the wine shop."

"They must have camped out in the lobby and waited for him." Philippa looked over Rina's shoulder. "I'm surprised they got in. Zurie sent out a memo about extra security being around while Dominic and his team are here. They're supposed to control access to the guesthouse."

"Actually, I'm surprised the lobby isn't packed. I've been fielding questions about him all week. Good thing he's not the type who shies away from attention."

Dominic waited patiently as a middle-aged woman who worked at the dog spa pulled two of his cookbooks from her bag.

His smile was genuine and his demeanor easygoing as he signed them, then took more pictures and chatted with his fans.

Rina nudged her. "There's Zurie."

Crisp and efficient-looking in a white blouse, navy slacks and matching pumps, Zurie exuded an all-business mindset and a natural, inner radiance.

In her late thirties, she and Rina had the same delicate features. As she greeted a few of the locals, her dark hair swung near her shoulders.

Spotting Philippa and Rina, she walked over to them.

"I was just coming to find you," Zurie said to Philippa. "Did you hear the news?"

"No." Philippa glanced briefly to Rina for a clue, but she just offered up a shrug.

"Dominic and his people wanted more exposure for this afternoon. They leaked his arrival and handed out special passes for the demo."

"This was supposed to be for my staff. Something casual with minimum setup."

"I know." Zurie sighed. "By the time I heard about it, things were already in motion, so we just have to deal with the situation. It's only twenty to twenty-five people, but you have nothing to worry about. I was assured that Dominic's team would handle rearranging the set up."

Philippa held back a response. Whether or not Dominic's team were handling the adjustments wasn't the problem. The changes were made without anyone consulting her. And what about her staff? They were looking forward to having direct access to him. Had she known this was how Dominic and his team operated, she would have spelled out her definition of collaboration in the contract.

Philippa turned toward Pasture Lane. "I still better check on things."

Zurie laid a hand on Philippa's arm, stalling her departure. "They also scheduled a meet and greet with Mayor Ashford and some of the town's officials in the conference room after the demo."

Rina snorted a laugh. "By town officials, you mean his entire family. After last week's town hall meeting, you might need referees."

Referees? That didn't sound good. "Why? What happened?" Philippa asked.

"What didn't happen?" Zurie shook her head. "It all

started when the mayor's brother-in-law, who's on the school board, accused his ex, who just took a position in public works, of having the crosswalks painted off-white instead of bright white, and according to him they're crooked."

"He also said she did it just to annoy him," Rina added. "Forget about going to the movies for entertainment. Just bring a bag of popcorn to the next town hall meeting and pull up a seat."

"You got that right." Zurie gave Rina a knowing look. "Lately, the level of drama has been unbelievable."

Actually, it was highly believable. With many of the mayor's immediate and extended family holding key positions in Bolan, it wasn't the first time a meeting had resembled a family squabble. But they also loved to schmooze with important people. As a celebrity, Dominic was catnip for them.

"I'll make sure the meeting room is ready." Philippa put the task on her mental checklist.

"And there's one more thing," Zurie said. "Now that this is a bigger deal, someone needs to introduce Dominic before he starts the demo. Dominic's publicist and I think you should do it."

And the hits just keep on coming... "Why me?" Philippa asked. "I don't know him that well. Sure, we used to know each other, but that was a long time ago."

Zurie shot her a puzzled look. "You don't have to know him to read his bio. And you were the one who invited him to do this."

She'd asked him as part of their agreement. And she'd clearly spelled out the expectation. This demo was supposed to help decrease her staff's starry-eyed excitement over him, not increase his exposure.

Philippa glanced over her shoulder and ran into Dominic's gaze. He smiled at her, and she struggled to take her eyes off him.

Looking away, she broke from the trance. He was in celebrity-chef mode. Promoting himself. Doing his job. That smile had nothing to do with her.

Dominic's legs tensed as he suppressed the urge to go after Philippa. He adjusted his stance and smiled as he autographed one of his cookbooks for a fan.

Philippa had looked bothered, and he could probably guess why—the change of opening the cooking demo to the public.

This was Bailey and the new publicist's doing. He hadn't found out about the so-called "minor adjustment" until three hours ago, after his plane had landed at the airport in Baltimore.

He rarely got a moment that was less about him promoting his brand and more of a conversation about food, cooking techniques and career advice, like he and Philippa had outlined in their emails that past week. He'd been looking forward to the low-key demo. And seeing Philippa.

How had things gotten twisted around so damn fast with the demo?

Once again when he talked to her, he would have to apologize over something that shouldn't have happened. He would have rather started a conversation about her recommendations for the party. They were perfect.

Her suggestion to feature an upscale menu with a casual feel to reflect the mood of the event fit perfectly with the farm-to-fork theme he had in mind.

He'd longed to call Philippa and tell her that, and

work through a few details about the recipes with her, but he and Philippa weren't that close. They didn't brainstorm ideas anymore. She wanted to move through the next few weeks as if how they'd interacted before had never happened. That they'd never anticipated each other's thoughts and next steps like they were their own.

Right then, she probably thought he was on board with making the demo more about him and less about her staff. He needed her to know that it wasn't that way at all. Even though he wasn't happy about them ignoring their past, it was important to him that she was comfortable with their present working relationship. He had to talk to her before the demo started.

In between signing autographs, Dominic glanced around the area. Amber, the publicity assistant the firm sent down to handle the event—where was she?

Somehow Bailey had managed to clone herself as the young woman who was probably just a minute or two out of college, all the way down to her chin-length wavy hair. Amber had even given him Bailey's patented death stare before reminding him he couldn't walk away from the crowd on his own when he felt done with signing autographs. He had to wait for her to pull him out so he didn't come off as the bad guy.

Minutes later, he spotted the petite young Black woman wearing a plum-colored business suit. She was busy talking on her phone.

He gave a subtle head tilt toward Pasture Lane, letting her know he was ready to go.

She lifted her finger and nodded, indicating he needed to wait a minute.

Dominic smothered impatience and turned his attention to a woman with short dark hair and silver poodle earrings, nudging people aside to squeeze in beside him.

"Can I get a photo?" she asked.

"Of course." He leaned in closer to the woman, and as she took the picture with her phone, he flashed a camera-ready smile.

A few more photos and autographs later, Amber appeared at his side. She raised her voice above the hubbub reverberating around them. "Thank you for coming. Dominic has to prep for the demo now. Those of you with tickets should remain here in the lobby until the doors to the restaurant open."

A groan of disappointment rose from the crowd.

Dominic waved goodbye. "Thank you, and thanks for watching the show."

Uniformed security for Tillbridge deftly stepped between him and the crowd as he followed the young woman into Pasture Lane.

In the dining area, a long, blue-cloth-covered table with portable burners and a smokeless table grill had been set up toward the back along with metal cabinets for heated and chilled foods.

Bethany, the blonde servers' supervisor he'd met the last time he was there, worked with her people. They arranged the light wood tables, most of which were clustered near the demo area.

Teale, dressed in a black, logo embroidered *Dinner with Dominic* pullover and red-and-black chef's pants with a flame design, approached with a huge smile. "Good. You're here."

"And you can relax," Eve, also in the same-style crew uniform but with blue-and-black pants with a frost design, chimed in. "We're good to go with the changes.

We were also able to find the last-minute ingredients we needed in Pasture Lane's kitchen to make the peanut-crusted bourbon chicken and the no-bake cheesecake shooters."

"But it wasn't easy." Teale mocked wiping her brow. "We owe Jeremy big-time for helping us."

"Bourbon chicken and cheesecake shooters?" Dominic frowned. "Those recipes are from my cookbook. I'm featuring items from Frost & Flame's current menu."

"We had to make another minor adjustment." Amber interjected. "I know you were planning to talk more about technique in a restaurant setting, but now that we have the general public in the room, we need the focus to be more relatable, like what's in your cookbooks."

Dominic faced Amber. "Any other adjustments I need to know about?"

"Just a couple of small ones. VIPs will be at the front table to your right as you face the audience—the mayor and his wife, the head of the local chamber of commerce, the fire chief. And on the left, there will be a table with a couple of food reporters from DC and a local journalist and her photographer. The rest of the tables near you will be guests who are staying at Tillbridge and locals from the area. The restaurant staff will be in back. Oh, and as a surprise, we have cookbooks for the VIPs and special invites."

"Hold on," he said. "This demo was originally scheduled for the staff. Why are they sitting in the back?"

"The special invites have tickets. They're expecting the royal treatment."

Dominic barely held back his irritation. "The staff who just worked their tails off to serve brunch and then clean up so I could do this demo for them also deserve the royal treatment."

Amber offered an apologetic shrug. "I know it doesn't seem fair, but if we don't give the VIPs and special invites prime access, there could be a backlash. They could talk to the press."

Teale quirked a brow. "And what about the employees of this restaurant? You think they won't?"

Dominic stalled their conversation with a raised hand. "There's only one thing I care about. The promise I made to Chef Gayle, and we will deliver on it."

Amber opened her mouth as if to object, then her shoulders fell with an exhale. "Okay. I'll make it open seating, except the VIPs and journalists have to sit up front. But the cookbooks—we couldn't get a larger number here in time. I had to make an agreement with the bookstore in Bolan to borrow from their stock and replace them before your book signing there next week. Maybe we can take care of the staff later."

He shook his head. "Later isn't good enough. I don't want them treated like they're second-class to everyone else."

"I may have a solution for the cookbook situation," Eve spoke to Amber. "Why don't we talk about it and let these two work on the specifics for the demo?"

As Eve guided Amber away, Dominic released a measured breath.

Teale studied him. "You okay?"

"I've been better. I know this situation has taken up a lot of your time. When you and Eve volunteered to handle this demo for me, I didn't anticipate things going sideways."

"Really?" Teale laughed. "We absolutely did. Last-minute details always pop up when publicity is involved."

Her positive attitude restored a bit of his optimism. "Thanks for rolling with the changes."

Eve and Teale's ability to handle challenges was what made them good at their jobs.

They'd been with him for over three years, almost from the start of *Dinner with Dominic*, and had been instrumental in helping him establish the basic premise of the show. Him and interesting guests, such as creatives, adventurers and innovators, cooking a meal together at the guest's house and talking about life and experiences. Their conversations explored a range of topics. Ways to make a difference in the world. Comic book icons. The dos and don'ts of dating. What makes life an adventure? Is it okay to be insecure about today and optimistic about tomorrow? Best movie lines ever.

The episode always ended with him, the guest and a few friends kicking back and enjoying the food they'd prepared.

Teale's creative vision was instrumental in coming up with food-and-drink themes to match the topics of the show. She also assisted with development of Frost & Flame's seasonal menus.

Eve, the organization whiz, made sure they had the right cooking tools, equipment and ingredients as well as dishes for showcasing the food.

Minutes later, Teale had him up to speed on the setup for preparing the chicken dish and cheesecake shooters along with the brown-butter lime shrimp that had originally been on the demo menu.

Jeremy walked out of the kitchen with a bowl of parsley. "Hey, Chef." He spoke to Dominic, but his gaze quickly settled on Teale. "You mentioned you might need more of this. I found some in the prep walk-in. We've got more coming in tomorrow."

"Great. Thanks." Teale beamed up at Jeremy.

"You're welcome. I'm happy to help." Jeremy grinned back as he followed her to one of the food cabinets to put the parsley away.

Dominic suppressed a wry chuckle.

The sous chef wouldn't be the first to become distracted by Teale. Hopefully, the guy wouldn't have issues concentrating over the next few weeks. Otherwise, Philippa might not be happy about that. Where was she?

Dominic cleared his throat as he walked over and interrupted them. "Have either of you seen Chef Gayle?"

"I think she's in her office," Jeremy replied. "But the blinds are closed. That usually means she doesn't want to be disturbed."

But this was his only chance for a quick check-in with Philippa before the demo started. With all the unexpected shifts in the presentation, letting her know that despite the addition of an outside audience, her people would have most of his attention was worth bothering her about.

Amber strode over to him. "I have a compromise. I got my hands on some numbered tickets. We'll hold a drawing for a few of the cookbooks. After the demo, the VIPs will get some one-on-one time with you in the meeting room down the hall. You'll autograph the cookbooks I've set aside for them, take some pictures and then meet with the journalists."

"That sounds reasonable." Dominic glanced back at the double doors leading to the kitchen. There went his chance to talk to Philippa.

"Good. The cookbooks for the giveaway are in an admin office. You need to autograph them with a generic signature."

Dominic followed Amber. The give-and-take of satisfying the public and the press, that was his part of the compromise for the demo. But so was making sure Philippa was satisfied. Hopefully, he could accomplish both.

Chapter 7

Philippa fastened the last black button on her crisp new lime-green kitchen jacket, then pulled down the hem with a snap. So much for a simple staff presentation. Not only was she expected to introduce Dominic, per Zurie's request, she now had to stay for the entire demonstration and possibly hang out afterward with him and the VIPs.

The change of events also interfered with the plan of her taking care of prep for that night's main dinner entrées. She'd wanted to prevent her cooks from having to scramble to get things ready after Dominic's demo.

She didn't have time for this type of Hollywood-style hype. He had a large team to do the work on his show and at his restaurant. She was a chef in charge of a busy restaurant with a modest-sized staff. Something Dominic and his people obviously hadn't taken into consideration when they upscaled the event.

Philippa snatched the empty packaging for the jacket from her desk. Underneath it was the bio for Dominic that his publicist had dropped off not too long ago.

Chef extraordinaire. Bestselling author. Star of an acclaimed cooking show. A pampered chef focused on his public persona. Was that who she was dealing with for the next few weeks?

She tossed the packaging in the trash and picked up the bio. After opening the blinds covering the window, she stepped out of her office.

A few of the staff walked by.

"I don't care what he makes," one of the blonde servers said to a thin, lanky kitchen helper. "I just want to hear his voice as he describes it. He could make mud pies sound irresistible."

Philippa kept her face neutral as she followed behind them, but inside, she gave an inner eye roll.

"I'm just glad he's not a disappointment in person, like some celebrities," the kitchen helper responded. "The way he stood up for us about where we could sit in the dining room proves he actually cares about people who work in the kitchen."

Stood up for them? Was there not enough seats? When she'd checked on things with Dominic's team and her staff, they'd said everything was good.

Philippa flagged down Quinn, who was walking past.

As usual, whenever Philippa talked to her, a slightly startled look came into the young woman's wide gray eyes. "Yes, Chef."

"I heard something about there being a problem with seating for the demo," Philippa said as she and Quinn walked toward the dining room. "Is everything okay?"

"Oh, yes, it's fine now." Quinn nodded quickly as she

smoothed a strand of curly ebony hair behind her ear. "There was just some mix-up with the publicity person. She said all the Pasture Lane employees would have to sit in the back and let everyone else sit up front. But Dominic set her straight. And Eve said we're getting some cool *Dinner with Dominic* swag next week. Kitchen towels, water bottles, that kind of stuff."

"Oh? That's nice." When she and Dominic had talked about the demo, he hadn't mentioned giving her people swag.

"It is. It's so exciting that he's here. I can't wait to see what he's cooking for us today."

As Quinn rushed into the dining room, Philippa hung back and peered through the window near the top of the right-hand door.

Her staff sat intermingled with the rest of the attendees.

"How does it look out there?"

The resonant tone of Dominic's voice coming from behind her ignited a frisson of awareness that moved along Philippa's spine and tingled across her nape.

"It's a full house." She calmed an unsteady breath and faced him.

Up close, he looked even better than he had in the lobby. But hints of fatigue were in his eyes. Last week, he'd flown in after working at his restaurant the night before. Had he done the same this weekend? She hadn't taken his present work schedule into consideration when she'd asked him to do the demo.

"Thank you…"

"I'm sorry…"

They both spoke at the same time.

Dominic gestured for her to speak first.

"I appreciate you adding this to your full schedule. And for making sure my staff have front-row seats. If they weren't already fans of chef extraordinaire, Dominic Crawford, they are now."

He grimaced. "Chef extraordinaire?"

She'd meant to tease him, but from his slight wince, her attempt had fallen flat. "That didn't come out right. I didn't mean it in a bad way." Philippa held up the paper in her hand. "I was just referring to the intro Amber gave me."

"I should have guessed." He smiled, but as he glanced at the paper a shadow of discomfort moved across his face. "You don't have to say all that. Owner of Frost & Flame is fine."

"And have Amber come after me? No, thank you."

Dominic huffed a low chuckle. "Yeah, she's insistent." He took a step forward and the subtle notes of his cologne wafted into the space between them. "About the changes with the demo. I—"

The door opened behind Philippa, pitching her forward, and her hand with the paper landed on his solid chest.

Dominic took hold of her arms. "You okay?"

As she looked into his eyes, familiarity washed over her. The automatic desire to lean into him almost overwhelmed her.

Amber peeked past the door. "Chef Gayle, good. You're right where you're supposed to be."

Averting her gaze from his, Philippa moved out of Dominic's grasp. "Is it time?" The high pitch of her voice made her clear her throat.

"Almost. We're still waiting on the mayor," Amber

replied. "I'll tap on the door when he's arrived. Oh, wait. He just walked in…"

"Good. He's here." Heart tripping in her chest, Philippa slipped past Amber and hurried out the door.

The mayor settled into a chair at a table on the right.

As more people in the audience started to notice her, noise decreased in the room.

Philippa plastered on a smile. "Good afternoon, everyone. Welcome to today's demo." She willed her fingers to open, unclenching Dominic's bio in her hand. "Chef extraordinaire, Dominic Crawford…"

He definitely felt extraordinary a minute ago… Giving herself a mental shake, she put aside the memory of how hard his chest had felt and his heat seeping into her palm.

When she finished reading the bio, the audience applauded, and she moved closer to the side wall.

Dominic came out the double doors of the kitchen. Smiling, he walked behind the table set up for the demonstration. "Alright. Are we ready?"

"Yes," some members of the audience responded, while others cheered and clapped louder.

Rina came up beside Philippa and deftly nudged her toward an empty table.

"What are you doing?"

"Saving you from yourself and a ton of rumors. You look like you're about to make a run for it."

"No, I don't."

"Tell that to your face."

As they sat down, Philippa flashed a cheery smile. "Is this better?"

"In a stalker-clown kind of way."

"I can't win with you. But how I look doesn't matter. No one in this room is here to see me. They're here for him."

Exuding magnetic charm and swagger, Dominic picked up a sauté pan and set it on one of the burners. "Alright. Let's do this. I'm going to make you two of my favorite dishes. And then I'm going to top it off with something sweet. First up, peanut-crusted bourbon chicken. The key to making good food is quality ingredients and seasonings that enhance their natural flavor."

Dominic chopped, cut and mixed—a perfectly choreographed dance that he explained step-by-step.

Philippa couldn't stop herself from being drawn in as she watched him. Her kitchen helper had been right. The smooth, confident tone of his voice had an almost seductive quality that made his description of the food sound incredible.

Dominic took the browned chicken from the skillet and placed it in a shallow baking pan. "This needs to finish cooking in the oven." He handed the pan to Teale. "We'll sample this in about twenty minutes. Next up is a dish that's popular at Frost & Flame—brown-butter lime shrimp with Carolina Gold rice grits…"

That dish sounded familiar. Years ago, Dominic had been perfecting recipes that he'd jotted down in a notebook. She used to tease him about how many times he'd tweaked the brown-butter-and-citrus combination for multiple seafood recipes.

Soon, a citrusy, buttery scent filled the air. It was as if she could taste the tang of the lime juice Dominic mixed in with the nutty, rich taste of the browned butter.

A short time later, samples of both entrées were passed to the audience.

Philippa immediately took a bite of the shrimp dish.

The reality of the flavors she'd imagined with the shrimp and the creamy risotto-like texture of the rice grits lifted her to a state of food bliss. And the herbs—he'd figured out the right combination.

Happiness for him made her smile.

Rina nudged her. "I know, right? You can't help but smile, eating this food."

A smile and the hmm... What did he used to say? *If you get those two things from someone after they've taken the first bite, you know you've gotten it right?*

As Dominic whipped up the chocolate cheesecake shooters, he opened the floor to Q&A.

"What inspired the theme for your restaurant?" someone in the audience asked.

"Years ago, I worked at a resort on the beach. The sunrises looked like fire hovering over the crystal-blue waves. It reminded me of fire and ice..."

Just like with the shrimp, another memory emerged in Philippa's mind of her and Dominic sitting on the beach together at sunrise, snuggled in a blanket. She could see his vision—the foam on the waves of the blue ocean had looked like ice under the fiery-orange rays of the sun.

While the island had awakened, they'd talked about everything, including wanting their own restaurants. New York, DC, Miami, Atlanta. Those were the places they'd envisioned themselves carving out their futures. Not Hollywood or a small town outside Baltimore. They'd made plans but the unexpected had unplanned their dreams.

"Chef Crawford. I'm Anna Ashford, senior reporter for the *Bolan Town Talk*."

The mayor's sister-in-law, a blonde in her late thirties, wore what she considered her uniform, a dark blazer with pushed-up sleeves over a T-shirt. Today, she'd paired it with jeans, and no doubt she also had on boots that looked new but were artfully worn as if she'd traveled miles in them instead of just up and down the streets of Bolan.

"I'm one of the few who has access to the private movie screening." Anna's attitude oozed with privilege. "I'd love to know if any of the items you prepared today will be served at the party?"

"Senior reporter?" Philippa whispered. "Isn't she the only reporter?"

"I guess she gave herself a promotion," Rina whispered as she got up. "And as much as I would love to stay and hear her riveting questions, I have to get back to Brewed Haven. See you later."

"Bye." Philippa gave Rina a small wave. No one said she had to stay for this part of the demo. Maybe she could escape, too.

Anna continued to dominate the Q&A. "How does it feel to be reunited with our very own Chef Gayle? That private island resort you just mentioned. Weren't the two of you there—together?"

Philippa froze midrise from the chair. Surprise and unease halted the air in her chest. What had Anna dug up about them? Whatever it was, he had to shut it down. Completely. As the audience's attention shifted between her and Dominic, Philippa sought out his gaze.

His attention remained on Anna as he flashed an affable smile. "Yes, Chef Gayle and I were both at Coral Cove. As far as the screening party—it's always a privilege to collaborate with a colleague and a talented chef."

Both at Coral Cove? Why had he mentioned the name

of the resort? All he'd done was pour gasoline on the gossip fire Anna was trying to start.

"Well," Amber interrupted, "unfortunately, our time has come to an end. Let's show some appreciation for Chef Dominic Crawford."

The audience applauded.

Philippa stood, planning to leave the restaurant by the front, avoiding Anna or anyone else with questions.

A few steps from the table, Amber zoomed in front of Philippa. A tight smile cut across her face. "Chef Gayle, would you mind coming with me please? I really need to talk to you about the setup for the meet and greet."

"I was just going there now." Philippa pointed to the front exit.

"We should go through the kitchen." Amber laid a hand on her back and nudged her that direction.

Their speed walk was a blur as the crowd got out of the way.

Annoying Anna moved toward them, took one look at Amber's face and backed up.

Inside the kitchen, Amber led the way to the back past the dish room and out the side door.

Dominic stood in the corridor.

His gaze met Philippa's. Before she could question what was going on, Amber motioned that they should walk farther down. They stopped near a corner at the end of the hall, and Amber pinned them both to the wall with a stare. She reminded Philippa of someone, but who?

"What is Coral Cove and what happened there?" Amber asked.

Dominic gestured to Philippa that she should answer.

Caught off guard, she responded with the first thing

that came to mind, "Well…it's a resort. We worked there…"

"It *was* a resort," Dominic clarified. "Now it's an aquatic research station."

Philippa tried to imagine the elegant resort no longer existing. "Really? When did that happen?"

"Two years ago," he replied. "The owners—"

Waving her hand, Amber cut him off. "I don't need to know the history of the place. What went on with the two of you while you were there? Were you just friends or more than friends?"

"We were more than friends," Dominic replied.

"Just friends," Philippa asserted at the same time. Did he forget that they weren't talking about their relationship?

Amber shook her head. "No. You need to decide what you want that local reporter and every media outlet covering celebrity entertainment to know. Until you get your stories straight, if anyone asks you about Coral Cove, your answer is you were both there. You're old acquaintances, and it's a privilege to be able to collaborate with each other as colleagues. Period. Don't elaborate." She looked to Dominic. "During the meet and greet, I'll handle the journalist from the *Bolan Town Talk*."

"Got it. Can you give me and Philippa a minute?"

"Sure. But make it quick." Amber walked down the corridor, the sharp clicks of her heels echoing on the tiles.

"What was that?" Philippa asked.

"That's a publicist's assistant who's ticked off that we were caught off guard by a journalist."

"She's not the only one." Philippa faced him. "Why did you give Anna the name of the resort?"

"I didn't. She mentioned private island resort. Nine times out of ten, she already knew the name, and if she didn't, as a journalist, she was going to find out."

"Anna isn't a journalist. She's a nosy woman who eats gossip for breakfast, lunch, dinner and a snack, and all you've done is given her an appetite for more about us." As Philippa paced, she lifted her hands then let them drop back to her sides. "The reason I agreed for us to work together was to *not* bring attention to us or our past relationship. And now you've ruined everything."

Dominic's brows shot up. "I ruined everything? You mean your master plan of us working together *not* bringing attention to us? Exactly how was that supposed to work?"

"It was a master plan." His skeptical expression fueled an outburst. "Don't give me that look. You don't know what it's like to live in a small community. Nothing ever happens here, and when it does, like a celebrity chef coming to town, everyone is all over it. That may be great for you, but as someone who knows you, that sucks for me. Especially since there's some silly rumor floating around about me hating you and us holding hands in my office yesterday."

"You think I don't understand?" A laugh shot out of him, but irritation flickered in his eyes. "Los Angeles is the ultimate big little town when it comes to rumors. It's the reason why I have a publicity firm on my payroll. One that could have handled this if you and I would have talked about Coral Cove in the first place."

"Oh, so this is my fault."

"It's not about fault. It's about fact."

"Fact? What fact?"

Dominic strode over to Philippa.

He leaned in near her cheek, and she immediately detected the exact notes of citrus in his cologne. *Mandarin.* "The fact that we can't forget about our past."

Opening her mouth to object, she drew in a deep breath, and her breasts nearly grazed his chest. Philippa's traitorous heart leaped with excitement.

Dominic moved back to look at her face, and the intense longing in his brought a rush of warmth to her cheeks.

Dropping her gaze, she stalled on his full, kissable mouth. Her own tingled in remembrance of the firm pressure of his lips, teasing and coaxing hers to open to him. The slow drift and glide of his tongue, drawing her into a deepening kiss. As desire pooled inside of her, Philippa dragged her gaze back up to his.

Want and frustration were in Dominic's eyes as he quirked a brow with an I-told-you-so expression.

A buzzing vibration came from near his hip.

Shaking his head as if in answer to an internal question, he stepped back and took his phone from his pocket. "It's Amber."

Philippa took several steps back as she fiddled with her collar, letting in a bit of cool air. "The VIP meet and greet. You should go."

Dominic moved as if to take a step forward, but as if sensing she needed distance, he paused. "We can't pretend it didn't happen. Coral Cove…us."

He was right.

Philippa tamped down the last of her weakening resistance. "When do you want to talk?"

Chapter 8

Dominic sat on the end of the rectangular table in the meeting room at the guesthouse.

Teale, Eve and Matt, one of the show's location scouts, sat with him.

The meet and greet with the VIPs after the demo had ended an hour and a half ago. After the gathering, they'd commandeered the room to discuss plans for the farm-to-fork episodes of *Dinner with Dominic*.

As Matt went over the details of the locations where they were planning to film segments of the show, Dominic adjusted his position in the navy-padded chair and glanced at his phone.

5:15 p.m.

Philippa was supposed to meet him at seven, but she'd sent a text earlier letting him know that she would be late. Something had come up at Pasture Lane. Would she make it, or was this her way of trying to get out of talking with him?

She'd been so adamant about them not speaking about Coral Cove when she'd agreed to them working together. After the local reporter's questions, hopefully she realized they couldn't avoid the topic any longer. And then there was what had happened between them in the hallway after the demo.

He'd only planned to challenge her belief that nothing existed between them. To give her a small nudge by proving a point. But then he'd almost kissed her. It had taken everything inside of him not to slide his arms around Philippa and bring her closer. From the look on her face, she'd been willing to go past that line, but he wasn't. Not as long as she was in denial about their situation.

Matt shifted his dark-rimmed glasses from the top of his lightly tanned, shaved head to his thin nose. He flipped through notes on his tablet. "The second bee farm is further away from here, but it's worth the effort. Easier access, more room to set up our trailers. And based on what we discussed at our last meeting, it ticks more of the boxes as far as what we want to feature with the farm-to-fork theme—hive science, an organic garden, honey tasting. Oh, and the owner claims she's psychic."

Teale gave him a WTH look. "And one *other* benefit to consider is they have the best chili-infused honey I've ever tasted. I'm definitely seeing it woven into the screening menu."

"Chili-infused honey at a psychic-owned bee farm. Can't pass that up." Dominic chuckled. "Just make sure the permit situation looks good. Since we're on a tight schedule, we don't want to invest time and energy into something that's a long shot instead of closer to a sure thing. I'm sure Jill feels the same way."

Jill Allen, the director of the show along with Brianne, the assistant director, had both expressed concerns about the timeframe for filming the episodes.

"Locations is on it," Matt replied, referring to the team led by his boss, the locations manager. "But getting permits and fees on all the places on our list looks really promising."

"Oh?" Teale raised a brow. "Did the bee psychic tell you that?"

"No." Matt grinned. "I just don't think we'll have any hiccups."

Teale, Eve and Dominic joined Matt in knocking on the table to ward off bad luck.

Next, Eve briefed them on the status of the studio kitchen.

At first, the production team had tossed around the idea of taping the informational segments at the bee farm and other locations in Maryland and then filming the actual cooking segments in LA. But doing it all in Maryland was a better fit since they were planning to use local ingredients and would have to ship them to LA for the cooking segments.

Trying to find a suitable place had been difficult. But Eve and Teale, who'd been sharing one of the two-room cottages at Tillbridge, had come up with the idea of using a cottage to film the show.

As it turned out, the Tillbridges were in the process of remodeling the cottage Tristan Tillbridge used to live in. The empty space was the perfect blank canvas to create a temporary studio. It would also become their base of operations, and he'd sleep there instead of the guesthouse.

A half hour later, the meeting ended.

In high spirits, Teale, Eve and Matt gathered their things. They had plans to hang out at the Montecito Steakhouse, the local spot just outside town.

As Dominic rose from the chair, he glanced at his phone. No other texts from Philippa had popped up. They were still on to meet up in a little over an hour.

What was the best approach with her? Ease into the conversation? Listen to her first? Go all-in with the facts and share some solutions? Philippa was so closed off from him. It was hard to know which way to go.

Eve handed him the key card to the cottage. "Security started guarding the cottage this morning. They also have a set of keys. As far as inside the place, I've already blocked off what will go where in the kitchen. The refrigerators came in today. And the guesthouse staff brought in some furniture."

"Good. Maybe I'll move there now instead of tomorrow night."

"You can, but apologies in advance. You won't have much privacy tomorrow, especially in the morning. They're installing the lights, and in the afternoon, the cabinets and the kitchen island. The appliances are being delivered, too. Work crews will be in and out for most of the day."

"Not a problem." Dominic slipped the key card into his front pocket. "First thing in the morning might be a good time for me to look around." Last weekend, he'd been too busy with work to take in the view. So far, he'd only seen the pastures and horses from a car or the guestroom.

Eve paused before going out the door. "And there's a surprise for you in the fridge at the cottage. The cocktail mixers you're supposed to taste test—they arrived this morning. I stored them there instead of one of Pasture Lane's walk-ins."

"Thanks."

He'd forgotten he was supposed to do that today. The company that made the handcrafted products wanted Frost & Flame to feature them at the bar and consider possibly serving their mixers exclusively.

Tasting them was his last work task of the day. But he could use a break. If he hurried, he could pack his bags upstairs and reach the cottage before sundown. He might even have time to take a short walk before meeting with Philippa. Would she mind meeting him there instead of upstairs?

He sent Philippa a text about the cottage.

Walking down the corridor, he went by Pasture Lane Restaurant.

A small group of people engaged in animated conversation stood outside the glass doors preparing to walk inside.

Dominic kept his head down and veered right toward the modern lobby with country-living accents.

A man and a woman in navy button-downs with the Tillbridge logo—a white horse and *T* with a lasso— stood behind the curved reception desk assisting guests.

More people sat in a seating area furnished with two blue couches surrounding a stained natural-wood coffee table.

No one noticed him. *So far, so good...*

For now, he could get away with not having constant security. Once they started taping segments on location, guards would have to monitor the area to prevent interruptions.

As he got on the elevator alone, his phone rang.

Bailey...

It had been a long day. He just wanted to relax until it was time to see Philippa.

Dominic sent Bailey a text.

Busy.

The doors shut as Bailey responded.

Okay. Call you tomorrow. First thing.

The doors reopened as another text came in.

Philippa's response to his question about the cottage.

I'll meet you there.

Chapter 9

Sitting in the driver's seat of her red four-door, Philippa stared at her text message to Dominic on her phone.

An expensive package on her doorstep that she had to pick up. A pounding migraine that wouldn't go away. A moody, hungry goldfish that she had to feed. All of them were plausible excuses for her to send him another text backing out of the meeting. She'd have to buy the goldfish.

But a convoluted version of her and Dominic's history together appearing in the *Bolan Town Talk* was even more intimidating. They needed to get their stories straight, just like Amber had said.

A short time later, she arrived at the back of the cottage.

Uniformed guards from Tillbridge unclipped the metal cord barring entry to the driveway.

She'd stayed there a few months ago after a heavy

rainstorm caused severe flooding and she couldn't get home safely. The guesthouse had been full, and the only space available had been the cottage.

At first, being stuck there on her first two days off in ages, and not being able to catch up on laundry, had been frustrating.

But then Zurie had sent over food and personal items and forbidden Philippa to go anywhere near Pasture Lane. She'd watched Netflix, ate when she was hungry and slept like the dead. When she'd left the cottage, she'd felt recharged.

Philippa parked behind a black SUV, then got out, leaving her purse in the car.

As she walked toward the back door, it opened. Dominic stepped out on the small porch wearing a brown T-shirt, jeans and casual boots.

Suddenly, she felt underdressed in her work cargo pants, fitted gray T-shirt and the gray-and-green tennis shoes she'd exchanged for her clogs.

He tucked his hands into his front pockets. "You made it."

"Sorry I'm late."

"That's okay. I know how it is, trying to leave the restaurant on a Saturday night. I'm glad you were able to make it."

He let her go in first.

Philippa walked down the back hallway and stopped at the entrance to the kitchen.

Track lighting illuminated the semigutted, beige-tiled space. A refrigerator was the only appliance. The white marble counters were bare except for a single-cup coffee maker tucked off to the side. The cabinets had missing doors, and there was a space where a kitchen island used to be. The adjoining living room with polished wood floors was completely empty.

"You're staying here? But they're still renovating."

"Yes." Dominic glanced around. "But the bedrooms are done, and it will look more like a set kitchen tomorrow after they install the island and bring in the appliances."

"Set kitchen? You're taping your show here, too?"

He nodded. "The team looked at other places, but this one suits our requirements. We can mold it temporarily into what we need since it's empty. And it's a win for the Tillbridges, too, since we're footing the bill. Once we're done, it won't take much to convert this to a standard kitchen. Basically, they're getting an upgrade out of the deal. Do you want to sit?"

She was about to ask *where* when she spotted the tall white bistro table with chairs in the adjoining dining area. Bottles and a package of small plastic cups sat on top of it with a small notebook. "Sure."

As they got closer to the table, she could read some of the labels on the bottles. "Pomegranate habanero, tomato watermelon, mango pineapple. What are these?"

"They're cocktail mixers. The company that makes them wants us to feature them at the bar in the restaurant. I didn't know how long you would be, so I was just about to taste test them. I could use some help."

"Sure. But I have to skip the alcohol. I'm tired and I'm driving."

Dominic chuckled, a rich deep sound that made her feel warm all over. "Not a problem. Non-alcoholic is the way to go for me, too, if I want to get up in the morning."

"Do you have ice?"

"Sure do. I'll get it. Can you set up the cups?"

She took a seat in one of the tall chairs that were next to each other and removed cups from the package.

He returned with napkins and an ice bin with two bottled waters resting inside of it. "Which mixer do you want to try first?"

"I think I need a warm-up before I try anything with habanero in it. How about the mango one?"

"Let's do it." He set the things he carried on the table, then sat in the chair. The wide position of his legs and his broad shoulders shrank the space around them to the size of skin-tingling intimacy.

They sampled the mango-pineapple mixer first, taking sips of water in between as they moved through the rest.

Clearly in business mode, his expression was deeply contemplative as he asked Philippa her opinion about the taste and texture of the products and jotted down her answers. The notebook was well used.

Dominic had a notebook at Coral Cove, too. He'd used it to scribble down ideas and new recipes. He hadn't been so serious while doing it. But he hadn't been running his own enterprise back then.

Dominic sipped water from a bottle. "Which one is your top choice?"

"The mango-pineapple one. You?"

"The tomato-watermelon mixer surprised me. The sweetness of the watermelon and the savoriness of the heirloom tomatoes really comes through. And that hint of basil right underneath. That's not easy to achieve with a bottled product."

As Philippa looked at him, she caught a glimpse of the younger Dominic, itching to set the world on fire. And he had.

He quirked a brow. "What?"

"Your excitement about what you're doing. It's grown even more. Choosing to pursue a career in Los Angeles was the right move for you."

"Los Angeles has been good to me, but a career there wasn't the plan."

"But you auditioned for a reality television show."

He stacked their used cups. "Actually, I didn't."

"So how did it happen?"

"I was visiting a friend in New York. Someone videoed me showing off in the kitchen making a stir fry—cutting vegetables, flipping the food in the pan. They posted it online, and it went viral. A scout for the *Best Chef* franchise saw it, tracked me down at Coral Cove and offered me a spot on the show. It was an opportunity to experience something different, so I went. But it definitely wasn't what I expected."

"What do you mean?"

"Well, for instance, you watched an hour-long show…"

Actually, she'd never watched a single episode of any of his shows, past or present, but there was no need to tell him that.

"But for the contestants, that was actually a twelve-to fifteen-hour day, not only planning recipes and cooking but also filming scenes or waiting around on set as the crew taped everything from multiple angles. And *Best Chef Wins* isn't about cooks preparing food, or the competition. It's about entertainment. The producers create the narrative for the contestants and their relationships with each other, true or not." A hint of bitterness entered his tone. "The more conflict, the better."

She had no idea the drama on cooking shows was so contrived. "That must have been hard."

"It was eye-opening." Dominic gave a barely there smile. "During the show, I was too caught up in trying to keep pace with the day-to-day to notice. It was afterward when I saw their true motives. I was portrayed as the cocky but likable one of the group. And who did everyone supposedly confide their fears to, only to privately worry on camera how I might use the information to win the competition?"

"You."

"Exactly. Of course I didn't, but when someone lost to me, they always blamed it on me knowing their weaknesses."

And what about his relationship with one of the contestants. Was that real or fake? No. That was none of her business and had nothing to do with what they needed to discuss.

Philippa tightened the twist tie on the package of cups. "I misjudged you this afternoon. You do know what it's like to have people fabricate things about you."

Chuckling wryly, he sat back and rested a booted foot on the bottom rung of the chair. "Yeah, I do have a little experience in that department."

"So how do you think we should handle our situation?"

"Amber has already gotten the ball rolling. She's finding out what could entice this journalist from the *Bolan Town Talk* away from our story, at least for a little while longer."

"A lingering case of food poisoning would be better than dealing with Anna. She almost ruined Chloe Daniels's engagement to Tristan Tillbridge."

"We can handle her. We just have to control the narrative."

"And how do we do that?"

"If the subject of us comes up in an interview or even a casual conversation, we just have to tell *our* story, as close to the truth as we're willing to get."

Our story... The way Dominic said it sparked recollections of the passion they'd shared. And the wonderfulness of letting go and losing herself in it.

Dominic shifted on his chair. His leg brushed hers, and she shivered as she pulled herself out of the memory.

"You're cold?" He stood. "You should have told me. I'll turn down the AC."

As he walked to the control panel on the other side of the room, Philippa continuously hit the delete button in her thoughts. No. She shouldn't notice the muscles rippling underneath his T-shirt. Or the way his jeans fit with the right amount of snugness, showcasing his long legs and all of his wonderful assets.

Needing to do something with her hands and her wandering gaze, Philippa focused on tidying the table. "Do you want these in the refrigerator?"

She picked up two of the mixers and swiveled around to get up. Hands full, she bumped into him.

"Oh!" Philippa bobbled the bottles. The top to the mango-pineapple mixer popped off sloshing orange-colored liquid on her chest.

"Whoa." As she started to lose her grip, Dominic stepped forward and made a grab for the mixers. "I've got it."

Bottles trapped in both of their grasps between them, the back of his hand grazed the tip of her breast. Tingles radiated and her breath hitched. *Headlights.* She had them. Philippa clutched the bottles tighter.

He did, too. "You can let go."

Let go of the bottles? Nope. She would just hold on to them. *And do what?* Keep them in front of her breasts all night? Nothing unusual about that, right?

Giving in to cold, hard reality, she released the bottles.

Dominic turned and put them on the counter.

Hands dripping with mango-pineapple mixer, she plucked the front of her T-shirt from her body, a futile attempt to hide her full-on high beams. "Sorry, I made a mess."

"I'll clean it up. Are you o—" Dominic glanced over at her. His gaze dropped to her chest, and for a few long seconds, he didn't blink. "You need a shirt."

He strode toward the beige-carpeted hallway.

She hesitated. It wasn't like she could refuse. Or leave. They still hadn't worked out a game plan for explaining their past connection.

Past? Ignoring the naysaying voice in her head that had shades of Rina's cackling laughter, she followed Dominic.

Instead of entering the main bedroom at the end, he went into the bedroom on the left.

She waited on the opposite side of the hall, near the bathroom.

Moments later, he came out with a sky-blue T-shirt.

"Here you go." Offering a quick smile, he handed it to her.

"Thanks." Philippa ducked into the bathroom and shut the door.

Taking off the shirt, but leaving on her black sports bra, she cleaned up the best she could with a white hand towel.

As she slipped on Dominic's T-shirt that fell low on her thighs, the fresh smell of laundry soap enveloped her instead of his wonderful cologne. A small pang of disappointment hit.

Stop. What are you thinking? Of course, he wouldn't give you a shirt he'd recently worn and hadn't washed yet.

As she scrubbed the stain out of her own, the soft fabric of his shirt brushed over her skin. She conjured up the image of that very shirt taut against him. Suddenly it felt like she was standing over a hot stove instead of a bathroom sink.

Setting aside her T-shirt, she splashed cold water on her face. After wringing out her shirt, she hung it on an empty towel rack to dry.

Philippa walked out into the hallway and toward the kitchen.

With his back to her, Dominic wiped down the counter. He'd changed his shirt to a burgundy one.

He glanced over his shoulder and just stared at her.

Even from a distance, she could see the tightness angling his jawline. And the longing in his eyes.

He'd mentioned that to solve their problem with Anna, they had to get as close to the truth as they were willing to get. But what would defining their feelings for each other cause or possibly cost them? They had to figure it out.

She walked into the kitchen, and he turned away from her, bowing his head. As he gripped the edge of the counter, the muscles in his arms grew taut.

Philippa came up behind him and reached out. As her hand grew closer to his back, she could feel tension radiating from him.

She flattened her palm below his shoulder. "Dominic."

He lifted his head. "Philippa, I can't—"

"I know."

"No, you don't." Frustration edged his tone. "You have no idea what it's like for me to see you after six years and find out I still care about you. And you don't understand what it's like for me to be near you and have to accept that you don't want to feel anything for me. And you don't know what it's like to have to pretend that doesn't matter."

She'd hurt him. But that hadn't been her intention. Unsure of what to say, Philippa wrapped her arms around him from behind. His unsteady breath vibrated into her cheek. "It does matter."

Dominic turned to face her and she let him go. Longing burned even brighter in his eyes. As if testing the waters, he slowly lowered his hands to her waist.

When she didn't move away, he slid his hands to her back. "What are you saying?"

"I was pretending, too. I was afraid of what would happen if I let you know how I really feel. I don't want to be afraid anymore."

Tired of trying to maintain a distance between them, she let the barriers drop. As she raised on her toes, Dominic wrapped his arms around her, and the press of his lips to hers was like a homecoming, heady, sweet and long overdue. She glided her hands up his chest to his nape, and he brought her closer, melding her to his muscled torso. The evidence of his need pressing urgently against her belly made Philippa moan into a deepening kiss that took her back to what they'd shared on the island. Real, uninhibited passion.

Dominic picked her straight up, and as he carried her through the living room into the hall, she wrapped her legs around his waist.

A feverish kiss interrupted the journey and when he set her down just short of the bedroom, she backed him up against the wall.

"Off," she murmured against his lips, tugging up the hem of his shirt.

Dominic pulled it over his head and came back in for another kiss.

Philippa caressed his hard chest and skimmed over the ridges of his abs, absorbing the heat rising from his skin. Him without the shirt was only a taste and not nearly enough. She unfastened his jeans and reached for the tab of his zipper.

Dominic took hold of her hands. "Not yet." The huskiness of his voice vibrated into her.

His open-mouthed kisses down the side of her neck made her shiver in anticipation.

Lifting her up, he carried her into the bedroom. In one quick, smooth movement, he backed her down on the bed.

She sank into the mattress, welcoming his weight along with the sweep of his lips and his bare palm gliding over her belly as he nudged up her shirt and bra. Molding his hand to the curve of her breast, he sucked the peak past his lips.

"Dominic…" She sighed his name, losing herself in the lush heat of his mouth.

He unfastened her cargo pants, and the downward slide of his palm made her heart speed up. As Dominic moved past the barrier keeping him from where she wanted him most, she arched into his touch.

For a few fleeting seconds, whispers from the past invaded her mind. *What if something goes wrong?*

No. This wasn't six years ago. This was different.

As he grazed his fingers over her, Philippa's worries dissolved, and she reveled in what Dominic freely gave to her. Pure ecstasy. It grew stronger with every stroke over her center and soft flick of his tongue over her nipple.

She climaxed and he captured her cries in a kiss.

They removed their clothing, and Dominic sheathed himself in protection.

As he glided inside of her, they both shook from the power of need.

He rolled his hips and she joined him in a familiar rhythm of pleasure. One where they inherently knew what would make the other moan, grasp tighter and tremble as they fought to control what they couldn't stop. Tumbling over the edge and free-falling into bliss.

Chapter 10

As Philippa snuggled closer to his chest, Dominic tightened his arm around her and smiled into the predawn darkness.

She'd stayed with him...

Last night, while she was in the shower, he'd come up with plenty of reasons for her not to leave. But when she'd come out of the bathroom, she'd snagged his burgundy shirt from the floor, set the alarm on her phone, and put it on the nightstand. Then she'd asked for something to tie her hair up with. He'd found a clean black bandana he sometimes wore in the restaurant kitchen. Once she tied up her hair, she'd crawled in bed beside him and promptly fallen asleep in his arms.

Unable to resist, Dominic pressed a soft lingering kiss to the top of her head. He could spend the entire day just holding her.

His phone dinged in a text. He eased partway from
Philippa, reached beside him and quickly snagged it
from the nightstand. It was Bailey.

Calling you.

It was four thirty in the morning. When Bailey had
said she was calling first thing, he'd thought she'd meant
at least seven his time. And why wasn't she asleep? It
was one thirty in the morning in California.

Using one hand, he texted her back.

Talk later?

A text bubble with dots appeared.

Calling you now. It's urgent. Pick up!

Was she actually shouting at him in a text?

Careful not to wake Philippa, he got out of bed and
found a pair of sweatpants in the dresser. Just as he
pulled them on, his phone buzzed in Bailey's call.

Dominic snagged the black shirt he'd loaned Philippa
last night from just under the bed before he slipped out
the room.

He answered the call as he shut the door behind him.
"Is whatever you have to tell me really that urgent it
couldn't wait a few more hours?"

"Seriously? You woke me up at four in the morning
just a week ago. No, it couldn't wait. I have good news.
It's still on the bubble, so don't mention this to anyone, but the producers of the *Best Chef Wins* franchise
want us to participate in a two-part crossover event.

A reunion show with you and the rest of the *Best Chef Wins Los Angeles* cast from five years ago, followed by a special reunion episode on *Dinner with Dominic*."

Good news? Reliving his *Best Chef Wins Los Angeles* days—definitely not on his version of that list. This conversation required a clear head. He needed caffeine.

Working from memory, Dominic walked down the hall in the dark. He headed for the kitchen as he slipped on his shirt.

"Hello," Bailey called out. "Did I lose you?"

"No. I'm here. Why are the producers not cutting this deal with the winner? I was the runner-up."

"The winner doesn't have his own hit show and his restaurant closed two years ago. And according to my sources, *Best Chef Wins* needs a ratings boost."

As Bailey outlined what the collaboration would do for the *Best Chef Wins* franchise and *Dinner with Dominic*, he set up the coffee maker with a brew pod and a black Flame & Frost embossed mug.

"Let me guess," he said. "The publicity firm thinks getting involved with this will be good for my brand."

"You say that like it's a bad thing."

"You know how I feel about my experience on that show."

"Yes, but this time, you're calling the shots, and they only want to highlight your strengths. You're known for really connecting with your guests, and that's what they're looking for with these episodes."

"They want drama. *Best Chef Wins* is a reality show. What's the catch?"

"There isn't one. It's a straightforward agreement. Part one would air as a network episode for *Best Chef Wins*. A look back at the past, visit the set type of thing.

Part two would air on your show with you interviewing each of your fellow contestants while they prepare their signature dishes. At the end, all of you will share a meal celebrating the five-year anniversary of the season."

That sounded too easy. "Are you sure they don't want anything else?"

"The only request they may have is for you to spend a little more time talking with Destiny since the two of you were in a relationship."

And there was the catch—he knew there had to be one.

"There was no relationship between us. The producers of the show spun it that way."

"But the two of you did date each other."

"We weren't dating. We went out a few times *after* the show ended."

Two years ago, Destiny had come into the restaurant. She had found popularity through her single-girl-life themed vlog and hanging out with other reality show stars famous for being famous. She'd claimed she had a publishing deal in the works to write a cookbook and had asked for his help. Going for coffee had evolved into brainstorming sessions over dinner and her attending a couple of events with him.

But the chemistry hadn't been there. Not like it was with him and Philippa.

"You can't change fan perceptions about what they think happened on or after the show," Bailey insisted. "Your season of *Best Chef Wins* had been over for three years when you started seeing her, and fans of the show were still thrilled about Des and Dom."

Des and Dom—he hated the nickname the press had given them and the pure insanity that had come with it. Once their season of the show had aired, every time he'd walked out the door, there was someone sticking a camera in his face asking him questions about his supposed relationship with Destiny.

When they'd started seeing each other two years ago, it had started all over again. Members of the paparazzi had camped out in front of their homes and his restaurant. She'd craved the attention.

Remembering those moments set Dominic's teeth on edge. "If creating some story about Destiny and I is part of *Best Chef*'s plans for a ratings boost, this conversation is over."

"It's not like the two of you would have to start dating again. Maybe a dinner or two before the show airs to create some curiosity, that's all."

"No."

"But this could kill the deal."

"My show isn't the one that needs the ratings boost."

During the silence, Dominic removed the full mug of coffee from the maker and took a sip. "You still there?"

"Yes. I just needed a minute to bang my head on the desk. Fine. I will insist they include in your contract that you and Destiny are not a package deal."

"Not so fast. What about the schedule? When do they want to start taping?"

"In three months, if they can get all the contracts signed in the next couple of weeks. The shows would air in late fall. Perfect timing with the opening of the Atlanta restaurant."

Bailey saw perfect timing. He saw a scheduling disaster that wouldn't allow him a break between taping episodes of his own show, running Frost & Flame LA, and planning the opening of Frost & Flame Atlanta.

His caffeine buzz started to wane and weariness kicked in.

But mentioning the tight schedule to Bailey would just earn him a pep talk he wasn't in the mood to hear. He'd tackle that issue another day. "Keep me in the loop."

"I will."

A hint of light peeked through the blinds covering the windows in the living room. His schedule wasn't perfect, but his morning was, so far. Philippa was down the hall, and he didn't have to hide how he felt about her.

"Hey, what did you think of the cocktail mixers?" Bailey asked. "Are we doing business with the company?"

The image of Philippa, sleeping in his bed interrupted Dominic's response. He wanted a moment to just be with her before they had to jump into their day. He could wake her up with a cup of hazelnut-flavored coffee.

But hashing out a few details with Bailey about the contract for the mixers wouldn't take long.

Feeling lighter about the future, Dominic took another cup from the cabinet. "I haven't made up my mind yet. I have questions…"

Philippa bolted upright on the mattress and gasped for air, her mind still reeling from the bad dream. Her heart knocked harder against her rib cage as she looked around the unfamiliar room. The pieces fell into place.

I'm okay. I'm safe… She was in the spare bedroom at the guest cottage at Tillbridge. She'd spent the night with Dominic.

A shudder ran through her as she remembered the

weird nightmare. She'd been in a restaurant kitchen, cooking eggs, but instead of her chef's uniform, she'd been wearing a purple sleepshirt.

Suddenly, the gray tiles had turned into quicksand, sucking her down. She couldn't cry out, and no one noticed she was in trouble. They'd kept doing their job as the floor had slowly entombed her in darkness.

The same stuck, smothering sensation that had come over her in the dream gripped Philippa now. Needing to move, she untangled her legs from the covers and sat on the edge of the bed.

Twilight turned the room a shadowy bluish gray.

She caught a glimpse of her wide-eyed reflection in the dresser against the wall. As she recalled the dream, the memory of the purple sleepshirt hovered in her thoughts.

The door opened.

"You're awake." Smiling, Dominic walked in carrying a steaming mug. "I'd hoped you wouldn't be."

Philippa pushed aside the nightmare and smiled back. "Why?"

"I had plans." Dominic leaned down and kissed her neck.

She breathed him in along with the scent of... *hazelnut coffee*... "Mmm, is that for me?"

"It is." He handed her the cup and sat beside her as she took a sip of the perfectly sweetened brew.

The warmth spreading inside of her chased away an inner chill leftover from the nightmare. "Thank you."

"You're welcome." Dominic slid an arm around her.

She leaned into him, and for a long moment they sat in companionable silence.

He pressed his lips to her temple and held her a bit closer. "I guess last night changes things?"

The uncertainty in his voice made her glance over at him. But what did she expect? Six years ago, she'd let him believe they'd just had a three-month fling, nothing special.

"It does." Philippa laid her hand on his thigh. "We can't claim that we're just colleagues anymore. What's our story now?"

"I think we need more time to figure that out." Laying his hand over hers, he intertwined their fingers. "We don't have to rush to explain our situation to anyone. We just have to take measures to keep our personal life private."

"So, what's the plan? Are we leaving our windows open so we can sneak in and out of each other's bedrooms?" She laughed but Dominic didn't. Her humor dissipated. "Oh."

His expression grew serious. "The guards outside the cottage have signed nondisclosure agreements, but the NDA is slanted toward protecting me. I'll have new ones drawn up that cover you, too. I'm also replacing the guards with ones from an LA-based firm we use whenever we need them. They work mainly with public figures and value discretion as part of their reputation."

For a few long seconds, Philippa remained speechless. She hadn't envisioned spending the night with him becoming a major privacy issue. "Okay...if that's best."

"I know. It's a lot. You normally don't have to think this way. If you'd rather not get involved with me because it's more than you bargained for, I'll understand." He gave a small smile that didn't reach his eyes.

Their situation had become more intense than she

could handle with just one cup of coffee. But she was already involved. She couldn't wind the clock back and pretend she didn't care about him. "I do want to spend time with you while you're here. Can we take it one day at a time?"

Dominic's shoulders relaxed and he exhaled as if he'd been holding a pent-up breath. "We can definitely do that." As he leaned in, his gaze held hers. "But just so you know, I plan on taking advantage of every minute, you're willing to give me."

"I like the sound of that."

Closing the distance, she pressed her mouth to his.

Dominic cupped her cheek, and as the kiss deepened, he started to lean her back on the mattress.

The heat of the mug in Philippa's hand and the room growing a bit brighter made her hesitate. She spoke against his lips. "I would love for you to take advantage of me now, but I have to go home and get ready for work."

He eased back. "Work… I guess we do have to do that today. And you should probably leave before things get too active around Tillbridge."

Tillbridge...the staff. Always being careful. Keeping secrets. That's what they'd face over the next few weeks. As she handed him the coffee cup, his eyes reflected the same resignation she felt. What was she getting herself into?

But as daunting as it seemed, she didn't want to give up what they'd shared last night. She hadn't felt this level of anticipation and desire or been able to just let go like that with a guy in…six years.

A short time later, she stood with Dominic in the back entryway. She wore the burgundy shirt and held her damp one in her hand. "I'll see you later." They were meeting that afternoon with Rachel and Zurie at the outdoor arena where the screening event was taking place.

"See you then." When she turned to walk away, Dominic caught her hand, and she let him pull her back to him for a long goodbye kiss.

As Philippa left the driveway headed for home, happiness made her smile into the sun rising just over the horizon.

Farther down the road, horses grazed in the pasture to her right, and one of the staff from the stable worked near the run-in, an open wood shelter on the far side of the field.

The employees at the stable arrived long before sunup. On a Sunday, a few of the staff at Tillbridge, including the ones at Pasture Lane, would have started work nearly a half hour ago at five thirty.

Still, a flicker of apprehension over the possibility of being spotted close to the cottage tempted her to push down on the accelerator.

Stop being paranoid... She had the road to herself. And even if someone did see her, it wasn't like she was driving around with a flashing sign telling everyone where she'd just came from.

The red light blinked on the gas indicator.

Crap. She'd planned on getting gas yesterday after work.

The white-and-red sign for the Bolan Quick Stop and Shop shone up ahead. Philippa made a left into the entrance and pulled up next to a free gas pump. After grabbing her debit card from her wallet, she got out and swiped it through the card reader.

As she pumped gas, diesel fumes from tractor trailers rolling slowly from the rear parking lot to the exit swarmed in the breeze.

Customers walking out of the store carrying coffee and giant cinnamon-roll breakfast sandwiches snagged her attention.

She'd heard the owner of the establishment, one of the mayor's cousins, had installed kitchen equipment in the back room to make them fresh.

At one time, Pasture Lane had served breakfast sandwiches from the restaurant's food van at the stable. But despite their popularity, they didn't make enough revenue to justify being open there in the morning. For sentimental reasons, she'd resisted making the decision to end serving breakfast using the van. The lime green vehicle had been her first food enterprise at Tillbridge before Pasture Lane Restaurant had been built almost five years ago.

The gas nozzle clicked, indicating the tank was full. She put it back on the pump, closed up her tank and pressed the yes button for a receipt on the transaction screen. Nothing came out of the slot.

Recently, overcharges on credit and debit cards at places like the Bolan Quick Stop and Shop had become an issue in the area. An interview with the police chief in the *Bolan Town Talk* had advised everyone to hold on to their receipts from the convenience stores as a precaution.

Philippa glanced down at Dominic's shirt, her pants and her tennis shoes. Not exactly fashionable, and the shirt obviously wasn't hers, but she was just running in for a receipt.

Inside the store, a combination of sunlight and bright

fluorescents illuminated the aisles filled with grocery and toiletry items, and a wide array of junk food.

An endcap featured Maryland T-shirts, shot glasses, and other tourist souvenirs. At the rear of the store, a bulb on the verge of going out blinked in one of the beverage refrigerators lining the wall.

Cinnamon and the overly sweet smell of multiple flavored coffees brewing in the large coffee makers on the side wall hovered in the air.

She joined the line behind the only two other customers in the store. The man being checked out at the counter by a tired, bored-looking, college-aged girl counted out coins from a sock to buy scratch-off tickets.

The dark-haired woman directly in front of Philippa sighed and muttered, "This is taking forever."

And from the looks of things—the man had switched from counting out quarters to pennies—it wasn't ending anytime soon.

Not in a hurry, Philippa weighed her options. She had time to grab an orange juice. And maybe she'd check out the cinnamon roll sandwiches in the glass case near the coffee.

The Bolan Quick Stop and Shop wasn't serving restaurant-quality meals like Pasture Lane, but it was still smart to keep an eye on any operation, large or small, that served food in the area. Especially since they were all vying for local dollars.

Philippa got out of line. As she walked down one of the narrow, center aisles toward the beverage refrigerator, a row of small, blue-and-white rectangular boxes on the shelf caught her eye. Her steps faltered.

An urge she couldn't control made her reach toward the shelf as memories of the nightmare that had awakened her at the bungalow flooded into her mind. They faded into a recollection of her wearing faded blue leggings and her favorite purple sleep shirt under her winter coat. She'd dragged herself out of bed and gone to the drugstore for flu medicine, but then—

"Philippa?" Dominic strode toward her from the end of the aisle.

Startled, she jerked her hand back and knocked some of the pregnancy tests off the shelf.

She quickly bent down and gathered them from the floor, but she dropped one.

Dominic picked it up.

As he put it on the shelf, Philippa remained frozen for a moment. "What are you doing here?"

He held up her phone. "You forgot this on the nightstand. The security guard knew which way you were headed, so he pointed me this direction. I recognized your car at the pump." His gaze flickered to the pregnancy tests in her hand. "Are you okay?"

Still reconciling her memory with the dream, she struggled to answer.

"I'm fine." Philippa stuck the tests on the shelf, and then she took her phone. "Thank you. I should pay for my gas." Unable to meet his gaze, she slipped past him and went to the register.

Before Dominic left the store, he stopped beside her. "I'll meet you outside."

Still trapped in what she'd just recalled from her past, Philippa went through the motions of paying the cashier.

She'd never really forgotten about what happened back then. She'd just banished the memories to a place so deep in her mind, it had felt that way. But the confusion and sadness hitting her now struck almost as painfully as they had back then.

Outside, he stood near the driver-side door of her car.

Philippa paused in front of him. "Dominic... I..." How could she explain?

Grimness and concern shadowed his unwavering gaze. "Whatever it is. It doesn't change how I feel about you. Just tell me the truth."

Chapter 11

Dominic drove his black SUV rental behind Philippa's car down the narrow, two-lane road.

Their conversation outside the quick mart ten minutes earlier played through his mind.

Just tell me the truth...

I will...but not here.

Assumptions about what she'd say twisted knots in his gut. The worst-case scenario of Philippa planning to trap him into a pregnancy didn't sit right as a possibility. That left only one logical reason why she would need a pregnancy test. Philippa was possibly already pregnant. If she was, who was the father? Someone local? Was he still in her life?

Philippa turned left onto a long, paved driveway. Yards away sat a white house with gray trim and shutters nestled in the trees.

Instead of driving toward the side-facing garage, Philippa kept going straight, past the house.

A smaller version of it with gray shutters on the front windows, a single-door garage and a porch surrounded by a white railing came into view.

She parked outside the garage, and he pulled in behind her.

They both got out of their cars, and Dominic followed her up the stairs to the wide porch.

She pointed to a grouping of wicker furniture with aqua cushions off to the side. "Do you mind if we sit out here?"

"This is fine with me."

"Good." She perched on the edge of the bench seat.

Signs of a fragile unease he'd never spotted in Philippa before made him want to pull her back up to her feet and hold her.

Dominic tamped down the urge and sat in the chair beside her.

He'd meant what he'd said earlier. Whatever she had to say wouldn't change the way he felt about her. It would impact their relationship moving forward. But he was there for her, even if she needed him as just a friend.

Dominic spoke first. "I don't care if you're pregnant. I just need to know if you're still with him."

"What?" Her eyes popped wide. "I'm not pregnant."

"But you were looking at pregnancy tests."

Philippa looked down for a long moment. "I'm not pregnant now…but I was six years ago when I left Coral Cove."

Her confession stunned him into silence.

She rushed on. "But I didn't know until three weeks

after I left. I was in DC by then, living with a room-mate. One day, we both were home, sick with the flu, and we ran out of medicine. I walked to the store up the street, and when I was there, I noticed the pregnancy tests, and it hit me. I was late. I grabbed one along with the medicine. But I didn't get a chance to use it. When I got home, I passed out."

Going to the store on her own even though she was sick. He could easily imagine her doing that. "Did some-one take you to a hospital?"

"Yes. I was weak from dehydration." She looked up at him. "A nurse asked if I could be pregnant. Between the stress of moving to DC and being too sick to keep down my birth control pills, I didn't know. They did a blood test."

Philippa stood and walked to the porch railing. As she leaned her hands on it, she stared out at the trees.

An image flashed through his mind of the two of them on a secluded area of beach at Coral Cove. While they'd watched the sunrise, one heated kiss had led them into doing more without a condom.

They weren't too concerned about the slipup. He and Philippa had been tested before the interview audition, and they were both disease-free. And she was on the pill. They'd used condoms as an extra precaution...except that one time.

Hope and concern hit him all at once. Did they have a child? Dominic got up.

Just as he went to ask, she met his gaze, and the bleak-ness he saw in her eyes made his chest ache. "What happened?"

She swallowed hard. "A week later, I started cramp-ing and then..."

Not enough words existed to express what he wanted to say to her. He grasped her hand and squeezed. "I'm sorry. I should have been with you. I called, but when you didn't answer, I gave up. I should have tried harder to reach you."

"No. Us not communicating with each other—that's on me." Philippa squeezed back. "The day you called was when I found out I was pregnant, but I didn't know how to tell you. You were at Coral Cove. I'd just moved to DC. A baby would have completely changed our futures. And afterward… I was dealing with so much. Telling you then would have just made it harder for me to get through it."

Needing her close, he tugged Philippa toward him. As they held each other, he breathed against the heaviness in his chest.

If she would have answered her phone that day and told him she was pregnant, there wouldn't have been a debate over what he would do. He would have chosen Philippa and their child. And if that would have meant giving up Coral Cove, he would have done it and not looked back.

And the loss…he would have done whatever he could to help her through it.

Dominic held her tighter. It hurt like hell to know she had borne the pain on her own for something he'd been a part of. From her reaction that morning at the mini mart, it still affected her.

He leaned back to look at her. "This morning, did seeing the pregnancy tests in the store trigger something?"

"Not on its own." Philippa's gaze dropped to her hands as she rested them on his chest. "I had a nightmare last night. In my dream, I was wearing the same purple sleep shirt I had on when it...when I..."

His heart ached for her as she blinked as if holding back tears.

"All these years later, I don't know why I'm not better at dealing with it." She shook her head. "I was just a few weeks along. It wasn't like I had to make any decisions or changes. Think about it. If my roommate and I hadn't run out of medicine that day, I might not have realized I was pregnant. I might have just thought I was having a heavier cycle than usual because I hadn't been taking my pills on a regular basis."

If only she hadn't—? Is that what she'd been telling herself all these years to cope with what had happened to her?

He cupped her cheek. "But you did know. You went through a difficult situation, and it came up for you now in an unexpected way. You're allowed to feel whatever you need to process it."

"But I didn't think I could still feel what I felt back then. The panic over what I was going to do. The fear that I wasn't ready. And when it came to an end, I was sad, but a part of me was also...relieved." She closed her eyes for a moment and tears leaked out. "I would have been responsible for helping that tiny being find its place in the world, but I had no idea where I was going or what I wanted for myself. Do you hate me for that?"

"No. Never." He dropped to eye level and cupped her face. "But you can't keep judging yourself for thinking that way. Being honest with yourself is a strength not a weakness."

A red van came up the driveway.

"That's Charlotte, my landlady." Philippa stepped

away from him and faced the house. She swiped tears from her cheeks.

The van with Buttons & Lace Boutique in gold script on the side pulled up behind his rental.

An older woman with a silvery-blond bob, wearing blue leggings, flats and an oversized pink blouse stepped out of the driver side.

Charlotte left the engine running and stood by the car. "Hey, Philippa." She waved. "How are you?"

"I'm fine." Philippa waved back. "Are you on your way to the shop?"

"Yes. I have some inventory to take care of." A youthful glow of excitement lit up Charlotte's face. "You and Rina have to stop by and check out my new shoe section. There's a pair of sandals with your name on them. How's the water heater? Any more problems?"

"No, it's heating up fine. Thank you."

"Glad to hear it." Charlotte's gaze landed on Dominic. "Hello."

As she studied him, her genuine smile made it easier for Dominic to prompt his mouth to curve upward. "Hello."

"Well, I better get going. Let me know if you need anything." Charlotte got into the van. As she reversed out of the driveway, she waved again, and drove back toward the larger house.

Philippa laughed quietly as she returned Charlotte's wave.

"What's so funny?" he asked.

"The water heater was fixed last month."

"So she was being nosy? From the look on her face, I'm assuming she knows who I am? Does this mean by noon the whole town will know I was here?"

"Not so much nosy as being protective of me, and yes, she does know who you are. I saw one of your cookbooks in her kitchen. But Charlotte Henry is definitely not a gossip. She made Chloe's wedding dress and took care of the bridesmaids' dresses and not a word of it got out. She's like a vault."

Usually people who were great at keeping secrets had a few of their own. Maybe that's why Charlotte was so good at it. But the important thing was that Philippa trusted her. And it was good to know that the older woman cared about her. But he did, too. Did Philippa realize that?

Dominic took hold of Philippa's hand, and she turned to face him. The tears were gone, but hints of the emotional toll of their conversation showed on her face. "Do you have to go in to Tillbridge today? If not, I can cover for you at the meeting this afternoon with Rachel. You can take the day off."

"The screening party is only weeks away and we have a lot to do. I'm a part of it, and I'm going to pull my weight." Philippa laid her hand near his shoulder. "I have the morning off. That's enough of a break. Don't worry about me. I'm fine."

But the urge to look after her was too close to the surface. He hadn't been there when she'd needed him the most, and there was no way for him to make up for failing her back then. But from this point on, while he was with Philippa, her peace of mind, her needs, were his priority.

Dominic kissed her forehead. "I don't doubt that you can't handle anything, but I'm here for you, in any way you want me to be. Just tell me what you need."

* * *

Philippa stopped at the traffic light on the street bordering downtown Bolan.

A little over a couple of hours ago, after reassuring Dominic that she was fine, he'd left her house. She'd gotten some chores in before getting ready for work. With plenty of time on her hands, she'd taken a detour into town.

Just before she'd backed out of the driveway, Dominic had sent her a text, asking if she was okay.

Once again, she'd told him she was fine, and for the most part, she was. Telling Dominic everything had been hard. Reliving the moment in her mind had been harder. But she didn't regret talking about it with him.

Philippa made the turn onto Main Street.

At nine on a Sunday, people leisurely strolled the square, an area in the middle of town with neatly cut grass, flowering bushes and old-fashioned-styled streetlamps lining the paths. Sun glistened off the water cascading down the stone-fountain centerpiece surrounded by park benches.

Other pedestrians window-shopped Buttons & Lace Boutique, the floral shop across the street and the Bolan Book Attic, the bookstore in town. They would open along with the other small businesses linked together in strip-mall fashion later that morning.

But on the corner farther down, a steady stream of customers entered and exited Brewed Haven. The standalone, two-story, light-colored brick building with large storefront windows was known for its pies, delicious pastries and other desserts and was the go-to place for coffee. The restaurant was also the weekend hot spot for meals throughout the day.

Philippa spotted a space in front of the flower shop and parallel parked. Leaving her chef's jacket in the car, she got out and walked up the street toward Brewed Haven. Instead of her Birkenstocks, she'd put on her black steel-toed boots with lime-green laces that morning.

Halfway there she passed the bookstore.

A poster featuring Dominic, advertising his upcoming book signing along with his book sat in the window.

Just tell me what you need...

He'd looked so sincere and concerned when he'd told her that. Was there something she didn't have before she'd told him everything that he could give her now? She didn't have an answer to that question, along with the others taking up residence in her mind. Talking with Rina would help. But first, she had to tell Rina what had happened with Dominic six years ago.

Would Rina understand she hadn't avoided telling her? That she'd just trained herself not to think about certain parts of her past? Lately, she'd teased Rina about her "eminent" future of having enough kids with Scott to fill an entire sports team roster. Now that her memories had resurfaced, would it feel awkward to laugh and tease Rina about it?

And what about her current relationship with Dominic? He'd said how he felt about her wouldn't change, and she believed that. But before he'd left, she'd sensed a shift in him. Maybe the shock over what she'd told him had settled in. He'd mentioned she had a right to process her feelings, but he did, too.

At the corner opposite Brewed Haven, Philippa crossed the street, and as she drew closer to the cafe, the scent of freshly brewed coffee wafted in the air.

She opened the glass door and walked inside.

A short line of people waited at the curved station. Baristas wearing jeans and purple T-shirts with the cafe's yellow coffee cup logo filled orders for drinks and grabbed pastries for customers from the glass case underneath the counter.

On the right, a sprinkling of customers sat in the purple booths lined along the wall and at the light wood tables with purple-and-yellow floral centerpieces, enjoying brunch.

The sound of familiar, happy laughter drew Philippa's attention to the smaller alcove on the opposite side of the cafe, where more customers sat at round tables or on the beige couches decorated with purple throw pillows tucked under the side windows.

Rina, dressed similarly to her staff and wearing a yellow apron chatted with a dark-haired man at one of the tables. He pointed to his open laptop in front of him, and she nodded in agreement to what he said.

Not wanting to interrupt, Philippa stepped forward to join the coffee line.

"Hey, Philippa." Mace Calderone tapped her arm.

"Hi, Mace." Philippa took in his beige-and-brown deputy sheriff's uniform. "Taking a coffee break?"

The tan-skinned, dark-haired deputy smiled. "Yeah, I got a long one ahead of me. Plus, I was up early this morning. Zurie wanted to go over the security plan for the movie screening. She said you guys have a meeting with the planner this afternoon?"

"Yes. We're going over the kitchen-trailer setup at the arena with Dominic and his team."

"Dominic's a busy man. Before I met with Zurie this

morning, I dropped by to check in with the security people at the cottage. They said he was out."

Did he know she'd stayed at the cottage or that Dominic had left the cottage that morning to find her? Or was she reading too much into Mace's steady gaze. "He has a lot on his plate with the screening and taping episodes of his show here."

Mace tipped his head with a nod. "I'm sure he does."

"What is this? A family reunion?" Rina nudged Mace's arm, then gave Philippa a tight hug. "You didn't tell me you were coming by."

Philippa returned the embrace. "It's my morning off. Jeremy and Quinn are taking care of brunch."

"Lucky girl, you could have slept in." Rina slumped her shoulders in mock exhaustion. "I haven't done that in weeks. I hope the reason you're here was worth giving that up."

"I wanted to talk to you about something."

"Next customer, please," the barista called out.

Philippa was next. She stepped out of line. "Mace, you go ahead."

"You sure?"

"Yes. You know how it is. I have to grab Rina while I can catch her."

"True." Smiling, he headed for the counter. "I'll see you two later."

Rina poked her. "You know I'm never too busy for you. Do you want to eat? There isn't a waiting list yet. We can sit in the dining area."

"Can we talk in your office?" Customers walked in for coffee, and Philippa and Rina scooted more to the side. "It's private."

"Okay. Then, we should probably walk and talk, so

there won't be any interruptions. Hold on. I'll let Darby know I'm stepping out. And I'll grab us some coffee."

A few minutes later, full cups in hand, they walked down the street toward the square.

As they passed by Buttons & Lace, Rina gripped her arm. "I heard Charlotte expanded her shoe section. Did you know?"

"I found out from her when she came by the house this morning. She said we have to stop by."

"Has Charlotte eased up on acting like a mother hen?"

When Philippa had first moved in, Charlotte had checked in on her almost every day. "A little. She just wants to make sure I'm comfortable."

Rina looped her arm through Philippa's. "I still think you should have moved into my spare room."

"And spend my time night gardening with you and making friends with the raccoons? No, thank you."

"It wouldn't have been that bad."

"Oh, yes it would have. And as much as Scott likes me, I think he would prefer to be the only one night gardening with you."

"Yeah, and he's really good at it." Mischievous humor beamed in Rina's face.

Philippa couldn't hold back a laugh. Leave it to Rina to put her in a good mood.

They crossed the street, then settled on a bench near the water fountain. In companionable silence, they people watched and drank their coffees.

As Philippa sipped the hazelnut-flavored brew in her cup, she thought of the coffee Dominic had brought her that morning. She turned toward Rina. "Dominic and I slept together last night."

Rina stared at her with a neutral expression. "Well... okay."

"I tell you I've slept with my ex, and that's all you can say?"

"Until you say more, I'm not sure if that's a good thing or a bad thing."

Philippa looked from Rina to the fountain. In true best-friend fashion, Rina had managed to encapsulate what was really on her mind. "Last night, it was a good thing. This morning was...tough."

"Oh, no. Were you two pretending to have a casual, non-awkward conversation when you first woke up?"

"No, actually he brought me hazelnut coffee."

"He remembered that's your favorite?" Smiling, Rina turned to face Philippa. "What happened after that?"

Like ripping off a Band-Aid, there was no easy way through it. "I left. Stopped for gas at the Bolan Quick Stop and Shop, and started looking at pregnancy tests on the shelf. And that's where Dominic found me when he came in to give me my phone."

Rina mouth dropped open. "Tell me that didn't happen."

"It did."

"But why were you looking at pregnancy tests? Was there a problem with the protection he used?"

"No, the condoms worked just fine."

"Plural, condoms. Okay, busy night. But you're still on birth control, right? Sure, a pregnancy can still happen but it's rare, like in the single digits."

"It is." Philippa paused to gather her words. "But it happened to me six years ago...with Dominic."

Taking advantage of Rina's stunned silence, Philippa

told her about what had happened back then and what occurred that morning.

Rina laid her hand on Philippa's arm. Empathy filled her face. "I'm so sorry. I can't imagine all that you went through."

Philippa almost brushed Rina's caring aside, but what Dominic had said about her being allowed to feel whatever she needed to process it, even after all these years, came to mind. "It wasn't easy. I struggled for a while. But landing at Tillbridge, meeting you and then getting to know you better when I took over the food van. It all helped."

"I'm so glad you found your way here." Eyes bright as if she was about to cry, Rina pulled Philippa into a big hug.

"I am, too." Philippa held her coffee cup out of the way and breathed against Rina's tightening hold. "Please, let me go."

"Never. You're my best friend. And, no matter what, I'm always here for you."

"No, really. Let me go. You're suffocating me."

"Oh, sorry." Rina released her.

Philippa took a huge breath. "Thank you. Aside from Dominic, you're the only person I've told."

"Are you glad you told him?"

"I am. In the moment, it wasn't easy, but now it feels like a weight has been lifted. Like telling him was the last thing I needed to do to put it behind me."

"How did he take it?"

"He was kind and supportive. And wanted me to tell him what I needed." Philippa paused, not quite sure what to say next. Dominic had been wonderful. Still, the way he'd acted right before he left felt off.

"But? And don't say nothing." Rina circled her finger in the air. "You've got that I'm-bothered-by-something look on your face. Just say it. He was kind, supportive and asked what you needed, but…"

"Before Dominic left, he kissed me on the forehead."

"He kissed you goodbye. What's the problem? You didn't want him to?"

"No, I did. But he's never kissed me on the forehead like that. Ever. It was like he was pitying me. I don't know." Philippa sunk against the back of the bench seat. "Maybe I'm judging him based on how I think he should act. I'm sure what I told him wasn't easy to hear. Just like me, he has a right to process what I told him in a way that's best for him."

"He does. But I'm wondering… He asked what you needed. What did you tell him?"

"I didn't give him an answer. I didn't have one."

Rina offered up a shrug. "Maybe he wasn't pitying you. He could be confused. For a guy, when the person they care about has been hurt or is hurting—their go-to is to try and fix something. But he can't fix the past and make it better for you. That's probably hard for him and rather than say or do the wrong thing, he's staying in the neutral zone."

Was Dominic confused, and that's what the kiss really reflected? Philippa took a sip of lukewarm coffee. "He's confused? I'm confused. I don't know what I need from him."

Rina sat back on the bench and sighed. "You wouldn't be the first to have felt that way. I hate to tell you, but you might not know what you need from him until you need it."

Chapter 12

Philippa sat beside Tristan in the golf cart as he reversed out of a space in the parking lot of the guesthouse, a two-story white building with green trim and a green pitched roof. At three in the afternoon on a Sunday, most of the guests had checked out at the end of brunch a half hour ago.

He sped across the lot toward the narrow-paved trail bisecting two fenced-in, grassy fields that comprised the north pasture. A breeze ruffled the ends of her hair, secured by a green headband. Her dark T-shirt and pants absorbed the rays of the sun, but the same breeze kept her cool.

A navy ball cap with the Tillbridge logo covered his short black hair and shielded Tristan's face, which was a medium brown after hours in the sun. His blue short-sleeved Tillbridge T-shirt and slightly faded jeans had a few smudges of dirt on them, and his boots had a layer of dust. Even though he was a co-owner of the Tillbridge operation, the tall, lean former bull rider was hands-on with his job of stable manager.

He glanced at Philippa. "Sorry I was late picking you up. I hadn't planned on going to this meeting. I was grooming horses when Zurie called and said I had to take her place."

"You didn't have to come for me. I could have driven." Uneven pavers jostled the cart and Philippa held on to the edge of the seat.

"No. Driving yourself there would have been a waste of gas. Besides, you can tell me about this event planner we're meeting with. Zurie was a little too happy to take care of a leak in one of the guestrooms and pass this task to me. From her tone, I'm guessing she's had enough of—Rachel. Is that her name?"

"Yes, that's it."

"You've been working with her. Is she that difficult?"

Still a tad annoyed by how Rachel had handled replacing her with Dominic but not wanting to trash her name, Philippa chose her words wisely. "Let's just say you're probably on-target with your guess about why Zurie wanted out of the meeting."

He chuckled. "Noted. The planner may be a pain, but Zurie's had nothing but good to say about Dominic and his team. I met him this morning. He came by with the location scout to talk about taping some general footage at the stable. Seems like a good man. He's not full of it like a few of the celebrities I've met while hanging with Chloe."

Since the filming of *Shadow Valley*, Chloe's notoriety had risen. Despite the pressure of fame, Tristan seemed to take it all in stride. But it hadn't been that way when the two first met. How long had it taken him to find his place in her life and career? Would she be able to do the same if she and Dominic remained together?

Philippa set the thought aside. She was getting ahead of herself. They were in new territory, as Rina had pointed out. A place where maybe they weren't meant to be a couple. Usually she didn't believe in fate, but the peace she'd started to feel after telling him everything that morning had only grown stronger.

Maybe Dominic showing up in her life again wasn't about them getting back together but about her finding true closure about what happened six years ago.

Tristan stopped near a metal pasture gate on the right. As he went to put the golf cart in Park, she stopped him. "I'll do it. What's the code?"

"One-two-two-eight. Thanks."

"You're welcome." Philippa got out, keyed in the code and swung the wide gate open.

As she waited for Tristan to drive through it, bittersweet acceptance hovered inside of her as she thought about things possibly coming to an end with Dominic. She breathed more of it in, along with the pungent mix of grass and horse manure.

Some people hated it, but to her, it smelled like a fresh start. Just like it had the very first day she'd arrived at Tillbridge.

After closing the gate, she got back into the golf cart, and Tristan drove toward the two-hundred-foot, sandstone-colored structure. It had been built to accommodate the needs of filming the movie. Now it was in the process of being transformed into a showpiece for the stable.

The state-of-the-art, temperature-controlled facility would not only house an arena large enough to train horses, but it would also be able to accommodate the needs of competitors training for rodeos and horse shows.

From what Rina had told her, the indoor arena was something Tristan had wanted for years.

"How is the renovation going?" she asked. "Last time I was here, they were painting the walls and installing the flooring."

"They finished most of it last week. They're working on that and the offices now." As Tristan maneuvered around a small hole in the grass, he pointed to the left of the building. "After the screening party is over, we'll start on the covered corridors that will lead to the outdoor arena and the new stable."

"Will you move the stable offices here?"

"I'm not sure. We're still considering it along with kicking things up a notch with more support for competitors—top trainers, specialized clinics for learning opportunities and hosting small events. Ideally, this would become one of the go-to places in the region."

Tristan parked in the front paved lot of the building, next to the four-seater golf cart Quinn, Jeremy, Eve and Teale had used to get to the arena. A red car was parked farther down, but she didn't see Dominic's rental. Had he hitched a ride with someone?

They got out of the cart, and Philippa walked ahead of Tristan down the sidewalk and through the glass-door entrance.

Cool air rushed over her as she stepped inside of the dark wood lobby with a reception desk to the right.

The impressive view of sophistication and practicality drew Philippa forward to the wide glass overlooking the main area.

A series of dark wood beams supported a white arched ceiling and two rows of translucent panels down the center of it. The beams continued down the wood walls that were in shades of light and warm brown wood. A dark wood ladder-railing fence surrounded the sand-covered area in the middle. Round, drop-down lights helped illuminate the space, and on the opposite end, a wide barn-style door sat partially open, letting in the sun.

Tristan joined her at the window. "They're up there, in the viewing box."

She followed where he pointed to the right. In the middle of bench-style bleachers along the wall was a room with a big window overlooking the arena.

Philippa caught a glimpse of Dominic, and happiness along with a small seed of anxiety tugged in her chest. Maybe the whole kiss on the forehead had just been a fluke reaction in the moment and she shouldn't read anything into it.

She followed Tristan through the door exiting the lobby. A walkway to the right, along the arena fence, took them past the wood bleachers. Instead of walking through the short tunnel to the wide corridor ahead, they went into a door on the left and up a short flight of stairs.

Tristan opened the door, and as she entered the wood-floored room with a sandstone fireplace, her gaze met Dominic's.

Something akin to sadness briefly flashed across his

face before he looked back to the group. No. Not sadness. Was it pity or guilt? Her heart sank.

Rachel walked up to Tristan with a wide smile. "Hello. We met a few months ago. I'm Rachel Everett."

"Tristan Tillbridge." He shook hands with the event planner.

Rachel looked to Philippa, and her smile dimmed. "Chef Gayle. You made it."

Before Philippa could respond, Dominic jumped in. "We appreciate you making time for this." His tone was formal and stilted as he looked to Philippa. "Especially since you have a lot on your plate today…like a busy schedule at Pasture Lane."

Teale and Eve exchanged perplexed looks, as if they'd missed something.

Quinn and Jeremy glanced at Philippa with slightly worried expressions.

Philippa answered him and her staff with a reassuring nod and a smile, "Everything's great at the restaurant and I'm excited to hear about the layout for the event."

Rachel took over the conversation, turning to the window and explaining how the sand in the arena would be covered with raised, temporary flooring.

A lot on my plate? They'd had an important conversation that morning. And yes, she'd cried, but she wasn't falling apart. She was fine. How many times did she have to tell him that? Philippa fought the urge to confront Dominic and tell him again. Not that she could if she wanted to—for some reason, he was keeping his distance from her.

As Rachel finished going over the seating arrangements, she turned back to the group. "Lighting is an issue. So we'll have to create it with candles in the centerpieces on the tables. They're going to be huge. Maybe we should just use big ol' candelabras." She released a breezy laugh. "But of course, I won't. That would be tacky. One thing we do have going for us are the skylights in the ceiling. Guess it breaks up the monotony for the people riding their horses in a circle."

Standing next to Philippa, Tristan crossed his arms over his chest. "They're not cosmetic. Natural light reduces the glare and shadows in the arena that could spook the horses."

"Right, the horses." Rachel flashed a bright smile. "And what about in here?" She opened her arms, encompassing the space. "Are there decorating plans for this room? This is where the stars of the film will meet with our largest donors before the event starts."

Tristan gave a nod. "Brown leather side chairs, a matching love seat and coffee table, plus stools in front of the window. They're arriving in two weeks. That's plenty of time before the event."

"Brown? That's so…rustic." Rachel's nose twitched with the same finicky expression she wore when she called Philippa's catering menu *decent*. "I'll make arrangements for something better to be brought in for the event."

"And what about our furniture?" Tristan asked.

Rachel focused on tapping info into her phone. "I suggest you get a PODS."

On the way down the corridor toward the back of the arena, Tristan murmured to Philippa, "Get a PODS. Is she for real? It's not like we don't have more important things on our task list besides changing out furniture she doesn't approve of just weeks ahead of the event."

"I know exactly how you feel."

He tapped a message into his phone. "Now I understand why Zurie bailed on this meeting. She probably suspected Rachel had demands. Zurie owes me."

Outside the barn-style door at the rear of the arena, the group discussion about the setup of the mobile kitchens, thankfully, didn't require as much input from Rachel. And they were all in agreement about the staging area for the servers and where they would enter and leave the arena.

Philippa made a note in her phone about service for VIPs in the viewing box. The kitchenette in the space wasn't outfitted to handle the small cocktail hour. Equipment would have to be brought in.

She stumbled.

Dominic suddenly appeared at her side and took her arm. "Careful. Are you good?"

Philippa gritted her teeth and resisted the urge to yell at him *I'm fine!* "Yes, thank you."

She marched away from him, more than ready to leave with Tristan.

Back at Pasture Lane, she grabbed the tablet they used for ordering out of her desk.

Dominic walked into her office. "Do you have a minute to talk about the portable kitchens?"

That was the last thing they needed to discuss, but the party, not their personal life came first. "If you can talk while I work. Sure."

She grabbed her zip-up, hooded blue sweatshirt from a hook behind the door and strode from the office.

Dominic followed her into the walk-in refrigerator, impervious to the cold in his short sleeves.

Philippa counted blocks of cheese on the metal shelf. "I'm listening."

"You're doing inventory. I could help. Do you want me to input the numbers while you count?"

Asking if he could assist her was a legitimate question. But under the present circumstances, it struck a nerve. "I can't do this. I won't do this." She left the tablet on the shelf and advanced on Dominic.

"Is there something wrong with the inventory?" he asked.

His honestly puzzled expression deflated some of her irritation. "No. But there's something going on with you. I realize finding out about the pregnancy this morning was a lot to take in. And just like you gave me permission to process how I felt about it, I respect that you need the same. But if you're feeling sorry for me or maybe guilty for not being there six years ago—don't."

Dominic opened his mouth as if to deny it, then paused. "That's not how I meant to make you feel. I'm just trying to..." He reached out to touch her. His hand and his shoulders fell with a long breath. "Maybe I do feel guilty. I just want you to know that I meant what I said about being here for you now."

"What I want you to know is that after telling you everything that happened, I feel like a burden was lifted from me that I didn't even realize I was carrying. You gave that to me. And I'm so grateful."

His brow lifted in surprise. "I did?"

"Yes." Philippa laid her hand on the middle of his chest. "And the last thing I want is for you to carry around guilt for whatever you think you did wrong." What she had to tell him next wasn't easy to say, but it had to be said. "As much as I want to be with you now, if guilt is all you feel when you look at me, we can't be together. But we can still work on this party as friends."

"No." Dominic laid his hand over hers, and his heart thumped against her palm. "I don't feel guilt when I look at you. From the moment I saw you again, all I've wanted is to be with you. And what you told me didn't change that. I was trying not to be selfish by putting my feelings first. I thought maybe you needed space or time away from me. I didn't know."

Rina was right. He *was* confused about what to do for her. She moved closer to him. "What I need... No, what I want is you."

"If that's what you want, you got me, Philippa. You always have." He intertwined his fingers with hers on his chest. "So where do we go from here?"

The outside handle on the walk-in door rattled and they moved apart.

Quinn opened the door and peeked inside. "Chef, we have a big problem."

"What's going on?" As Philippa rushed out of the refrigerator, Dominic was close behind.

"We're maxed out with reservations," Quinn said.

"And the waitlist is filling up," Bethany added, walking up next to Quinn. "And the front desk said people are hanging out in the lobby."

"That's odd." Philippa mentally ran through the event calendar in Bolan. Nothing stood out. "Did we miss a big event?"

"I asked the last person who called in for a reservation." Bethany's gaze slid to Dominic. "Someone spread a rumor that you're in the kitchen tonight."

"Where did that come from?" Philippa looked to Dominic.

He shrugged. "I don't know anything about it. If publicity had planned something, they would have told me before now."

"Maybe it's not that bad," Quinn piped in with hopefulness in her tone. "Maybe the people in the lobby are just waiting to see Dominic for an autograph or a picture."

Bethany massaged her temples. Anxiety reflected in her flushed face. "The hungry masses are going to slaughter us."

Philippa silently agreed with Bethany. "I'll go to the lobby and let people know the rumor isn't true. As far as the incoming reservations, we'll just have to tell them the truth as well. People will be upset with us, but we just have to remind them, we didn't advertise he'd be here."

"They're not going to accept that as an excuse," Dominic spoke to Philippa. "There's only one way around this. They came here for food. Let's give it to them."

"No." She shook her head. "You haven't had time to prepare a menu, and you're not familiar with ours. I can't ask you to put yourself in a bad position."

"I won't be in a bad position if it's a collaborative effort. Pasture Lane is *your* restaurant. You and your staff know the menu inside and out. I'll just follow your lead."

"And in the front of the house, we could squeeze in extra tables to cut down the wait," Bethany said. "And a few of the housekeeping and front desk staff have experience working in the restaurant. I could check in with their supervisors and see if they can spare them."

Philippa started to object, but what she saw in Dominic's eyes stopped her. He wasn't jumping in to help out of guilt that a rumor was spread about him being there. He genuinely wanted to do it, and he was up for a challenge. Back in the day, they were a good team on the front lines of the kitchen at Coral Cove. Did they still have it? If they were a little rusty, they could work out the kinks now instead of at the screening party.

Philippa swallowed the *no* to Dominic's offer that had been hovering on her lips. "Okay. Let's do this."

Chapter 13

Dominic tied a black apron around his waist. Pasture Lane was opening in a few minutes, and they seemed ready.

Earlier he'd called Teale and Eve to see if they could help. Eve was busy, but Teale was available to assist, and Jeremy had come in with her. The two of them would monitor the orders coming in and the plates going out.

Dominic walked to the center cooking station in the kitchen, double-checked the burners and the grill in front of him, and made sure he had ample pans, oils and the seasonings he would need nearby.

He glanced toward the front of the kitchen where Philippa conferred with Zurie.

They'd already worked out a plan. He, Philippa and Quinn would handle the main entrées while the rest of the cooks took care of the side dishes.

Philippa joined him at the station a few feet over.

She already had her game face on but gave him a quick smile as she adjusted the orders monitor attached to a rail above.

Determination settled inside of him. He wouldn't let her down. This was his chance to make up for being a bonehead. He'd realized after their talk in the walk-in, that when she'd cried on the porch at her house, he'd viewed it as her falling apart. And he'd assumed it was his job to pick up the pieces to make up for not being there for Philippa. He hadn't considered her sharing what happened would free her of something that was keeping her from being more of herself.

"First order up," Jeremy called out.

Dominic's focus kicked in as he read the order for pan-seared steak and grilled salmon on the monitor in front of him. "Firing steak."

"Firing salmon," Philippa said.

Although he wasn't in his own kitchen, as time passed, he quickly settled into the practiced rhythm of starting one order, moving on to the next and the next and then back again to plate up the finished products. Managing the hectic pace came as naturally to him as breathing. Innate and necessary. He needed the heat rising around him along with aromas of impending perfection. And Philippa standing beside him made the moment even better.

Her joy. Her skill. Her eye for making good even more wonderful. The confidence she'd gained over the years as a leader in her own kitchen. It fueled the adrenaline running through him. A ping of happiness and something Dominic had never felt before swelled in his chest. She was…phenomenal. And she was his again. At least temporarily.

Teale hurried over to him, carrying a plate with a pan-seared steak, the most popular entrée of the night. "A mistake was made on an order. We need to kill this on the fly."

Dominic quickly put the steak in a pan and tamped down judgment. There was no accounting for taste. If the customer wanted it extremely well-done, he'd give it to them.

As he handed a clean plate with the steak back to Teale, a couple of flashes of red appeared on the monitor in front of him, an indication that the maximum time it should take to complete some of the orders was almost up. He glanced at Quinn's station.

She was falling behind.

"How much longer on the vegetarians for thirty-nine and forty?" Jeremy asked.

"Ten out," Quinn responded.

That was way too long. He caught Philippa's eye.

From her concerned expression, she also realized they were dangerously close to being in the weeds. "Can you handle this for minute?" she asked him.

"Got it." Focus on maximum, he dialed in, cooking her parts of the menu as well as his while she jumped over to help Quinn catch up.

"Eighty-six the baked potatoes," one of the cooks handling the sides called out.

They were out of baked potatoes already? *Damn.* Dominic slid perfectly grilled salmon from a spatula onto a plate. They were running low on a few items and were already at the point of stretching others. Would they make it?

After what seemed like forever and no time at all, Teale shouted, "Last order out. We're done."

Whoops erupted in the kitchen, and smiles became infectious.

Philippa's smile was the best of all.

He winked at her, and she laughed and fanned her face.

Cheers grew louder as the staff started to applaud him and Philippa. They both redirected the accolades back to the staff.

Bethany hurried over to him wearing a rosy-cheeked smile. "The mayor is here with a few of his family and friends. He's wondering if you could come out and say hello to everyone."

Dominic waved off the request. "This is Philippa's restaurant, not mine. I was just helping out."

And he wasn't taking credit for something that shouldn't have happened in the first place. Things had worked out in Pasture Lane's favor, but it could have easily gone sideways. And more importantly, he wanted to finish his conversation with Philippa to make sure they were on the same page with their relationship.

"You should go out there." Philippa nudged him.

"No. This was a team effort."

"And right now, you're our star player, Chef Extraordinaire." With a bit of tease in her smile, she nudged his arm again. "You're up. And tonight, everybody wins. Go make people happy."

Make people happy. If he didn't go out there, people might leave unhappy. And that could reflect on Philippa and her people. After all the work they'd put in to make dinner a success, they deserved nothing but praise for their performance.

He spoke to Bethany, "Please tell them I'm on my way."

"Sweet." Bethany rushed back to the front of the house.

As he took off his apron, he looked at Philippa. "I won't be long. Can you wait for me?"

"I'm not going anywhere." He followed her gaze to the stacked dirty pans, utensils and food-splattered surfaces. "We're going to be here awhile."

In the dining room, he chatted, smiled and took pictures. When customers complimented him about the food, he gave credit where it was due—to Philippa and her staff. But not everyone heard him. They were too enamored with the idea of him being their chef for the night.

Close to an hour later, he finally slipped back into the kitchen.

The cooking stations were already clean. Kitchen helpers scrubbed ovens and other equipment. A combination of staff members from Pasture Lane and departments in the guesthouse helped at the dish machine.

The door to Philippa's office was closed, and he glanced through the window.

Quinn sat in the gray chair in front of the desk. Philippa leaned back on the edge of the desk, facing Quinn as she talked to her. As Quinn looked down at her hands in her lap, Philippa patted the young woman's shoulder in a comforting gesture.

Quinn had looked rattled when she'd fallen behind during dinner. Was she upset about that?

Just as he started to walk away, the office door opened, and Quinn walked out.

Head down, she passed him but not before he saw her blotchy cheeks and the bleakness in her red-rimmed eyes.

Dominic went into Philippa's office. "Is Quinn alright?"

"She will be. She's embarrassed about falling behind on the line at dinner."

"Tonight was intense. It could have happened to any one of us."

"That's what I told her." Philippa released a sigh. "One of the things that tripped her up tonight was being intimidated. She doesn't see herself as good enough, but she is. And comparing herself to Jeremy isn't helping. I advised her to stop dwelling on what she sees as her faults and focus on the type of leader she wants to be in the kitchen. On the other hand, sometimes I wish Jeremy would push himself a little harder. They both have so much potential, they're just scratching the surface."

In that moment, he saw glimpses of Chef LeBlanc in her. "What you're noticing in Jeremy, Chef LeBlanc spotted in me. She told me I had a choice to make. I could stay comfortable where I was and just be a good sous chef and an okay head chef someday. Or I could reach for something more, risk falling flat on my ass and probably achieve something better than I ever expected."

"That definitely sounds like Chef LeBlanc." Philippa released a wry laugh. "She was good at sharing advice involving choices."

He leaned back on the edge of the desk beside her. "What did Chef LeBlanc tell you?"

Philippa's smile faded a little. "I'll tell you another time. You asked me to wait for you. I'm assuming you want an answer to the question you asked me in the walk-in?"

"I do."

She leaned in, bringing her shoulder close to his. "I still think we should take things a day at a time and just enjoy being with each other."

For the part of him that not only wanted her but also to gain an understanding of who she was now, what she was suggesting sounded too simple. But maybe that's what she wanted. Uncomplicated. And he'd respect her wishes, especially if it moved them to the enjoying part of their relationship a lot quicker. He just wanted to get back to holding her in his arms without any reservations between them.

Dominic bumped his shoulder against hers. "It's a deal."

Chapter 14

Philippa sat at her desk, taking advantage of down-time after lunch to work on a draft of the food order for the party. It was massive, and they still had more menu items to decide on. But finishing the menu wouldn't take long since she and Dominic saw eye-to-eye on almost everything.

Her gaze drifted to the spot on the edge of the desk where they'd sat four days ago and agreed to keep seeing each other. Things had been good between them personally since then. And the planning for the event was falling right into place. But they could use a lot more couple's time outside of work.

His schedule had ramped up and his days were packed. He was running his LA restaurant long-distance and planning to open a new restaurant in Atlanta. Plus he was traveling to local farms and other places near Bolan to record segments that would be included in upcoming farm-to-fork themed episodes on his show. And on top of all that, he was still working out details for the screening party with her and their teams.

And now that the cottage was fully outfitted as a set kitchen, privacy there was almost nonexistent. It also served as workspace for the film crew and someone was always around. By the time he was alone, Dominic was tired. Their intimate moments, so far, had consisted of a few passionate kisses in the walk-in like the one they'd shared yesterday. He'd stopped by on his way to tape a segment at a family-owned operation that specialized in growing herbs for their line of preservative free seasonings.

It had been nice, and the kiss had added a spark to her morning, but she really missed him. And she was concerned about him not getting a break from work outside the few hours he slept.

"Earth to Philippa." Rina waved at her from the doorway.

"Hey. Why are you just standing there? Come in."

Rina shut the door behind her, then dropped into the gray chair. "I wasn't just standing there. I called your name twice, but you didn't hear me. I came to tell you that I changed your dessert order. You'd requested twelve rhubarb pies and two apple ones. I figured it was a mistake because I know you use more apple pies than that in a week, so I switched it around."

"I ordered twelve rhubarb pies? I must have been really distracted or something when I placed the order. Thanks for catching it."

"Does that 'distraction or something' have anything to do with the person who put that glow on your face?"

Philippa started to deny it, but as she thought of Dominic, she could feel happiness shimmering inside of her. "Is it that obvious?"

"Yes," Rina laughed. "They can probably see that glow from outer space."

"Great. I wonder what people are saying. I'm surprised Anna hasn't mentioned it in the *Town Talk*."

"If people are gossiping, I haven't heard about it. And all Anna talks about nowadays is the exclusive Dominic's people promised her at the party."

"That was the trade-off for her not pushing for a story about us at Coral Cove. I hope they know what they're doing. Backstage access. No limitations, and everyone in attendance is fair game for an interview if they're willing to give her one."

"Wow. No wonder she's keeping her mouth shut. But you smiling for no reason instead of frowning over work is worth talking about."

"Did I really frown that much before?"

Rina's good-natured expression came with a small shrug. "You were preoccupied with running this place, so it was understandable. But I'm also happy something else is also on your mind. I want details."

"There are none." Philippa sat back in the chair and explained the situation between her and Dominic.

When she finished, Rina slowly nodded. "Sounds familiar. The struggle for quality time together pretty much comes with the territory of being with someone connected to the entertainment industry. Tristan has experienced it with Chloe, and I have, too, with Scott."

"Any suggestions besides being understanding about Dominic's career? And I already mentioned to him about trying to spend more time together."

"When Scott's been working full-on for weeks, he forgets the benefits of slowing down for a few days. So I give him a few helpful reminders about what he's missing."

From the gleam in Rina's eyes, it was easy to imagine the theme of those helpful reminders.

Philippa laughed. "I'll keep that suggestion in mind."

The conversation switched to the screening party.

"I have news." Rina leaned in. "Scott called me this morning. He is going to make it back in time for the party. I'm so excited."

Tillbridge Horse Stable and Guesthouse was one of the major donors buying a table for the event, plus they'd contributed directly to Holland's scholarship fund.

"That's great. Do you know what you're wearing?"

"I'm still debating. Chloe said the dress code is on the formal side of dressy casual. A nice cocktail dress would probably work."

"Or a jumpsuit."

Rina's brow raised with interest. "I hadn't thought of that. Something that skews toward elegance. I'll stop by Buttons & Lace and talk to Charlotte. Last time I was there, I only saw casual jumpsuits, but she could probably order something for me."

Eager to stop by the boutique before going back to Brewed Haven, Rina gave Philippa a quick hug and left.

As Philippa refocused on work, her phone rang.

It was Dominic.

Smiling she answered, "Hey, stranger."

"Stranger? You just saw me yesterday."

"Did I? The kiss in the walk-in was so quick, I thought I imagined it."

He chuckled, and the sound curled through her, fading softly like whispers of smoke. "Well, I guess you should come see me for a refresher."

"Are you standing in my walk-in right now?"

"No, but I'm at the cottage. We had to delay filming at the bee farm. Apparently, the bees weren't having a good day, so we're testing a mac and cheese recipe for the show. We're using the fresh cheese we picked up from the dairy. Can you take a break and come give us an opinion?"

"Does giving an opinion come with a kiss for dessert?"

"I can probably come up with something."

"I'm on my way."

In the car, her conversation with Rina about being with a celebrity drifted into her thoughts along with Rina giving Scott "reminders."

Philippa chuckled. No wonder Scott was racking up frequent flyer miles coming back to Maryland so often. But if all went as Scott and Rina had planned, he would move to Bolan and the two of them would be together.

But with her and Dominic the situation was different. He was committed to his show and his restaurants.

If it was this difficult for Dominic to fit an afternoon into his schedule, a long-distance relationship would be even harder. *Sounds like what Chef LeBlanc had mentioned all over again...*

Whoa. Hold on. Philippa pulled herself out of the downward spiral the thought started to take her. It wasn't the same. They were established in their careers now and didn't have to work so hard to prove themselves. With a few adjustments and coordinating, they could at least try to make it work. But she was getting way too ahead of herself. What had she told Dominic?

They were taking it one day at a time and that meant not projecting into the future. At least, not yet.

At the entrance to the cottage, security opened the barrier and waved her in. The vans that the crew were using to get around town weren't taking up space behind Dominic's rental like they had been lately. Did that mean there were fewer people around today?

Philippa parked, then went inside the back door, which was unlocked. Inside the entryway, she followed the smell of delicious food wafting in the air to the kitchen.

Now that the white-topped granite island, a full complement of high-end appliances, and wood cabinets were installed, the brightly lit space was an intimate and welcoming atmosphere.

In the living room area, rolled-up black cables, camera equipment, and folded-up director's chairs sat near the side walls.

Teale and Dominic stood at the island, dressed in their work clothes. On top of the granite surface, steam rose from four square casserole dishes of mac and cheese, baked to a perfect golden brown. Bottles of water were also on the island.

Teale waved. "Hi, Philippa."

"Hello." Philippa stood next to Dominic.

He glanced over at her and smiled. "Thanks for agreeing to give us another opinion."

"Mac and cheese. I wouldn't miss it. So, are you not featuring the mac and cheese bites we're serving during cocktail hour at the party?"

"We're featuring both," Dominic replied. "The bites and a variation of traditional baked mac and cheese. We're trying to decide on the variation."

"What have you narrowed it down to so far?"

Teale pointed to the dishes as Dominic spooned a modest amount from the first one on three small plates. "We have traditional mac and cheese as the control. The variation we choose has to stack up to it as far as texture, mouthfeel and flavor. The first variation is sun-dried tomato and truffle oil. The second is seafood. We used a mixture of lobster and crab."

Philippa accepted the plate and a fork from Dominic. They all took bites. The traditional dish with a blending of different cheeses hit high marks on every level.

After sips of water, they moved on to the second. After more sips of water, they tasted the third.

"What do you think?" Teale asked.

Philippa set her fork on her plate. "Well, the tartness of the sun-dried tomatoes and the earthy flavor of truffle oil really blends well together. With the seafood variation, I'm tasting a Creole-type seasoning that's balancing out the sweetness of the lobster and crab. I like that, too."

Dominic studied her as he took a sip of bottled water. He set it down and placed the cap on it. "What's your pick?"

Her pick? The two of them spending the afternoon alone someplace where kisses were the priority, along with sharing a plate of mac and cheese while tucked under the bed covers. And maybe a nap to help erase the shadows from under his eyes. But unfortunately, those options weren't on the menu.

She pointed to the seafood variation. "That one. The Creole seasoning gives it just the right amount of kick."

Teale smiled. "I like that one, too." Her phone rang on the counter, and she checked the screen. "I need to take this." She walked into the living room space.

Unable to resist temptation, Philippa put a little more of the traditional mac and cheese on her plate. "Change is nice, but I don't think anything can beat a really good basic mac and cheese."

She ate a bite of the pasta dish. As she licked cheese sauce from her lower lip, she glanced up and saw Dominic staring at her mouth.

He cleared his throat. "Yeah, I agree. There's nothing like an original."

The huskiness in his tone raised daring, desire, and her curiosity. Clearly Rina's reminders had snagged Scott's attention when it came to making time for enjoyment as a couple. Did the busy Chef Extraordinaire need the same kind of nudge? It wouldn't hurt to try. And it could be fun.

"What type of cheese is in this? I can't quite place it. Wait don't tell me." Philippa took another bite of food. She released a quiet moan, making a show of drawing the fork slowly from her mouth. "Oh, I got it. Cheddar, Swiss and Parmesan...and Gouda. Definitely, Gouda."

As Dominic looked at her, he swallowed hard. "Yeah, definitely Gouda. You got that right."

He lifted his bottled water partway to his mouth before realizing the cap was still on.

She barely repressed a smile.

As he took a sip of water, she leaned in and whispered to him, "You know, this mac and cheese may be the best thing I've ever had. Well, maybe not the best. There is something that's much, much better and I really enjoyed it."

Dominic put the cap back on the water and set it down. "There is?"

She took him in from head to booted feet and back

up again. "Oh definitely." As she met his gaze, she pictured what she wanted him to see. Desire enveloping her from the inside out.

The look in Dominic's eyes made her heart speed up. He glanced around to Teale.

Her back was to them as she chatted on the phone.

He moved closer and flattened his palm low on Philippa's back. "I think we should go to the main room down the hall. We're using it for storage." He leaned near her cheek, and his faintly whiskered one grazed over hers. "I've got some new cookware you should see. And I should probably deliver on the promise of dessert."

Dominic moved his hand a bit lower, and a rush of desire made her shiver. As much as she wanted to take him up on his offer right then, she wasn't ready to concede in the flirting game yet. She was holding out for a bigger payoff.

Philippa brushed her lips lightly over his ear as she whispered to him, "I'd love to check out your impressive cookware and sample dessert, but I have to go." She stepped out of reach with a smile on her face.

"Wait. You're leaving?"

"Yes. Priorities. You know how it is."

Dominic's incredulous expression pulled a laugh out of her.

The look on his face shifted to one of understanding, and a sinful smile curled up his lips. "Priorities. That's a good one. You do know what they say about payback, don't you?"

"You mean like turnabout is fair play?"

Dominic took a step toward her. "Exactly."

"I'm still a little confused by what you mean. If you care to explain it to me. I'll be home around eight."

His steady gaze stayed on her as she backed out of the kitchen.

As she reached her car, a text from him pinged on her phone.

You're in trouble.

Internally, she happy danced as she texted back.

I'm counting on it.

See you at eight.

The hours crawled by at a snail's pace until she finally left Pasture Lane. She had enough time to get ready for Dominic. What should she wear? Something flirty or downright sexy?

Eight o'clock at her place, she checked her hair and makeup in the mirror hanging by the entryway. Behind her, the low light from a corner lamp in the living room added a rosy glow to the beige furniture with an assortment of throw pillows with a pink, blue and green design.

She adjusted the shoulder strap of her coral-pink sundress. Flirty—that was the right choice, wasn't it?

Five after eight came and went, and her heart practically sank to her bare feet. Had something come up and he couldn't get away?

The sound of tires crunching on gravel made her heart leap and she peeked out the living room window.

Dominic got out of a black SUV, and as he walked up the steps, the car pulled out of the driveway.

She opened the door before he had a chance to ring the bell.

He was still dressed in his uniform.

He walked in and she backed up. From the look in his eyes as he shut and locked the door behind him, she really was in trouble. The good kind.

"Oh…" Desire and anticipation took away her ability to form sentences.

A faint trace of humor broke through the desire in Dominic's eyes. "'Oh'? After the torture you put me through, is that all you have to say to me?"

"Sorry…not sorry." Laughing, Philippa made a run for it, and he chased her down the adjoining hallway. Sure, she deserved payback for teasing him, but why make it easy for him?

She reached her bedroom near the end of the hall, and Dominic was on her heels. But as she backed farther inside the room lit up softly by a bedside lamp, he paused.

Instead of coming for her, he started unbuttoning his gray chef's jacket, holding her gaze as he took his time. After he dropped the jacket, he moved on to his black pull-on shirt.

Riveted by the ripple of muscles in his abs, chest and arms, she dropped down on the bed.

As his shirt joined his jacket on the floor, he moved on to unfasten his boots. A self-assured smile ghosted over his mouth as she continued to watch him.

When the rest of his clothing finally joined the pile on the floor, he approached the bed. In between heated kisses, he removed hers.

Dominic nudged her back and stretched out beside her on the bed.

Philippa's breathing shallowed as the evidence of his desire pressed to her thigh. Her own need made her tremble as his slow caresses and the brush of his lips moved down her throat and whispered over the tips of her breasts...her belly...and between her thighs.

She arched up as he teased, pleased, and took his time. Breathy moans poured out of her as Dominic kept her hovering on the precipice. It wasn't enough. She ached for her climax that was just out of reach.

Impatience...her greatest weakness next to him. He knew her too well.

Chapter 15

Philippa sat in the canvas director's chair in the portable trailer, remaining as still as possible as the auburn-haired makeup artist lined her lips.

What had she been thinking when she'd agreed to tape an episode of Dominic's show with him? Clearly, she hadn't been thinking. Probably because she'd been so into him. Holding back the smile that wanted to take over her mouth, Philippa let her mind wander through all that had taken place since the day of the mac and cheese tasting.

He'd started coming to her house at night whenever he could get away after a day of filming. But that wasn't a simple task. At the cottage, Dominic would slip into the back seat of the SUV driven by one of the private security specialists he'd brought in from LA. On their way to the hotel up the road where the security team was staying, they'd drop Dominic off at her place.

Once he arrived, they usually cooked a meal together, watched movies, talked…and made love. But he never stayed until morning.

Long before sunrise, the routine was repeated in reverse as the security specialist now going to the cottage for his guard duty shift would pick Dominic up.

The paparazzi or local journalists weren't hounding him yet, but as they ramped up for the event in two weeks and the stars of *Shadow Valley*, including Chloe Daniels, arrived in Bolan, more of them would be in town. Adhering to the current security plan would help keep him and Philippa off their radar for now.

"Okay, you're all set." The makeup artist removed the protective paper collar from around Philippa's neck.

The middle-aged woman had skillfully filled in Philippa's brows, enhanced her cheekbones and given her natural-looking lush lips.

"Thank you." Philippa rose from the chair, carrying a copy of the one-page script.

Walking out the wide trailer onto the grassy field overlooking the strawberry patch at Crossroads, a pick-your-own-fruit-and-vegetables farm near Bolan, she struggled to remember what to do next. The hoard of butterflies turning somersaults in her belly kept distracting her.

The film crew and other members of Dominic's team, including Eve, bustled in and out of the other three trailers and extended vans, also parked in the field, almost in a row.

Chloe was supposed to be there, too, but Philippa hadn't seen her since she'd arrived close to an hour ago. Or Dominic.

Farther down on the right, John, the blond production assistant, emerged from in between a trailer and a van. The slender, serious-looking guy was dressed in tennis shoes, jeans and a black *Dinner with Dominic* T-shirt with CREW printed on the back.

As he hurried over to her, he talked to someone on his headset as he looked at the screen of the computer tablet he carried. "Yes, the talent is ready. I'm bringing them to you now." John looked up and his face morphed into a smile. "Chef Gayle, you look great. Follow me."

Philippa fast-walked with him. Maybe she should have worn her tennis shoes instead of her boots with her chef's uniform. "How far do we have to walk to get to the set?"

"Oh, no, you don't have to walk. I'm zipping you over there in a golf cart, and I'll bring you back here afterward so the driver can take you home."

The two-hour journey there by private car had been nice, and the driver had been courteous. But it had also been lonely.

When Dominic and his director had talked her into this, she'd envisioned her and Dominic riding to the farm together, taking in the sights along the way. Of course, that didn't make sense. Coming to Crossroads Farms wasn't a romantic road trip.

As promised, John took her where today's set was located.

The area with empty stalls covered by green-and-white-striped awnings was where the farmers' market took place on the weekends. An intimate outdoor restaurant, reserved tables only, was also opened for lunch and dinner right next to it during that time. Customers enjoyed a limited menu featuring produce they picked, prepared tableside.

She and Rina had tried it out once and loved it, but the long drive there and back had been a bit much.

A tall bistro-style table sat in the middle of a grassy space amid the stalls. Cameras, lighting and other filming equipment along with a director's chair were positioned a few yards away from it.

John walked her to a spot off to the side. He left for a moment and returned with a canvas chair. "Have a seat. Someone will mic you up soon. I'll be nearby. Let me know if you need anything."

"Thank you."

Crew members bustled around the area. They moved equipment. Checked the lighting as well as the distances, from different angles, from the camera to the table.

Where was Dominic? Would he spend a few minutes with her before the filming started? It would help to see his face right now. As time passed without seeing him, her disappointment and anxiety started to increase.

"Hi, Philippa." Chloe waved.

As she strolled toward Philippa, a light breeze lifted her wavy black hair from her shoulders, and the skirt of her casual purple dress flowed around her thighs. She made traversing across the grass in heels appear effortless.

When she reached Philippa, she gave her a big hug. "Uh-oh. I know that look. It's called nervous."

Philippa returned the embrace, relieved to see a familiar face. "I can't believe I got talked into this."

As John appeared with a chair for Chloe, another young, dark-haired guy with kind hazel eyes came over with two lavalier microphones.

He turned to Philippa. "This needs to be inside your

jacket so it won't show on camera. Is it alright if I attached it?"

"That's fine." She opened the top buttons of her jacket and he clipped it on the inside, near the top of her chest.

He handed her a black box the size of a deck of cards. "This is the receiver. I'll let you tuck this into a pocket. That side one on your pants leg looks good."

Philippa stuck it in her pocket and buttoned it closed.

Chloe taped on her own mic and tucked the receiver into a discreet side pocket in the skirt of her dress.

After thanking John and the sound guy, she settled into the chair next to Philippa. "You're going to be just fine."

"I don't feel fine. I woke up feeling nauseous. I don't know how to act."

"That's the best part. You don't have to. From what I saw when I glanced at the script, it calls for you and Dominic to have an ordinary chef-to-chef conversation about food, just like you would if the crew and cameras weren't around."

"Let me guess. I'm supposed to pretend that they're not there."

"Yeah, that's the expectation." Chloe chuckled but empathy reflected in her brown eyes. "I know it's intimidating to have cameras in your face. But Dominic and I are experienced at doing this. Just follow our lead, and we'll get you through it."

A brunette, dressed like John, drove Dominic on set in a golf cart. After thanking the woman, he got out and strode toward Philippa and Chloe. He was more than impressive looking in a navy chef's jacket rolled up to his forearms, paired with black pants and boots.

As he approached the table, his gaze met Philippa's and he smiled.

Her heart kicked in a few extra beats. He looked so wonderful. She could sit there and stare at him forever.

"Hi, ladies. It's good to see you." Dominic gave Philippa an impersonal hug. He smelled just as wonderful as he looked. He turned and hugged Chloe. "Thanks for doing this on such short notice."

Chloe smoothed a curl from her forehead and smiled. "Happy to help. And you promised me food. How could I resist?"

Brianne, the show's dark haired assistant director, came over to them. After greeting everyone, she walked them through the scene. "Dominic, we'll do the intro for this clip later. Chloe, we want your genuine reaction to what you're tasting, so don't hold back." She looked to Philippa. "This is just a natural conversation between you, Dominic and Chloe about the menu. Do what you'd normally do in a food-tasting situation. Just pretend the rest of us aren't here."

Chloe arched a brow at Philippa with a friendly I-told-you-so look on her face.

It couldn't be that simple. Could it?

In a flurry of activity, the crew handled camera adjustments as the makeup artist and stylist made last-minute touch-ups to Dominic, Philippa and Chloe's hair and makeup.

Eve brought two picture-perfect salads to the table. Sliced orange-and-blush peaches added bright pops of color to the summer slaw, and lemon wedges along with lemony dressing gave the grilled romaine a fresh appeal.

Once the salads were in place, Eve and the stylist cleared the set.

As Dominic and Philippa took their places around the high table, he gave her hand a light squeeze, and she glanced at him.

His wink combined with a slight, sexy smile created chaos with her heart rate, already on overload from nerves.

Not helping... The mics hanging above them and the one clipped near her chest caused her to hold back in saying it. She stared at Dominic, hoping he'd get the hint.

His smile broadened, and from the look of satisfaction on his face, he knew what type of an effect he had on her.

Philippa's nerves lessened a bit as she released a quiet chuckle and slowly shook her head at him.

"Alright." Brianne peered at a monitor. "Looks good. Quiet everyone. Action."

As if he'd flipped a switch, Dominic kicked off the conversational scene. "Chef Gayle and I have narrowed the salad choices down to these two. A summer slaw with charred peppers and peaches with a miso dressing. And grilled romaine topped with applewood-smoked bacon, fresh Parmesan, a dusting of crushed sourdough croutons and drizzled with a creamy lemon dressing." He turned to Philippa. "So, which one do you think is best?"

Upbeat banter... That was something the script mentioned. She looked up from the salad at Dominic. But they didn't banter. They traded opinions and took sides.

"I like the slaw, but I'm leaning toward the grilled romaine. The combination of the char on the lettuce, the smokiness of the bacon and the zesty flavor of the lemon reminds me of summer grilling season. It's simple, but it also has upscale flair. It's almost a reflection of the event."

Dominic's eyes lit up with approval. "I definitely see and taste what you're saying, but I also think this summer slaw fits in with the event in the same way. It's a complex mix of flavors with the cabbage, peppers and peaches. But the peaches, along with the fresh cilantro, basil and mint, give it a fresh summer appeal, which gives the salad its name."

"But a name isn't what makes a recipe." Philippa smiled. "It's all about taste."

"True." He chuckled good-naturedly. "I think we're going to need help with this decision, which is why I gave Chloe Daniels a call."

"Hey, you two." Chloe waved as she approached them.

Hugs were exchanged, and then Dominic spelled out their dilemma.

Just like Chloe promised, she and Dominic took the lead, making it easier for Philippa to forget about the cameras and follow them through the conversation.

After Chloe tasted the salads, she set down her fork. "Wow. This is so hard. I love the fresh peaches in the slaw, but who can say no to bacon with the grilled romaine?" Her expression grew thoughtful. "Why can't we have both of them?"

That wasn't a bad idea. Philippa chimed in, "A sampling of both—I like it."

Dominic stroked his chin with a contemplative expression. Then he smiled. "I can get on board with that."

"Yay," Chloe cheered. "I can't wait to enjoy them at the party."

A beat or two later, Brianne yelled out. "Cut. Good job, guys."

Chloe looked Philippa up and down. "You go, girl. Handling yourself like a pro."

A smile took over Philippa's mouth as she exchanged a high five with her. "You two made it easy."

Dominic lightly placed his hand on Philippa's waist. "She's right. You were great. I knew you would be."

She leaned into him, and as his gaze dropped to her mouth, the temptation to kiss him almost overwhelmed her. "Thanks."

"I like all of this. And I want more." Chloe made a gesture encompassing them and the salads. "Tristan and I are going out for bar food at the Montecito. It's karaoke night. We don't sing. We sit in a corner and watch. Do you want to come with? It's usually calm—hardly anyone asks for a picture or an autograph."

Dominic looked to Philippa. "We'll be done here in a couple of hours. I'm in if you are."

"But don't you have a conference call with your sister tonight?" He'd mentioned it yesterday.

"I'll squeeze in a short one with her beforehand."

A night out with Dominic—like a date? No, it wouldn't be like a real date because they wouldn't be able to act like a couple. "Sure, I can make it."

"Sounds like a plan." Enthusiasm lit up his eyes. "What time are we meeting up?"

Hours later, Philippa tucked her keys into her shoulder bag and walked up the steps to the porch of the Montecito Steakhouse alone.

She entered the semifull corridor between the bar

and the dining area of the dark-wood-and-brick restaurant and veered left to the bar.

The place was fairly busy for a Thursday night. Most of the stools at the bar up-front were occupied with people watching the flat screens featuring sports channels. Empty tables dotted the semicrowded main floor, and a few people played pool and darts at the side of the room.

After changing four times, she'd chosen the right outfit. Thank goodness. Because of her job, she spent most of her days, buttoned up in a chef's jacket wearing a pair of clogs. Slipping into her strappy stilettos, form-fitting jeans, and pink-and-blue-patterned boho sleeveless blouse was a nice change, along with ditching the headband she wore in the kitchen. And she didn't have to worry about staying out too late. Tomorrow, she had the morning and most of the afternoon off.

She spotted Chloe waving her over to a corner booth on the other side of the room. Tristan sat beside her. Chloe still wore the same dress from the taping at the farm. Tristan was also casual in a tan shirt and jeans.

Over the past few years, Philippa had socialized with Tristan at staff gatherings and at Rina's house. She'd also hung out with Chloe numerous times in the past year, including helping to organize Chloe's bridal shower, but Philippa had never gone on a couples' outing with them.

It was a little strange. And joining them on her own made her feel a tad awkward.

"Hi… Hey." Chloe and Tristan greeted Philippa at the same time.

She gave them both a smile and a general wave before she took her bag off her shoulder and sat down.

Tucked in the middle of the curved seat next to

Tristan, Chloe patted the space next to her, prompting Philippa to slide closer.

As Tristan took a pull from his bottle of beer, he glanced toward the room, then back to Philippa. "I thought Dominic was coming?"

"His meeting with his sister ran longer than anticipated, but he's on his way. He said we should start without him." And coming in separate cars helped protect their undercover relationship.

"I'll put in a food order at the bar," Tristan said. "It's faster than waiting for a server." He looked to Philippa. "Cajun wings, ribs and loaded nachos okay?"

"Sounds good to me."

After finding out what Philippa wanted to drink and if Chloe wanted another glass of red wine, he headed for the bar.

Chloe sat back in the booth. "You did a really good job today with the segment. I honestly don't know what you were worried about."

"Thank you. It means a lot to hear you say that. I was so afraid of messing up."

"That was never going to happen. You held your own. Dominic wouldn't have asked you if he didn't think you could. He's the star of a hit show. It doesn't matter that you're his girlfriend, he can't afford to be charitable about who he puts in front of the camera."

"Girlfriend? No. Dominic and I are old acquaintances and colleagues."

"You do realize I can see right through Publicist 101–speak. And I felt the sparks between you two this afternoon, so I'm not buying it."

"That obvious, huh?"

"Just a tad." Chloe laughed, but then her expression

sobered. "But I get why you're not making things public. It can get rough. Coming back to Bolan is a relief for me. The novelty of me being with Tristan died down after the wedding. And a lot of the people around here don't care that I was in a movie. I'm just Chloe Tillbridge walking down the street. But that could change once *Shadow Valley* releases next week."

It may have been rough, but Chloe and Tristan gave off strong power-couple energy when they were together. "How do you and Tristan handle the attention so well?"

"One moment at a time." Chloe looked toward Tristan at the bar and smiled softly. "And he understands that what we share as a couple is fact. Anything that's put out for public consumption about us, especially in the media, is highly speculative." She glanced past Philippa and pointed. "He's here."

Philippa joined Chloe in waving down Dominic.

He wove through the tables and the crowd, making it to the corner booth without anyone stopping him, and sat next to Philippa.

He'd changed into dark jeans and a black pullover. Outfit-wise they were a perfect match on their first couples' date.

"Sorry I'm so late." His gaze met Philippa's before encompassing Chloe. "Next round's on me. Where's Tristan?"

"Waiting for drinks at the bar. I should go help him. Do you know what you want?" Chloe asked Dominic as she slid out the other side of the booth.

"Beer's fine."

Once Chloe left, Philippa looked to Dominic. A

small frown tugged down his mouth as he stared at his hand on the table. "Did your call with Bailey go okay?"

He gave her a lopsided smile. "It could have gone better."

"What happened?"

Dominic scratched over his brow. "I lost a big investor in the Atlanta restaurant."

"Oh, no, I'm sorry. Why are they pulling out?"

"Not sure." He released a harsh breath. "They just said the project wasn't a right fit for them anymore."

Philippa angled herself toward him. "Will this delay opening the restaurant?"

"Not if we can find another investor. I have to go back to LA day after tomorrow for a few meetings."

"How long will you be gone?"

"A few days, maybe. But I'll be back in time for the party. I'm sorry that I'm leaving at a critical time and dropping it all on you."

"You're not dropping anything on me. The menu's finalized. The food is ordered. Coordination for the setup and the help we need is on track. There isn't much left to do. But what about your show?"

"We might be able to squeeze in one more episode at the cottage after the screening party. We'll have to tape the rest of them at the set kitchen in LA. As far as the rest of the farm segments, the crew will film some general footage of the places I didn't get to visit, and we'll add my voice-over to them."

The dejected look on his face made her heart go out to him.

He'd really been looking forward to his upcoming visits to the bee farm and the local farm vineyard and winery. They were using honey from the bee farm in one of the sauces and serving wine from the vineyard at the party. He'd planned to highlight both on his show.

Under the table, Philippa laid her hand on his thigh in a comforting gesture. "Anything I can do to help?"

He laid his hand on hers. "No, but I have to tell you something." He opened his mouth to say more.

Tristan and Chloe returned with drinks, and a server followed with their food.

"We're back." Chloe set a bottle of beer in front of Dominic.

The server put down the food, plates and utensils as Chloe and Tristan slid into the booth.

Dominic gave Philippa's hand a brief squeeze before letting go. He leaned closer and spoke in a low voice for only her to hear. "Let's enjoy being out tonight. We'll talk later."

They all dug into the food.

Chloe talked about the upcoming, red-carpet premier of the movie in LA the following week. Tristan would attend with her.

"And review time is always interesting." Chloe shook her head. "I can't bring myself to read them when they go up."

"You were fantastic in *Shadow Valley*." Tristan kissed her cheek. "That's all you need to know."

Loud hoots of laughter traveled across the bar from a group headed toward seats near the pool table. A willowy tanned, dark-haired woman in a short flowy white dress and brown cowboy boots seemed to be the ringleader of the group.

Chloe stared that direction. "She looks familiar."

Something about her was familiar to Philippa, too. "Who is she?"

Dominic put down his beer. "Destiny Mitchell." Scowling, he stood. "I'll be right back." He stalked off toward the group.

"Wait. Isn't she his ex?" Chloe asked.

Tristan paused in the middle of eating nachos.

"Yes, that's her." Unease built inside of Philippa as Destiny threw her arms around Dominic.

"Well." Chloe's gaze narrowed. "She's definitely not invited to our table."

Chapter 16

Dominic reined in frustration as he deftly took Destiny's arms from around his neck and guided her to a less crowded area near the pool table. "What are you doing here?"

Destiny gave him a puzzled look. "Didn't your sister pass along that I wanted to talk to you?"

"She said you were calling me." And he'd told Bailey to tell Destiny *not* to call him. They had nothing to talk about.

Recently, the producers of *Best Chef Wins* had pushed back about featuring him and Destiny as a couple on the reunion show. She was all in. His answer was still a hard pass.

"New York is just a few hours away, and I wanted to have a conversation with you face-to-face. Come sit with us." She tilted her head to the side, a practiced, coy gesture aimed at breaking down resistance and getting what she wanted.

He'd quickly become immune to that during their few months together. Right around the time he'd found out her so-called friends were the ones feeding info about him and Destiny to the media. And that she knew about it. He also began to suspect her cookbook deal was nonexistent. She kept changing her story about whether she had a contract. All of that had led him to distance himself from her.

"I don't know if you're here on your own or if someone convinced you it was a good idea. Either way, you're wasting your time. I'm not doing the reunion if rekindling a fake relationship with you is part of it."

"Des and Dom." A woman hurried over to them. "I told my husband it was the two of you." She looked to Dominic. "I love your show and your cookbook. Can I get a picture with the two of you?"

"Sure." Destiny beamed.

One of Destiny's friends jumped up to take the photo.

The woman was so excited. He couldn't say no to a fan.

Making sure the woman was between him and Destiny, he conjured up a smile as the picture was taken.

"Thank you," the woman said. "My girlfriends back home in Colorado are going to be so jealous." She hurried back to her table.

Destiny turned to Dominic with a high-and-mighty expression. "Pleasing the fans. That's what the reunion show is about. That's why I've signed on to do it. You holding out is just selfish." She stalked back to her friends.

Selfish? He respected and appreciated his fans. He

wasn't holding out because he was selfish. He was holding out because he didn't want to perpetuate lies about his personal life. Especially now that he and Philippa were back together.

Dominic glanced back at the corner booth. Chloe sat alone. He spotted Tristan near the pool tables, talking to Bethany and her boyfriend, Adam, who was a groom at the stable.

Did Philippa leave? Dominic swore under his breath as he wove through the crowd. He should have told Philippa about the reunion show and Destiny. He'd almost mentioned it when he sat down earlier in the booth and he and Philippa were alone. But then Chloe and Tristan and the food had showed up.

At the booth, her purse was gone. His heart dropped. "Where did Philippa go?"

Chloe glanced up at him as she ate a loaded chip. She held up her finger, telling him to wait as she chewed. Finally she finished. "Ladies' room. And that's all I know."

Dominic exhaled in relief as he dropped down on the padded seat. "Can you at least tell me if she's upset?"

Chloe said nothing, but the look she gave him said everything.

He should know the answer to that question. "Destiny being here is not what it looks like."

"So I should hold off on digging up my vintage Des & Dom T-shirt?"

"Definitely?" Did she really have one?

Chloe picked up a pile of nachos with a fork and put it on her plate. "Balancing reality and perception are what we have to do. I get it. But people outside our industry don't always see it that way. I almost lost Tristan because I wasn't viewing my situation from his perspective."

"What did you do to fix it?"

"I set boundaries with other people. And I made sure he was clear on where we stood as a couple. He knows I have obligations, but he also understands that he's an important part of my life. The last thing a relationship needs is doubt." Her gaze shifted from him to across the room. "She's coming back." Chloe's gaze came back to him. "Whatever you need to say to straighten things out with her, don't wait. Tell her now. You might not get another chance."

"I know." He'd already made the mistake of not telling her earlier about the situation with Destiny and the reunion. He wouldn't do that again.

Tristan returned and slid back into the booth next to Chloe. He looked between her and Dominic. "So... is everything okay?"

Chloe held a chip near Tristan's mouth. "It will be when you order more appetizers."

Tristan grinned. "Already on it. Cheese fries and jalapeño poppers are on the way." He ate the chip and Chloe kissed him.

Stay ahead of the curve and take nothing for granted. Tristan had the right game plan. Envy and disappointment in himself pinged solidly in Dominic. He had to get his act together if he didn't want to lose Philippa.

She arrived at the table, and he stood to let her in the booth.

As she scooted next to Chloe, she plunked her purse down next to him, as if putting a barrier between them.

Ignoring him, she looked toward the karaoke DJ set up off to the side.

Just as he leaned in to speak to her, music blasted through the speakers and the crowd grew livelier.

A small group of women stood near the area huddled around a song menu. Laughing, they all pointed to each other as if trying to determine who should go first.

A moment later one of them stood in front of the monitor with a mic.

Strains of a ballad sung by Adele floated through the bar. The self-conscious woman quietly sang the opening line slightly off key. But as her friends cheered her on, she settled into the lyrics and grew more confident.

Philippa swayed in her seat to the music.

Was it corny to get up and dance to karaoke? No one in the bar was, but did it matter? Especially if he could erase any doubts in Philippa's mind about his commitment to their relationship?

Dominic stood and held his hand out to Philippa. "Dance with me?"

Her eyes popped wide as she swallowed a bite of nachos. "To this? Now?"

"Yes. Now. And the song doesn't matter. I want to dance...with you."

Smiling, Chloe nudged her. "Go on."

Philippa took his hand and got up. He led her to a clear spot a few feet from the karaoke equipment, then pulled her close, holding her by the waist.

She hesitated a beat before resting her hands on his chest. Hints of confusion and concern were in her gaze as she glanced around the bar. "Maybe we shouldn't do this. People are staring."

"I don't care. I'm with you, not Destiny. And I want everyone here and outside this place to know we're together. I don't want to pretend we're not anymore."

Maybe it wasn't the ideal way to break the news of their relationship, but he was tired of pretending.

Nodding in agreement, Philippa relaxed in his arms.

As he brought her closer and laid his forehead to hers, Philippa slid her hands up and around his neck and closed her eyes.

The ballad about true love floated over them, and soon they swayed slowly, nearly cheek to cheek.

I could hold you for a million years to make you feel my love...

The lyrics of the song reflected everything he wanted her to know and hoped their relationship could be.

During a break in the song where the lyrics paused, the music swelled and so did a strange feeling in his chest.

"I love you." Stunned that the declaration slipped out of him, he missed a step.

As she looked up at him, surprise and a soft, happy smile lit up Philippa's face. "I love you, too."

Relief came over him, and he kissed her softly, fighting the urge to deepen the kiss as her lips curved into a smile against his.

"Hey, you two," Chloe stage-whispered as she danced nearby with Tristan. "Cut that out, or go make out in the car already."

Philippa glanced at Chloe and laughed, a pure sound, filled with joy.

As her eyes met his, a mix of emotions hit him all at once. Desire, love, the need to take care of her and keep her safe—they intertwined inside of him along with a hint of fear.

He couldn't mess this up. No matter what, he'd make sure she was happy. He'd show her in every way he could just how much she mattered to him. How much he needed her. Starting when they got to her place later on. Dominic kissed her again. But until then, he'd have to be content with a dance.

That night, at Philippa's house, they went inside and he locked the door.

"Tonight was fun." Philippa leaned over to slip off her sandals.

"It was."

She stood up straight, and the lure of her lush lips was too much of a temptation. He gave into it and pressed his mouth to hers. The kiss took them from zero to burning passion in an instant.

In the bedroom, they undressed each other, and his world narrowed to fervent caresses and heated kisses. Gliding into Philippa, he was lost, blinded by need that he couldn't control.

Afterward, sated from passion, he held her in his arms, content and happy for the first time in…he couldn't remember. And he didn't want to give it up to travel back to LA. Or to be on a reunion show.

You holding out is just selfish…

Destiny's words played in his mind. Bailey had said pretty much the same thing when he'd wanted to pull out of the screening party.

What they called *selfish* felt like self-preservation, because lately it had started to feel as if he had nothing. But around Philippa it felt as if he had something. And whatever it was, he didn't want to lose it.

A couple of hours before sunrise, Philippa stuck a hazelnut coffee pod in the coffee maker on her black granite counter. She started the machine and the scent that always perked up her morning filled the air.

Her growling stomach had woken her up earlier. Maybe it was because of all the extra activity she'd put in with Dominic last night. Unable to go back to sleep, she'd gotten up without waking him. He'd looked so peaceful in her bed. She'd lingered, taking in the sight of him.

And that's when the idea had come to her. Breakfast.

They hadn't shared a morning meal at her house yet. And they had time to enjoy it before his security showed up to take him back to Tillbridge.

As she sipped coffee, she sorted through a mental list of current ingredients in her kitchen and settled on what to make.

Reaching into the hammered-copper bread box, she took out the loaf of brioche. Then she grabbed a bowl from under the counter and took a whisk from the drawer. From memory, she mixed milk, eggs, vanilla, sugar and spices in a bowl. In no time, slices of brioche sizzled in a skillet with butter and syrup warmed in a pan on the stove.

Dominic walked into the kitchen, sniffing the air. "French toast?"

"Yes. And you're just in time."

As she slid the golden, toasted slices from the non-stick skillet onto a couple of plates, Dominic hugged her from behind and kissed the side of her neck. "Thank you."

"You're welcome."

A short time later, they sat on the high-backed stools next to the tall kitchen counter and communed over their food in companionable silence.

Cinnamon, nutmeg, allspice and buttery sweetness flowed over her taste buds.

Dominic swirled the last bit of his French toast around his plate, gathering up leftover syrup. "I haven't tasted French toast like this in a while." He finished the bite. "Allspice, huh? How much?"

"Just a dash."

He chuckled. "Got it. So this is one of those recipes that lives in your head, no measurements needed."

"Yeah. I've been making it since I arrived at Till-bridge."

He sat back on the high-backed stool. "How did you end up at Tillbridge?"

During their past conversations, they hadn't gotten to that topic.

"Well." She pulled the pieces of the story together in her mind. "I'd decided to leave DC and move to Phila-delphia. I was driving there. I didn't have to be to work for two weeks. I already had a place to live, so I was taking my time. Someone had mentioned that the best chili they'd ever tasted had come from this food van at a horse stable. I was intrigued."

"So, like all foodies lured by the claim of the best, you had to check it out."

Philippa chuckled. "Yeah, I did. And I met the van's cook, Hollis Prescott, or Hollie as everyone called him. He was seventy years old with the energy of someone half his age. He'd worked for Tillbridge as a groom for years, and he was also known for his food. He used to cook meals for the staff on a grill, set up near the parking lot.

"Five years before I met him, a horse had crushed his foot. It became too difficult for him to do his job and he had to retire. But he missed being around everyone, and they missed his food, so he started going to the stable during the week to cook for them. He purchased the van so he wouldn't have to miss a day because of cold or bad weather. Eventually, it turned into a bona fide business."

Dominic picked up their plates. "So many great places start out like that. Someone cooking for the love of it and it turning into something more."

In her mind, she could see Hollie's smile light up his brown face through his white beard. "He really did cook with love and didn't mind sharing it. When I told him why I'd come to his food van, he invited me to come back the next day to see how he made his famous chili. I did, and ended up helping serve it to his customers."

"Smart man. He put you to work." Dominic rinsed the plates in the sink and put them in the dishwasher.

"I didn't mind. I loved talking to him. He'd led a fascinating life. He'd grown up in Texas. Joined the navy at eighteen. Got out and joined the merchant marines. He'd married twice. Lost both wives and didn't have any children. After he lost his second wife, the love of his life, he'd been on his way to Maine to become a deckhand on a lobster boat. A wrong turn had put him at Tillbridge, and he never left."

Dominic came back to the stool and sat down. "Sounds like what happened was meant to be."

He took hold of her hand on the counter and intertwined their fingers. It was a natural gesture that happened with ease, as if they'd sat there hundreds of times and he'd done that very thing.

Philippa continued the story. "I didn't want to leave, either, after helping him for two more days. I came by the van the third day to say goodbye to Hollie, but it was closed. I found out he'd had a heart attack. I went to see him and decided to stay the night. He was so upbeat and optimistic about his surgery. I just knew he'd make it."

As if sensing what was coming next, Dominic held her hand a bit tighter.

"I was devastated. I'd envisioned coming back to see him, helping him in the van and enjoying one of our long talks." Remembered sadness tightened Philippa's throat.

"I kept thinking about our talks as I was driving to Philadelphia and halfway there, I turned back.

"The Tillbridges were in charge of Hollie's affairs. I wanted to buy the van from them and take over where Hollie had left off. They said they couldn't sell it to me, but they could give it to me. Before the surgery, Hollie had updated his will and he'd left it to me. He believed I'd come back. Less than year later, I was opening Pasture Lane."

Pride and respect for her bloomed inside of him. "I'm not surprised you were successful." Her kissed her hand. "How did the restaurant happen? Did you approach the Tillbridge's with the idea?"

"I—"

The sound of a car engine filtered in, and they both looked to the front of the house.

Breakfast was over. Dominic had to leave.

Philippa smiled through her disappointment. "Your ride is here."

Chapter 17

Dominic battled reluctance as he retrieved his wallet and phone from Philippa's bedroom. He sent a text to the security specialist waiting in the SUV that he was on his way out to meet them.

Waking up to be with Philippa and having breakfast together had been so relaxing. And he'd enjoyed finding out more about her career and the things she'd experienced along the way.

But the moment had ended too soon. And since he was flying to California tomorrow, they wouldn't get a chance to kick back like this for a while considering the upcoming event and their schedules.

Dominic went back down the hall and joined her at the front door. He indulged in a long kiss with Philippa.

It would have to tide him over at least for a few hours. He and the crew were filming at the bee farm that morning.

Maybe he and Philippa could meet up for a late lunch. "What time are you going into the restaurant today?"

"Close to the start of dinner. I have a ton of house-work to do." As Philippa leaned away, she caressed up and down his back. "Quinn is in charge until I get there, I'm hoping the responsibility will boost her confidence."

Dominic squashed his planned lunch invitation. "Can we meet up later tonight at the cottage? I promise to kick everyone out by eight."

"I'll come by, but I'm not staying the night. You need to get some sleep before you leave."

He was flying out of Baltimore at four in the morn-ing by private jet, and he'd hit the ground running once he landed in LA. "True. And if you stayed, you'd wake up earlier than you needed to because of me."

"Yeah, that wouldn't be any fun." She looped her arms around his neck. "But I will miss kissing you before you leave. I like your goodbye kisses."

He squeezed her waist. "Just my goodbye kisses?"

"Well…" She gave him a teasing contemplative look. "I guess your hello kisses are decent, too. On the scale of one to ten maybe they're a four."

"A four? Oh really?" He tickled Philippa's waist and nibbled a sensitive spot on the side of her neck.

Releasing a squeal of laughter, she squirmed in his arms. "Wait…stop."

"Not until you change your score."

"Intimidating the judge—that's not fair!"

Chuckling, he doubled down on the tickling.

"Okay." Philippa laughed breathlessly. "Four and a half." She escaped from his hold.

Dominic caught her by the waist again, brought her flush against him, and captured her mouth. The feel of her soft curves changed teasing into want and the kiss quickly grew heated.

Releasing a moan of disappointment, she flattened her hands to his chest and eased out of the kiss. "Go. The bees are waiting."

Dominic took a deep breath and reined himself in. Philippa's lips, swollen from the kiss, made him want to say to hell with everything but being with her.

He let her go. "See you tonight."

In the driveway, on the way to the SUV, his phone rang.

He checked the screen then answered it. "Hey, Eve, what's up?"

"Apparently, not the bees. The psychic bee farmer says today's not a good day either for us to film. Or more accurately, she said, it's not a good plan for *you* to be there today. Isn't that weird? Anyway, Brianna and Matt are working on moving up filming at the vineyard to today instead. I had a question about the wine pairings we're featuring in that segment…"

His mind drifted away from what Eve was telling him, and an idea started to form. He couldn't stop a grin. "I'm taking the morning and afternoon off."

"Excuse me?"

"And everyone else can, too. I'll be at the cottage in time to tape the episode like we planned."

"That's fine with me, but Brianne…"

"She'll be fine. I'll let everyone know. See you tonight."

He ended the call, released the security specialist to return to the cottage until he called him, and then sent the team a text.

No frills or explanations, just what he told Eve. He'd

never skipped out before, but it was his show, and he had a say in his schedule. The bee farmer cancelled. He could shift his afternoon conference calls to another day. It was too easy.

After he sent it, a weight lifted from his chest, and something he hadn't felt in a long time took its place. Freedom.

Dominic jogged back up the stairs to the porch. He rang the doorbell.

A short time later, Philippa opened the door. She was clearly surprised to see him. "Hey."

Dominic strode across the threshold, cupped her face, and laid a kiss on her that left them both breathless.

"How was that for a hello kiss?" he asked.

A dreamy expression covered Philippa's face as she blinked back at him. "That was perfect. Did you come all the way back here for that?"

He stroked her face. "Yes, kind of. Need help with your housework? I have the morning and afternoon off."

That afternoon, Dominic stirred sugar into a pitcher of fresh lemonade in Philippa's kitchen.

After they'd finished the chicken sandwiches he'd made for lunch earlier, he'd been cleaning the refrigerator and discovered a half-dozen lemons starting to dry out in the back of the crisper drawer. With all he and Philippa had accomplished in and outside the house, lemonade was the perfect reward.

Working together they'd knocked out cleaning the rooms, doing a couple of loads of laundry, and clipping a few of the hedges in half the time it would have taken Philippa on her own. Now they could just relax.

He'd even gotten the rest of the story about her and Pasture Lane Restaurant. Business at the food van had become so successful, she'd started selling basic pre-made dinners at night to the locals. But instead of driving back home, many of the people started utilizing the few tables she'd set up or took chairs out of their truck and tailgated.

Once Zurie had decided to build the guesthouse, it was clear a restaurant needed to be a part of it. Philippa and Zurie had approached each other at the same time. They'd negotiated terms—Philippa would have full control over the development and running of the restaurant and receive a percentage of the profits on top of her salary. From its opening day, Pasture Lane had been a success.

After pouring the lemonade into two glasses with ice, he carried them to the front porch where Philippa sat on the bench seat.

A light breeze ruffled the leaves on the trees and recently trimmed flowering hedges lined near the porch.

She looked up at him, and the gleam of happiness that had been in her eyes since their hello kiss grew even brighter. "Okay. Now you're just showing off. You cleaned, cooked, did lawn work, and now you've made fresh lemonade."

"I'm not showing off. I'm spoiling you."

She accepted the glass he handed her. "I could get used to this."

He sat on the bench seat next to her. According to Philippa, the area around them had once been farmland. The time he'd spent at Tillbridge and traveling through the countryside to visit farms, he could easily imagine cows and horses as part of the landscape. And maybe a modest-sized garden off to the side.

Dominic stretched his arm behind Philippa's back and took a sip of lemonade. "I wouldn't mind doing this again. I'm really enjoying today."

She made a face. "Even the vacuuming?"

"I'm happy about being here with you. But I have to admit, the vacuuming was pretty satisfying."

"Seriously?" She gave him a baffled look. "You find housecleaning satisfying?"

"Not always." He pulled her close and kissed her temple. "But today, wasn't just about cleaning. There was so much more to it."

Philippa's expression grew even more puzzled. "I don't understand."

He searched for the words to explain. "This place reflects who you are, and every room tells a story. The throw pillows in the living room reflect your love of color. The number of serving bowls and platters in your cabinet are a dead giveaway that you want to share your love of food. And the scent of lavender and lemon balm in your bedroom," he traced his finger over her smooth cheek. "That's the place where you're the most peaceful. This isn't just a home. It's your sanctuary."

"But isn't your house a sanctuary for you, too?"

"In a way, I guess. It serves its purpose. It's where I leave and come home to at night. It's functional."

"Oh?" For a brief second, something akin to sadness passed through Philippa's face before she covered it with a smile. She laid her head on his shoulder. "Well, that's important, too. Especially if functional was what you wanted."

When he'd bought the house a few years ago, he'd

designed the studio kitchen the building contractors had added on to the house for the filming of his show.

As far as the rest of the place, he'd filled out an extensive questionnaire for the interior decorator about his style preferences and intended uses for the rooms. Weeks later, he walked into a place with clean lines and a few eye-catching details.

In the private plane the next morning, when it lifted from the runway into the dark sky, a sadness that mirrored what he'd spotted in Philippa's eyes when he'd described his house to her came over him.

Years ago, a functional house, and a functional life had suited him. Now he yearned for something that he didn't know how to describe. But the one thing he did know, whatever it was. He wanted it with Philippa.

Chapter 18

Dominic walked past the host stand into the dining area of Flame & Frost LA. Afternoon heat mingling underneath his gray suit and light gray dress shirt, minus the tie, quickly dissipated.

At three in the afternoon on a Monday, the lunch crowd in the space that was a combination of clean lines, dark wood and tinted glass had thinned out.

The perfect time for a meeting, at least it was in Bailey's eyes. He would have rather been in the restaurant's kitchen. Cooking was one thing that could jolt him awake after a long flight. Earlier that afternoon, he'd made the mistake of sitting down on the couch in his home office after a series of conference calls and conked right out. He'd even slept through the reminder he'd set on his phone, making him late for the meeting.

Dreaming of holding Philippa in his arms, then waking up on his couch had been a huge disappointment. He missed her.

As he walked through the dining area, servers wearing uniforms in different combinations of the restaurant's ice-blue-and-black, and red-and-black color schemes walked briskly, delivering food from pass-through windows in front of the restaurant's two open kitchens on the right and left.

On one side near the pass-through, in a glass-enclosed cooking station, one of the cooks made a show of lighting the pan while preparing one of the restaurant's popular flambéed desserts.

In the glass-enclosed station on the opposite side of the restaurant, another cook chopped, sliced and diced vegetables at lightning speed. He twirled the knife as he finished preparing one of the restaurant's signature salads.

Artful 3D images of both cooks hovered up top near the ceiling.

Today, no one flagged him to a table for a conversation. Most of the high-profile patrons would show up for dinner, and he'd have to make the rounds then, acknowledging them.

Dominic spotted Bailey in a teal dress, having lunch at a four top with the businessman who'd flown in from New York. He gravitated in that direction.

Bailey saw him and flashed a smile that leaned more toward business than personal. "Here he is, Mr. Henshaw." She looked toward the middle-aged dark-haired man at the table. "Let me introduce you to my brother, Chef Dominic Crawford."

"Mr. Henshaw, it's a pleasure. My apologies for being late." Dominic shook hands with the businessman.

"It's a pleasure to meet you as well."

Bailey sat down and both men took their seats.

"How was lunch?" Dominic glanced over Bailey's half-empty plate with her usual order of a grilled pineapple-and-chicken salad.

From the potato tourne garnish still on the plate, Henshaw had ordered a ribeye.

"How was the steak?" Dominic asked.

"It was great." Henshaw gave an appreciative smile. "One of the best I've tasted. The seasoning was perfect."

A tall brunette server came by the table. As she cleared Bailey and Henshaw's plates, she glanced to Dominic. "Would you like me to bring you something, Chef?"

He really wasn't hungry, but a chef who didn't eat in his own restaurant was a bad sign.

Dominic looked to Henshaw and Bailey. "Have you decided on dessert yet?"

Bailey responded, "No, we haven't."

"Would you like me to bring an order of the flambé sampler?" the server asked.

That was exactly what Dominic had planned to suggest. "Please."

He made small talk with Henshaw and Bailey about flight delays, airports and the weather. As they conversed, the server returned with shooter glasses of peach cherry jubilee topped with fresh rum whipped cream, bananas Foster, and candied bacon and apples over vanilla ice cream.

Henshaw took a bite of the peach cherry jubilee and his brows shot up. "Wow. This takes me back. My grandmother had a peach orchard. She was a whiz when it came to making desserts with all of the fruit."

Dominic's thoughts took him on his own journey. Sitting on Philippa's porch, imagining what a house in the country might look like, he'd envisioned a garden. But a place with an orchard...

Bailey surreptitiously kicking his leg under the table brought him back.

She smiled at Henshaw. "Dominic definitely has some innovative ideas brewing."

Picking up on what he believed was the thread of the conversation, he added. "I do. Right now, my team and I are developing a farm-to-fork menu for an event."

"Oh, really?" Henshaw replied.

"Yes. We're striving to bring out those memories of home, like when you tasted the peach-cherry jubilee." Dominic leaned in. "When I was in Maryland..."

Dominic and Bailey said goodbye to Henshaw in the lobby of the restaurant.

As soon as the man walked out the door, Bailey looked to Dominic. "Can I talk to you please?"

Instead of heading for his upstairs office overlooking the dining room, she stalked into the nearby admin office used by the host staff.

As soon as he shut the door, she whirled around and faced him. "What was that?"

"What was what?"

"You talked for almost an hour about taste memories, orchards, houses in the country and cows. Oh, and bees?"

"You asked me to tell him about the ideas I had brewing."

"For Frost & Flame Atlanta. Not from your field trips in Nowheresville, Maryland."

"First of all, it's Bolan, Maryland. And second, hell yeah, my mind is in Maryland. I'm a week away from the *Shadow Valley* movie screening, but you pulled me out here for meetings. And maybe, if you wanted me to talk about brewing ideas the way you want me to, you should have let me get some sleep before you scheduled this meeting." Fatigue and frustration made him impervious to her patented death stare.

Bailey closed her eyes a moment and released a heavy breath. "If Mom and Dad didn't love you so much, I would trade you in for a better brother."

"You love me too much to get rid of me."

"I love my sensible brother who understands the value of investors, but he's not here. Seriously? Bees? Why?"

Maybe he had gone overboard, drawing out the whole ecosystem thing on a napkin. "We've been trying to tape a segment at a bee farm, but something always goes wrong, like yesterday. I ended up taking the morning and afternoon off."

"Really? You took time off? What did you do?"

From the look on her face, she might have already heard, and even if she hadn't, he wasn't going to lie about it. "I spent the time with Philippa."

"Philippa—that reminds me. I got a call from someone I know who works for one of the producers of *Best Chef Wins*. Destiny Mitchell pitched them an idea for a new show called *A Date with Destiny*. How a single girl goes from the heartbreak of being part of a love triangle to finding true love one meal at a time."

"Love triangle..." He was about to ask with who, but Bailey's face clued him in. "You mean me, her and Philippa."

"Ding, ding, ding. You win! And there's pictures and videos of the three of you at some dive bar to back up her claim. You're kissing Philippa and Destiny is confronting you about it before she stalks away."

"What? That didn't happen. Philippa and I were enjoying a night out with friends when Destiny showed up at the bar with her entourage. She hunted me down after you told her I was in Bolan. So far, Philippa hasn't called me about any issues with paparazzi or the press. But I should still warn her."

"Well, lucky for all of us, the latest Kardashian news cycle is on an upswing, and not very many people care about your little love triangle. It's already yesterday's news, at least until the reunion episode, where I'm sure Destiny will cry her eyes out to help pitch her new show."

"So, they're going ahead with the reunion show?"

"In one form or another. But that isn't your focus, and neither is Bolan. The screening party is done from a project perspective. You just have to execute it, and once you do, you're not ever going back. I need your eye on the ball that's important—Atlanta."

Dominic started to object about not ever going back to Bolan. But in the world of celebrity, long-distance relationships often had a short shelf life. But he also couldn't envision not seeing Philippa again.

For the next three days, Dominic stayed on task with the restaurant and investor meetings, while brief conversations and texts with Philippa tided him over. But she was wearing down, carrying the load of the restaurant plus preparing for the screening party.

On the night before the event, they chatted by video as he sat on the couch and she lay in bed.

She yawned. "The trout and the rest of the vegetables came in today. So that's everything."

"Are Jeremy and Ben good on cutting the short ribs tomorrow?" Ben, a sous chef at Frost & Flame LA, had flown to Maryland that morning.

"Yep. They'll get it done." Philippa's eyelids drooped. "And..." She fell asleep.

There was no point in waking her.

He could end the call. But he stayed on, watching her sleep. Her nose wiggled with a soft, quiet snort, and he stifled a chuckle. She looked cute.

"Good night, Philippa," he whispered, tracing over her cheek on the screen.

The time where he could hold her in his arms again couldn't come fast enough.

Chapter 19

Philippa stood in the viewing box at the indoor arena overlooking the dining area for the party. Nine hours ahead of the event that started at eight, the raised flooring, round tables, groupings of potted green plants and flowers provided hints of the coming transformation.

She turned and glanced behind her at the glass enclosed space.

Rachel had decorated the viewing box with a deep blue, U-shaped sectional, surrounding a large coffee table. Four tall bistro tables were also positioned along the side wall.

The adjoining bathrooms were clean, polished and stocked with artfully arranged baskets on the counter that possessed multiple convenience items including breath mints, deodorant and sewing kits.

Hopefully, the food service areas and all the staff would remain just as ready. She'd just completed a walk-through of the portable kitchens, making sure all the equipment worked, and pots, pans and utensils had been stocked, along with dishware. The only thing missing were disposable gloves.

In a couple of hours, Jeremy, Ben, Teale and a couple of kitchen workers would arrive at the portable kitchens to complete the advanced prep that hadn't already been done. Quinn was supervising normal operations at Pasture Lane through lunch. Once that ended at two, she'd oversee closing the restaurant with Bethany, and then both of them would come to the arena.

The only missing piece was Dominic. His last text message was to tell her he was on his way to the airport. By now, the private jet he was taking was already in the air.

"There you are." Zurie came into the viewing box. "I'm just checking in. How are things?"

"So far, so good."

Zurie glanced out the window. "Rachel may have her quirks, but she definitely knows what she's doing. I can't wait to see the finished product. And I can't wait to get my hands on the short ribs you guys are making tonight. When I sampled the test recipe, they were amazing," Zurie stage-whispered. "Maybe you could send a few extra plates of that entrée to our table."

Philippa laughed. "I'll see what I can do."

While everyone at the party would receive the salad and dessert sampler plates, multiple entreés would be plated in smaller portions and brought to the table by servers on a tray. The servers would make at least three passes, giving the guests an opportunity to try different entrées or have a second or third portion of what they enjoyed.

Close to noon at Pasture Lane, as she supervised the packing of ingredients in a van and a refrigerated truck on the back dock, she glanced at her phone. Dominic's plane should have landed.

Later in the day, back in the kitchen, she checked on Quinn at the expeditor station and the lunch service.

"I'm going to the arena," Philippa said. "Call me if you need something."

"Okay, I will." Quinn stopped a server from picking up a plate in the window. Using a cloth, she wiped a spot of gravy off the rim as she spoke to the server. "Jackie's in the weeds. Can you help her out and take her order to table six? It's about to become a dead plate."

The server snagged the two orders and took them to the dining room.

Good call... Since their talk, Quinn seemed more focused, and her confidence had improved.

Philippa's phone buzzed in her pocket. It was a text from Dominic.

Running late. We're stuck in traffic.

But at least he's on his way. She answered.

No problem. We're good here. Can't wait to see you.

A moment later a GIF of the spaghetti scene from the movie *Lady and The Tramp*, appeared on her phone.

Philippa laughed and some of the tension lifted from her shoulders. Tonight was going to turn out great. She could feel it.

At the arena, Quinn walking into the portable trailer

made Philippa stop seasoning the trout and look at the time. Where was Dominic?

She'd sent him a text, but he hadn't responded. He hadn't answered her calls either. Cell phone dead spots sometimes happened on the back roads to Tillbridge. If the driver had taken one as a shortcut, Dominic might not realize she was trying to contact him or be able to call. But if they were on a back road, that would mean Dominic was closer to getting there.

Moments later, the chime ringtone she'd recently programmed for Dominic played on her phone in her front pocket. Relief sang through her as she stripped off her disposable gloves to answer it. "Hi, are you almost here?"

"I'm still near Baltimore." The sound of passing traffic came through the phone.

"Are you stuck behind an accident?"

"No, but I was in one."

"What? Are you okay?"

Ben, searing short ribs nearby, glanced at her.

The wail of sirens on Dominic's end of the line fueled tingles of dread.

Swallowing panic, she left the kitchen trailer. "Dominic."

"I'm here."

"Are you okay? What happened?"

"My driver had a heart attack. One minute, he was driving, and the next, he slumped over the wheel."

"Oh, my…" Shocked, she stared at the two connected kitchen trailers just yards away. The ones Dominic would have been in if he were there. "Is he alright? What about you?"

"He's on his way to the hospital. I'm on my way there, too. I have a cut on my head. I need stitches."

Stitches? Dominic must have hit his head really hard. He could have a concussion. "Which hospital are you going to? I'll meet you." Philippa rushed toward the makeshift parking area where she'd left the golf cart.

"No, Philippa. You can't. The screening party. You have to stay there."

He was right. She couldn't leave. "I'll find someone who can pick you up."

"I'll call the car service. I need to make sure they know what happened, anyway. I'll ask them to send another driver to pick me up from the hospital."

"No. I'm finding someone."

A golf cart was coming across the field. It was Zurie.

Unable to stay put, Philippa started jogging toward her.

Zurie slowed to a stop beside her, concern on her face. "What's happened?"

Philippa filled her in.

"Let me talk to him." Zurie took the phone and got the pertinent details from him. "Got it. Just sit tight at the hospital. Someone will be there to get you. And you have my number? If anything changes, call me." She ended the call and gave Philippa her phone. "I'll call Mace. I'm sure he can pick him up."

"Thank you." Philippa's hand trembled as she put the phone in her pocket.

"Hey." Zurie reached out and squeezed Philippa's arm. "He's okay. He's on his way to the hospital. They'll take care of him, and Mace will get him here safely."

"I know. I should tell his team what happened. And mine."

"Take a minute before you do that. Let me call Mace, and then I'll come talk to you."

Philippa forced herself to breathe as she slowly walked back to the trailers, trying to envision what happened with Dominic and the driver. What *could* have happened.

I almost lost him... Her heart filled her throat.

A few deep breaths later, she rounded up Teale, Ben, Jeremy and Quinn and told them about Dominic's accident.

Teale grew pale. "He's going to the hospital, but he's okay, right?"

"As far as I know he just needs a few stitches."

Jeremy wrapped a protective arm around Teale's shoulders and whispered in her ear. Nodding, she leaned on him a moment, and then he let her go.

"What do you need us to do?" Jeremy asked.

"I'll need you and Teale to take over Dominic's two trailers. Quinn and Ben, I'll need you with me. You're all experienced supervisors, so I need you to take the lead with the cooks and kitchen staff that are working with us today and reassure them that we're still on track. Dominic and I picked you to work with us on this event because we knew we could count on you. And that's why I'm not worried. I know you'll do a fantastic job."

The group dispersed and walked to their assigned trailers.

Philippa took a moment to mentally lean into what she'd just told them. It wasn't lip service. Jeremy and Teale were in sync with each other and would easily take over Dominic's place. Ben was professional, precise and had good instincts about what had to be done, and Quinn was reliable and would also rise to the occasion. Having the four of them in place would allow her to oversee the entire food production process and keep an eye on quality control.

Anxious moments later, Zurie tracked her down. "Mace is on his way to Dominic."

"Good." Philippa released a pent-up breath. Knowing Dominic was taken care of and that he was counting on her, she focused.

As Philippa checked over the salads in one of the trailer's refrigerators, Eve showed up dressed to work.

"I heard about Dominic. What do you need me to do?"

Grateful to have another pair of experienced hands and Eve's eye for presentation, she assigned her to quality control and to keep things moving smoothly in the staging area set up in the corridor.

Time sped up as the start of the event grew closer. The atmosphere became even more intense when the party started and trays of food were taken from the trailers to the corridor.

Philippa settled into the calming space of what she loved to do—create moments of solidarity for people with food. A moment where first bites ignited shared smiles and conversations. Where new taste memories were born and people would look back and say "Remember that meal?"

She made sure the honey-lemon dressing was drizzled just right over the salads. Monitored the cooking of the seared trout, making sure it was crispy and succulent as it rested on a twirl of veggie noodles. She ensured the glazed short ribs sat perfectly on creamy, Carolina Gold rice grits. That in the staging area, puffs of whipped cream sat like fluffy clouds on top of the fruit-based desserts.

As the last of the desserts left the table in the staging area, she closed her eyes and breathed. A happy high-pitched squeal made her open her eyes.

Rina hurried over to her, looking fabulous in a blue-green sleeveless jumpsuit and heels. "You killed it! Everything was beyond wonderful. I'm so proud of you." She briefly hugged Philippa, then leaned away. "And I have good news. Mace has Dominic. They're on the way. Dominic is fine."

"Thank you." Her whispered prayer came with an unexpected rush of latent adrenaline and relief. Happiness almost loosed tears.

Rina snatched a clean cloth napkin from the servers' backup stash on a table and put it in Philippa's hand. "No time for that. Dry your eyes. Wipe your face. And take off that apron. Holland Ainsley wants to acknowledge you onstage."

"But…"

"No *but*s. Come on." Rina tugged her down the corridor toward the front of the arena.

As they reached the hall archway leading to the arena, Philippa saw Dominic.

Her mind went blank to anyone or anything else as she ran to him. He took her in his arms.

His warmth and strength surrounded her, and she took in a shaky inhale, breathing him in. "Are you okay?" Not waiting for an answer, she cupped his cheek and kissed him. The firm press of Dominic's lips reassuring her that he was. Philippa leaned away and carefully skimmed over the bandage near his right temple.

"I'm fine." He smiled down at her. "They even did a

scan at the hospital to make sure my head's okay. I just needed a few stitches, that's all."

Rachel came partway into the tunnel and smiled. "Dominic, you're okay."

"Yeah, I'm good."

Rachel beckoned. "Come on. Holland's waiting."

Philippa took Dominic's hand and stepped forward, but he didn't move. She looked back at him.

He smiled wider. "Not me. Just you."

She glanced to Rachel, who beckoned again. "Chef Gayle, come on. Holland's announcing your name."

Dominic nudged Philippa along, but she held on to him. "Go on." He kissed the back of her hand. "I'll be here when you're done. Promise."

Nodding, Philippa slipped her hand from his and followed Rachel.

A short time later, applause erupted, and pride swelled inside of him. Rachel had already told him how smooth everything had gone and that the attendees were raving about the food.

But he'd never worried or doubted her ability to handle the event without him. She'd been there for every step of the planning, and even made it easier for him. They shared the same vision, work ethic and level of passion. They made a good team.

Philippa came back to him with a happy grin on her face. "Wow. Did you hear that?"

"I did." He gave her a lingering kiss. "I'm really proud of you."

"Thank you, but I didn't do it on my own. Everyone helped. They heard what happened, and they really stepped up. I need to thank them. Are you coming?

They were worried about you, especially Teale, Eve and Ben."

"No, I don't want the focus to be on me and what happened. I want you guys to celebrate the moment." His head throbbed, but he resisted touching the bandage. "I'm heading to your place. If that's alright."

Happiness flooded her face, and something tugged in his chest. "Of course it is. Do remember the codes for the door and the alarm?"

She refreshed his memory and hurried down the corridor to thank the staff.

As she walked away, some of the tension he'd carried since the accident left him.

Mace and Zurie came down the stairs from the viewing box and walked over to him.

Zurie looked around, then back to Dominic. "Where's Philippa? Did she see you?"

"She just went to thank everyone."

"I know she's glad you're okay," Zurie said. "We all are. I can't believe what happened."

"Neither can I. One minute, the driver, Pete, was talking about his grandkids, then the car started slowing down, and he slumped over. Seconds after that, we were rear-ended and spinning off the road."

Zurie's mouth dropped open. "It's amazing no one aside from the driver is in the hospital. That poor man."

Mace nodded. "I talked to one of the deputies on the scene. She said the driver taking his foot off the accelerator saved you both."

And Dominic was grateful for that. He'd felt so helpless in the back seat when Pete slumped over. The feeling had only grown during the seconds afterward, when he realized how much danger they were in with traffic speeding down the interstate around them.

Then the car had started to spin, but his mind had slowed, and Philippa's face came into his thoughts along with a sadness that he might not ever see her again.

Dominic breathed away the awful memory. "Any word on Pete's condition?" he asked Mace.

"Not yet. He's still in surgery. I can't get an update directly from the hospital, but the deputy said she'd call me once she heard something."

"And his family? Were they able to reach them?"

"They got a hold of his wife. She's at the hospital."

"Good." Pete had family with him. Hopefully, he would pull through.

Suddenly, a wave of soreness and tiredness hit Dominic and he massaged near his temple.

"Do want me to take you home?" Mace asked.

"If you do, you'll miss the start of the movie."

"She'll fill me in on what I missed later." Mace briefly kissed Zurie then turned back to Dominic. "Are you going to the cottage?"

"No." A longing to go where he wanted to be the most settled over him. "I'm going to Philippa's."

By the time Mace dropped Dominic off, his head was throbbing full force. After a long, hot shower, he found some pain reliever in the cabinet, took it, crawled into bed and immediately conked out.

A few hours later, the dipping of the mattress woke him up.

Slipping under the covers, Philippa glanced his direction. "Sorry, I didn't mean to wake you."

"That's okay. Come here. Let me hold you."

She snuggled close to him. The clean smell of soap-scented oil wafted from her. "I'm so glad you're okay."

"Me, too." There was so much more that he needed to tell her, but fatigue took hold of him again. One thought lingered as his eyelids closed. Holding Philippa in his arms felt like home.

The thought was still on his mind in the morning when he drifted into the kitchen.

Philippa, standing at the stove in a blue silky button-down sleep shirt, making eggs, was a beautiful sight. And one that he couldn't imagine not seeing again.

Dominic wrapped his arms around her from behind, and she leaned into him. He'd missed her so much when he'd been in LA. He didn't want to be apart from her again.

Reaching out, he turned off the burner under the skillet and turned her around by the waist to face him.

A surprised smile lit up her face. "What—?"

He kissed her hard and deep, savoring the sweep of his tongue over hers and the soft curves of her mouth.

Dominic eased away and stared into her eyes. "Come back with me to California. Before you say anything, hear me out. We're good together. And I don't want to miss a moment of being with you. I want to be there when you rise to the top—a bigger restaurant. A ton of cookbooks with your name on them. Your own show. And not just work. I want to share a home with you that tells the story of us. I want to build a life with you."

He'd meant to lay out his plan with more finesse, but the words had poured out of him.

"Oh, Dominic." An inner struggle played out in her eyes. As Philippa skimmed her fingers over the bandage on his head, her bottom lip trembled.

His heart started to sink. "Please, don't say no."

Soft emotions covered her face as she cupped his cheek. "I'm not saying no. I want all of those things with you. But I can't leave Tillbridge. At least not right away. I need some time. Five or six months, maybe. Is that okay with you?"

"Of course it is." Dominic held her close.

Every day they were apart, he'd wish for time to move faster to get her there. But in the end, they would be together, and that's what mattered.

Chapter 20

Philippa tidied her desk. Pasture Lane had closed after dinner over an hour ago. The staff were on their way out. She could finally go home to Dominic.

Home... It sounded so right to put that word and his name in the same sentence. But in a few months, home wouldn't be in Maryland. It would be in California with Dominic.

Two days had passed since she'd said yes, but she hadn't told anyone. She'd tried, but she couldn't say it. Maybe the uncertainty would go away if she wrote out her exit plan. One that would assure everyone that Pasture Lane would continue to thrive.

Leaving Rina would be even harder. Not that they wouldn't remain friends. And since she wasn't leaving Maryland for at least six months, and Scott hadn't made the move from California yet, she and Rina could end up doing the long-distance-boyfriend commute together.

A vision of her and Rina, laughing on a plane bound for California came to mind. They would feed off each other's excitement, ready to see the guys they love.

But those trips wouldn't go on forever.

The image in her mind of her and Rina faded, and her optimism about the move went with it. Philippa shook it off. Expanding her career was a good thing. Being with Dominic was a wonderful thing. She was just experiencing a bit of anxiety over making a change.

The clang of oven racks being dropped on a metal table echoed into the office, and Philippa glanced out the window.

Jeremy wiped out the ovens on the other side of the kitchen.

That was strange. One of the kitchen helpers should have done that, and Jeremy was good about checking to make sure they did a good job. But he had been a little off the entire day.

Her phone rang. It was Dominic. He was probably wondering how much longer she would be. Philippa answered the call.

"Hey, I'm on my way out now. What about you?"

"We just wrapped up. I know you and I were planning to go straight home tonight, but apparently, I'm buying at the Montecito. Can you meet me there? We won't stay long."

"Sure. Can you give me twenty minutes or so?"

"That works. The crew is still packing up. I can swing by and get you."

Another loud clang from the kitchen drew her attention. "No. I'll meet you there. I need to talk to Jeremy."

"Everything okay?"

"I don't know. He's been quiet and moody. That's not like him."

"But it's understandable."

"Why?"

"Hold on a sec." During the pause, doors opened and shut on his end of the phone. "It isn't a secret, but Teale accepted a job offer. A designer luggage company is paying her to vlog her travels while cooking in places off the beaten path."

"Wow, that's exciting." More clanging reverberated from the kitchen. "But I'm guessing that means the end of her and Jeremy's relationship."

"Probably. I hate to lose her, too, for different reasons, obviously. They're not paying her much, and she's only guaranteed the position for six months, but this is her dream opportunity. She has to take it."

Years ago, Philippa had felt the same about going to Coral Cove for the interview audition. But honestly, despite everything that had happened with her and Dominic, if she was having a conversation with her twenty-two-year-old self, she wouldn't discourage her from taking healthy risks.

"She absolutely has to." Philippa turned off her computer. "I'm sure Jeremy understands, but that doesn't make it any easier for him."

"Or for Teale. Part of the reason why the team wants to go to the Montecito tonight is to cheer her up. She's really down about the breakup." Dominic released a long exhale. "I'm glad we were finally able to figure things out and that we're on our way to a new chapter."

"We are." Philippa waited for her own surge of gratefulness, but she wrestled with the same anxiety she'd felt a minute ago.

"A part of me thinks we should sit them down and tell them not to give up on each other."

A laugh slipped out of her. "You and I as relationship counselors? I don't know about that. We didn't exactly take the easy road to get here."

He chuckled softly. "Yeah, you're probably right. I have to go. Bailey's calling me on the other line. So I'll see you later?"

"Yes. I'll be there. Love you."

"Love you, too."

Love. The warmth Philippa felt in hearing and saying the important four-letter word wrapped around her heart like a hug. Yeah, anxiety on the verge of a huge shift like she was taking was absolutely normal. And what she and Dominic felt for each other would see her through it.

Philippa left her office. As the boss, it wasn't her place to pry into Jeremy's personal business, but she did need to address his earlier mood with the staff.

As she approached Jeremy, he glanced up from wiping out an oven on the other side of the table. "Hey, Chef."

"Hey. Are you heading out soon? It's been a long day."

"I just wanted to hit a few things I noticed. I'm off tomorrow, so staying late is no big deal."

"So, how do you think dinner service went tonight?"

"Things were slower than usual. And the line wasn't as focused as they should have been. They made a lot of mistakes."

"There was something I noticed that could have influenced what was happening on the line."

"Oh?" Jeremy paused.

"You seemed on edge."

"I did? I didn't mean to be. I guess I'm a little preoccupied." He picked up a metal rack from the table and slid it into the oven. "I don't know if you heard, but Teale is leaving Dominic's team."

"I heard she accepted a new position. It sounds like a great opportunity."

"Yeah, it is." He gave a lopsided grin. "She's going to have a great time traveling to all those places, meeting people, cooking, discovering all kinds of different ingredients and trying new stuff. Like she said, it's a dream job." He picked up a white kitchen towel from the table, staring down at it as he wiped his hands. "She asked me to go with her."

"She did?"

He looked up. "But of course I said no. I have a really nice apartment and a car I just paid off. And responsibilities. You're counting on me. And I like working here with you at Pasture Lane. I've learned a lot. I can't just walk away from everything. Sure, I've got some savings I could dip into, but what about when I get back? I could get another apartment, but there's no guarantee that you'd have a spot for me in six months. It's too risky."

Philippa caught the hint of conflict in his eyes. Who was he trying to convince? Her or himself?

Yes, she'd been counting on Jeremy to be there after she left Pasture Lane. But like she'd mentioned to Dominic, one of the things that she'd always wanted for Jeremy as her sous chef was for him to push himself a little harder.

Philippa joined Jeremy on the other side of the table. "Set aside the risky part for a minute. Do you want to go? Would it make you happy?"

"Yes." Jeremy shrugged. "Obviously, I like Teale and want to be with her, but there's so much more to know about food and people and the recipes that are part of their culture. I could bring that back with me."

Dominic had said that what she saw in Jeremy, Chef LeBlanc had noticed in him. What was the advice he'd said she'd given him?

Philippa borrowed from it as she faced Jeremy. "Do you mind if I give you some advice?"

"No. I'm glad to get it."

"You can stay here and be comfortable, and that's perfectly okay. But don't let the risk of going with Teale scare you if going with her is something you really want to do, especially if you think you'll be happy doing it. Find someone to sublet your apartment. Let someone you trust take care of your car. And if it helps, your job will be here when you get back, if you still want it."

"You'll hold my job for me?"

"Yes." Jeremy getting his job back, she'd set that up with Zurie before she left. "With all the new knowledge you'll gain, it's nothing but a benefit to Pasture Lane if you come back and work for me. Think about it and let me know what you decide." She reached toward him and patted the table in a encouraging gesture. "I support you either way."

A pondering, more hopeful expression took over his face. "Okay. I'll think about it."

"Good." As she turned to walk away, a feeling of doing the right thing came over her.

"Chef Gayle."

She paused.

Jeremy gave a nod. "Thanks."

A half hour later, as Philippa pulled out of the parking lot at Tillbridge, Jeremy sped out ahead of her in his truck. Farther down the road, he turned left just like she planned to do, headed toward the Montecito.

If he was choosing to go with Teale, he was probably making the best choice and she was glad for him. She and everyone else would miss having him in the kitchen as a leader, but maybe this was the perfect opportunity to mentor Quinn and help her elevate her skills. The night of the movie screening, Quinn had really stepped up and impressed her. Gradually giving Quinn more responsibility while encouraging her to attend culinary workshops and other learning opportunities would help bring out her abilities even more.

As Philippa braked at the stop sign, then made the turn, reality swept in. She wouldn't be around to mentor Quinn. Someone else would have to do it. But would they see the same potential in her? And if Jeremy came back, what if the new head chef didn't encourage him to expand on what he'd learned traveling the world.

Worry, resignation and sadness bored down inside of Philippa. The letting-go process was hard. But it was worth it, right?

Set aside the risky part for a minute. Do you want to go? Would it make you happy?

Her advice to Jeremy still looped through her thoughts as she parked in the lot at the Montecito. She turned off the engine but remained in the car. Jeremy had said yes without hesitation, but when Dominic had presented his LA plan to her, she'd felt torn between wanting to be with him and remaining at Tillbridge. Jeremy had said he wanted to be with Teale…but the opportunity made him happy, too.

Did she feel the same way about the LA plan?

A knock on the window startled her out of her thoughts.

Dominic smiled, motioning she should unlock the door.

She did and he opened it.

As soon as she got out, Dominic shut the door behind her, then kissed her.

Philippa laid her hand to his chest as desire and bittersweetness swelled.

As if sensing it, he eased out of the kiss and leaned away. The parking lot lights illuminated the empathy on his face. "Are you sad about Jeremy? I saw him and Teale a minute ago. They're not telling everyone, but they told me that he's going with her. And he also mentioned how you're supporting him." Dominic cupped her cheek and tipped up her face. "You did a good thing. The right thing." He pressed his lips briefly to hers. "Come on. Let's go inside."

Dominic held her hand and took a step toward the Montecito.

"Wait." She tugged him back. "I can't go with you."

"Are you sure you don't want to come in? The team was looking forward to seeing you. We'll make it quick. Once I pay the bar tab, we can leave."

Sadness pushed in on Philippa's chest. She couldn't go inside and pretend that everything was okay. She had to tell him now. "No. I mean I can't leave Tillbridge and go with you to LA."

Dominic stood back in front of her. "I know you're worried about what will happen to Pasture Lane. If you have to stay on a few months longer to help everyone move past the transition without Jeremy, we'll figure it out." He gave her hand a squeeze. "I know it's hard to let go, but you can't let Jeremy leaving be the excuse that keeps you from moving on."

"It's not." As she let that sink in, the truth she'd been denying for the past two days emerged. "Being a part of your world has been exciting. But it's not me. Being here. Doing what I do at Tillbridge. It's enough for me."

"But what about us? Don't you want that?" As he let go of her hand, he visibly swallowed. "I don't want a long-distance relationship with you."

"And I don't want that with you."

"Then, why are you playing small when you could have everything, including us being together?"

"Playing small?" She took a step back. "Is that what you think I've been doing here all these years?"

"I'm not saying what you achieved with Pasture Lane isn't important." Frustration leaped in his eyes. "But in LA, you would have a chance at other opportunities. That's all that I meant."

"Shows, cookbooks, a restaurant in a larger city—those things don't feel bigger to me. Leaving here and giving up my dreams would be playing small. I'm happy where I am. Are you?" The last comment hadn't been intended. It had just slipped out.

Dominic gave her a look, as if she'd shocked him by asking the question. Bleakness came into his eyes before he glanced away. When he met her gaze again, it was gone. "Are we really doing this?"

Ending their relationship in a restaurant parking lot? It was almost fitting. And it was like a cruel joke. Philippa took a shaky breath. "I think we are."

Dominic closed his eyes a moment. "Okay."

"Okay."

He started to walk away, but in three quick strides,

he returned to Philippa and cupped her face. The hard press of his lips to hers stole her breath and broke her heart as she tasted the saltiness of tears.

In need of air, they broke apart. Breathing hard, he laid his forehead to hers. "I have to go."

Hands tucked in his front pockets, he stalked toward the Montecito.

Tears blurred her eyes as she got back in the car and watched him go inside. Philippa swiped them from her face, started the car and drove out of the parking lot.

Before she realized it, she was pulling into Rina's driveway. She turned off the engine.

Scott walked out of the house and onto the brightly lit porch. As he glanced back, Rina came out, comfortable for the night in shorts and T-shirt.

Philippa gripped the keys still in the ignition. She was intruding. She should go.

But as Rina came closer, Philippa got out.

Rina paused and stared at her. "Oh no. What's wrong?"

"Dominic and I, we... I..." Philippa couldn't even say it.

"Oh, honey." Rina rushed over and hugged her. "I got you. It's okay." She rocked Philippa like a child, then put an arm around Philippa's shoulders and guided her to the house.

They sat on the couch in the living room.

Philippa's eyes felt gritty and tight, but there were no more tears. They were trapped in the icy ball of disbelief lodged in her chest. "I shouldn't have interrupted you and Scott."

"Don't worry about that." Rina grabbed hold of Philippa's hand. "What happened?"

Philippa took a deep breath and poured out her heart.

Chapter 21

Dominic walked into his upstairs office at Frost & Flame, grateful the dinner meeting downstairs with him, Bailey and the latest potential investor she'd found for Frost & Flame Atlanta was over. It was their third meeting that week, each of them beginning to feel like a command performance where he hyped his vision, and she backed him up with a set of impressive numbers.

He took off his blue suit blazer and laid it over the arm of the black leather sofa. As he unbuttoned and rolled up the sleeves of his crisp white dress shirt, he glanced at his desk. A full in-box waited for him. He was going to be there awhile.

But instead of sitting down, he stuck his hands in his front pockets and stared out the dark tinted window overlooking the dining room. But in its place, he saw Pasture Lane's kitchen in his mind. And Philippa. He longed to hold her. And to change how things had ended between them two weeks ago.

Then, why are you playing small when you could have everything?

A part of him had known he'd messed up when he said it, but he'd been frustrated and hurt that she'd changed her mind about joining forces with him and building a life together. All he could think about was that she was pushing him away again, like she had before she'd left Coral Cove.

No. Leaving here and giving up my dreams would be playing small. I'm happy where I am. Are you?

Her question in the Montecito parking lot lingered in his mind.

Was he happy about losing her again? He wasn't. But Philippa claimed she was happy at Pasture Lane. And he had responsibilities that demanded his full attention. There was no point in stretching out the inevitable with a long-distance relationship. They not only lived on opposite coasts, but they were also moving in different directions.

The door to his office opened and closed.

In the reflection of the window, he watched Bailey walk toward him looking like she owned the world in a scarlet business suit.

She stood beside him. "Russ is on his way to the airport. I think he'll still be raving over the ribeye steak he had for dinner when he gets back to New York."

"I'm glad he enjoyed it." He looked to Bailey. "So?"

The one-word question encapsulated what was on both their minds. Did they have a new investor?

She crossed her arms over her chest. "He didn't say

no. But he didn't say yes either. Honestly, I give him until he lands to give us his answer. No."

"But you just said he was raving about the food. And he seemed impressed by the numbers."

"Yes, Russ was impressed by all of that. But what he wasn't impressed with was you."

"He said that?"

"He didn't have to. I could see it on his face, just like I could with the other two potential investors when you were talking about the future of the restaurant. Hell. I wasn't even impressed."

"Not impressed?" Irritation poured heat into his face and out of the collar of his open shirt. "I didn't talk about farm-to-fork concepts, so that can't be the problem. Let me guess. I didn't smile or laugh in all the right places?"

"Actually, you did. Like I'd given you a script. You're not feeling it, and we can all tell."

"All? You make it sound like there's a hoard of people in on this."

"Well, let's see…" Bailey counted off on her fingers. "There's Eve, Brianne and the rest of the production crew for your show. And the entire restaurant staff, they're totally confused. I heard you haven't cooked in the restaurant for over a week and barely come downstairs to greet the VIPs or the rest of the customers."

"Because I'm busy." He jabbed his finger in the air toward his desk. "I've got a full load of work waiting for me, or hasn't anyone noticed?"

"You've been twice as busy, and it never affected your performance before. You have to face—"

"Don't say it. You're about to bring Tillbridge into the conversation, and I don't want to hear it. I don't want to be here all night." Dominic went to his desk. "You mentioned earlier you left papers for me to sign."

Bailey slammed her palm down on the stack in his in-box. "Screw the papers. And this isn't just about Tillbridge."

Her eyes growing bright as if they were about to well with tears cooled his anger. Bailey never cried. Not even when they were kids and she fell off her bike, skinning both of her knees.

He walked over to her. "Bailey, what's wrong?"

Laying her hand to her stomach, she took a breath, quickly recomposing herself. "You're not listening. The problem is you. You haven't been yourself for a while. I thought you were tired or on the edge of burnout, so that's why I got you the contract for the screening party."

"Got me the contract? You said Holland requested me."

"She was perfectly content with what Tillbridge had to offer, but she went along with the change as a favor to me. And then I used every bargaining chip I had to get the production company to kick in the budget for you to tape your farm-to-fork episodes there. I thought running around the countryside would re-inspire you."

She'd sent him to Tillbridge? He turned away from her a moment as he ran his hand across his nape. "So when I asked you to get me out of the contract and you wouldn't, it had nothing to do with money or my image?"

"No."

"And Philippa? How did she fit into your plan?"

"She didn't. I found out that she was the chef at the property the same day the contract arrived for you to sign. I'd hoped that she was far enough in your rearview that it wouldn't matter. If anything, I thought seeing her would remind you of how much you'd enjoyed your sous chef days at Coral Cove, and those memories might inspire you, too. I was just trying to do the right thing."

He couldn't be mad at her for that. Bailey was a handful, but she also truly cared about him.

Dominic pulled her in for a mutual one-armed hug. "You could have just told me to take a vacation."

Bailey playfully pushed him away. "Like you would have listened to me." Her small smile faded as sincerity came into her eyes. "But you have to listen to me now. Go away for a few days. Unplug. Work things out in your head. Figure out your future. Sleep. Do whatever it is you want to do. Then come back recharged. We need you. I need you."

He had felt more worn down than usual since returning from Maryland. A chance to get away from it all sounded great. "But we have episodes to shoot for the show and meetings lined up. And we still haven't found someone to replace Teale."

"Piece of cake. I'll handle it. Really, I've got this." She patted his arm. "Just go."

Dominic walked out the back door onto the porch of the beach bungalow, carrying a bowl of cubed, fresh mango. As he sat on the lower step in his blue-and-white swim shorts, warm white sand caved around his bare feet. An afternoon breeze filled with ocean brine whispered over him.

He'd slept past noon. It had taken three days for his body to adjust and not automatically wake him up before dawn with his schedule running through his mind. Bailey had been right. He'd needed this.

After polishing off the mango, he set the bowl on the step and walked the beach. The private island, owned by a friend of a friend, wasn't Coral Cove, but the palm and cassia trees landscaped into the front of the bungalow had stirred up the good memories of being there as a sous chef. The sumptuous meals he'd cooked for the guests. The skills he'd learned from Chef LeBlanc. Supervising the staff. The place he'd shared with five other people in Bridgetown that was basically a shack. Those experiences had launched him to where he was now.

Lured by the rise and fall of the glittering ocean, he went into it, diving in where the sand dropped off and the water grew deep. Sometime later, he swam in on the gentle push of a wave, and as he walked back up on the beach, a peacefulness reminiscent of being at Coral Cove washed over him. He'd had responsibilities back then, but inside he'd been carefree.

But he'd felt it before…with Philippa.

He imagined seeing the two of them walking in the surf, laughing, kicking up water and chasing each other. Her laughing as he carried her into the waves. But what he saw was from six years ago. The Philippa he knew back then belonged on the beach in his memories. The woman he knew now was right where she was supposed to be, in the countryside, under the bright blue sky and the radiance of the sun. She was in the kitchen at Pasture Lane, sharing the food she loved and mentoring her staff. And more importantly, she knew that was where she belonged.

As far as himself… The guy who'd walked the beaches of Coral Cove with Philippa no longer existed, either. And as good as it had been for him, he had no desire to rewind the clock and go back in time to the island resort. But he wanted to feel that sense of light-ness in his heart and soul and the purpose he'd once felt. He'd lost that along the way. And found it with Philippa.

I'm happy... Are you?

Two days later, as the sun started to dip low into the ocean, he held his phone in his hand. It had remained off since he'd been there, but he had an important call to make.

Bailey thought she needed him, but she didn't. And now it was time for her to rise and take over what she'd put her time and heart in to build. His restaurant enter-prise. She'd still have his name and his support, but the vision would be hers, not his.

He dialed her number.

She picked up on the third ring. "Hi." Bailey's tone was light almost playful. "Love you. But I'm hanging up unless it's an emergency. You're on vacation."

"It's not an emergency, but…"

Bailey hung up.

A chuckle huffed out of him. He'd walked into that one. Dominic called her again.

She answered, and he jumped right in. "Hang up again, and I'm sending someone to your house to take all your favorite stuff, including the stash of peanut-butter-cup ice cream."

"My ice cream? Wow. You don't have to take it that far. I'm listening."

The importance of his decision and big-brother pro-tectiveness made him pause. No, he wasn't abandoning her. Bailey really didn't need him. She needed him to step out of her way.

Dominic smiled as he watched the sun slip farther below the horizon. "I've worked out my future…"

Chapter 22

Philippa reversed the golf cart out of a space in the parking lot of the guesthouse. At six in the morning, only three people were in the lot—a couple, packing their bags into an SUV, and a man who had jogged to his car, grabbed something from the front of it, and was now jogging back to the guesthouse.

Tristan had called her last night and asked her to come to the indoor arena. Tillbridge was planning some sort of event there next month that would require food.

As she sped down the narrow-paved trail, she recalled riding to the arena a few weeks ago with Tristan for the meeting with Rachel...and seeing Dominic there. On that day, frustration and confusion had almost kept them apart, but what they felt for each other had allowed them to figure it out, to listen and talk. And find their way back to each other.

But what if she'd known then that they wouldn't make it? Would she have chosen for them to just remain friends? It would have been safer that way, but then she would have missed out on the good moments they'd shared while he was there. Like when they'd told each other "I love you" on the dance floor at the Montecito.

Reconciling the good with the bad of what happened between her and Dominic was something she was learning to do. Hopefully with time, it would become easier.

Using the updated code Tristan had given her, she entered the field through the pasture gate, then drove to the arena. Another golf cart was in the parking lot.

Tristan was already there.

Inside the building, she walked through the dark wood lobby and out the door near the reception desk leading to the main part of the arena.

Glimpsing Tristan standing in the viewing box, she veered right, then up the stairs to get there.

The door was already open and she walked inside. "Good morning, Tristan."

"Hey Philippa." He glanced up from typing a message on his phone and smiled. "Thanks again for meeting me."

"No problem. So what is this event again? I didn't see it on the schedule."

"It just came up and it's not booked yet. Right now, I'm just trying to get a feel on if we should agree to do it. It would take place out back. We'd have to use trailers again, like we did with the screening party. Let's head back there. I need a visual reference."

They left the viewing box and she walked with him down the wide corridor. "Can you give me an idea about the menu? The type of food they want will determine the setup."

His phone rang and Tristan glanced at the screen. "I should take this." He answered. "Hey, Rick. Yep... Nope... I know you need her back. Yes, I fed her..."

Was that one of the stable's boarding clients? If they were that worried, they must have been new to Tillbridge. The staff at the stable took great care of the horses.

Tristan glanced at Philippa as he continued to talk. "You're fifteen minutes out? I'll see if I can speed things up. Hold on a sec." He paused and waved Philippa forward. "Go on ahead. You can get a jump on things. I'll meet you out there."

"Okay." Philippa kept walking. A jump on what? He still hadn't told her about the event or the menu. As she approached the back door, the sound of mooing cows floated through the corridor.

She was hearing things. Tristan would have mentioned cows.

But she heard the sound again. Philippa cautiously pushed open the door and peeked outside.

A dairy cow standing in a portable corral mooed at her.

Confusion made her open the door wider.

Close to the corral, a small tree in a black pot sat next to a round cafe table. On top of the table was a basket filled with fresh carrots, red peppers and tomatoes.

Movement to the left drew her attention, and her breath caught in her chest. It was Dominic.

A smile shadowed his lips. "Hello, Philippa." He looked good, a bit thinner but rested.

Just as she was about to ask him why he was there,

a plausible answer came to mind. Was he part of the event Tristan was talking about? Tristan had mentioned wanting to get a feel on if they should agree to do it. Maybe this meeting was really about determining if she and Dominic could still work together.

If that was the case, she could handle it. Catering events at Tillbridge was her responsibility, and this was about professionalism. Not her feelings. She and Dominic made a good team in the kitchen. They just weren't destined to have a personal relationship.

A dull ache swelled in her chest. Her mind accepted the truth, now she just had to make her heart understand.

As Dominic approached her, she quelled her mixed emotions and schooled her face. "Tristan had to take a call. He'll be here in a minute." She shifted her attention from him to the cow. "He mentioned an event, but he didn't give me any details about it. I'm assuming it's a farm-to-fork theme like we created for the screening event?"

"No. It's about hoping you'll forgive me."

"What?" Philippa looked up at him. Clearly she was hearing things. "Can you repeat that?"

As he stepped closer, sincerity filled his gaze. "I'm sorry. I'm sorry for what I said to you before I left. And I'm sorry that I hurt you instead of facing the truth about my life. You asked me if I was happy where I was. I wasn't. I thought the solution was for you to move to California so we could be together, but by asking you to do that, I was limiting your happiness. I was the one who needed to make a change. Not you."

Hope intensified, but as Philippa glanced at the cow

and the table, she grew confused. "What are you trying to tell me. And what's all of this?"

"This is what I want."

"So you want...cows?"

He laughed. "Cows, chickens, and maybe even a goat grazing next to a house with a big kitchen, and a garden in the backyard. Or even an orchard."

The enthusiasm in his voice made Philippa see it in her mind. "But what about your restaurants and your show?"

"I'm grateful for Frost & Flame and *Dinner with Dominic*, but it's time for me to move on to what I really want. And I want it with you." He cupped her cheek, but a huge welt on his wrist stole her attention.

She grasped his hand and took it from her cheek. "Oh my gosh, Dominic. What happened?"

"The bees at the bee farm. I guess the owner was right about them not being happy. At least not with me. I went there yesterday to get honey to put in the basket, and this bee flew out of nowhere and stung me. But it's all good. The staff at the farm shot me up with an EpiPen, and then Tristan took me to the emergency room."

"Emergency room?" Concern raised her voice an octave.

"I'm fine, now. I'm slightly allergic to bee venom."

"Cross-cultivating bees is definitely off the list of things we'll be doing at the farm slash orchard."

"So is that a yes to us getting back together?"

It had taken six years for Dominic to come back into her life, and Philippa couldn't imagine another day without him. "It is."

Dominic slipped his arms around her, and the joy growing inside of her reflected on his face.

As they met halfway for a kiss, the potent smell of manure wafted in the air.

He glanced at the cow and grimaced. "Whoa. That's strong. Maybe we'll skip the cows and just visit Lula at Rick's farm."

Philippa laughed. Her city guy had a lot to learn about living in the country. "Deal. No bees. No cows. And no gardening in the dark with a family of raccoons."

"What?"

"Never mind." A truck with a livestock trailer driving through the pasture caught her attention. "I think it's time for Lula to go home."

As she went to move away, Dominic held her in place. "I love you."

Philippa stared up at him, and what had lived in her heart from the first moment she'd looked into his cinnamon-colored eyes filled her heart. "I love you, too."

Chapter 23

Two years later...

Philippa unwrapped the corn on the cob in the foil. Steam filled with savory goodness rose from the lightly charred, golden kernels. She flashed a smile at the cameras in the studio kitchen in the cottage at Tillbridge. "Chili lime corn on the cob. The perfect addition to your next barbecue."

Dominic stood beside her. "Sweet and spicy. Just the way I like it," he murmured.

She glanced at him, and he stared at her instead of at the camera or the dish they'd just made. Passion and heat flashed in his eyes and her breath hitched.

"Cut. That's a wrap," Brianne said.

Dominic swooped in for a kiss and Philippa leaned into him.

"Alright, you two. Get a room." Brianne smiled as she called out to them from near one of the cameras.

Chuckling, Dominic's lips drifted toward Philippa's ear. "That's not a bad idea."

"I agree. After the late nights we've been putting in. I could use a nap." Smiling, Philippa laid her hand to the middle of Dominic's chest as he cupped her waist. "But someone's waiting for us."

Philippa looked beyond the cameras, and he followed her gaze.

Tristan stood at the opening of the hallway.

Dominic gave her a squeeze and kissed her cheek. "Go ahead. I need to talk to Brianne about the segment we're shooting tomorrow."

Drawn like a magnet, Philippa went to Tristan, who held a baby close to his chest. "Look, Angel." He pointed to Philippa. "Your mama's here."

Philippa's heart swelled as Angelique Renee Crawford cooed and smiled at her. "Hi, sweetie." She took the now-squirming baby in her arms and held her near her shoulder. "Thanks for watching her on such short notice."

The young woman who usually watched Angelique on set, in the nursery outfitted in the cottage's main bedroom, had fallen ill with a cold.

"No problem. I enjoyed it." Tristan transferred a small towel from his shoulder to Philippa's. "She ate not too long ago, and I changed her diaper."

Dominic walked up beside them. "How's my girl?" As he talked to her, Angelique stared at her daddy and he stared back, both enthralled with each other.

Philippa completely understood the sentiment. Some days she woke up, thought about her life now and almost had to pinch herself because it was so wonderful. A large part of that happiness came from being with Dominic, and now, Angelique.

Since their small wedding at Tillbridge a little over a year and half ago with their family and friends in attendance, Dominic had completely stepped away from the day-to-day running of Frost & Flame LA and Frost & Flame Atlanta. Head chefs oversaw the establishments, and Bailey managed the entire restaurant enterprise and any projects associated with them.

Dominic also had a new show, *Farm to Fork with Dominic Crawford.* Just like he dropped in from time to time to cook at Pasture Lane, she sometimes appeared as a guest on the show. He was taping at the cottage until he could move into the studio kitchen attached to their dream home that was being built. They were located a short distance from Rina and Scott.

"I better get back to the stable," Tristan said. "Are you two still coming to the house for dinner tonight? Chloe's been texting me all morning from the set in Canada. She can't wait to get back here, especially to see Angelique."

"We'll be there." Laughing, Philippa gave into Angelique reaching for her dad and handed her to Dominic. "Should we bring anything besides this little handful?"

"Nope. Rina and Scott are helping out. Just show up around seven."

A couple of hours later, back at the house they were renting in Bolan, Philippa tiptoed out of the nursery where Angelique slept.

As she shut the door behind her, Dominic embraced her from behind.

She leaned into him. "Hey, we have some time before

dinner at Tristan and Chloe's. We can test that brussels sprout recipe you were interested in."

"We could." He kissed her earlobe, and the warmth of his mouth radiated over her cheek. "Or we can take that nice, long nap you mentioned...among other things."

"But we really should get ahead on..." Words slipped away as Dominic trailed his lips down the side of her throat and slid his hand under her shirt.

"You were saying?" he murmured.

His palm gliding along her belly and moving upward erased the rest from her mind. He still possessed the ability to easily distract her.

Philippa turned in Dominic's arms and faced him. "I was saying that you're right."

In one smooth movement, he leaned down and swept her up in his arms.

As she looped her hands around his neck, she suppressed a squeak to a quiet laugh. "What are you doing?"

He carried her down the hall to their bedroom. "Not wasting a minute of my time with you."

In bed, as they lay in each other's arms, Dominic's deep kisses and caresses made her heart pound faster. She arched up her hips, hoping to coax him to where she needed him most. "Please..."

He gave her what she wanted, gliding inside of her, but then he paused, staring into her eyes. "How did I get so lucky?"

Philippa cupped his cheek, seeing their journey from Coral Cove to now. She knew the answer. "It wasn't luck. It was love."

* * * * *